KADE'S REDEMPTION

COPYRIGHT

OPENING QUOTE

Maybe I'm amazed at the way you love me all the time. Maybe I'm afraid of the way I love you. Maybe I'm amazed at the way you pulled me out of time. You hung me on a line. Maybe I'm amazed at the way I really need you. Maybe I'm a man. Maybe I'm a lonely man who's in the middle of something that he doesn't really understand. And maybe I'm a man. And maybe you're the only woman who could ever help me. Won't you help me to understand?

Maybe I'm Amazed by James Dornan

CHAPTER ONE

~*~ KADE ~*~

I take a deep breath and let it out on a sigh as I close the door of my giant house behind me. I keep breathing deeply, inhaling the impossibly fresh scent of wood. Like it was cut just now. I've never understood how a house in existence before I was born could possibly still smell like it was just built.

This house is my dad's pride and joy, though. A close second behind my mother, me, and the rest of our family and pack. I've always wondered exactly how he keeps it smelling so new, but he only ever says that it's a secret he'll tell me when he passes the responsibility of Alpha to me. Along with the rest of the history and secrets of the Deimos Pack. My pack.

My legacy.

I can't wait. I already feel a little like I disappointed him when I didn't feel a mate bond with anyone when I turned eighteen like I was supposed to. He's told me for months, since my birthday, that he could never be disappointed by that. But I hate the feeling of letting him down. It makes me want to do everything in my power to prove myself to him.

I drop my backpack and rub my chest for the thousandth time. I've had chest pain ever since I stepped out onto the football field of Palisade Falls High School hours ago. I'm a senior, and the Varsity team's star quarterback. I've brought them to Georgia's State Football Tournament four years in a row. I have skills the coaches have never seen.

The thought makes me chuckle. If only they knew I'm part Wolf. I wonder what they'd think. Truth is, I'm probably cheating a little. I'm tough, but even more so because of my Wolf side. I'm fast, but that's amplified by my Wolf. I can read people well. I'm very observant. I can smell emotions, especially my opponent's nerves and fear. All of those skills are enhanced, though, thanks to my Wolf.

I, along with my twin brother and our little sister, and every other Wolf cub in this pack, spent years being homeschooled and honing our shifting skills. We spent most of our lives, at least until it was time for high school, learning how to control ourselves. How to live amongst Humans without freaking them out with our almost superhuman strength and agility. We learned how to control our shifting so we didn't do it by accident in front of Humans. Be more Human than Wolf.

I don't shift into some scary, hairy werewolf like Hollywood would have everyone assume when they think Shifter. That's not what I am. I'm a Human. I look Human. I talk like a Human. I eat like a Human. But I have the ability to shift into a Wolf. A real Wolf. Large and four-legged Wolf. All growl. All fur. Just as majestic. If I were to shift into a Wolf, no one would be able to tell the difference between me and any other Wolf. Except, perhaps, my size.

My father is one of the most powerful attorneys in the country. His name became well-known when he took on the Federal Government and made them responsible for the abuse that Wolves were suffering at the hands of those running a Refuge near our home. He won.

The Refuge became ours after one of the people who took it over passed and the other decided to take over his father's place as the Chief of Police. I remember being taken there all the time when I was young. Now it's my place of sanctuary. Peace.

My father, Connor Deimos, is also a Human. I haven't been told much about our history other than my father was the first Human Alpha of not only our pack, but any pack that we know of or have heard of. My mother, Belle, was a full Wolf Luna. The two of them were the beginning of our pack. They allied with my older brother Fenn's pack. He's a full Wolf and an Alpha, just like my father. His mate, Aryan, is the first Human Luna of their pack and of any that we've heard of.

We've grown exponentially over the years. Our territory has expanded beyond even my father's wildest imagination. We have more allies with other Wolf and Shifter packs all over the country than I think anyone can truly grasp. Everyone knows how protective my father is of our kind. Just that simple quality about him made packs flock to him, offering friendship and an allegiance. My father is truly a legend.

I grip my chest and rub as another pain stabs it. "What the fuck?" I growl through gritted teeth.

I managed to get through practice, but I've been in pain and sick since I started it three hours ago. Of all the Shifters in the Deimos Pack that are in high school, I'm the only one who chose to play football as a sport. My best friend plays baseball, as do a few others. Most play basketball, my twin included. The rest don't play any sports.

I head for the kitchen to grab a bottle of water. Maybe I'm thirsty or something. I've never had pain in my chest like this. I feel like I'm having a heart attack. Almost like my fucking heart is being ripped out and squeezed right in front of me.

I grit my teeth and groan when another sharp pain hits me. My mind suddenly feels like it's spinning. It's like people are screaming and yelling, but I can't make out what they're saying. There are so many flashing images in front of me, I can't grasp one. It's all chaos, but it's the pain in my heart that doubles me over.

"Holy fucking hell." I barely get my water to my lips before my entire body experiences the heart-wrenching agony.

I'm not sure if I blacked out or if I figured out how to time travel, but when I open my eyes, the sun has long ago set. The room is pitch-black. I feel nothing but emptiness. Some bizarre overwhelming sadness that has the power to destroy me. I have the strangest urge to allow it to. Like nothing at all matters anymore.

"Fuck, what the hell is wrong with me?" I grip the counter and pull myself up. It takes me a long time to stand, and when I finally get there, I have to lean on the counter to steady myself. The light switch is too far away. I don't care enough about it to attempt to reach it.

6

I grip my head with one hand, afraid to completely let go of the counter. My Wolf is painfully howling in my head. I can feel a deep-rooted fear and sadness from him. I don't know if what I'm feeling is something going on with him, but I'm scared to death.

Before I have a chance to ask him, though, I hear the front door of the house open. I look up and see Dominick, my best friend, carrying my little sister, Jordan. They both look like they've literally walked through Hell and fought Demon after Demon before crawling home. He flicks the light to the kitchen on when he sees me.

I want to move to them, but I can't. I can't even talk. My Wolf howling has grown more paralyzingly melancholy. The emptiness I feel is worse than the pain. It's ripping me to shreds. I can feel my cheeks are wet, but I don't feel the tears falling.

"What's happening?" I manage to ask.

He makes it to the counter and sets Jordan on it in front of him. She clings to him like he's the only thing keeping her from completely falling apart. She's trembling. She's bloodied and bruised. Her clothes are ripped to shreds. She's barely covered. I push Dominick aside and put my arms around my sister. She wraps her small body around me as she shivers and cries.

"We have a problem, Kade," Dominick whispers. "A huge fucking problem." Tears swim in his eyes.

"Tell me. Tell my why the fuck I feel like I just went through a fight for my life and now have an overbearing emptiness trying to overpower me."

Dominick tries to steady himself. He grips the counter for support. I rub my hand up and down Jordan's back soothingly and tangle my fingers in her hair. She bursts into a fresh wave of body-wracking, hysterical sobs that force my Wolf to howl with her.

I start to tremble myself. Whatever the hell is going on, my Wolf has blocked me from it. I can't feel him. All I can do is hear him. And what I hear is heartbreaking enough. He's trying to protect me. Which means he knows that whatever it is will destroy me. That whatever he feels with all that I'm feeling with shatter me in unimaginable ways.

"They're gone," Dominick whispers. The tears he fought start to fall as he meets my eyes. "We were raided. Your father went after the pack who did it. He took all who could fight. He left your mom and sister-in-law

7

here to protect the young kids and cubs. He left a couple of our strongest warriors with them. He thought the pack who raided us would flee, but they left a few here to finish the destruction." He pauses to try and choke back the sobs, but a few escape.

I'm frozen. I'm trying to follow, but can't. "When? Why didn't I know?"

Dominick steadies himself. Like me, the tears are falling. "When we got home from school, it was already starting. They'd come in with such force, it overwhelmed us. Your mom started howling. Your sister-in-law started screaming. Your brother and father were trying to gather everyone while fighting off those they could. It was chaos, Kade."

I can feel his pain, and that same empty feeling I have slams into me with such force, I stumble. "Dominick. Fuck. Just fucking tell me. Where's my family?" I'm shaking uncontrollably.

He takes a breath as he wraps his arms around me and Jordan. "Dead, Kade. Aryan, Luna Belle, Fenn, Alpha Connor. Zeke. All of them. Dead." He cries into my shoulder as I start to numb. "Aryan and Belle. They were killed trying to protect the kids. Those that were left to help them were slaughtered. I could hear both Alphas howling and then growling so fucking viciously, I thought they'd tear the world apart. I was with Jordan, but when I turned, she was gone. I heard her screaming. I shifted and followed. By the time I caught up, the battle was in full fucking force, Kade. They'd taken Jordan and another girl and trapped them in a goddamn cage that they'd strung up in a fucking tree."

The more he talks, the more I feel the numbness turn to all out anger, then rage. I'm still trembling as Jordan sobs into my shoulder, but it's not because of the overpowering sense of sorrow. It's fury.

My entire family. Slaughtered. My pack. Friends I've known since I was just a cub. My cousins. I don't need him to tell me. I can feel it. I can feel it all. I can see it in my mind. Shifters, Wolves, Humans. All on the ground covered in blood. The images my Wolf blocked. I can see it all as he weakens too much to keep them from me any longer.

Bile rises in my throat. I try to hold myself together for my sister's sake. I don't want to scare her. "Who did this?" I growl so dangerously, I make myself fearful of what my next actions will be.

"I don't know, man. I don't. I fought off so many fucking attacks trying to get to Jordan. In the end, I couldn't. It was the girl she was *locked in the cage with that got her out. She saved her, but... she didn't make it. I grabbed Jordan and ran. I watched them take out the Alphas. They took out the Betas. They fucking just took everyone out. Like it was nothing. No effort. The pack house." He lets out a pained sob. "It's a fucking a bloodbath, Kade. I tried calling for you. I don't know why you didn't hear it."*

I say nothing because I know.

My father.

It was a last-ditch effort to protect me and our pack. He blocked my bond the best he could until his dying breath. Although I could feel something was wrong, I didn't feel it all until it was too late. It slammed into me all at once, but I know exactly what happened. He did it because he knew I'd run after them. He blocked me because he knew if anything happened, I'd need to lead. I couldn't do that if I was dead.

If it takes my entire life, I will find whoever did this to my family. I will find them and kill them all. One by one. Painfully. So they feel each and every single drop of everything the three of us huddled together in this kitchen feel.

~ ~ ~

I sit up in bed clutching my chest and gasping. The silk sheets under me are soaked. My body is dripping sweat. My eyes dart around my room as I leap out of the bed, shifting into my Wolf in mid-air. I land silently and survey my surroundings from the darkest corner of my room. A place I can see every single movement and can attack if I need to.

Nothing moves. I'm not entirely certain I'm breathing. I thank the Moon Goddess my fur is a sleek black, though. It makes me hard to see when I'm in Wolf form. I'm light and very graceful on my paws. It makes me silent and very deadly. Very difficult for an attacker to actually succeed in his goal of getting to me.

I jump when I hear the shrill sound of my alarm. It takes me several more moments to actually make any movement towards it. When I do, my steps are slow and deliberate. It's not until I'm near my bed that I shift to my Human form once more and reach for my phone.

"Fuck, Kade," I whisper as I finally come back to myself. "It was a dream. A fucking dream."

9

Nightmare is more like it. One that is becoming increasingly more frequent. It's like I'm reliving everything that happened fourteen years ago over and over again. Like that fucking movie, Groundhog's Day.

I rub my head after shutting off my alarm and head straight for the shower. I turn it on as cold as I can stand it and step in. I let the water wash off the sweat and cool me down. I don't know why, but I always feel like I'm standing in the sun and it's a hundred degrees after a nightmare like that.

It takes me a few minutes to come down enough to reach over and make my water warmer. Even still, I stand under the spray a long while before I finally start to do anything about actually cleaning myself. After I finally get done, I step out to dry off. I wipe the steam off the mirror and stare at myself.

As I suspected, I look tired. I'm thirty-two years old. I'm tall like my father was. I'm almost six feet four. I'm muscular. I spend a lot of time in my home gym and training with my pack. I make certain we're all in tip top shape in case we ever need to defend our territory or help another of our allies. If someone is falling behind, they get more training. One on one with me. There aren't a lot of Shifters in my pack who like that idea. I'm a well-known asshole.

But the safety of my pack is of utmost importance. I'll never allow my pack to be caught off guard again. Not like we were the day my entire fucking life changed forever. The day I lost my whole family and almost all of my pack.

After Jordan and Dominick told me what happened, a few more of our pack started trickling in. We lost both of our Betas along with anyone else who could take the lead in the absence of our Alphas. My twin brother was among those killed. The only ones left in my entire family were me and my little sister.

I was forced to take over as Alpha before I really had a chance to comprehend the devastation. I had to call in our closest allies. I made Dominick my Beta. By the time we were semi-organized, my over a hundred member pack had become less than twenty, and our attackers were long gone.

It's been fourteen years since that day, and I'm still no closer to figuring out who attacked us. I had heard rumors of some ghost pack, but no one knows who they are. They go into a territory, take it over, and blend seamlessly back into whatever the fuck corner of Hell they appear from.

I sigh when my phone rings. Though I ignore it, I tear my thoughts away from the past and try to focus on now. I splash cold water on my face and finish drying myself off. I run the towel through my short dark hair before wrapping it around my waist.

By the time I'm done shaving, my dark brown eyes look more lively. I'm starting to feel slightly more like myself. I glance at the time and groan, deciding to forego my morning routine. I can miss my sit-ups and push-ups for a day. Not like I'm not already well-defined. I begin to get dressed.

One of the other huge changes in my life after becoming Alpha was figuring out just how in the hell to take care of my pack. Using my father's life insurance, and the other money he'd managed to put aside, wasn't going to last long. Even if I hadn't refused to allow Dominick or Jordan to put their inheritance towards anything but college and their needs, we wouldn't have gotten all that far.

I knew if I wanted to grow and rise to the status he'd brought us to, I had to figure something out. No fucking way I was letting him down. I know my family is looking down on me. Fuck. They're my Spirit Guides. They can drop in whenever they want in their ethereal forms. I vowed to do everything I could to make them proud. Show them I could be and would be an Alpha worthy of the title. Just like my father and older brother.

So, after fixing the pack house, I bought the local diner near our territory that was going out of business. The owners were retiring, but I hated seeing the place close. I grew up eating there. The owners were damn near like my own grandparents. I paid more than they were asking, did a little remodeling, and fixed some damage to the building. It gave those that were left in my pack something to do. They all loved the place as much as I did. An added bonus is that it's near the pack house, so they can always find their way home.

The owners were able to retire with more money than they expected. I felt better knowing they were taken care of. After a couple of years, I graduated from a community college and had enough income from the diner to start my own company.

Deimos Publishing was born. Within a year, I owned several publishing companies around the nation that were struggling. And five years after that, I was worldwide. Now, not only is Deimos Publishing well-known and respected, but we're the largest publishing company in the world.

My pack, with the help of the allies we had and more that we've gained, has once again grown. We're among the largest, if not the largest, pack in the world. We are the most well-to-do. Our territory expands farther now than it had even with my father. I know he, and all of those we lost that day, are proud of where we are now.

I'm still haunted by what happened, though. I still hear the cries of my pack at night when I'm going to sleep. I can hear my mother's howls; my sister-in-law's screams. I can feel my father's bravery; the courage of our pack. I feel my brother's courage.

While my father was, and still is, the bravest and strongest man I know, there is one thing I took from that day that I know he isn't proud of. Something he has never agreed to. But it's my way of protecting innocent people from the danger my pack brings. We still have an unknown enemy out there. An unpredictable phantom.

While my father may have been the strongest Human I have ever known, he was still Human. Shifters are inherently stronger in every aspect than a Human could ever be. While Humans can be a pack's greatest strength, helping us to remember our humanity and keep our power and tempers in check, they can also be our greatest weakness.

So, I've made a no Human rule. Humans and Shifters cannot and will not mate.

Ever.

CHAPTER TWO

~*~ KAIA ~*~

I've never been more grateful for being in a hurry to clean my room last night. I wanted to hurry and get to my graduation party. I was so excited for it. I threw everything in my closet that was on my bedroom floor. Clothing, old books, school work I never finished. I didn't need to. I had all straight A's.

Graduation yesterday was an amazing feeling. Especially since I was Valedictorian. School has always come easy to me, but I was so proud of the graduation accomplishment. Seeing my parent's pride as they watched my speech, which was mostly about the support they gave me, was one of the best things of my life.

I choke back a quiet sob as I listen from underneath the pile of clothing I'm under. I heard some commotion as I was getting ready. I ran to the stairs. My mom was screaming. My dad was fighting with someone. I was just about to run downstairs to help when one of them shot my mother.

Right in front of me.

I slapped a hand over my mouth and ran back to my room. I silently closed the door, but I heard someone screaming about checking the house. I dove into my closet and buried myself in the stuff I threw in here.

I heard someone come in here and search for me. I felt them kick at the pile I'm under. I thought I was found when whoever it was hit my rib cage. I don't know how I kept the pain they inflicted from coming out of my mouth in the form of a whimper, or moan, or scream. Anything.

I haven't moved from this spot. The only reason I know what time it is is because of my phone. I can at least see the time. I know it's three in the morning. I haven't heard any noises in a couple of hours, but I'm terrified to come out of my hiding spot.

I need to get help, though. I know that. I need to see if my parents somehow survived the attack. I need to see if the people who were here are still here. I take a deep breath and slowly move. I'm careful not to make noise. I hope nothing falls and alerts anyone if there's anyone still in the house.

My bladder is full. I slowly sit up after unburying myself. My closet door was left open. I look around the dark room. The bright moonlight is streaming through my window. I let my eyes fall on it.

Ever since I was a child, I've had a connection to the moon. I've sent up silent prayers to it almost every single night. I've never told anyone, but I can hear the moon answer me. A soft voice. Beautiful.

Sometimes, I can see her. She's a Wolf. A pretty, majestic gray Wolf. She guides me. Helps me when I don't think anyone else can understand. Sometimes, I feel like she's hugging me. I've drawn her so many times in my sketchbook. I even have a silver bracelet I wear with a wolf charm and a moon charm on it.

Sometimes, I see a person. I call him the Man in the Moon. He's tall. He's very strong. I can see that he has well-defined features and dark eyes. There's some stubble on his face. He never says anything, but sometimes I see him. He's fleeting. He's never there for long.

I'm sure people would think I'm insane. It's the reason I've never said a word about it to anyone. I might be crazy, but they are a comfort to me. I don't want to lose them. If I'm having a bad day, they are there for me.

I take a deep breath and stand. I quietly let it out and rush for the bathroom in my room. After using it and being as quiet as possible, I don't flush. I don't want to make any noise. I still hear nothing but silence, but that doesn't mean someone isn't listening for me.

Hurrying silently back into my room, I glance back up at the moon. "Now would be a good time to help me out, Moon Wolf. I don't know what to do," I whisper. I listen for any motion or noises that aren't my own.

Pack some things, little one, the Moon Wolf says. *They're coming back.*

I bite my lip. My body feels numb. The light reflects off something shiny and gold. I kneel to pick it up. It's a metallic, gold, metal star. I look over my shoulder towards my door before standing. I quickly walk to the door, pocketing the gold star. It's a badge. A sheriff's badge. Whoever was here was one of the only people who can help me. It explains the uniforms I saw. I was sure I imagined that.

Which means I'm on my own. No one can help me. No one except my Moon Wolf. I wipe my eyes when they begin to sting with tears. I have to be strong. I need to know what happened to my parents. I lean my ear against my door before I quietly start to open it.

No. No, little one. The Moon Wolf appears next to me. She's never done that before. She's always just been in my mind.

I jump back with wide eyes and cover my mouth so I don't shriek. "Wh-what?"

She nudges me back from the door. *You must get out. You don't have time. They're coming. Go. Run.*

"But I need to see if my parents are okay."

They are dead. Please. Please, run. You must get out. Go. Now! Run!

The intensity of her words spurs me into action. I don't know if I'm dreaming. Maybe I am. But I do as she pleads for me to do. I grab my backpack and throw my sketchbook into it. My head snaps to my door again when I hear voices.

I choke on a sob. "What do I do?" I scream-whisper.

Run, Kaia! Out the window! The Moon Wolf nudges me towards my window. She's large. She comes just past my waist on all four paws. *Go! Hurry!*

I hurry to my window and open it as quietly and quickly as I can. I shakily climb out onto the roof. My window overlooks the back of the

15

house. I live just on the edge of the woods. It's easy to get lost. Which is just what I need to do. I look back at the Moon Wolf.

Hurry, sweet child. Into the woods! She's standing near the door.

"I lost my fucking badge. Just hurry up and start clean-up. I'll be down in a minute," a deep male voice says.

The Moon Wolf looks at me. *Go!* An ethereal blue and white glow lights up around her. Sparkles almost. Shimmers. Something I would never be able to explain or believe if I didn't see it with my own two eyes.

I leave her, even though I don't want to. She makes me feel safe. I run as quietly as possible to the corner of the house. I look around before jumping down as silently as possible onto the connected garage. I can see three Sheriff's department squad cars in the front yard. I wipe my eyes, unsure what's happening as I feel in the pocket of my jeans. I still have the badge I found.

I crouch and make my way to the edge of the garage. There's a trellis near the back of it. I quickly adjust my backpack straps over both shoulders and make my way down. As soon as I hit the ground, I start to run, but the Moon Wolf steps in front of me.

Stay back!

I plaster myself against the garage and close my eyes. I can feel I'm being searched for. I chance taking a glance towards my bedroom, but see nothing. At least not right away. My eyes widen when I see someone at the edge of the roof.

"Oh, God," I whisper. "He's wearing a uniform! I really did see that!"

Run! Run, Kaia! To the woods!

I don't hesitate, though my feet feel rooted to the ground. I force myself to move. To obey. Everything slows down. I feel like I'm running through quicksand. The bullets that start whizzing by me look to me as if they are bouncing off an invisible shield.

But that's impossible.

I look over my shoulder as I run and decide I have to be dreaming. It looks like I'm in a protective, invisible, impenetrable bubble that nothing can get through. Someone I've never seen before is behind me. He's tall. Muscular. His hair is dark. He looks like a slightly older version of the mystery Man in the Moon. I feel safe with him. Just as safe as I do with the Moon Wolf.

Which is why I feel like I have to be dreaming. None of this can be real. None of it. My parents are still alive. I'm going to wake up. They'll be waiting to take pictures of me before I drive to the party. I'm not being shot at. There's really not a Wolf and a strange man behind me.

Protecting me from the bullets.

Guiding me.

Don't look back! Run! Run! the man says. I can't see his lips move, but I can hear him in my head.

I snap my head forward and run, but not before I see that the man shooting at me is now chasing me. And so are two, maybe three, other people. I pump my legs as fast as they can carry me and hit the tree line. It's dark. I don't know where I'm going, but the Moon Wolf dives in front of me. Her light guides me. I follow her.

I feel the hand of the man on my back. I expect it to be cold, but it's not. It's warm. Soothing. Even though he has the same glow and shimmers surrounding him as the Moon Wolf does. He has to be a ghost. So does she. They can't be real.

Can they? Can any of this be real?

I shake my head. I'll wake up. Any minute now, I'll wake up. I know I will. It will all be okay. I'll be warm in my bed with memories of the best night of my life at the graduation party floating in my head. I'll wake up with the warm sun streaming through my windows. Any minute now.

But I don't. I don't wake up. My lungs feel like they're going to collapse. I'm starting to wheeze. I slow down because I need air. My ribs hurt. My stomach hurts. My chest hurts. My legs burn.

Run, girl. Don't you stop, the man says. *Keep going. They're behind us. We're almost to safety.* He propels me forward. I can feel him. I can feel his hands on my hips as the Moon Wolf runs ahead of me, lighting my way.

"I'm tired," I say as I cry. The tears blur my vision. "I can't breathe!"

He keeps pushing me. *Run, Kaia. You're almost fucking there. Run for me. He'll protect you. He's waiting. You just need to get to him. Don't you give up on me! Don't give up on him!*

I nod and keep running.

Take a breath, the Moon Wolf says. *We're almost there, sweetheart. In through your nose. Out through your mouth. You can do it!*

I do it. In through my nose. Out through my mouth. I repeat the mantra as I run. I'm not sure how far I've gone, but I listen to them. I don't stop. When I stumble, the man catches me and pushes me on.

I run through a small creek. Up hills. I jump across small crevices. When I feel like I'm going to fall after tripping, the man catches me, and I briefly feel as if I'm flying. Like he's carrying me when I just don't feel like I can jump far enough; high enough.

"Can't... run... anymore...," I pant.

The Moon Wolf looks back at me. *You must, Kaia!*

"Can't!" I stumble again and fall when my feet don't quite make it to the other side of a crevice I attempt to jump.

Kaia! the man yells.

I scream as I roll down a muddy hill.

Kaia! The man kneels down next to me when I stop rolling.

The Moon Wolf nuzzles my face. *Kaia, get up. You have to get up, sweetheart.*

I try to obey, but my body doesn't listen to the command. "Can't..." I fall back into the mud. My ankle screams in protest when I try to put weight on it. "Ow!"

They're coming, Kaia! Get up! He'll help you! We have to get to him! the Moon Wolf yells. *Connor! Help her!*

"Connor...," I whisper.

Kaia, come on. His hands grip my hips. He pulls me up. I don't know how, but the pain in my ankle seems to fade. *You need to get to the pack. Come on, Kaia. Run! Now!*

"The pack?" I shake my head like I'm coming out of a daze. I must have hit my head. Connor pushes me up the side of the crevice I fell into. I scramble to my feet and start running again.

Watch out! the Moon Wolf screams.

I turn, but the warning isn't in time. A hard body that feels like steel plows into me. I scream and curl into myself because it's all I can do. I cover my head as a hard boot meets my stomach. My legs. My arms.

Kade! the Moon Wolf screams. *Kade!*

"Did you think you could get away from us? Huh? You're just as stupid as your parents!" a male voice I've never heard growls at me as he kicks at me. Dirt flies into my mouth.

"Please, stop!" I scream. I spit out the dirt and keep my face covered. I'll wake up. Anytime now. I'll wake up.

Someone grabs my arms, but I keep a tight grip on my head. I'm slammed repeatedly into the ground. "You're finished! You're never going to be able to identify us! Just like your parents!"

I don't have any idea what they're talking about, but I can't scream anymore. The pain in my head from hitting the ground makes any sound impossible. I can't even keep a grip on my hair to cover my face.

I know more people have joined the man because I feel more people hitting me. I feel more kicks. I hear more voices. What they are saying, though, is so distant. So far away. I'm fading. I've squeezed my eyes closed so the dirt flying around me doesn't get into them, but I can't open them anymore even if I try.

The pain is so intense, I don't even know where it's resonating from. My legs. My back. My stomach. My chest. My face. My arms. My head. The tears fall as I take blow after blow, but all I see is darkness. A heavy weight falls over me like a blanket.

I still hear the Moon Wolf screaming for someone named Kade. I hear her howling. But I can't open my eyes. I can't even move now. I want to get up. I want to listen to Connor and run. He told me to run. Keep running. Don't stop.

But I did stop. I feel like I failed him. I feel broken. Not just my bones. My soul. My heart. All of me.

Kaia, Connor whispers. I feel his hand in my hair. How much time has gone by? *Kaia. Stay with me, sweetheart. Stay with me. He's coming. He's on his way. Just hold on.*

I try to hold onto his voice. Grasp it like a lifeline. But even it's fading. The further I sink into the darkness, the harder it is to feel him, or the pain. Anything.

But I try. I try to focus on the agony my body is experiencing because at least I'll know I'm still alive, but even that is difficult. It's fading. Everything is fading.

"Who's coming?" I manage to whisper. Though, I'm not really sure if the words left my mouth or if I only said them in my head.

Kade, Connor whispers. The name pulls at my heart. I don't know why.

Just as suddenly as he says it, the image of the Man in the Moon appears. I reach for it. It's barely there, but I can make out his features just enough to know who he is. I can see his muscle tone. I can see the sharp edges of his facial features. It's shimmery. It's not as solid as Connor and the Moon Wolf. It's wavy. Almost like a mirage someone would see in the distance walking through a desert.

Just as quickly as it appears, it fades. Just like it always does. Only this time, I feel my heart shatter into a million pieces at the loss. I can't feel Connor anymore. I don't hear the Moon Wolf screaming for the man named Kade. Her painful and heartbroken howls cease to hit my ears.

"Kade…," I whisper before I hear and feel nothing at all.

I'm going to wake up.

Anytime now.

The sun. It's going to be warming me.

Wake up! I scream to myself. *Wake up!*

CHAPTER THREE

~*~ KADE ~*~

I bolt upright, panting. I look around my room and rub my chest, completely unsure what woke me up this time. It wasn't the same dream I had last night. This dream was different. I felt at peace. A little frustrated, but I was at peace.

I was dreaming of *her*. A beautiful, almost raven-haired beauty. But she's blurry. I can't quite see her clearly. I can just make out the edges of her figure. She's small. Very petite. Sometimes, I can make out her eyes. They're big and a coffee brown. Sometimes I can make out her lips. Plump. Kissable. But just as my lips are about to meet hers, or just before I am able to touch her, she vanishes into a shimmery mist and floats away. Almost like she was a dream.

And then I wake up and realize she was just a dream. Like I just did. Only, I usually don't feel like I'm being pulled towards something. I don't feel like I'm being called. I don't feel uneasy. I usually wake up and feel soothed.

Not this time. I'm on edge. I scrub my hands down my face and let out a breath. Knowing I won't be able to go back to sleep, I decide to go for a run. It's the weekend, so I have time to myself. No meetings. No clients with new books coming across my desk.

I can't really complain. I don't really spend that much time in my office anymore. I have a CEO for that. Someone who is the front man for my company while I stay behind the scenes where I want to be. So I can train my pack and make sure they're all where I feel they should be. I don't actually take meetings or manuscripts unless I need to.

After I throw a pair of sweats on and a t-shirt, I make my way down the stairs of my house in the dark. This is the house I grew up in. Even though I have great night vision, thanks to my Wolf, and I've made several expansions to it, I still know it like the back of my hand and could walk through it with my eyes closed.

I make my way to the front door and grab my running shoes. Just as I'm putting them on, though, is when I hear it. When I hear her. Her pained howl. Her screams.

Kade! Kade, hurry!

"Mom?" I look around me. "Mom, where are you?"

Kade! The woods at the edge of Deimos' territory! Kade, hurry!

I don't question her. It's not the first time I've heard her or my father's voice telling me to hurry to help someone, either a Wolf or Human or Shifter, who needed me. They both may be gone, but that doesn't mean they haven't guided me in some ways.

Usually, I can see the ghost or shadow of one of them. Usually, they guide me. This time is different. My heart hurts. Just like that fucking day that changed my entire life. My Wolf is howling.

Mate! Mate! he growls. Then I feel it. I feel like my heart is being tugged. Like the piece that was missing is suddenly there. I can feel her. Her fear. Her panic. The pain. Excruciating agony. I feel her fading.

"Shit… Shit!" I throw on my shoes and open my bond with my pack. I don't know what is going on, but I feel a threat. *Dominick! Grab some of our warriors! We need to move!*

I can feel the second he wakes up. *What?* he asks me. *What the fuck is happening, Alpha?*

Get up! Now!

Alpha? One of the guards I have on patrol hears me. Fuck. Good. *Where do you need us?*

Head for the woods at the edge of our territory, Jamie, I tell him. *I'll need some guys.*

What area? he asks.

Fuck, I don't know, I answer.

I got it, Alpha, Dominick says. *Coming, now.*

I focus on the girl, but I've lost her. I know it's the same girl I see in my dreams, I feel it, but she's faded. Just like she always does right before I reach her. I try focusing on my mom, but all I can feel is her rising fear. Or maybe it's mine.

"I need a direction, mom," I say out loud. "I can't feel you or her." I run outside as several members from my pack meet me, including my Beta, Dominick.

"Where are we going?" Dominick asks.

I take a deep breath and focus. Suddenly, a black Wolf with a bit of gray fur appears in front of me. I know I'm the only one who can see him. *Fenn. Brother. Tell me where to go.*

Southeast. Follow me.

"Fenn?" Dominick asks. He watches me closely.

"Long story," I say. "Let's go." I watch Fenn as he takes off. *Southeast, Jamie.*

Got it, Alpha, he responds.

I run with four of my best warriors and my Beta, following the spirit of my brother, Fenn, as he bounds through the woods. The guards around the house and the pack house are all on high alert. Just how they should be.

You need to shift, brother, Fenn says to me. *We need to be fast.*

I do as I'm told. The others follow me with no question and shift as I did. In our Wolf forms, we run as fast as our paws will carry us. We leap over fallen trees and other obstacles. It felt like my heart hurt before, but it's almost blindingly painful now. The closer I get to the edge of our territory, the more I can feel her.

Mate, I growl. The mate bond is strong.

Mate? What? Dominick asks as he falls in step next to me. *Are you sensing your mate?*

Yes. She's near. And she's hurt. Badly.

Fuck, Kade. I don't know what the fuck is happening. You better explain it to me when we get home. Dominick leaps over a creek with such grace I almost forget to watch where I'm going.

He's always been far more graceful than me or any other Wolf I've ever seen. It's a strange thing because he's one of the least graceful Humans I've ever met. I'm sure it has something to do with the fact that his damn nose is always in a book or reading one on his phone.

We land on the other side and continue running. I still can't hear my mother or feel her, so I keep my eyes glued to Fenn as he leads us where we need to go. We have to be nearly there. We're almost to the edge of our territory.

I feel her. She's really fucking hurt. I push myself and run faster.

You're right. She's really fucking hurt. Kade, hurry up! Jamie yells at me.

I follow Fenn, but I can't help but notice the pain my pack is starting to feel. It's slamming into me just as much as hers is. Except it's not physical. It feels like their hearts are breaking. Like they are losing someone important to them. I can hear their Wolves start whining and whimpering. I can feel their confusion. I try to soothe them, but I can't. I feel it just as much as they do.

Only far more. The further she fades, the more my heart breaks. The feeling I felt at finally feeling that mate bond after so many years of believing I'd never feel it was very short-lived. Feeling like I'm losing her before I even met her, though, is one of the two worst pains I've ever felt.

No. I'm not fucking losing her. She's close. The closer I get to her, the more I can start to feel my mother. I can feel my father now, too. *We're close. Hang on, my mate. I'm almost there.* I don't know if she can hear me, but I hope she can. I hope my voice brings her some kind of comfort and gives her the strength she needs to fight.

We break into a small clearing. I see her. My father looks up at me with a pained expression. My mother is whimpering next to her and nuzzling her. Fenn is sitting next to my father. My sister-in-law, Aryan, is keeping watch.

I can't see her face, but I don't need to. I know she's the girl I see in my dreams. Jamie looks up at me. He's shifted to his Human form. The three warriors he has with him have all shifted and are all surrounding her.

"I… fuck… Kade, I don't know what to do here," Jamie says. "She's Human."

I shift back to my Human form with a shake of my head. "I can see that." I drop to my knees next to her, and my breath catches. She doesn't look alive. I wouldn't think she was if I didn't feel her.

"No, I mean, she's Human," Jamie says. "She's not a Shifter."

As soon as he says the words, I feel it like a sledgehammer to my heart. She's my mate. I can feel that with every fiber of my being. She is the completion to my heart and soul. She's the one I've been waiting for my entire life.

But she's Human.

There isn't an ounce of Wolf in her. If there were, I'd feel it. We would all feel it. We would know. I inwardly curse the Moon Goddess. She has one fucking sick and twisted sense of humor. First, she takes my entire family, except my little sister, away from me. Then, as if that isn't enough, she decides to give me a fucking Human mate.

"What do we do, Kade?" Dominick asks.

And for once, I don't fucking know. Leave her here? My Wolf howls in my head. He doesn't like that idea any more than my traitor of a heart does. We have a no Human rule for a reason. A very good one. I look up at my father and sister-in-law.

Don't do this, Kade. Don't do this to yourself. I never wanted you to be unhappy and reject your mate because of what happened to me and Aryan. Finding the only one in the world fated to be your mate, your destiny is not just the greatest feeling in the world, Kade. It should be treasured. It doesn't matter if she's Human or Shifter or a Wolf. It's the greatest power. She's special. The Moon Goddess wouldn't have chosen her for someone as powerful as you if she weren't. She could be your strength when you feel it waning. Just like you can be hers. Just like your mother was mine, and I hers. He looks down at the girl. And that's what she is. A fucking girl. She can't be any older than eighteen. Probably why I never felt her until now. *Even if she weren't your mate, you can't leave her here to die.*

I know he's right. I can't leave her here. She needs help. I don't know what happened to her, but she's been beaten pretty badly. I doubt she'll survive the night if I don't get her home and under the care of someone.

Or if you don't heal her yourself, my Wolf growls.

"Fuck," I whisper. He's right. I have that power. It's one of the perks of being fated mates. At least on the Shifter side of things. I can heal her, but since she's a Human, she'd never be able to do the same. I don't even know if I can do it since she's Human.

But it doesn't really matter because I can't leave her. No one would forgive me. My pack. My Wolf. My family watching over me. Fuck. I'd never forgive myself. So, no. No. I can't leave her here. She'll never survive.

I look up at my father, mother, brother, and sister-in-law. They are all watching me intently, waiting for my decision. Though, I know they already know. They know I could never leave her to die.

And then I hear his voice. *Kade, she's your fucking mate. Pick her up. Take her home.*

I shake my head. I don't hear him often, but when I do, it always cuts me right down to my core. I scrub a hand over my face. I don't know why the fuck Fenn, Aryan, and my mother and father can appear before me and guide me, but he never does. He's just in my head. I don't really even know if he actually says anything or if it's just my conscience.

Fuck, I miss you, Zeke. I look down at the girl and know right away I'm not going to be able to move her. Not without healing her first. At least enough to get her out of here. I put one hand on her stomach and the other on her shoulder.

"What do you need, Kade?" Jamie asks.

I look up at him. "Someone did this to her. We need to know who and why." I look at the spirits of my family. I don't know how much they'll be able to tell me, but I'm missing a lot. I don't like it.

The girl moans quietly. I'm sure it's because she feels a surge of warmth flooding through her as I heal her enough to be able to move her. Her head lolls towards me. Her eyelids flutter, but she doesn't open them. I close my eyes and focus on her injuries. I need to deal with one thing at a time because my mind is racing out of fucking control. I'm pissed off for more reasons than I can count, and I'm not looking forward to the conversation I'm about to have with Dominick.

When I open them, the only one with me is Dominick. The girl is healed enough to get her out of the open. My Spirit Guides are gone.

Probably because they all know I'm pissed at them, too. Fuck. I'm pissed at the world. The entire fucking universe.

I force myself to calm, though, and gently lift the girl in my arms. Her whimpers cut me. My heart is bleeding. My Wolf whimpers right along with her, and I feel that just as much. I want to get her fucking home so I can think.

"Talk to me, Kade," Dominick says, falling in step with me as I carry her. "Are you seeing your family and shit?"

I let out a long sigh and nod. "I tell you damn near everything, Dom. You know that. But you're my sister's mate. I know if I tell you everything, you'll tell her because you're a good man. You don't keep shit from her. It's something I respect about you. I don't want Jordan worried."

He raises a brow. "You think you saying your family is guiding you is going to worry her?"

"It's not just guidance, Dominick. I see them. I see their spirits. You don't know how fucking often they've saved us from a fate I couldn't see. How many times they have told me to turn left when I would have taken us straight. How many times my father has gotten our pack to circle around our enemies instead of running right fucking into them like I would have led us. Fuck. I've been the Alpha for fourteen years, and I'm still nowhere near my father's level. Connor Deimos is still the Alpha of this pack. I'm just acting in his absence."

"No. You're the Alpha of this pack. And you're a fucking good one because you aren't afraid to listen to your pack. You aren't afraid to listen to those guiding you. Past Alpha's or not. You listen to your mom. Your brother. Fuck, I'd bet Zeke is guiding you just as much, Kade."

I swallow hard, keeping my focus ahead of me and senses on her. "He's the only one I don't see. I see Fenn. Aryan. I see my mom. My dad. But I don't see Zeke. Sometimes, I can hear his voice. Or at least I think I do. Then I question it because I don't fucking know. It pisses me off because everyone but him has come back. They've all made the pain of losing them bearable. They've helped me and guided me in rebuilding our pack. But not him. Not Zeke. I've thought so many fucking times that maybe he fucking made it. Sometimes, I think I feel him. That twin bond they talk so fucking much about, you know? But it's fleeting. It's there, then it's gone. Just like his fucking voice."

"Maybe he's not dead," Dominick says. He swallows just as hard as I had.

"But you'd think I'd be able to feel him. I mean, of all people, right? I'm his fucking twin." I fall silent and shift the girl in my arms when she stirs. After a few moments, I take a breath. "They can't feel him either."

"Who?"

I nod towards the sky. "My Spirit Guides. It's like he vanished. If he was taken hostage, I would know. So would they. If he was still alive, I'd feel him. I believe that. They'd tell me."

"Unless his bond with you and the pack has been broken. At the very least, severely damaged. Maybe when you hear him, it's him thinking about you, but he quickly shuts that down because he thinks you're gone."

I just nod and blink. I've had the same thought myself, but it doesn't explain why my family can't feel him or go to him. They would have mentioned it if they were able to. I shake my head as we emerge from the trees in front of the house. No. I can't let myself have false hope. He can't be alive. It's been fourteen years. I'd know.

Jordan pokes her head out of the door. When she sees us, her eyes dart around before she opens it wide and lets us in. I've taught my sister very well. Always be aware of surroundings. Fight if you need to. Every woman in this pack gets the same training as the men. I will never be unprepared in the event of an attack. Everyone will be able to protect themselves and others.

Jordan looks up at me with watery eyes. "Your mate?"

"So says the Moon Goddess," I growl in response. I glare down at the girl as I walk past Jordan.

Dominick and Jordan don't follow. It's for the best. My mind is spinning. Having her as close to me as she is right now is wreaking havoc on every part of me. Including my carefully crafted Alpha persona. I have to keep telling myself and my Wolf that she is a Human. A fucking Human. No Humans in this pack. We need to protect them. That's our damn job. I will not let another spill their blood because they came up against a power that is superhuman compared to theirs.

I love my father, but he overestimated his strength. I will never allow another Human to do that. Of course, I'm not stupid. I am not the only Shifter with a Human mate. I didn't expect to have a Human mate, but

I'm not changing the rules. I'm the Alpha. The rule applies to me just like everyone else. Probably more.

But a few pack members have chosen to move away from the safety of our territory in order to be with their Human mate. While I've never forced them to leave the pack or break their bond with it, some have. It was just as painful for me as it was them. Their bond breaking with us is like a piece of my heart being taken with them.

Others, though, have simply chosen to leave to be with their mates in the Human world, which is what I wanted and wished for. They still have a connection with the pack, but they aren't with us. It's my way of showing my pack that I love them all. While my rule stands, I understand better than anyone that we don't choose our mates. I've given them an option.

One I don't have. I can't leave my pack to be with my Human mate. And I won't let a Human be in a world she doesn't belong. Not one as dangerous as this one. I think once more how giving me a Human mate when everyone, including the fucking Moon Goddess, knows my reason for rule, is cruel. Unjust.

I bring the girl to my room. Probably my first mistake, but I can't bring myself to be away from her. I don't have the strength to fight the bond I have with her right now. Healing takes energy. And it's energy I was lacking already by waking so early and abruptly. I know I need to recover.

Which is what leads to what I'm sure is mistake number two. I crawl into bed behind her and pull her close to me. She's shivering, but she also needs more healing. I can feel the broken bones and bruising scattered through her body. I got her here to help her. I need to finish the job. Afterwards, I'll send her back where she came from.

You know you can't do that. You need to figure out why the fuck she was running in the first place. From who. And you can't send her away anyway. She's our mate. Like it or not. My Wolf is as much of an asshole as I am. I guess since we're one, it makes perfect sense.

I have a rule for a reason. Do you want to see her suffer the same fate dad and Aryan did? Or the other Humans in our pack did? I sure as fuck don't. I'll help her figure out what happened. I'll deal with why. But I'm rejecting her as our mate. There is no place for Humans in this world. It's too dangerous.

He snaps viciously in my head. Too bad for him that he can't actually hurt me. I suppose I have some luck on my side for that one. I can feel his anger vibrating throughout me as he growls. He'd probably tear my head off.

But it's not him I'm worried about. I reach up and rub my chest. As soon as I thought of rejecting her, that intense fucking pain stabbed its way through my heart once more. Dammit, though. I know I'm right. What the fuck kind of mate would I be if I set her up to suffer a fate she would never be able to control?

A poor one not worth his salt. I won't do that to her. My rejection of her will suck for a while, I'm sure. It will be painful. But she's a Human. She knows nothing of my world. Humans are kept away from us because if they knew we exist, their bright fucking lives in the sun would be tarnished.

I ignore the pain I feel at the very idea of rejecting her. I've gotten good at ignoring pain. Fighting through it. I put my arm back around her and focus on healing her. I feel her relaxing against me. She presses her back into me like she's trying to get closer to the warm and soothing feeling that's overpowering her pain. I keep her close to me because I need to in order to heal her and grab the blanket on the bed. I wrap it around us both and force myself to relax. I need to rest if I expect to help her at all.

So, I close my eyes and let my power help her. As each and every bone begins to mend, I fall into a deep slumber, though not as deep as hers.

I won't admit that the woman in my arms feels like she's meant to be there. That I finally found the person I don't ever want to let go.

CHAPTER FOUR

~*~ KAIA ~*~

"Mmm...," I murmur. A warm, soothing feeling courses through me like gentle waves. My mind is fuzzy, but it's tranquil. Like a calm ocean breeze fluttering my hair. Or floating in a pool with my eyes closed and nothing on my mind. Just... peace.

I'm surrounded by the most beautiful scent. Something I've never smelled before. It's intoxicating. Spicy musk with some kind of woodsy smell. Oak. Purely male. Purely powerful. Yet the most reassuring scent. Enveloping. Like I'm safe. Protected. Cherished.

"Mmm..." I turn slightly onto my back and yawn with a soft smile as I open my eyes slowly. I haven't woken up feeling this relaxed in a long time. Maybe graduation did something good for me. No stress. At least until I start college.

But not until after I travel. I want to see the world. I've been planning it for many years. My mom always tells me I'm a free spirit. I've always loved being outside. She always says that is the reason we got a house just at the edge of Blood Mountain. So I could have plenty of room to run. When I came up with the idea of travel, they both supported my decision whole-heartedly. They're even helping me plan my trip.

As my eyes focus, the smile falls from my lips. My eyes widen. I sit up with a start. This isn't my room. I've never seen this room in my life. It's huge. Where my room is light and full of life, this room is dark and looks like a Vampire would be happy here.

The curtain over the giant window is black and blocks the sun. I only know it's daytime because the curtains don't block all of the light coming in at the sides. The room is lit up just enough for me to make out that the walls are painted a deep red. The carpet is black. The trim on the doorframe and windowpane also looks black. The bedspread is that same deep red on the walls. The posts and headboard are black and red.

My eyes dart around as they adjust. I take everything in. There's a huge, black dresser near the far wall and matching nightstands on both of the sides of the bed. In the middle of the nightstands is a single candle in a silver candle holder with an intricate design I can't quite make out. There is a larger silver candelabra in the middle of the giant dresser.

"This isn't my bedroom," I whisper.

"You're correct. It's mine," a deep, rumbling, all man, very dominant voice says.

My head snaps towards the edge of the room behind me. My hand flies to my throat. I try to inhale, but my lungs don't seem to be working any longer. The man stands and struts towards me in such a deliberate manner that I can't help but stare at his movements. They are graceful. Beautiful. Even.

The man is tall. I can tell he's built so well that any man in the world would be completely jealous and strive to be him. The black t-shirt he's wearing stretches across his muscles and looks like it might tear at any moment. The jeans that hang low on his hips hug perfectly to every single inch of him.

As he draws closer, my heartbeat quickens. I'm shocked because what I feel isn't fear. I should be terrified of this man who oozes power and control walking towards me with purpose and a sexy, slow gait, but I'm not. I'm intrigued.

He stops at the edge of the bed and sits down slowly next to me. "How do you feel?"

I blink a few times. My lungs finally remember to draw air. I take a few shallow breaths. The man is beautiful. His jaw is strong and chiseled, just like the rest of him. He has just the right amount of scruff on his jaw. And his eyes... They are a beautiful dark chocolate brown with specks of gold. I could drown in them.

Him.

I could drown in him. I am drowning in him. Sinking deeper and deeper, and I don't even want to come up for air. My heart feels like it's being pulled towards his. Like if I'm not near him, I'll die. I feel like I've known him my entire life. My soul recognizes his on a level far greater than what I understand. An attraction that baffles me.

It hits me so suddenly who he is, though, that I jolt. "The Man in the Moon..." The words are soft, even to my own ears, but he hears me.

"Not exactly the Man in the Moon. I'm Kade," he says. "And you are?"

I swallow. Hard. I can't take my eyes off of his. It's like there are golden sparkles where his pupils should be. Like he's reflecting firelight, only there aren't any flames near us. I force myself to look away and down at my hands.

I take a breath and swallow again. "K-Kaia."

"Well, K-Kaia." He chuckles. "I'm glad you're feeling better."

I furrow my eyebrows and look up at him. "Feeling better?"

He raises an eyebrow. "Yes. Feeling better. You've been out for a while."

This causes me deeper confusion. "Out?" I look around the room. "Where am I?"

He's silent for a few moments until I look back at him. "What do you remember?" he finally asks me.

I shrug. "I just graduated. I was getting ready for the party. I was super excited because I'm turning eighteen." I look around again. "This doesn't look like a party."

He chuckles. "Hardly." He falls silent once more. When I look back at him, he's sitting with his elbows on his knees. He takes a breath that I can hear is shaky, and all I want to do is hug him. I'm convinced there is something wrong with me. Or that I'm really dreaming. "Why did you call me the Man in the Moon?" he asks me after several moments of silence. He doesn't look at me, though, and I already miss his eyes.

Yep. Crazy.

I look down at my hands and let out a breath. I don't know how much I should say. I don't know him. The strange feeling I have, the bizarre pull towards him, is difficult to comprehend. Instead of answering him, I bite my lip and hug the comforter to myself. I don't know what to say.

I don't need to see him turn to look over his shoulder at me. I can feel those eyes on me again. "So far, I've asked you four questions. You've answered one. So, we're going to try this again."

My eyes snap to his. His tone requires it. I have the overwhelming need to apologize. Instead, I think of each question and force my eyes from his once more. "I'm confused. Okay. But confused. I don't understand why I was out, as you say, or for how long, or why. I don't remember anything, though I feel like I'm supposed to remember something, or you wouldn't ask me what I remember." I take a deep breath, hoping that will appease him, and that he won't ask me again about my reasoning for calling him what I did.

"We're up to three of four." His tone is condescending and immediately gets under my skin.

I glare up at him. His cocky grin infuriates me. "You want me to answer the last question so you can tell me I'm stupid and crazy?"

He shakes his head. The stupidly sexy arrogance doesn't fall from his perfect lips. Instead, he grins more. "Nope. I want you to answer because I asked. And I don't do very well with disobedience."

I scoff. "Refusing to answer your question is hardly disobedience. It's me protecting myself from a complete stranger."

He laughs. The sound both fills me with joy and pisses me off. "But you do know me, don't you, Kaia? You feel like you've known me your entire life and can't quite figure out why."

He knows something I don't. He knows a lot of things I don't. Being put at such a disadvantage makes me uncomfortable. I turn away from him again. He stands and strides to the other side of the room. I watch him because the thought of him leaving me alone in this room fills me with a strange sense of emptiness and dread.

The room is suddenly bathed in a soft glow of warm light that brings a different ambiance to the incredibly dark room. I feel like this is

34

very much Kade. I know nothing about him, but this bedroom screams the man in front of me. It's dark and broody just like he is.

He walks back to the bed with the same sense of grace and purpose he had earlier. He's not in any hurry. He sits down once more and keeps his eyes completely focused on me. In the light, I can see the danger I hadn't before. Kade is a large man. Intimidating. There is nothing about his posture that is gentle as I'd thought before. He's all solid. Hard.

I don't understand why I don't want to run.

Or why the hell I don't feel truly afraid of him. I don't know how I know that Kade won't hurt me. No matter how intimidating he is. My brain screams at me to shrink away, but I don't. I don't hold his gaze, but I don't curl into myself either.

"Why did you call me the Man in the Moon?"

I know instinctively that he's not going to drop it. Maybe if I tell him, he'll tell me why I'm here instead of at home planning my trip to Europe. I draw my knees up to my chest and keep the blanket tucked around me. It smells like him, and I don't know why, but that scent makes me feel safe.

I sigh. "Because... I..." I take a deep breath and hide my face a little from him. "Because ever since I was a little girl, I..." His eyes burn into me. I blush and shiver. "I have never told another soul this..., but... I saw a figure, mostly just a face. It was never completely clear. It was like it... shimmered?" I shrug and say nothing more.

"And you think it was me." It's a statement. A direct one. Accusing. I can hear the growl. I can hear his disapproval. His opinion of me.

"It was you," I whisper. He says nothing, but his eyes stay laser-focused on me. I bite the inside of my cheek as tears suddenly sting my eyes. Thinking of the Man in the Moon makes me think of the Moon Wolf and the man. Which makes me remember running. "Where am I?" I ask again. Only this time, it's a whisper, and I choke on the sob.

"What do you remember?" he asks again, just as he had before.

This time, the tears that threaten to fall nearly make it. I glare at him as viciously as I can. "You sit there and expect me to answer your questions, but you won't answer a single one of mine? Obviously, I've gone through something traumatic! I'm waking up in a strange bed, in a strange room, with a man I've seen in my dreams and in stupid visions that make me feel insane!" I throw the covers off. Thankfully, I'm still wearing clothes, though they are worse for wear. They've certainly seen better days.

I crawl out of the massive bed with every intention of putting distance between me and him. He makes my heart do strange things. My head gets fuzzy. I have a magnetic pull to him, or something, and I need to think of something other than how good he smells or looks.

My feet hit the floor just as the anger at him for being a condescending asshole fades. Tears stream from my eyes, but I will not allow him to see them. I won't look at him. I need to get out of here. I don't know where I am, but I'll figure it out. I'll get home. Back to my parents. They're probably missing me. I'm sure the cops are out looking for me.

The thought of the cops makes it feel like there is a knife being stabbed through my heart. I cry out a pained sob because it hurts. Images I don't understand flash through my mind. I drop to my knees and start crying even harder

Dark like midnight.

I'm running.

The Moon Wolf.

The man.

Cops.

I try to catch my breath as so many different things flash through my mind like bursts of light. Things that don't make sense and feel like a dream. Like they are so far away that I can see them, but not quite make them out or make sense of them.

Kade cups my cheek gently in his and tilts my face up so I'm forced to look at him. Focus. I sniffle and take several deep breaths focusing on the golden fleck in his eyes. I'm locked onto him. Once more, it's like I'm drowning in him. Like he's surrounding me.

"What do you remember?" he asks again. Only this time, his voice is soothing. Deep. Raspy. There's a dominance, but it's nothing like it was the first few times he asked me.

I don't bother moving from the place on the floor that I dropped. I cry harder because I can't answer him. All I can see are flashes that I can't really decipher. I close my eyes and shake my head to try and clear it, but all that does is cause more confusing images to surge into me.

I shake my head. "I… I don't know!" I hold my head. I feel him helping me to my feet and sitting me on the edge of the bed. The bed dips as he sits next to me once more.

"Take a breath." His hand snakes around my waist. He pulls me closer to him, and the action calms me. It's like he draped a warm, invisible blanket around me.

I follow his command and take a breath. And then another. Followed by one more. Slow, deep breath after breath until my heart has returned to a normal pace. Part of me hates the fact that this intimidating giant of a man has that effect on me. The other part just wants to melt into him and never move from his side again.

I sniffle and wipe my eyes. I don't want to show weakness in front of him. Maybe if I explain what happened, he'll finally tell me where I am and why. Maybe he can help me make sense of the things I'm seeing.

"I remember things. I don't know what they are or mean." I struggle with how much to tell him. Telling him about the Moon Wolf and Man is something I'm hesitant to do. It's not just that it's private. It's that I've told no one. It's a secret between me and the Moon Wolf and Man.

"Tell me what you remember, Kaia."

I shake my head and swallow. "Just bits and pieces. There were cops at my house. I ran. They shot at me." I hug myself.

"Try to remember," he says quietly. "I can't help you if I don't know. And right now, all I know is that you were left for dead at the edge of my terr-" He cuts himself off and clears his throat. "My property."

The words left for dead make me whimper, but it's the memory it brings with it. I feel my entire body deflate, and I cover my face with my hand, wrapping my other arm around myself. The sobs this time are gut-wrenching and sound like pained howls to my ears because I remember it all.

"Th-they k-killed m-my p-p-p-parents!" I wouldn't be able to stop the words if I tried. They all come flying out of me with the speed of light. "Th-they sh-shot them! I don't kn-know wh-why!" I know I sound hysterical, but I can't stop. "I hid! Th-they tr-tried to f-find me." I cry harder and louder. "Sh-she told me t-to run. I r-ran! Th-they saw m-me. Th-they sh-shot at me. H-he pro-protected me!" I choke on the hysterical cries as I talk and cough. Kade grips my hip. "Th-they said to r-run to the w-woods. Th-that h-he would h-help. But I f-failed th-them! I c-couldn't get th-there. Th-they caught me!" I rock back and forth as I cry.

Thankfully, Kade says nothing. Instead, he keeps me held tightly to his side while I cry. I don't know how long he sits with me, but he doesn't move the entire time. He doesn't say anything, but he doesn't leave.

"Thank you for telling me," he says quietly after a long while of silence.

He looks up as a young woman with dark, raven colored hair comes in. She's a small woman. Maybe around my height. She looks friendly with the soft smile that falls across her red lips. Even with her coal-colored eyes that contrast with the almost ivory color of her skin tone.

She doesn't say anything, though. She sets a pile of clothing on the chair Kade had been sitting in earlier. There is also a bottle of shampoo and conditioner along with a hairbrush and a small make-up kit.

Kade watches her every move until she finally looks back at him. "Kaia. This is Jordan. She's my sister." He looks down at me. His deep and rich voice further calms me. "She's brought a few things you'll need. I have some things to take care of, and you need rest. You're not finished healing, and you need to sort through everything you just remembered. Jordan is here to help you. She'll get you anything you need." He stands. I instantly miss his touch. Strength. His warmth. He strides to the door.

"Why do I see you in my dreams?" I whisper because while I want to know the answer, I'm also afraid of it.

Kade doesn't answer. Disappointment washes over me, but I know I have no right to feel it. I didn't ask loudly enough for him to hear. That was intentional. It doesn't stop me from sniffling and biting my lip, though. I look down at my feet and blink back tears. Partially over everything I remembered, but mostly because Kade is walking away, and I want him to stay.

"Kade," Jordan says as she sits down next to me. Her voice is laced with warning.

Kade stops at the door and looks over his shoulder. He glares at his sister. Those pretty eyes are filled with disdain. Anger. I expect a chill to run down my spine when he flicks them at me, but there isn't.

There isn't because when I look into his eyes, I see something I'm sure I'm not supposed to. Confusion. Like there is a war being fought in

38

his mind. Like he wants to answer the question I was so sure he didn't hear, but he won't. Or maybe he can't.

But it's not the confusion that grips my heart and squeezes. It's something deeper. Something stronger. Something I don't understand because just as quickly as I see it, he blinks. It's gone. Like a flash of lighting that struck something, and then went back to its home in the sky to wait and ruin something else.

Kade is hiding something. I know it. I can feel it. I will find out, even if it's the last thing I do. As he leaves the room, I fear it will be.

With that fleeting glance at me before he left, I know one thing. I don't doubt Kade will help me like he says he is going to. What I do doubt is if my heart will survive.

CHAPTER FIVE

~*~ KADE ~*~

I shut the door to my bedroom as I close my eyes. I lean against it and let out a long breath. I cross my arms over my chest and lean my head against the door. "You don't need to look so fucking smug," I say to Dominick without opening my eyes.

I don't need to see him to know he's there. Even if I couldn't smell him, there is no way he would let Jordan do this alone. Bonding with Kaia is going to be hard. She's the Beta's mate. While everyone in this pack can feel a bond with my mate, the Luna, in our pack, the Beta's mate has always felt it the strongest. When I reject her, which I will, Jordan will be just as destroyed as I am.

But giving Kaia someone to talk to is important. If she's going to trust me to help her, she needs someone she can lean on since it will not be me. I can't allow myself to get close to her. I can't let our bond with one another grow. It will be better for all of us this way, but especially Kaia.

"You're really walking out without answering her question?"

I open my eyes and glare at him. "There's nothing to answer. She doesn't need to know."

"You know that's bullshit. She deserves an answer. She's the Luna of this pack."

I walk towards my office without saying anything to him. A small part of me knows he's right. It's a part I refuse to listen to, though. I will not allow a Human to be put into harm's way. Especially one that is my mate. I may not be able to have her completely, but I can still protect her from a life she doesn't deserve. A life filled with constant training for a war I plan on waging as soon as I find the pack responsible for the deaths and loss my pack and I endured.

I close the door behind me and stalk to my desk. This room is my new sanctuary. My sanctuary used to be my bedroom, but now that her scent is all over it, I'll never be able to go back in there again. Fucking vanilla and honeysuckle.

I sigh when I feel a cold draft against my side. "Don't start with me, dad," I growl.

Oh, it's not me you're going to have to face, son.

The words send a shiver down my spine just before I feel her presence. But it's not anger. It's not biting bitterness. It's not even a cold rage. I can deal with all of those just fine. What I cannot deal with is the emotion wafting off her right now and crashing into me like a tidal wave.

I'm so disappointed in you, Kade. You're better than this. You're the Alpha of this pack. And she is your Luna. You know you are stronger with your mate. We've proven that so many times.

I take a breath and glare down at my mother. It's not the first time I've felt angry with her or my father for leaving me, but today it's more intense. *Are you kidding me? Mom, you and dad were killed! How can you say that you were stronger together? If that were the case, you'd still be here! And the Alpha of this pack? Fuck! He's the Alpha of this pack.* I point at my father without looking at him. *I'll never live up to him!*

Kade! That's enough! my father yells. His voice reverberates through my head, but it just pisses me off more.

I whirl to him, shooting him the same intense glare. *You and Aryan were killed because you didn't have Shifter strength and power, dad!*

Aryan and I were killed protecting this pack, Kade! he yells at me. The same glare I give him is reflected back at me. *We were killed no differently than the Shifters and Wolves who were part of our pack! Every single member of the pack brought their own strength. Human. Wolf.*

41

Shifter. It didn't matter. They made us strong. They bonded us together. They reminded us we were not just the Wolf. We were Human, too. Your way of thinking is not only an insult to myself and Aryan, but to every single life we lost that day. Human, Wolf, Shifter alike! You cannot keep continuing on with this bullshit that we were killed because we were Human! You fucking know better!

I shut my mouth. It's not like he hasn't told this to me before. It's an argument we've had plenty of times. One I know I won't win. It doesn't matter, though. My mind is made up. I lost my entire life that day. He'd have been faster, stronger, unstoppable if he'd been a full Shifter. I wouldn't have lost so much.

I choose to change the subject. *When are you going to tell me which pack ruined my life?*

He glares at me even more darkly and shakes his head. *When you grow the fuck up. Which is obviously not today.* He tangles his finger in my mother's fur as they disappear.

But not before I see the hurt in my mother's eyes that she tries to hide when she turns her head and buries it into my father's hip. "Fuck…" I reach for them both as they fade. "Mom, I'm sorry!"

It's okay, Kade, I hear her whisper. I can hear that it isn't. I really upset her this time, but it's the crushing feeling of her heartbreak that makes me hang my head in shame.

For the first time since I implemented my rule, I question it. And not because of the sexy girl in my bedroom. Because that voice that keeps niggling in the back of my mind is telling me how right my father is. He's not the only one who was killed that day. Neither was Aryan. We lost Wolves. We lost Shifters. We lost Humans. There was no prejudice.

I scrub my hands down my face. "Fuck." I take a deep breath. I can feel my Wolf whining and rejecting every single thought I have about sending Kaia away.

We need to protect her. She's our mate, he growls.

Shut-up, would you? I rub my eyes as if that will make him stop. But I know better. He's a stubborn fucker. Just like I am. He never agreed with my decision in the first place. If we weren't one entity, I'm sure he'd have jumped ship long ago.

She's our mate. Go to her. Tell her. Mark her as ours!

I'm about to snap again at him, but someone knocks on my door, providing a distraction at the perfect time. "Yeah," I call.

A timid looking girl pokes her head in. "Sorry to bother you, Alpha. One of our guards brought this from the area where you found Luna."

I growl low at her being called Luna. The girl jumps at my tone. I sigh. "Give it here."

She lowers her eyes and quickly makes her way to my desk. She puts a brown backpack that has seen better days on my desk and scurries from my office. She quickly closes the door behind her. I hear her let out a relieved sigh and sigh myself. I'm going to have to apologize later. I don't run this pack based on fear. I can be hard. Cold. I can be the world's biggest asshole, but I have never and will never give anyone in my pack a reason to fear me.

I search through the pockets on the outside and find nothing. I open it and find only a sketchbook with Kaia's name etched on the cover. I put it down and put my elbows on my desk. I run my fingers through my short hair and tug a little in frustration before dropping my hands back on the desk.

Dominick. My office, I request through the mind link I have with every single member of my pack.

A few moments later, Dominick enters my office. "You requested the presence of my company?"

I smile and chuckle. Leave it to him to bring me out of a foul mood. There's a reason he's both my best friend and Beta. "Take a seat. I promised you a conversation."

He barks out a laugh as he sits. "Give me a shot of the good whiskey you keep hidden, and maybe I'll stay."

I laugh because I know he would anyway, but I reach down and take out a bottle of thirty-five year old Karuizawa Emerald Geisha Bourbon Cask. I grab two shot glasses and set them on my desk. I fill each glass and put the bottle back.

I hand him one. "Better?"

He grins as he takes a sip. "Much. How much did this bottle cost you?"

I shrug. "Fifty-five grand."

He laughs. "Just fifty-five grand. No fucking big deal." He takes another sip. "Alright. Talk."

I down my shot with a sigh. "Well, you know she's my mate."

"Got that. Maybe your ridiculous rule can burn in Hell where it belongs."

"Fuck you. It's not going anywhere. It's just been more reinforced."

He finishes his drink and sets the cup down. He leans back in the leather chair in front of my desk and crosses his arms over his chest. "When I felt the mate bond with Jordan, it was unlike anything I've ever felt. The pull was more than magnetic. It was fucking irresistible. Like I was a drug addict, and she was the hit I couldn't live without. I couldn't wait to make her mine. I was fucking crazed. Anyone else even so much as glanced at her, I wanted to rip out their heart and feed it to them. How the hell are you sitting there like it doesn't faze you at all? Like you can reject her officially, and it doesn't bother you in the slightest."

I let out a long breath and lean back in my own chair. I close my eyes. "It does, Dom. Every time I think of it, my Wolf howls so painfully that it nearly brings me to my knees. My heart feels like it's shattering over and over again."

"Then why the hell are you doing this?"

"To protect her."

"That's fucking bullshit, Kade. It's -"

I hold up a hand to silence him. "I just got into it with my parents. I don't need it from you, too."

He's silent for a few moments before he lets out a breath of his own. "So, you can see them, too. Fourteen fucking years, and you didn't think to tell me."

My eyes snap open. "What?"

He's glaring at me. "Jordan, Kade. Jordan sees them, too."

I just stare at him as my mouth falls open. "What? Why didn't she tell me?"

He raises a challenging eyebrow that no one would get away with but him. "Why didn't you tell her? Maybe you'll answer your own damn question."

I suddenly have a massive headache. I reach up and rub my temples. "Because I didn't want her to be upset that I could see them if she wasn't able to. And how the fuck do you bring that shit up?"

"You're Alpha, Kade. You can link with her and see it yourself. Not like you've never done that shit with anyone to see what was going on when you felt like it was something significant that you needed to know."

"You know I don't like doing it. And you know she fucking feels it. No matter how subtle I do it with her. She hates it and feels like I don't trust her. That's the last thing I want her to feel. She's been through enough. You know how hard she took everything."

"You act like you didn't take it just as hard."

I fall silent because he's right. Jordan and I were both distraught. There isn't a day that goes by that we don't think of that day. The fact that we can both function today is really saying something considering where we started.

Although, when anyone mentions my twin brother, I feel the pain of losing the other half of me all over again. The plans we made to lead together burned to the ground that day. I still don't feel like he's dead, but him not being here with me still breaks me.

I scrub my hands over my face again. "Sometimes, I hear Zeke's voice."

Dominick's eyes widen. "What?"

I nod and look at him again. "Like he's alive. But he can't be, right? I'd be able to find him if he were. Or he'd somehow tell me. But you asked me last night. You wanted an explanation. My parents guide me. Fenn. Aryan. I've never seen Zeke. He doesn't exactly guide me. I do hear him sometimes. Maybe it's in my head. I don't know. As for my mate. I think you figured that one out on your own."

"The entire pack knows. You know you're going to have to address this. Pack have left because of your rule."

I sigh. "They are still under pack protection. Even those that completely broke from the pack. You know I'd never completely abandon anyone. I'm not addressing anything. What I am going to do is figure out what the hell made her run. She said there were cops shooting at her. They killed her parents. She hid until she ran. She was led by someone or something. I have suspicions on who."

He watches me a few moments before he finally runs his fingers through his hair, messing it up even more than it already is. "So, you're going to gloss over the part where she is your mate, you have a stupid rule of no Human mates that you refuse to change, your parents are guiding you as they are your sister, and that you still hear your brother's voice but can't feel him so you think it's in your head."

I hear the sarcasm dripping from his voice but ignore it. "Yep."

He chuckles and leans forward, putting his elbows on his knees. "Fine. But this is not going to go away. Who are these cops? Would she recognize them?"

"I don't know. I doubt it. She was running, and they were shooting at her."

"Why?"

"I don't think she knows. She said she hid from them. They tried to find her. She didn't say it, but she said that she was led out of there. I think it was by my mom and dad."

Dominick raises an eyebrow. "And that little revelation doesn't change things a little for you?"

I glare as I stand. "We need to figure out why the hell cops killed her parents and tried to kill her. That's our focus." I say nothing more as I walk to my office door.

He finally sighs and follows. "I am going on record here and saying this is stupid."

I pause at my door. "Helping a girl in trouble is stupid?"

He returns the glare I gave him earlier. "Ignoring the big elephant in the fucking room is stupid. I'm all for protecting our Luna." He holds up a hand to silence my protests when I open my mouth. "Which is what she fucking is, whether you and your stubborn ass want to believe or not."

I shake my head and open the door. I walk in silence with him following to the garage. I jump in my black Mercedes Benz GT sports car and wait for him to get into the passenger side before I take off.

"Do you even know where you're going?"

I shoot him my best look of perplexity. "You do know I'm an Alpha. I can block her from hearing me and my thoughts and still hear hers. I don't like that level of intrusion, but I needed to know."

We both fall silent as I drive to her house. I know it's at the foot of the mountain and near the edge of the woods. I heard her thoughts quite clearly. Her mother always thought her spirit was wild. She wanted to give her a home that had a lot of room for her to explore. Run.

I use my connection to her to find the house. It's not that far from our pack house. I chuckle because it's fitting. One more thing the Moon Goddess seems to find funny. My mate is not only a Human, but she's this fucking close to me.

And she has been her entire life.

"The place is crawling with cops," Dominick says. "She was passed out for all of yesterday and most of today. What are they still doing here? Don't they usually leave the house after they clear out the bodies and gather their evidence? Does that take two days?"

I watch the activity as I drive slowly by. "I wouldn't think so. But I'm not a cop." I find what looks to be a driveway and turn down it. I follow it to a clearing in front of an old, abandoned house and park. I get out. Dominick follows, but I can feel his questions and uncertainty slamming into me.

He won't say anything, though. He'll follow and pick up on my signals. It's yet one more thing that makes him such a good Beta and even better friend. So, as I sneak through the woods towards the house, I don't need to look back to know he's right behind me.

When we get to the edge of the property Kaia's house sits on, I kneel behind some bushes. Dominick kneels next to me, sniffing the air. He glances at me a few times, but I don't say anything. I let him tell me what he's sensing because I am sure it's the same thing as I am.

Why am I smelling Shifters, Kade? he finally asks.

Because you are.

He looks at me in complete horror. *What the fuck is the girl into? She's Human. She shouldn't have anything to do with Shifters!*

I nod, not taking my eyes off the activity going on in front of us. *Did you pick up the scent I did at the house we parked at?*

Yeah, but I ignored it. I thought someone from our pack ventured down here to explore. The house is abandoned. Maybe they came down here to get away or something. The scent is strong.

That's because it belonged to someone from the Deimos Pack. Someone who left when I imposed my rule. I kept track of everyone. Even those that broke the bond. Most of them didn't totally break it. They just left. It was hard enough on all of us when I made them leave the pack house. *But they all understood. I wanted to protect them. I couldn't let them be in our territory. Too dangerous.*

But you asked for them to be close. Fuck, Kade. Why am I only just learning this shit? I'm not only your best friend, I'm your Beta. And your fucking brother-in-law.

I glance at him. *To protect you, Dominick. And my sister. I don't want everyone in the fucking pack knowing where I sent pack members I told to leave. For all they know, they are no longer a part of the Deimos Pack. If anything happens, no one knows shit. Only me.*

He scoffs. *You mean, only you so if we ever get captured by any other pack or threat, the only one they'd torture for information is you.*

I don't look at him. *It's my job as Alpha to protect my pack.*

And it's my job as Beta to protect you. You know, keep you from making stupid mistakes and foolish decisions. Like keeping shit from me you shouldn't. If you didn't actually kick anyone out of the pack for having a Human mate, why the fuck does the rule exist?

I sigh in exasperation and glare. *To protect the Humans, Dominick. What if we were attacked? Humans can't shift. They can't fight off a Shifter. It's not fucking possible. We've seen it. Shifters are too strong. And even stronger now than they were then, Dom. Humans do not belong in this world.*

So, what are you going to do about your mate, Kade? Huh? What if she has nothing and no one?

It's not like the thought hasn't crossed my mind. But I do know that I can't leave my pack. And I won't let her be in the type of danger she would be being around me. I shake my head. *I don't know.*

You're being ridiculous. I wish Aryan would smack you upside the head like she used to when we were kids and causing chaos. Because you really fucking deserve it.

I chuckle. The truth is, she has a few times. Of course, I didn't feel it like I did when she wasn't a spirit. But the motion was still there. And my mind remembers the sting. I still flinch just as I would when I was a kid. But it's the disappointment I feel the most. The same I felt from my mother earlier today. It's that feeling that does more for me than anything else. And for the second time today, it has me questioning myself; my decision.

I quickly shake it off as soon as I see the cops leaving the scene. I watch as one of them looks towards where Dominick and I are hiding, but he makes no move towards us. He does tilt his head up, though. Like he can smell us on the light breeze, even though we are downwind. I'm immediately uncomfortable and on alert. Not because I think he might sense us, but because I can smell him. I know he's a Shifter. And he's from a pack I don't recognize.

I can hear Dominick's Wolf whining and growling along with my own, so I know he feels exactly as I do. We wait for them all to leave before we move. We stealthily walk to the house and around back. I check the door and sigh when it's locked.

"We can go through the window." Dominick points up. He's standing a few feet behind me.

I step back to him and look up. I know instantaneously that it is her room.

Kaia.

I can smell her sweet scent. My heart pounds at the thought of her. My stomach tightens. My cock jumps in on the betrayal and twitches. Fuck her for making me feel any of this. I ignore it all and look around for a way to get up to her second floor window. I could jump and make it, but using that kind of power in broad daylight is something I will never do. No matter how isolated we are. We aren't home. I don't know who the fuck is watching.

I see a trellis on the side of the garage and make my way to it. I quickly climb it. Dominick follows. We swiftly make our way across the roof, keeping a lookout for anything suspicious. Seeing nothing and no one watching, we duck into the open window of Kaia's bedroom.

And stop dead in our tracks.

"Holy fuck," I say in disbelief.

"Think they were looking for something? Jesus."

The room has been ransacked. Clothes are strewn everywhere. Her pictures that I assume had been hanging on her wall at one point are on the floor. They are shattered. Paintings are cut to shreds. Her bed is flipped upside down. The blankets are shredded. The mattress is torn apart.

"What the hell is the point of this?" I ask.

"I don't know. They have to think she has something they want."

I spot a duffel bag and pick it up. I hand it to Dominick. "I'm going to look around the house. Get some things you think she'll need. I'm not good with women."

He scoffs. "Fuck. You are too. They fall at your damn feet."

"Don't mean I know what the hell they need. Other than my cock." I shoot him a smirk. He laughs and shakes his head as he starts picking through her clothing.

I head out of her room, stepping over the door that's been kicked off its hinges and broken in half. Just as I thought, the rest of the house has been destroyed. I can smell the stench of blood over the overpowering scent of the Shifters that were in this house. But subtly, underneath it all, is the scent of my pack. I sniff the air and stay alert as I search the house for something, anything, to tell me what the fuck happened here and why.

My eyes fall on a picture in a silver frame. My heart feels like someone is squeezing it. In the photograph is who I assume are Kaia's parents. With them is Aisha and Evan Roman. Evan is a Shifter. He left after I implemented my rule because his wife was Human. And he had a daughter, Leia. He wanted to protect them just as much as I did. He moved his family to the foot of Blood Mountain. The house I parked at was his.

He was killed in a car accident a couple of years ago. As was his wife and daughter. The fact that they are with Kaia's parents, though, and their daughter is hugging Kaia, creates a lot of questions in my mind.

Above and beyond the stench of the unknown pack and smell of blood, I sense something else. It takes me a moment to place it, but when I do, my heart starts racing. On the mantle is a timer. And attached to the timer is TNT.

"Time to go, Dominick!" I yell up the stairs.

Moments later, we're exiting the house through the back. The sun has set. Thankfully, we're shrouded in darkness as we run towards my car. Jumping in, I peel out and quickly speed home. The framed picture is tucked safely at my side. The only thing left from the house that is now lighting up the night sky. I can hear sirens in the distance, but there's no chance of them saving the house. It's gone.

As I navigate up the winding mountain roads towards home, I arrange all of the questions I have running through my head. The biggest one, though, is Kaia's relationship with Leia Roman. It might be insignificant, but instincts tell me it's not.

50

And my instincts are never wrong.

CHAPTER SIX

~*~ KAIA ~*~

"And this is, uh, well, it's the house where all of our friends are," Jordan says as she leads me into a large house.

Jordan, apparently Kade's little sister, has been giving me a tour of the property. At least the houses. The house Kade lives in with Dominick and Jordan is huge. It's very much Kade. Just like his room. Dark and broody with a touch of elegance and light that he tries hard to hide. In his house, the windows are tall. It smells like freshly cut wood throughout the whole house. Like it was just built today.

Of course, that can't be true. Jordan told me their father built it years before with his own hands. It was not only his pride and joy, it's Kade's as well. He built more onto it since his parents were killed. Jordan wouldn't tell me how it happened, but she did say that it was a heartbreaking day. They not only lost their mother and father, but also their sister-in-law and both of their brothers, one of them being Kade's twin.

I can't imagine how difficult it would be to lose a twin. It was hard enough losing my only friend. I push Leia out of my mind and cross my arms over my chest as I follow Jordan. I blink away the tears that always come when I think of her and focus on the house I'm being shown.

"Kade has expanded this, too. As more people started staying."

I look around the house. Much like his house, it's dark with a touch of elegance. Dark woods. Dark drapes. Tall windows. That beautiful smell of pine. Fresh. Like a forest should smell. Fitting since we are literally in the middle of the woods at the foot of a giant mountain.

"Why are so many people here?" I ask. I'm genuinely curious.

Jordan bites her lip. "He's… very kind. He likes to make sure those close to him are taken care of and always have a place to call home."

I nod. I can't deny that small bit of knowledge into Kade makes my heart flutter. I don't understand why, but it makes me feel closer to him somehow. Who am I kidding? I don't understand much of anything about this place. I am smart enough to realize that Connor and the Moon Wolf are somehow connected to this group of people. I understand that Kade is powerful somehow, and that he helps people.

I follow Jordan into a large room where a lot of people are gathered. It appears to be a game room. There's a pool table. There's even an ice hockey table. There's a TV mounted to the wall that is larger than any I've ever seen in my life. And every gaming system known to man is laid out neatly underneath.

Two guys look to be in a very intense battle of Mario Kart. A couple of the kids are giggling about Pokémon as they play on what I assume is their parents' iPads. A few people see me. They seem to stare at me in shock. Some lower their eyes. Others turn to whisper to each other, their eyes focused on me. I'm immediately uncomfortable and start backing out of the room.

Jordan glares at everyone and turns to me. "This is where a lot of them come to hang out." She leads me down a hallway and away from the game room.

I look over my shoulder. "Why were they looking at me like that?"

She nibbles her lip. "You're new." She offers nothing else, but I feel she's holding back. I got the same feeling from Kade when I questioned him.

A tall and well-built man comes towards us. He looks to be near Kade's age, but I can't quite figure out what that is. Maybe thirties. I move behind Jordan.

The man nods to me as he passes. "Luna," he rumbles. His voice is so low that I can feel my body vibrating from it.

I narrow my eyes and glare at his retreating back. "Did he just call me crazy?"

Jordan giggles and shakes her head. "No. I think you're thinking loca. Which is a Spanish word for crazy."

I turn back to her and fall into step beside her again. "I thought it was some shortened version of lunatic. Which is sort of how I feel right now, so I guess I shouldn't be insulted."

She looks over her shoulder and smiles softly as she looks at me. She stops and turns towards me. "Luna is another word for new beginnings. It can also mean silver. But the most common definition comes from the Latin word meaning moon. Luna is also another name for Dianna, who was the Roman Moon Goddess."

I tilt my head. "So, he was calling me the Goddess of the Moon? Why?"

Jordan bites her lip and looks down. "A term of endearment?" She offers me a small smile as she starts walking again. She turns. "This hall holds portraits of men and women we honor. Those who have…" She pauses as she chews her lip. "Who have moved onto better opportunities."

"Like… died?"

She shakes her head. "No. Nothing like that. They just aren't here anymore with us. They've moved and gotten a job somewhere that they love or started a family and wanted to live on their own. But we don't want anyone to forget them or where their origins began. So, we hang their portraits in this hall. Kade likes to come here and look at them sometimes."

"How come?"

She smiles but says nothing. I step to the side as two girls hurry down the hall. They have to be about my age. They look very young. They giggle as they hurry past us, holding hands. They both glance back at me before they turn the corner.

But not before I hear a tidbit of what they are saying. "That's our Luna!" They sound beyond excited.

"There's that word again." I start to follow them, but as I'm turning around, a portrait catches my eye. I slap a hand over my mouth. "Oh my God."

Jordan puts a hand on my shoulder. "Are you okay, Kaia?"

I look at her and drop my hand from my mouth. "Who are you people? Why are my best friend's parents on your wall with her as a baby? Is this some kind of cult?"

"What?" Jordan looks horrified. "Oh God. No! No, Kaia. That's not what we are." She shakes her head.

"Then what is this?" I gesture to the portrait.

"Jordan?" a deep male voice calls from somewhere in the house. It sounds like his voice is bouncing off the walls.

"That's Dom." Jordan smiles wide. "He's my m- um… my husband."

"Jordan! You up here?" A man with a little scruff on his face dressed in black jeans and a black t-shirt pops around the corner. His arms remind me a little of a tree trunk covered in tattoos. His hair is dark. His eyes are a piercing blue. I swear to God all the guys here are tall and muscular. It must be something in the trees.

"Hi, sweetie!" Jordan kisses her husband. Dominick. She told me his name earlier. She said he went somewhere with Kade.

Dominick wraps one arm around Jordan's waist and pulls her to his side. The move is as possessive as it is dominant and loving. It makes me wish I had that. And I must be insane because when I think of the man doing it, I think of Kade. Someone I don't even know.

But you do know me, don't you? I hear his voice in my head where it's been all day. I've never heard his voice before. I just saw him when I looked at the moon. Hearing it, though, feels right. It's like a missing piece to a very strange puzzle I've questioned most all of my life. It sends shockwaves of desire throughout my whole body. They all settle between my thighs, making me blush.

Until I met him, I always thought he was a type of guardian angel. Sort of like the Moon Wolf. Now I know that Kade is so much more. I may not understand the depth, but I know my connection to him is deeper than him just being a type of Spirit Guide.

But all of that is irrelevant to me right now. "Why are my best friend's parents on your wall with her as a baby?"

Dominick looks at Jordan, who looks down at her feet. He clears his throat as he looks at me. "The portraits in this hall are people we're close to that we have chosen to honor."

I glare at him and cross my arms over my chest. "That tells me nothing. How are they involved with…" I look around. "With this? Whatever the hell this is."

Dominick returns my glare. "We're a close knit group. We protect our own. We help our own succeed. And we do a lot of shit for everyone outside our walls, Kaia." The tone of his voice makes me look down immediately. Not out of fear. Out of shame for everything I'm thinking that he obviously senses. "That's a question you need to ask Kade. I won't answer it. Neither will anyone else here. Not because we're being disrespectful to you. But because that is a conversation you need to have with him."

I just nod and choke down my anger and suspicion. I'm confused. I don't understand what's happening. All I really know right now is that the police are after me for something. They killed my parents. They left me for dead. And I was told Kade would help. That his people would. That his people have a portrait of my best friend and her parents on their wall. And above all else, I feel an odd sense of belonging here.

It doesn't make sense. Nothing makes sense. But it is late. Maybe I just need some sleep. I've had a very difficult day. I've remembered things I would have preferred to forget completely. Remembering creates questions. Questions I don't have answers to. Questions that Connor and the Moon Wolf seem to be avoiding just as much as Dominick and Jordan. I haven't seen either of them since they led me away.

I follow Dominick and Jordan as they hold hands. They lead me back to Kade's house. It's pitch black outside and cold. I rub my hands over my arms wishing for the thousandth time in less than a minute that I had what Jordan does with Dominick. He's holding her so close to him. I know she's warm. I can feel it.

And that feeling in itself is unsettling. I can feel her warmth. It doesn't warm me, but I can feel it. I don't even need to see his arm around her. I can feel her warmth being radiated somehow to me.

I let out a long, quiet breath as we enter the house. Dominick and Jordan lead me to Kade's bedroom and tell me to have a good night before they continue on their way to their bedroom, which is in another wing of the gigantic house.

I take a deep breath before opening the door to Kade's bedroom and stop in my tracks. Standing next to the dresser is the most beautiful body I've ever seen. He is toned. Everything I thought was underneath his shirt is on display right now. He's just as big as Dominick. Taller. His muscles ripple. The dark blue jeans he wears are slung low on his hips.

When he turns, his beauty takes my breath away. I've never seen a more gorgeous being. Breathtaking. I can't take my eyes off him. I try to, but they refuse to obey the commands of my mind. The only thing I want to do is trace the ridges of his stomach. And see just where that sexy V-shape that disappears below his waistband leads.

I mentally shake myself and politely turn away as he starts to pull on a shirt. I can feel his eyes on me, though. Everywhere they touch erupts in goosebumps until my entire body is covered in them.

"I'll get out of here in a minute." His deep voice oozes sexiness and makes me shiver. The thought of him leaving, though, fills me with emptiness.

My eyes snap to his. "You don't have to," I say quietly. "It's your bedroom. I could sleep in one of the guest rooms."

"Don't worry about it. I'll sleep in my office." Underneath the sexy grovel is a cold tone that I hate.

I hug myself and look down at my feet. "You really don't have to." I take a deep breath and make my eyes lift to his again. "I was hoping we could… talk?"

Kade starts putting things he's folded and placed on the bed into a large duffel bag. "About what?"

"I remembered… everything." I bite my lip and take a few cautious steps towards the bed. "I thought maybe you could help me make sense of it."

He's quiet for so long, I wonder if he's ignoring me. He continues neatly placing things into his bag. "Okay. Talk." He doesn't look at me, but the words soothe my too fast beating heart.

I sit at the foot of the bed and fold my hands into my lap. I focus on the large dresser in front of me. The handles are silver and have an intricate wolf design that looks to be howling at the moon. It's so pretty. I could stare at it all night if I let myself.

I don't. I need answers. "I just need the blanks filled in. Starting with why the police were chasing me and left me for dead. I'm not sure you can answer that."

"I can't. At least not yet. But I am working on it. Until I find out, you'll stay here. Where you'll be safe. No one knows you're here. And even if they did, they wouldn't dare come against me. It would be suicide. Everyone knows that."

I nod. The words should chill me to the bone, but they don't. They further soothe me. I trust him and what he says. I close my eyes for a moment and let the scent of him and this room give me the strength I need to continue with this conversation.

I open them again and let out a quiet puff. "Why did I see you in the moon? Before I even met you?"

I don't look at him, but I can hear the sharp intake of breath. He continues putting things slowly into his bag. After a few moments, he finally takes a breath. "That's a very complicated answer that I don't think you're ready to hear."

I don't know why, but his answer breaks me a little. An intense sadness seems to flow through me. "Okay." I lower my voice to a whisper. "Sounds like an excuse to me." I'm too tired to fight for answers, though. "What about the reason you have a portrait of my best friend and her parents?" This is something I will fight for.

He sighs. "What are you talking about?"

I turn to him but don't move from where I'm sitting. "In the big house with all of the people. You have a hallway full of people that Jordan said you are close to and honor in some way after they move on to jobs or something. One of them is a portrait of my best friend when she was a baby and her parents."

"Every person in that hallway is someone close to me. If they are in that hallway, then I guess it means I know them." He doesn't look at me. He zips his bag.

"I don't understand what this is. Why are there so many people here? Jordan said it's nothing like a cult or -"

He cuts me off with a sharp glare. "It's not a fucking cult. Everyone here is like family to me. Friends. They are here because they need to be. Because this is their home. Where they belong. If they wanted to leave, I'd never fucking stop them. They are free to come and go as they please. I don't proclaim to be a fucking God." He slings the bag over his shoulder and starts walking to the door.

I jump to my feet. I don't want him to leave. "Kade! Please, just talk to me!" I step in front of him, putting my hands on his chest.

"Why? So, you can continue to throw around insults because you've been thrown into a world you don't understand? Is it not up to your prissy standards?" He towers over me. He doesn't take a step back. He stands directly in front of me, giving me a vicious glare.

I shake my head and pull my hand back from his chest as if he's burned me. "I just want to understand! I'm scared! This is so scary for me! People are after me, and I don't know why, Kade! Please, just help me to understand! I just want things to make sense!"

"You want things to make sense, Kaia?" He lets the bag fall from his shoulder and hit the floor. He steps even closer until his chest is touching me. I refuse to move, even though my whole body is screaming at me to. He grips my arms. "You want me to give you all the answers? You want me to tell you the reason you see me in the moon is because I'm your fated mate? That the Wolf and Human guiding you through the woods and protecting you are my mother and father? Is that what you want me to say, Kaia? You want me to tell you the reason you feel like you can't breathe without me is because of the mate bond? Huh? That I'm a Shifter?"

My head is spinning. I shake it. "A wh-what?"

"A Shifter, Kaia. I am part Human. Part Wolf. All those fucking horror stories you heard about werewolves? Well, guess what? That's me. I'm the big bad Wolf of your nightmares. And you're the lucky Human who gets to be my mate."

The venom dripping from his voice sends ice through my veins, but I refuse to allow him to see he's scaring me. Something is telling me that he's lashing out and trying to push me away. Trying to keep me from getting the answers I seek.

I take a step back and turn. I walk to the door because I won't allow him to think he has all of the control. "Maybe when you aren't so angry, you'll talk to me." I don't intend to whisper, but I do. I hate that it betrays the fear he just instilled in me.

He grabs my arm. "Where do you think you're going?" he growls.

I yank my arm away and spin on him. I shove him. Again, though, he doesn't move. I should have known he wouldn't. So, I stand my ground again. "I just got chased by four cops with guns who were shooting at me! Four of them, at least I think it was four of them, caught me and tried to kill me. Why? I don't know. I don't know what I did. I don't know what my parents did. And you think after that your words will scare me? You think after all I went through and survived that you can just try and intimidate me and freak me out? I will get answers because I deserve them! There is a reason I'm here. If you won't tell me, fine! I'll figure it out on my own! I didn't have any friends in school. I was too busy studying. Leia was my only friend. When I lost her, I felt like I lost a part of me! Do you have any idea what that's like? So, don't bother helping me! I'll survive! I'll make it by myself!" I turn and head for the door again, truly angry this time.

He grabs me again and hauls me against his hard chest. I could be mistaken, but I swear I see something in his eyes akin to admiration. A fire. An attraction. A firestorm of emotion that I can't quite decipher.

Before I have any time to figure it out, his lips are on mine. The kiss is capable of making me burst into flames and melt at his feet all at the same time. His tongue swipes at my lips then dives into my mouth. Like he's demanding my tongue to dance with his. It does just that on its own accord.

His fingers tangle in my hair. He tugs just enough to angle my head so he can dominate the kiss even more than he already is. My fingers grip his shirt for dear life. Because if I don't, I'm not sure I'll be able to stand. He was right earlier when he said I can't breathe without him. I feel like if he stops kissing me, I'll die.

Kade pulls back. His cold facade falls back into place quicker than I can recover from the knee buckling kiss. When he lets go and steps back, I fall to the ground with a gasp feeling as if my heart has been ripped out of my chest.

When I look up, Kade is slamming the door to his bedroom. His bag is gone. He's gone. I lay on the floor and cry.

I cry for my parents.

I cry for Leia.

But mostly I cry because I feel more alone than I have ever felt in my life. I felt alone after Leia died because she was the closest thing I had to a sister. I cry more as I remember my parents and what happened to them. I feel empty without them.

None of it compares to Kade kissing me like that and walking away. None of it. I don't know what he means by fated mates. I want to find out. I will find out. But the idea of doing it without Kade destroys me. It's like he took my soul when he walked out that door.

How is this possible? I don't know anything about him. So why do I feel like I'm drowning and he's the only thing that can save me before the wave crashes over me and buries me in its murky depths?

CHAPTER SEVEN

~*~ KADE ~*~

(Two Weeks Later)

"What do you mean you still have no leads?" I growl to the Chief of Police of Palisades Falls. "What else do I need to give you? Do I need to have my team do your whole fucking job? I already gave you eyewitness testimony."

"Kade, I understand you're upset, but these things take time. Especially since you've accused four cops of murder. A murder you didn't witness and are just giving me the hearsay testimony of the daughter of the deceased. A daughter who, by the way, is considered missing. You're lucky I haven't sent up a squad to pick her up."

"She has no family. Who the fuck reported her missing? Huh?"

"She's a suspect, too. Did you know that? The only reason I haven't gotten an arrest warrant is because I trust you as much as I did your father."

I run a hand down my face. "I suppose I should thank you for that."

"Fuck right you should. But I don't need the thank you. Give me time, Kade."

"You know I'll help however I can."

"I know."

"I'm serious. Resources. Extra surveillance. Whatever you need. Just get her out of this mess. She doesn't need this."

"I'll take care of it. But you need to give me the time I need. I'll take a couple of you guys to do that surveillance, though."

"You got it. I'll send them to you now."

"Thanks, Kade. We'll figure it out. Hopefully, no one finds out I know where she is. I could get in a lot of trouble for that. I'm close to retiring. I don't need that shit."

"I've got your back, Chief."

He chuckles. "Just like your father." He hangs up.

I put my phone in my pocket and keep pacing. I need to get Kaia out of here. Ever since I kissed her I've been avoiding her. Not that it matters much. I can still feel her. And what I feel tears me apart. I hurt her that night when I walked out after kissing her. I cut her deeply and gave myself some scars in the process.

I keep telling myself that I'm okay with her hating me. It will make it easier on her when I reject her as my mate when the time comes. She'll feel pain, but she won't be broken. She'll move on and live her life.

And we'll be destroyed. A shell of ourselves.

I ignore my Wolf and his growly whines. I head for the door to my office, which has been my bedroom ever since I walked out on Kaia. I miss my bedroom, but I can't bear being in it. It smells like her. When I look at my bed, all I see is her. I'd rather give up the bedroom completely than be subjected to that. I've already jacked off to the image of her far more than I care to admit. I also refuse to admit I've never come as hard to anyone as I do her.

I quickly make my way to the pack house to gather a couple of men to send to Chief Alexander. They'll report directly to him because I don't trust anyone else. I walk into the pack house and head directly to the game room. It's where most of them hang out.

I smell her before I see her, and it stops me dead in my tracks. Sitting in the corner of the room is Kaia dressed in ripped light-blue jeans that show off enough of her skin to see she's toned and perfectly bronzed from her time in the sun. Her pink tank top is like a beacon of light in my dark world.

And makes every possessive fiber of my being rise to the surface. I have no chance in hell to tamp it down before I'm crossing the room to her. She's reading a book, but I don't care what it's called or where she got it. I grip her wrists and pull her up.

She looks up at me in shock. "What are you doing?" she squeaks out.

I don't answer. I throw her over my shoulder and carry her out of the game room. My heart is racing, and I'm pissed off that so many others got to see her like this. Those that I'd seen staring at her are going to pay.

I pass by Jordan and Dominick on my way to our house. I can sense they follow me, but I don't give a shit. All I care about is Kaia putting more clothing on. Something. Anything that hides the curves that belong to me.

"Kade! What are you doing?" Kaia yells as she wiggles to get out of my grip. Like she has any chance of that happening.

I slap her ass and put her down on the floor in my living room as she squeaks and looks up at me with wide eyes, rubbing her ass. "I don't care what you do around here, but if you go to the other house, you better put some clothes on," I growl.

Her mouth drops open. "I am wearing clothes!"

"Clothes that show off far more fucking skin than you should ever be showing to anyone but me!" I storm up the stairs with her gawking at me. I run to my bedroom and slam the door open. I start rifling through the drawers for a long-sleeve shirt.

"What the hell is wrong with you?" Jordan says from behind me. "You just scared the hell out of that poor girl. Dominick is down there hugging her trying to get her to calm down because she's hyperventilating."

I turn a fierce glare on her. "Dominick needs to keep his fucking hands off her." I head for the door with a long-sleeve shirt clutched in my hand.

Jordan stands in front of me with her arms folded over her chest. She's a small girl, but my sister has never had a problem standing up to me. "You're acting like a crazed maniac. She's not yours. Remember?

You're being a coward and rejecting her on the next Blood Moon. Which is in three weeks. You have no claim to her."

I close my eyes and try to calm myself, but I can't. Her scent is everywhere. I clench the shirt tighter in my fist and walk out of the bedroom. I stride directly to my office. She hasn't been in this room. Maybe if I can get her scent out of my head, I can calm myself down and regain some ounce of control.

Of course, Jordan doesn't let me be alone. "Do you know what she's been doing since she's been here?"

"Do you think I don't?" I snap. I attempt to close the door to my office, but she manages to slip in like she owns the place.

"She's been in the library scouring it. Reading everything she can find on Shifters and our family history. Everything, Kade." She looks up at me with the same fire I'm shooting at her.

"So? It doesn't change anything. She's a Human. She can't be here longer than she needs to be."

"So, you're going to send her away knowing she has nothing and no one? Kade, come on. That isn't you."

"Fucking hell, Jordan! Do you think I won't take care of her? Check on her? It's easier for her to hate me. Because when I send her away, it's going to kill me! At least she'll be safe and happy!"

"Kade, I swear you're so stupid sometimes! Do you think it won't hurt her? She's your mate! You're hers! It will tear her to shreds if you go through with your plan!"

"But she'll get over it! She'll move on and live a happy life. Eventually, she'll forget she ever met me!"

Jordan screams in frustration and stomps her foot. She shoves past me with such force, she manages to knock me back a step. When she reaches the door, she turns to me. "If you honestly think that, Kade, you don't deserve the role of Alpha. How many people have left this pack to be with their mates because of your stupid rule? Not a single one of them has stayed and sent their mates away. Do you know why?" She doesn't wait for an answer. "Because like mom and dad always said. It doesn't matter if your mate is Human, Wolf, or a fucking gopher. You're stronger with your mate than without! Rejecting her weakens you. Which weakens the entire pack! Maybe think about that before you decide to keep being a complete idiotic coward!" She slams the door as she leaves.

I can't argue with her because I know she's right. I toss Kaia's shirt onto the couch and sink into a chair. I know rejecting Kaia will weaken me. If I'm not at my best, my entire pack feels it and becomes less confident in their abilities. It weakens them just as much.

But I can't allow a Human to be in my world. Her being my mate makes her a huge target. She can't shift and fight off a Shifter if she needs to. She doesn't have the strength, endurance, or speed that a Shifter does. I can't do that to her. That would be setting her up for a fate worse than death. I learned that lesson well with Aryan and my father. I won't do that to her.

I can feel her crying. I can feel the hurt I just caused her. It's stabbing through my heart like a dagger. Twisting and turning. I force myself to fight it off, though, because it helps her to hate me a little more. Hating me will make it easier.

You know that's not true. My Wolf whimpers and whines, allowing himself to feel everything she is like an asshole because he knows I'll feel it just as much. *She needs us. We need her. We can't will this pain away. It will only get worse.*

We have no choice. She can't stay. It's too dangerous.

I stand and shut down any other protests from myself or my Wolf. I take a steadying breath as I walk out of my office and down the stairs. My living room is empty. Not sensing anyone else in the house, I know instinctively Dominick took her to the pack house. I scrub my hands down my face and head towards the pack house once more.

Jordan is right. I have no claim over her. If I really intend to reject her, which I do, I can't allow myself to feel anything towards her. Especially possessiveness. She isn't mine. She never will be.

My heart tells me something different. My Wolf. My whole fucking body. Seeing her makes me want to claim her. Mark her. Make everyone, including her, see she belongs to me. I let that part of me take control when I carried her out of the pack house earlier. I can't allow that to happen again.

Just as I'm about to enter the pack house, my phone rings. I take it out without looking at the caller ID. "What?" I open the door and head for the game room again.

"Is that any way to talk to the woman you love?"

I stop and shake my head. "What?"

She laughs. "Kade, I'm lonely. Come see me."

I look at my phone and see Charlene's face. She's one of the many women I've taken to bed, but calling it love is something I'd never do. Charlene just happens to be the one I've been with the most. But it's because she's willing when I need to blow off steam. I haven't thought of another woman since I found my mate, though. The idea of being with anyone but Kaia repulses me.

Two weeks ago, though, I would have jumped at the chance to be with Charlene. She's gorgeous. I've always gone for women with long, dark hair and big eyes I could drown in. Curves I can grab a hold of while I'm sinking myself into her. After seeing Kaia in real life and not just my dreams, I finally understand why. I've never been with a blond or redhead. Just women with dark hair. Women just like Charlene.

I duck into an empty room. I don't turn on a light and keep my back to the door. "Charlene," I say smoothly and low. "When have I ever told you I love you?"

"Right, right. You've never said it. Finding your true love and all."

I chuckle because I can see her rolling her eyes. "You've always just been a pit stop on that path."

She laughs. I never realized until today just how much I hate her laugh. It grates on my nerves. "One you keep turning around and running back to."

"I won't deny that. But it's only because you're so eager and willing for me to sink my cock into you."

"And what a glorious cock it is. Now, come see me," she whines. "It's been far too long."

"I've been busy."

"You always say that. But everyone needs a break sometime, right?"

"I do need a break." I rub my forehead. "You have no idea how much."

"Then come see me. The mountain can live without you for a few hours. Let me make it all better."

I hear something crash behind me and turn quickly. "Kaia." My chest clenches as she scrambles to her feet from the floor where she must have tripped and fallen.

"Who?" Charlene asks, sounding annoyed.

I run towards the door and see Kaia sprinting down the hall. I hang up on Charlene and start going after her, but think better of it. Instead, I reign in my emotions, clutching my chest. Fucking hell. Her pain is killing me. I lean on the doorframe and close my eyes, focusing on anything but her as I rub my heart that feels like it's shattering all over again.

Go after her! Our mate is hurting! My Wolf screams at me.

I don't. I stay rooted to the ground because I can't chase her. It's better this way. One more nail in my coffin. It gives her more ammo when I send her on her way. The more she hates me, the better off she'll be.

"Fucked up again, I see."

"Shut-up, Dominick," I snap.

"When are you going to give up and rescind your damn rule?"

"I'm not. She deserves more than this life. She deserves far better than me."

"Well, I'll agree with the second part of that statement.'

I ignore him and stand to my full height. I can still feel her hurt, but I'll take it. At least it's manageable now. "I need a couple guys to do surveillance for Chief Alexander."

"Okay. I'll grab a couple and have them report to him."

"I was thinking it could be us."

He raises an eyebrow. "Because the further away from her you are, the better?"

I sigh. "Don't. Don't start with me."

"You know that even if she walks away hurt and hating you, you rejecting her will shatter her just as much as you. You breaking your bond with her will weaken the pack. It gives any of our enemies the perfect opportunity to attack."

"We're strong enough."

"Kade, come on."

I shake my head and stride past him. "We're strong enough. Come on. I want to start surveillance."

"Fuck. Fine. But I need to say goodbye to Jordan, and we are taking your car. If I'm sitting out all night, I'm doing it in fucking style." He walks ahead of me and doesn't wait for me as he walks into the house.

I head for the kitchen chuckling and take out snacks and drinks. He's right. If we're doing surveillance, we're doing it right. It's the least I can do for assigning him and myself to this instead of literally anyone else in our pack. I need to get away. It will help me clear my head.

As I'm making sandwiches, Kaia makes an appearance. She hovers by the door with something clutched to her chest. I look up and watch her a few moments before going back to concentrating on the sandwiches. When I'm done, I lick the mayo off my thumb and turn to wash the knife.

"What do you need?" I ask with my back to her.

"Um… I… found something. I… guess I thought it might help. I don't… really know what it is or means." Her voice is shaky and barely above a whisper. I guess I can't blame her. I probably scared the shit out of her with my act of possession earlier. I'm sure she's trying not to cry thinking of me with someone else.

I slowly wash the knife. "What did you find?" I put the knife in the drain rack and steel myself before turning to her.

The sight in front of me, stops my heart. Kaia is putting the sandwiches into a sandwich bag and packing all of my snacks into an insulated lunch bag. She turns to the refrigerator and pulls out the fruit and vegetable trays. She finds Tupperware bowls and starts filling them with a variety of the fruit and vegetables that I had no intention of taking with us.

I watch her in a state of admiration. She's so fucking pretty, but the fact that her heart is big enough to put up with my shit and still pack snacks and stuff pulls at places I didn't know existed until her.

She nods towards the picture frame she'd been holding. I pick it up and raise an eyebrow. "Your parents with you, Evan, Aisha, and Leia." I gave her the picture with her things, thinking it would bring her some sort of comfort. I was right. She sleeps with it on the pillow next to her. Where I should be. I shake my head to expel that thought. "Am I missing something?"

"Well, you still haven't told me why you have a portrait of Leia and her parents."

"Kaia -" I begin, letting out a frustrated breath, but she cuts me off.

"That's not what I found." She nods to it again. "Take the back off. I was going to clean the frame and polish the silver. I took the back off and found that."

I lean against the counter with my back to it and stand next to her. I take the back off as she finishes packing the fruit and vegetables. I only planned on taking sandwiches and chips. Kaia is giving us a full meal. She takes an ice pack out of the freezer and starts filling another lunch bag with drinks. Water. Soda. The iced coffee I have a slight obsession with.

I clear my throat and look back down at the frame. "What am I looking at? It looks just like the back of a frame."

"That's what I thought, too. But there's a false back. Sort of. It's like a little pouch. I wouldn't have noticed it if I didn't know what the back of the frame looks like. Or is supposed to look like." She turns and points to a slice in the top of the black foam.

"It goes all the way around the frame," I say as I inspect it. "How do you know it isn't part of the design?"

"Because I'm the one who bought it," she says quietly. "I bought it for Leia for her sixteenth birthday. Right before the car accident that killed her and her parents. I remember exactly what it looked like because I was being really specific in what I was looking for. I wanted it to be perfect and represent her. She loved the woods as much as I do. And her favorite color and metal was silver. Just like me. It's one of the things we bonded over." She wipes a tear from her eyes and smiles softly. Once more, she pulls at my heartstrings. "Anyway, the leaves engraved in the frame represent the woods. She loved this frame so much. She put this picture in there. When she… died… I wanted to make sure I got this. It was the most important thing to her."

I won't tell her or even lead on that I care, but learning these little things about her fills cracks in my armor I will never show anyone. I'll hold onto these moments when I let her go as a lifeline to help me survive. She'll never know that.

I run my fingers along the edge of the frame while she finishes packing everything. There's one part at the top that pulls away further than the rest of the frame. But unless I was looking for it, I would never know.

Inside the pouch is a small piece of paper that seems to be browning from lack of oxygen. I carefully remove it, though it's not easy with my large fingers and hands. When I do finally manage to remove it, Kaia is looking up at me. Waiting. I hand her the frame and carefully unfold the paper.

If you're reading this, it means my parents and I are dead.
I don't know who he is, but I heard them talking about someone
named Kade Deimos. That he could help.

Things are scary, Kaia.
I don't know what's happening, but I think people are after us.
Please. Find Kade. I know he can help.

My parents said we're running tonight. We're going to Kade.
But if we don't make it, you need to find him.

I know you'll find this note. I know you're the only one who can.
That's how I know that whatever is about to happen, you'll get help.

I love you, Kaia. You're like my sister. Always remember that.

Kaia wipes her eyes as I silently read. "Fuck," I whisper.

"Please, Kade. Please tell me what that means. I know you know." She begs me with large eyes full of the pain of losing the friend who was like family to her.

I open my mouth to speak, but just as I'm about to tell her everything she wants to know, Dominick walks into the kitchen. I close my mouth and turn to him. She doesn't need to know this. She isn't involved in it. She'll be gone soon anyway. This is something she needs to stay far away from.

"Ready to go?" Dominick asks.

I glance down at Kaia and almost give in again. But I don't. I can't. It could put her in too much danger. It's bad enough she's already learned about Shifters and our family history. She doesn't need to know the reason one of the members of my pack and his entire family were killed.

Not like I know that reason either, but if they hadn't been sent away, they'd still be here.

Safe.

Whatever or whoever they were running from wouldn't have been a factor. For fourteen years, I never once questioned my decision to make a no Human rule. Since Kaia entered my life, I've questioned it many times. Everything has been turned upside down. I'm rethinking every fucking decision I've ever made.

71

I let out a breath and put the note in my pocket. I take the lunch bags and say nothing to her as I leave the room. Dominick follows, confused. I can feel Kaia's eyes on my back as I leave her standing in the kitchen. I can feel her tears fall as if they are falling from my own eyes.

Leading Dominick to my car, I link with the rest of my pack and do something I know I'll hate myself for. But it needs to be done.

Listen up. No one, and I mean NO ONE tells Kaia anything about this pack, our history, Shifters, pack business, or anything else relating to us as Shifters. If you do, you face me.

Dominick watches me sadly. But just like every other Shifter in this pack, he won't disobey the orders of his Alpha. No matter how much he or I disagree with it.

CHAPTER EIGHT

~*~ KAIA ~*~

I watch Kade and Dominick leave and let the tears silently fall. I want to scream at him and demand he tell me all I want to know. All I deserve to know. But I don't. I don't because I know there's no point. Kade won't tell me anything if he doesn't want to. I should be grateful I've gotten what I have out of him.

I clean up the kitchen and take the picture. I noticed he put the note in his pocket. It saddens me because it's something of Leia's. I feel a loss at losing it. I feel broken. Even more than he already broke me.

I walk straight to the library because it's my place of solitude. Kade hasn't once set foot in here since I've been here. Then again, until today, I hadn't seen him much at all. Even at the pack house. That's what I've come to call it. It's what the books I've been reading say it is.

I curl up in one of the oversized chairs and grab the book I'd left on the table. I open it and continue reading about the mate bond and all it entails. I've already learned that Shifters have particular powers. They are faster, stronger, and often smarter than Humans. The old fable is that

Shifters are some kind of half Human and half Wolf. They call them Werewolves.

From what I've read about Kade's family, though, they don't shift like that. They shift from a Human into a Wolf. They aren't some slobbery, rabies infected creature that kills for sport. They are Humans with the mind of a Wolf and a Wolf with the mind of a Human. They are one unit. There aren't two separate entities. They are no different than a Human who is half Latin and half Italian.

I wipe my eyes and focus on the words in front of me. The mate bond. I found this book after Kade's punishing kiss two weeks ago. I haven't gotten very far in it because I also found a book that had to do with his family specifically. I think it was written by his sister-in-law, Aryan. It seemed like it was a journal of some sort chronicling where the Deimos Pack was born and how. I was immersed in it.

But I got back to this book a couple of days ago, and I'm just as enraptured. Everything I've been feeling makes so much sense now. The pain I feel without him near me. The earth-shattering sadness. The way I feel like a part of my soul leaves with him every time he walks out the door. The way I felt broken when he kissed me and left me on the ground after.

The way my body lights up whenever he's near. How I feel like I'm on fire whenever he looks at me. Whenever I think of him, I want to both shake him and make him talk to me, as well as touch myself until I get the release only he can bring me. I've done the latter a lot since I've met him. I feel like I should be ashamed, but I'm not.

The feelings I have are so confusing. I've never been with anyone before. In school, I was always focused on my studies. After Leia died, I was even more focused because I wanted to succeed for the both of us. We'd planned to travel together. I knew that she'd want to make sure I still went without her to enjoy everything I could in her memory.

That's not to say I didn't explore feelings and urges. I'm no stranger to giving myself orgasms. I'd even go so far to say that I'm pretty good at them. I've just never been with anyone. The feelings I have for Kade are nothing like the crushes I may have briefly experienced growing up. Thinking of the Man in the Moon, though, is what I envisioned as I was giving myself the release. Now that I know the Man in the Moon is Kade, the orgasms are so much stronger.

Now I understand why everything is so intensely up and down with him. According to this book, the mate bond is strong and fierce. When it hits, it feels like a magnetic pull. Shifters don't feel the bond until they are eighteen. I know Kade is older than that. Which makes me question why he didn't feel something for someone. Before I can get my answer, though, Jordan comes into the library. She doesn't look happy.

"Is everything okay?" I ask.

"It's fine. My brother is just stupid and frustrating and made an order to all of us."

I tilt my head. "An order? I just saw him. He didn't say anyth-" I cut myself off and lower my head, once again feeling like the outsider I am. "Oh. Because it's about me."

She opens her mouth like she's about to confirm my suspicion, but then I hear his voice. Connor, who I have learned is Kade and Jordan's father. *Careful, Jordan. You know better than to defy an Alpha's order.*

I sigh. "An Alpha's order," I say quietly. "The law of a pack."

Jordan's eyes snap to mine. "Wh-what? D-did you hear that?"

I figure there's no point in denying it. I'm part of this pack through my bond with Kade. I may never be completely welcome, but I know better than to lie. "Connor. Yours and Kade's father. He's the one who protected me from the bullets when I was running. Belle, your mother, is the Moon Wolf. She's been my Spirit Guide ever since I was just a child." I glance up. "He's standing right next to you."

"You can see them?" she squeaks.

I nod slowly but keep my eyes on my book. I haven't seen Connor or Belle since the night they led me to Kade. Or Kade to me. However it worked. I know that without them, I'd be dead. I know that without Kade's healing powers, I wouldn't have made it through the night. It's all things I have learned about in these books. Questions I have tried to ask Kade to clarify so I understand, but it hasn't worked that way.

Jordan and Dominick, on the other hand, as well as many of the pack members have been very forthcoming about my questions. It's how I've managed to get as far as I have with all of the clarification I've gotten.

My assumption, though, is that Kade just put an end to that. Which has successfully isolated me more than I already feel I am. I shouldn't be surprised. I was obviously getting too close and comfortable here. I don't doubt Kade wants me to leave as soon as possible. I haven't asked him outright, but I have heard grumblings about some law he made about no Human mates. It's a question I had intended to ask him with hopes I'd get something out of him. If I don't get a full explanation, I hoped Jordan would help.

It looks like that road has been violently closed, though. Which means I'll just have to rely on the books. I can't even rely on my Spirit Guide, the Moon Wolf. She hasn't been coming around lately when I've needed her or begged for her. It's yet one more thing that's broken my heart. I feel like I've lost another piece of myself.

This is completely unfair! She's his mate! He's being foolish! Jordan says through her mind link with her parents. I don't think she knows I can hear her.

But it's his orders, Jordan, Belle says. She sounds as sad as I feel.

It's stupid, mama! He's just being salty because of how he lost you all! But he needs to get fucking over it! Can't I disobey him just this once?

Jordan! Enough of this. No one agrees with him, Connor says. *But the order of an Alpha is final. Whether you agree or not is irrelevant. If you disobey, there will be punishments. You could be banished, Jordan. Sister of the Alpha or not.*

The statement causes me to hang my head even lower and Jordan to run out of the library in tears. I don't want anyone to get in trouble because of me. Especially if it means banishment. I'm not sure Kade would go that far. He only seems cold towards me.

I feel a hand on my shoulder and look up to see Connor. "I just wish he'd let me in," I whisper. "I'm learning so much. I…" I trail off as tears sting my eyes. *I can do this. If he'd just help me.*

Kade needs to figure this out and work through this on his own, Connor says to me.

I wish he'd just talk to me, but he won't. I sniffle. *Is it just because I'm Human? Or is it because I'm not what he wants? Am I repulsive or something to him?*

Oh my Moon Goddess, no! Belle exclaims. She lays her head on my leg. I can feel the weight of it. I wish I could feel her soft fur. It would be such a comfort to me right now.

Technically, though you are his mate, until he claims you, there are things that are pack business, a voice I've never heard before says.

I snap my head around and see a black Wolf with just a touch of gray. My eyes widen. *F-Fenn?* I have read about him, but never seen him. He's standing next to a beautiful woman with long, dark hair. She looks just as sad as Belle does and I feel.

He nods and tilts his head. *I don't mean to hurt you more, Kaia, but you're already walking over waters that are deep. One wrong step could send you straight to the bottom. You need to tread lightly. While he's been okay with you researching on your own, there are things he won't tell you because you aren't part of the pack.*

At least not yet, Aryan's soft voice says to me. I've never spoken with her either, but I have read a lot about her. She's a Human Luna. Like I guess I am.

Fenn continues. *And being brutally honest? He doesn't have to. He's the Alpha. He could have easily kept you in the dark about everything you have learned so far.*

Don't worry, I say. *I get it. I'm not part of this. I never will be.* I say nothing more as I take my book and leave the library with my head down. I can hear Belle's sad whine.

He'll come around, little one. I believe that, she says.

I hope the words are true because I feel like this is where I belong. From my understanding, it's part of the bond with the pack. Something I haven't quite felt all of, but from what I read, the closer I get to all of them, the more I'll feel like my roots are with them. Not just them, but also the territory. I'll feel like I'm part of them and their home.

I glance out the window when I reach Kade's room. I turn on the light and bite my lip. I feel awful that he's been sleeping on the couch in his office. I've been sneaking in there and tidying up when he isn't in there. I'm sure he thinks it's one of his staff, but it's a small way I feel like I can repay him for the kindness that he has shown me.

While I'd give anything to be near him, I also know that is wishful thinking right now. I don't understand how he can resist the bond we share. It's painful for me to not be near him. I want him so much, but it's not just physical. I long for his heart. Just him.

I hate what I'm about to do, but I quickly start grabbing all of my things. I know there is a room next door to this one. I've been contemplating moving into it, but I keep holding out hope that he'll come back to his room. To me...

He doesn't, though. Maybe if I'm not here, he'll feel more comfortable. This is his room. It's not fair for me to take it over. No matter how much he seems to not mind. He hasn't said a word about me being in here.

When I have all of my things, I take one last look around the room. I've never felt more comfortable anywhere. This room smells like him. I feel surrounded by him. Comforted by him, even though he's the one who cuts me so deeply and leaves such ugly scars. He doesn't even have to say anything. It's all in what he does.

I wish I could walk away. There are so many reasons I can't. One is because I have nowhere else to go. I don't have family. My parents are gone. Leia and her parents are gone. My mom and dad had no other siblings. Their parents are dead. I don't know if I was left any life insurance or inheritance. I haven't heard anything, but maybe that's because no one knows where I am.

And that's what Kade wants. Until we know what happened and who it was that tried killing me and did kill my parents, I trust that I'm better off right where I am. Not like I'd be able to survive out there on my own. I don't know the first thing about being an adult and being on my own. Being freshly graduated from high school, that thought is terrifying. I guess I always thought I'd have my parents to guide me and support me.

I suppose I thought I'd always have the Moon Wolf. Belle. I really don't know if I'd have her anymore. I think her entire purpose was to guide me to Kade. My mate. My destiny. The guy who seems to hate me. A Shifter…

I turn out the light and turn towards the guest bedroom. I find the light when I walk in and look around. The room is brighter. It's more me. The walls are a light blue. The room is filled with blues and grays. The windows are high, like they are throughout the house, but the curtains are lighter, which allows more light to come in.

The bedspread is a pretty dark blue and matches the gray wood of the furniture, bed frame, and posts perfectly, giving it a slight dark contrast to the brightness. I turn on the lamp on the nightstand next to the bed and quickly put my things away before turning off the larger light. I keep the curtains open. I love the moonlight streaming in with the soft light from the lamp.

I pull my jeans and bra off. I leave them neatly folded on top of the dresser and crawl into bed. The light blue sheets are as soft as they are in Kade's room. The comforter is just as heavy. But it's not the same. It doesn't smell like him. It's not as soothing as his room.

Even still. He deserves his bedroom. It's not fair for him to sleep in his office. He could choose a different room if he's insistent on letting me stay in his, but I still don't think that's fair. Despite everything, I don't want to uproot him from something as simple as his bedroom.

So, I take a deep breath and pull out my notebook. I snuggle into the pillows after propping them up behind me so I can sit and read. I want to go over everything I've learned so far. I need to make sense of it.

I open up the first page and start reading. My parents were killed by the police. I saw them. I can't get their faces out of my head. I drew them in my sketchbook. I hold the badge I found in my hand for a moment before putting it on the nightstand. I'm no closer to understanding why the police killed my parents. These people are supposed to be protectors. Instead, they brought about the greatest type of pain and harm.

I've told Kade that part, but I haven't shown him the badge. Truthfully, I'd forgotten about it until I saw it just a few moments ago while I was unpacking. If he's really going to help me, I need to show him. It has a number on it. I'm sure the number is significant. A number on a badge is something I've never thought of before because I've never needed to, but don't all police have specific numbers on their badge? I've never really spent time in the presence of one to pay enough attention to that detail, but I'm pretty sure they all have a number.

Belle and Connor, who I know now are my Spirit Guides, helped me get out of there. Connor protected me, but from what I know about Spirit Guides, they aren't allowed to interfere in fates. I am not sure if protecting me and leading me to Kade was interference or not, but it seems to be. Maybe that's the reason I haven't seen either of them since the night Kade found me after the police caught up to me and left me for dead after beating me up. Maybe it was a punishment for them.

I woke up in Kade's bed. I was out for a while, but I remember feeling warm and protected. I remember my mind screaming in pain at times right before a soothing feeling washed over me and made the agony go away. In one of the books I read, I learned that Kade, being my mate, has the ability to heal me. As a Shifter, he has the power to heal more quickly than a Human. As an Alpha, he can assist the rest of his pack in speeding up their ability to heal. So, I know the reason I woke up with no pain or bruising was because of him. Kade saved my life that night. I would have died without him.

I've learned the reason the pack was whispering the word Luna and looking at me is because that is what I am as Kade's mate. At least, what I would be if he made me his mate. Apparently, in order for him to do that, he needs to mark me with a bite to my neck. Not like a Vampire, but something to seal the bond.

I trace the words I wrote about being his mate and how the mate bond makes us both feel. It's like a magnetic force that is pulling us towards each other. Kade would feel a possessive and protective instinct for me as well as intense attraction he can't control. It explains why he threw me over his shoulder when he saw me and thought I was showing too much skin.

The idea of him seeing me like that and being so blinded by his attraction to me to think of anything else makes my skin heat, and my cheeks blush. My reaction to him is unlike anything I've ever felt before. The intensity of it scares me, but after reading about the mate bond, I understand it. It's impossible to resist it.

It's the reason I saw him in the moon, but never felt him. At least not until after he found me. I turned eighteen at exactly 3:27am. That is when he would have felt me. It's when I felt the draw to him, but I was also caught by my attackers shortly after. My heart called to his. My soul. He knew I needed help, but I was dying. So, while he felt the bond with me, he would have also felt it fading quickly with each breath I struggled to take.

It's because of the bond with him and the bond I'm forging with the pack that I don't want to leave. I don't think I'd be able to survive without him or the pack. Not because I'm weak. I could probably figure it out. I'm not a stupid person. It would be hard. But from what I've read, mates can't survive a broken bond. It weakens them to the point they don't want to live. Thinking of a life without Kade or this pack breaks my heart into so many pieces, I fear I'd never be able to put myself back together.

It's only been two weeks, and I already know I belong here. This is my home.

Kade.

Kade is my home.

As I sleepily start to drift off, visions of the members of the pack happy and laughing lift my spirits. I smile a small smile when I think of Kade. He may not be open to the idea of a Human mate, and I may not understand the reason fully yet, but I will. I hold onto Belle's words that Kade will come around. I have to believe that because the alternative is more than I can bear.

So, as I fall into the first peaceful sleep I've had since Kade healed me, I let myself grab onto one tiny word.

Hope.

CHAPTER NINE

~*~ KADE ~*~

The sun is just about to start rising when Dominick and I walk into our home. The sky is just beginning to lighten. The brilliant colors haven't painted it yet, but it won't be long. It makes my mood all the worse. I toss the plastic Tupperware into the sink.

"Fuck, Kade," Dominick hisses. "You trying to wake up the whole damn house?"

"Everyone should be awake anyway," I growl. There's only two other people in the house right now. The couple of staff who offered to clean and cook for me aren't due here for a couple of hours.

"You can deal with Jordan because I sure as fuck won't be if you wake her up. I'll gladly push you in front of me when her claws come out."

I glare at him but quiet down because I don't want to deal with Jordan. My little sister has a temper I'd rather leave alone. Especially today. "How the hell could it be that quiet? I mean, nothing." I shake my head. "I expected we'd see something I could bring to the Chief that he could use."

Dominick puts a hand on my arm and gives me a light squeeze. It's supposed to soothe me and has the desired effect. "You know as well as I do, these things take time." He lets my arm go after I take a calming breath. "Get some sleep. We'll go back out tonight. Tim and Seth have day surveillance. We'll find something."

I nod. Tim and Seth are two of my pack members who survived the attack on us so many years ago. It took us all time to recover, and I questioned if those that did survive would be as loyal to me as they were to my father. Tim and Seth eased my fears and have become two of my most trusted pack members.

With a yawn, Dominick and I both head for bed. At the top of the stairs, he veers off towards his and Jordan's wing of the house. I head for my office but stop when I see my bedroom door is open and the room next to it is as well. While my bedroom is dark, there is a subtle light coming from the one next to it.

I glance in my bedroom on my way by. Finding it empty, my heart clenches a little bit. I've grown used to seeing Kaia in my bed. Even if I refuse to sleep in it, my bed is where Kaia belongs. I walk the few steps to the room next to mine and glance in. I expect to see Kaia awake and reading or something, but she surprises me.

I inhale a sharp breath at her beauty and am forced to steady myself by gripping the doorframe. She's sleeping peacefully. A soft smile is on her face, lighting up her pretty features in a way I haven't yet seen. I grip my chest and take a steadying breath as my heartbeat quickens. She's breathtaking.

I should run.

I should sprint to my office and slam the door.

I should refuse to ever come out.

I don't do any of that. Of course, I give into my fucking urge to walk into the room. I'm immediately assaulted with her scent. A scent I've grown so accustomed to having around me that when I miss it, I step into my bedroom and inhale her like a fucking stalker.

Two weeks. That's all it's taken for this girl to flip my life upside down and make me question everything. Until her, I had a purpose. I know there's a war coming our way. It's why I work so hard to prepare my pack. Train them. I will not be caught off guard. I liked not having a distraction.

Kaia is the biggest distraction imaginable. She's not only Human. She's mine. My mate. I can never claim her as mine because of the danger she'd be put in. I'll never allow her to be hurt. But while she's here, I can't think of anything but her. All I can think of is figuring out who the hell attacked her and killed her parents. When I do, I'll feel better about sending her away. Until then, she stays here. And while she's here, she's a problem for me. For all of us. If I can't focus, I can't train. If I can't train, then it leaves us vulnerable.

"Christ…," I whisper to myself. I gently take the book and her notebook. I put it on the nightstand and carefully pull the blanket up. I fight myself on every level to not pick her up, carry her to my bedroom, wrap around her, and never let her go.

I let out a quiet breath and ignore the zing-like feeling that goes straight to my dick when I touch her skin. Before I do something stupid, like kiss her again or crawl into bed next to her, I straighten and reach for the light.

I stop, though, when my eyes catch sight of the gold, star-shaped Sheriff's badge. I glance at her to make sure she isn't waking up and quietly pick up the badge to study it. I commit the number on the badge to memory. Two-seven-one-three. After deciding the badge is real, I put it down. There's too much weight to it for it to be fake.

I glance at her notebook and see a bunch of notes written about the mate bond. "Fuck…," I whisper and quickly pick it up to see what she's learned. My eyes fall on the book.

I haven't minded her researching things on her own. Things about Shifters. My family history. Things that allowed her to figure out where we came from and what we stand for. But she's managed to find a book that deals directly with mate bonds and how they work. This book will tell her all she needs to know about when I can claim her.

And when I can reject her.

I pick up the book with her notebook. I contemplate taking her notebook with the book, but against my better judgment, I don't. I sit down in the overstuffed chair by the window and keep one eye on her as I flip through the pages to see what she's written down.

I feel a little like I'm invading her privacy on some level. Like I'm reading a journal or something. It's something I'd never do or have done, but I have to know what she's uncovered. If she's learned of my plans to reject her, I'm not certain I could go through with it. The closer we get to that day, the harder it's becoming for me as it is. If she found out about it, it would break me.

I keep telling myself I'm doing this for her own good, but I'm not sure I even believe myself anymore. The longer she's around, the more blurred things become for me. The stronger our bond gets. She may not feel it, but I do.

I read the things she's written. She's figured out a lot of things about my powers as a Shifter and her mate. She's figured out that there is a mind link between all Shifters in the pack. That Wolves, Shifters, and even Humans who belong to any pack can communicate with any other Wolf or Shifter in any other pack via that mind link.

She's even figured out that her link with the pack will grow, eventually, the more she is around them and bonds with them, even without being claimed by her mate within the pack. She knows that the Alpha can block his mind link with anyone. That any of us can link with just one Shifter or Wolf or even Human and have a conversation through the link with them without anyone else overhearing or being involved.

I sigh when I see she's figured out that I am blocking her link with me. My heart feels heavy when she questions why and blames herself for not being good enough for me somehow. Once again, her pain slams into me. I'm forced once more to tell myself that her hating me is for the best. It will help her move on.

Unfortunately, my heart and my head are not in sync. I stand as the sky starts getting brighter. I put her notebook down on her nightstand because I can't bring myself to take it. I keep the book and take a breath as I lean down.

I press my lips against the side of her neck and revel in the smoothness of her skin. *You're good enough, Kaia. Far too fucking good for me,* I whisper through my link with her. She murmurs and turns towards me. I can tell she's still asleep. I nuzzle and kiss the side of her neck softly. I open my eyes as I stand.

My heart seems to stop beating at the thought of leaving this room, but I reach out and turn the lamp off. I quickly leave the room and close the door gently behind me. I let out a shuddering breath and head for the library. For the millionth time, I hate everything I'm about to do, but I can't let her learn any more than she already has. I put the book away and grab the key hanging from the wall near the door. I'm surprised at the tears that sting my eyes as I lock the door.

I know she's spent a lot of time in there. It's become a sanctuary for her. It's not just the books about Shifters and the history of the Deimos Pack. I have a variety of books in there that I know she's read because I've seen her when she doesn't think I'm looking. Books like the first edition of *Of Mice and Men* and *Grapes of Wrath*. Locking this door has taken away one of the few things I've allowed her to use freely.

I rest my head against the cold wood of the heavy door until I've regained my composure. I put the key in my pocket. It's the only key to this room, so I don't need to worry about Jordan unlocking it for her, which is something I know she'd do.

I let out a breath and square my shoulders as I turn to walk to my office. I need to attempt to get some sleep before I join training, which should be starting now. Fenn, however, doesn't seem to agree. He's sitting in the middle of the hallway looking at me with as much disappointment as he's radiating.

So, you've made an order for people not to talk to her. And then taken away the one way she has to learn anything about us without asking you.

I level him with a glare. *I'm Alpha. You, of everyone, should understand pack business is none of hers.*

I do. But I also don't think you hiding shit about things that affect her is the right choice. Now, you know as well as I do that we can't infer. We can't tell her anything, just like we can't tell you certain things. We can only nudge her in the right direction like we do you. We already paid a price for interfering as much as we did with Aryan and leading her to you. Connor was never supposed to use his power to protect her, but he did. We got in trouble for that, and we don't want the Moon Goddess to take away our Spirit Guide privileges. But we can tell you that this decision is wrong, Kade. She is rumored to be the fated Luna of this pack. There are murmurings on this side that something big is coming. Something that both excites and brings fear to us who are watching over you all. And she may be connected to it.

I blink at him a few times in shock. *What are you talking about?*

He shakes his head. *I can't tell you more than that, Kade. Just…* He hangs his head as he starts to shimmer out of focus. *Just don't be too hasty with things with her.*

I shake my head and look up at the ceiling after he fades. *That doesn't help me at all, Fenn.*

He, of course, says nothing more. I rub the back of my neck and continue to my office. I close the door behind me and fall onto my couch with a deep sigh when I see the office is cleaned up. No one from my cleaning staff comes in here. This area has always been off limits.

I didn't tell Kaia that, though. She's been coming in here when I'm not here and picking up after me ever since I started sleeping in here. She has no idea I know that, but I caught her once. The sight touched me so much that I backed away and just let her. I don't expect it, but it's her way of showing kindness. No matter how much of an asshole I am to her, she still does it. And some messed up part of me fucking enjoys her taking care of me in that way.

I like knowing that some part of her still is affectionate.

~ ~ ~

After filling Chief Alexander in on everything we didn't find out on our surveillance and telling him about the badge, I did manage to sleep a little. At least enough to give me enough energy to help my warriors train the rest of the pack.

I quickly jog to the field behind the pack house. I fully expect everyone to be paired off with a warrior. What I do not expect to see in the slightest is Kaia paired off with Drake, one of my head trainers. He's in his twenties, but he's fast and strong. He learned quickly and very well. I definitely trust the guy to have my back, but I do not like him with his hands all over what's mine.

I stride towards them. Kaia's back is to me, but as soon as Drake sees me, he backs off. I don't have to say a word, so I must have one fuck of a scowl on my face. Drake doesn't often just back away from me.

I watch Kaia's head tilt in confusion and can sense the exact moment she senses me. Her back stiffens. Her breath hitches. She doesn't look over her shoulder, but she knows I'm near. I'm sure my scent is assaulting her just as hers is me.

"What are you doing?" I rumble low.

"L-learning to fight," she responds just barely above a whisper. "Dr-Drake said he'd teach me."

"Not anymore," I growl against her ear.

She shivers as her eyes fly to mine. She gives me a heated glare. "You've taken away my ability to ask you questions. Then I find out I can't talk to anyone else about things I'm curious about because they seem to fear the consequences. Now this? What is wrong with me learning to defend myself?"

I narrow my eyes as I grip her waist. As soon as my hands touch her, I want to kiss her. I want to throw her over my shoulder and make her mine. Show her exactly the reaction I have to her. And when she shivers under my touch despite the cold death stare she's shooting my way, I know she feels just as strongly.

I turn her so her back is facing me and pull her back against my chest. "Your stance is all wrong. Back straight."

Her breath shudders, but she does what I tell her to and straightens her back. "Like that?" she asks quietly.

"Bend your knees." I close my eyes for a moment and allow myself to bury my nose in her hair. I bend my knees and force her to follow. "Do you feel how different this position is? You can move in any direction quickly." I move us both to the right, and then back to the left as I open my eyes. I raise my head and focus on the lesson instead of the way her body fits perfectly with mine.

"It feels better," she says as she releases a breath. "More natural."

"That's what you want. Defending yourself should never feel unnatural." I slowly move one arm around her waist. The other I put across her chest and close to her neck.

"What are you doing?" She looks up at me with wide eyes.

"People aren't going to come up to you and try to fight you. As sexist as it sounds, you're a woman. They're going to grab you." I easily lift her off the ground.

"Kade!" she squeaks. A few of the pack look at us, but go back to what they were doing when I shoot them all a look.

"You have several advantages, Kaia. One of them is that your arms and legs are free. The other is that you're small. Even if I trap your arms, you still have the ability to get away." I set her down and reposition my arms so that hers are pinned against her body and pick her back up again. I rest my lips against her neck. "Kick. Squirm. Fight. Your foot would connect with my knee perfectly if you bend your leg a little. Your heel can directly connect with my shin. Your head would hit me in the nose. You'd break it if you head-butted hard enough. Twist your body. Fight me."

She shakes her head. "I don't want to hurt you."

"There isn't a chance in all of the Hells for that. Fight, Kaia," I growl. She takes a breath and hesitantly twists her body. I tighten my grip. "You're going to have to do better than that. I won't let go until you fight me."

She squirms more and manages to get loose slightly, but I just re-adjust so she's forced to do something other than twist her body. I want her to fight for her freedom and not be afraid. If she's serious about defending herself, then she better start trying.

"You're too strong, Kade!" She sniffles. "This was a bad idea."

"Fucking with Shifters? You're damn right it is. Doesn't mean I can't teach you some basics. Now, fucking fight, Kaia. I'm not letting you go until you do it right."

What if I don't want you to let me go? I can hear her thoughts as plain as day, but I won't allow her to think I did. Damn if it doesn't make my cock harder than it already is with her sweet little ass rubbing against it. And fuck if it doesn't do something to my heart.

After taking a breath, Kaia finally starts fighting. Taking my advice, she kicks her heel back into my shin. I grunt and let her go because it's what any Human would do. Kaia takes off running exactly as she should if she were being attacked by a Human.

But I'm not just any Human. I'm a Shifter. And getting involved with me means the possibility of her having to fight off a Shifter before I let her go. I know a war is coming. It's what my father has been telling me and guiding me towards my entire life.

So, switching to Shifter mode, I give her a taste of what it would be like to fight one. I let her run a little way away from me. When she starts to look over her shoulder to see if I'm following, I make my move. Before she can blink, I'm standing in front of her. She runs directly into my chest. Just as she's falling backwards, I catch her. I don't slam her to the ground, but I do put her down on it harder than I'm sure she expects. I straddle her and pin her arms above her head.

I lean down close to her face until my lips are brushing hers. The touch of her lips sends shockwaves through me. "Shifters are far stronger than Humans. Faster. That kick to my shin would have left a Human in tears. Not a Shifter. We barely feel it." I watch her eyes darken with the same amount of lust I'm feeling but widen in fear at my words. I press myself further against her to relieve some of the ache she causes below my belt.

She whimpers and licks her lip. "Kade…" She closes her eyes and arches slightly into me.

I brush my lips across her cheek to her ear. "That should scare the shit out of you," I whisper as I growl. "It's the entire reason I have a no Human rule, little girl. Humans cannot and never will be able to fight a Shifter."

"Then teach me. Teach me how to fight a Shifter."

Her tenacity might be one of her most attractive qualities. My dick twitches, begging me for more than what I'm allowing. I growl low once more, completely ignoring her effect on me, and leap to my feet. "Get up. You will never be able to fight a Shifter. What I can do however, is show you how to defend yourself."

She slowly follows me and stands. The pretty pink flush to her cheeks as she visibly tries to compose herself makes me feel slightly better at the painful hard-on she's caused me. I turn away from her and adjust myself, not really giving a shit who sees.

As long as it's not her.

I've noticed the others have all stopped to watch us. Leveling them all with a dangerous glare sends them all right back to work, though. After taking a few calming breaths, that's exactly what I do.

I remove my shirt and toss it. I don't miss the shuddering breath she takes when I turn back to her, or the way her eyes sweep across my body and come to a rest on the tattoo on my arm. But I don't give her time to take me in before I launch into more training.

I may not allow her to stay with me, but there's no way in fuck I'll let her leave here without knowing how to defend herself. It's the least I can do for the woman I've been in love with since I saw her come to me in my dreams.

CHAPTER TEN

~*~ KAIA ~*~

(Five Days Later)

I limp my way back to the house breathing slowly. Every muscle in my body hurts. My bruises have bruises. I'm pretty sure my ribs are broken.

Fuck that.

Every bone in my body is broken. All of them.

I stand at the bottom of the stairs breathing shallowly as I look up them. They look longer than usual. Steeper. I'm sure they've multiplied. There's more of them. That's why they look so daunting.

I hold my sides and start the climb.

The never-ending climb.

The climb to the summit of Mount Everest. Is that the tallest mountain? Or is it Mount Kilimanjaro? My brain literally isn't functioning any longer. I'm not even sure I could come up with the correct answer for two plus two. Five? Twelve? Who cares?

By the time I'm halfway up, I give up and accept my fate. I'm going to die. Right here on the stairs. So, I sit down panting and holding my ribs in an attempt to keep them from cracking more. Or maybe from falling out altogether.

I close my eyes and wait for death.

Of course, it couldn't just take me peacefully. No… Death has to come in the form of a six foot whatever the fuck Shifter God named Kade Deimos. All muscle. All perfect. Even though I'm sweating bullets and smell terrible, Kade still exudes sexiness and that stupidly incredible scent that makes me weak in the knees. I don't even need to open my eyes to know he's near. I can sense him just by how good he smells.

I feel his hands on my arms, but I fall even more limp. If that's possible. "Just let me die. You win. I can't keep up with you. I'm not worthy of being the mate of Shifter." The words that spill from my lips break my heart. The one organ that didn't hurt is now broken into a million more pieces than it probably already was. I didn't think I could feel it anymore. I guess I can.

His low rumble of a chuckle pisses me off and soothes me at the same time as he easily lifts me to my feet. Which also hurt. "Whoever said anything about you not being worthy?"

I finally open my eyes and sigh deeply. Kade takes most of my weight as he helps me up the stairs. "You. You, Kade. You say it all the time without words." I try to pull away, but he just holds me tighter. I'm too weak to fight. "I can get to my room myself."

"I don't doubt that. It just might take you an hour."

I glare up at him. He looks down at me with a stupid smirk. "But I'd still get there on my own. And prove to you that I'm not just a weak Human."

"There are many things about you that surprise me, Kaia. Your strength is one of them. There is a major difference between inner strength and physical strength." He passes by his room and opens the door to mine. "My father was the strongest man I have ever known. And he was killed. By a Shifter. My sister-in-law was killed by a Shifter, too. She was the strongest woman I've ever known. I will not allow that to happen to another Human on my watch."

He doesn't say anything else. He helps me to the bathroom and leans me against the counter. When his arm leaves my waist, I almost sink to the ground. I watch him run a bath for me, complete with relaxing bubbles.

Over the past five days, Kade has been teaching me self-defense. I honestly didn't realize it would be so hard. I've always wanted to learn ways to protect myself, so I'm grateful he's teaching me, but I also realize with heartbreaking clarity that I would never win a fight with a shifter. I'm not sure I'd even be able to injure one. I've kicked Kade and punched him as hard as I can because that's what he told me to do, but I have barely left a scratch on him.

While he's been incredibly tough on me on the field, he's been very kind off of it. He makes sure I eat enough and drink what I'm supposed to. He has even run a bath for me after every session with him. I haven't asked him questions, though, because I don't want to push him away. I'm relishing in how close we've become.

He shuts the water off after the jacuzzi tub is filled and turns to me. "Tonight is the last night of the Crescent Moon celebration. We each write down one thing we want to bring into existence during this lunar cycle, then toss it into the bonfire. Think you'll be able to make it?"

I shrug and look down. There has been four nights of celebrations so far. Each night has been different than the one before, but I've enjoyed them. The problem is, I'm afraid to enjoy them too much and allow myself to get too close to anyone because I'm not sure if or when it will end. While I feel myself getting closer to Kade and even believe he's warming up to me, he still throws statements out there about no Humans in his pack.

I'm sure his plans haven't changed. As soon as he figures out who is after me, he's going to send me away. I haven't had any time to use the library over the past few days, but maybe I should start looking up how to survive on my own instead of focusing on Shifters and the history of this pack.

Maybe I should find ways that a Human can survive without her fated Shifter mate. Everything I've read so far about it makes me think that we'll die without each other. We'll be so depressed that we'll just waste away.

I can't let myself believe that, though. If he really means no Humans, then I need to believe I'll be able to live without him. Without anyone, really, because I don't have another soul on this Earth to support me. I need to learn how to make my own way.

"It will be fun. You could use that after today. We all need to unwind after grueling workouts. Dominick will be barbecuing. He's a grill master. And you do need to eat."

I smile softly and look up at him. "Why are you so insistent on having me go to these celebrations?" I ask quietly.

He shrugs and crosses his arms over his chest. "Why not?"

"You don't want me. It's obvious." That's a lie. I've felt him against me. It's very difficult to deny his attraction to me. It's probably the reason he fights it so hard. He doesn't want a human for a mate, but his body completely disagrees. "So why have me participate in these things?"

"Maybe to give you some light in the darkness with everything that has happened." He lets his arms fall to his sides. He scowls, but I can see a little bit of the hurt he feels in his eyes. Hell, I can feel the hurt he feels. It's all part of the mate bond. "Come, or don't."

I watch him walk out of the bathroom and feel the immediate sense of loss I always feel when he's not near me. It's nearly crippling. Most of the time, I can't figure how I manage to stay standing, but I do.

I take a deep breath and start removing my clothing. A few moments later, I'm immersed in incredibly warm and comforting waters with bubbles up to my neck that I'm sure have healing powers of their own. I push the button to turn on the jets and feel all tension starting to release from my body. I allow myself to relax and the waters to work their magic.

I smile softly when Kade's face conjures itself in my mind. Not like it doesn't already permanently live there. He's taken up residence, and I'm sure he won't be going anywhere anytime soon.

I can't say I'm not happy with it. His smile warms my soul. At least when he lets me see it. His eyes light up. I love the golden sparkle in them that contrast the dark color. When he lets himself feel for me what I do for him, his eyes look like they are on fire.

I let my eyes fall closed as the familiar ache only he seems to be able to cause between my thighs begins. I allow my hand to slide down my body until my fingers hit that sweet bundle of nerves capable of bringing me immense pleasure. Before long, I'm imagining Kade just like I always do. His long, capable fingers sliding into me while his thumb flicks my clit back and forth.

94

I let out a quiet moan and arch into my hand as I thrust two fingers into myself. I spread my legs to give myself more access and start meeting my thrusts. I pant, feeling myself get closer and closer. I thrust faster. My hips jerk into my fingers at the same pace, but I'm as quiet as I can be.

"Oh, Kade," I whisper. Just his name on my lips brings me so close to the peak I'm about ready to jump off. "Yes, yes…," I moan. I give my clit more pressure and imagine it's his tongue. The tingle turns into an intense throb. My pussy clenches and pulses erratically. My head falls back as my release washes over me. "Kade!" I moan in a quiet whisper.

As I come, I swear I hear something drop. I jerk my head towards the door as I slowly thrust inside myself to bring myself down. Kade closed the door to the bathroom on his way out, though. I'm sure whatever it was must have been in another room.

Unsure of how much time has actually gone by, but feeling a lot better, I groan and quickly wash myself up. I'm surprised that most of the pain of the day has subsided along with the stress and sexual frustration.

I slowly rise from the tub and turn off the jets. I let the water drain while I dry off. I open the door to the bathroom and see that it's beginning to get dark. I dress as fast as I can in jeans and a long sleeve shirt. It tends to get a little cold in the mountains at night, no matter how warm the day is.

I smile a little because I can already hear everyone outside having fun and smell the barbecue. The other nights have been fun, but there was no all out party. There were snacks put out, but not a barbecue. It smells delicious and the happy laughter lifts my spirits. I'm sure that's exactly what Kade meant when he was talking about adding some light.

Things have been difficult. It's not easy dealing with a complete life upheaval and the loss of my parents on top of it. I'm still not sure how I'm functioning. Maybe it just hasn't completely hit me yet.

When I reach the bottom of the stairs, I grip the railing. I sense him. I can feel the hairs on the back of my neck stand at just as much attention as every cell in my body. His unique cologne mixes with his natural scent and makes me dizzy. It always tilts my world.

"I'm glad you decided to join us," he says as he appears at my side. His voice is husky and deep.

I shiver and fight the clenching of my stomach. The all too familiar tingle between my thighs forces me to swallow and do all I can to subtly cross my legs to ease the ache I just took care of not that long ago. If his voice does this to me, I wonder what it would be like if he fully opened himself up to me. I'm sure what I feel is just a taste of what could be.

"What is wrong with me?" I whisper softly as I look up at him.

He quirks an eyebrow and cocky smile like he knows exactly everything I'm thinking. "Where did that come from?"

Right. Like I'm telling you that. I chuckle and shake my head. "Nothing." I hug myself as I make my legs move and carry me outside.

Kade follows. "Dominick is just finishing some burgers. Steaks and some corn on the cob are on the grill now. If you tell him how you like your steaks, he'll cook it for you."

I nod and reach up to discreetly wipe away a tear. I'm not sure if I like Kade better being an asshole or this caring Kade. At least when he's being a jerk, I know where I stand. Kade like this makes me feel like he is starting to come around to the idea of a Human mate. It's not something I dare hope right now, but the up and down emotional rollercoaster he's put me on is hard to keep up with.

"Kade!" a stupidly voluptuous woman screeches as she pushes me aside and lunges for Kade. She plants her plump red lips against his as she throws her arms around him and presses her barely covered breasts against his chest. Her jean skirt rises up her thighs, showing off the bottom of her butt cheeks. She wraps her perfectly tanned legs around his waist.

I hold a hand over my mouth to keep from vomiting, but when I see his shocked eyes close and his hands fall to her hips, it's all that I needed to break me the rest of the way. I turn away before I burst into tears. I don't know who she is, but it's obvious they have something.

I slip behind a tree away from everyone and fall to my knees as I gasp for breath. Sobs wrack my body. Everything that's happened since my parents were killed slams into me with the force of an atom bomb. I don't know what keeps me from howling my pain as loudly as I can, but I am thankful for being able to hang onto what little dignity I have left.

The question I've been thinking since almost the day I was taken here plays over and over in my mind. Why do I stay? What's wrong with me that I don't just leave? Walk away from all of this and try to figure everything out on my own?

The truth is blindingly obvious and completely undeniable. I'm scared. I watched the police kill my parents. I am no closer to figuring out why. My parents were perfect. They weren't into anything illegal or crazy. Which means they had to have seen something. Maybe they knew something. Either way, I have no one to turn to.

I swallow lungfuls of air trying to calm myself, but the tears still fall. I can't get Kade and the way too busty woman out of my head. Every time I think of him kissing her it feels like he's stomping all over my heart. The pain I feel during the day trying to learn to defend myself and fight is nothing compared to what I feel right now. It's like a thick, twice my weight blanket has been draped over me, and I've been thrown into the river.

I can't breathe. I claw at the dirt and gasp, but my lungs burn and feel like they've been punctured. It's like a bunch of needles are being poked into every inch of my skin, but it's nothing compared to those being shoved into my heart.

"Oh my God, Kaia!" someone says. I feel warm hands on my back, but I don't move. Jordan. I know it's Jordan. She has a calming aura about her. "Kaia, look at me, sweetie."

"I c-can't." I'm lying in the dirt, but I don't care. "I h-hate h-him! I h-hate th-the mate b-bond!" Dirt is mixing with my tears, but I can't force myself to move. If it feels like this to see him kiss someone else, how is it going to feel without him? "Wh-why would I h-have one with so-someone who doesn't w-want me? What k-kind of cr-cruel twist of fucked-up-ness i-is that?" I cry.

"Oh, honey." Jordan wraps her arms around me. "The mate bond is such a special thing. I know Kade is… Well, he's an ass, but don't give up on him. This isn't usually how he is. He is trying to have everyone's best interest at heart. I think he might be a little scared, though he would never admit it."

I squeeze my eyes closed and shake my head. "He k-kissed…" I can't finish the sentence. Instead, the thought causes me to dry-heave. "Wh-why do I feel l-like I'm dy-dying?"

She runs her fingers through my hair and pulls me out of the dirt and into her. "Because you just saw the one soul who was made for yours kissing another woman. I know he hasn't claimed you, but you're still connected."

I hiccup and sob even harder, clutching her shirt. "It's st-stupid!"

"You're not thinking straight. Your head feels like it's spinning in a circle. You feel like your mind is racing, and you can't connect the dots. Your heart is beating rapidly. You feel flushed, even if it is freezing cold outside. Believe me, I understand." She hugs me a little tighter. "With everything that's happened to you, no one can really blame you for feeling like that. Even if you didn't have a mate bond pulling at you and were thrown into a world you don't understand, you'd still feel totally out of control, and disoriented, and like nothing at all makes sense. You've been through hell over the last month and haven't taken the time to truly process what happened and what it all means for you. Add in the future being so uncertain, and you've got one hell of a migraine."

I nod and try to regain my composure. I chant to myself over and over and over that he isn't mine because he really isn't. I need to study it more, but in order for the bond to be complete, there has to be some kind of marking. Or ritual. Or maybe it's as simple as consummating the relationship and receiving the mating bite. Until then, the bond isn't sealed. Everything I feel is barely a drop in the ocean to what being bonded to your mate is like. Like what Jordan and Dominick have.

I want that.

I want it with Kade.

I want to feel when he is happy, when he is sad, even when he is angry. To just feel anything from him that isn't just an echo. A feeling that slips through my fingers before I can grasp it. I just wish the asshole would be honest with himself and stop hiding.

Don't get me wrong, I understand his rule. I understand why he made it. He suffered an immense loss. So did Jordan, but she also had Kade and Dominick to lean on. Kade, being the new Alpha, probably held it all inside and kept it locked up tighter than a bank vault. So, I understand the reasons behind why he created it. But now, it seems more like a hindrance to the pack than making us… them… him… stronger.

If Kade refuses to give me the answers I need, then I will have to find them for myself. He may have told the pack not to answer my questions, but there is more than one way to find the information I am looking for. Maybe then I can figure out what I need to do with my life.

Mainly, if I have a future here.

With Kade.

CHAPTER ELEVEN

~*~ KADE ~*~

I don't have much of a chance to do anything other than catch Charlene when she launches herself at me. When her lips latch onto mine and her legs wrap around my waist, bile instantaneously rises up my throat. I close my eyes and swallow it down as I grip her hips and throw her off me.

She lands on her ass and looks up at me as I'm wiping my mouth and glaring down at her. "Kade, what the hell!" she yells up at me.

"Me? What the fuck was that, Charlene? Why the hell are you even here? I said I was fucking busy!" I growl.

"Busy having a party without your girlfriend?" she screeches.

The sound makes me want to cover my ears, but instead I growl. "Leave. I didn't invite you here. You and I are not a thing, and never have been."

Dominick looks down at her. "When the hell are you going to understand Kade doesn't have any respect for you? You've never been anything but a temporary sexual release. You knew the rules when you started fucking with him. And considering how many men you've been with, I doubt you'll miss him."

"You might miss my bank account." I look around for Kaia, but don't see her. I can feel her, though. And what I feel is not good. It goes in my favor. She's hurt and angry at me. But this is not what I want her to think of me. I shoot Charlene a withering glare that makes her shrink back as she stands. "Get.. the… fuck… out… Never come back here," I seethe.

She tries to win some fucking staring contest, but backs down quickly when my glare heats up exponentially and becomes murderous. She takes a few steps back with fear on her face that should have rightfully been there from the beginning.

Everyone in the area is watching her. The Den Makers have moved the kids further away from the crowd and are keeping them distracted. One thing I love about Den Makers is that they are not all women. Most of the Den Makers in our pack are men. It's a role I know Zeke wanted to incorporate when he got older.

Charlene made one fuck of a scene, and my pack is loyal. One wrong move, and she'll be escorted off the property. I'm pissed off enough that it may be in a damn body bag. I clench my fists as I watch her every move.

Leave it to Charlene to ruin a good night that started not long ago with me accidentally overhearing Kaia getting off. I don't think she realizes just how good a Shifter's hearing is. I've heard her before, but tonight, she was calling my name. I'll be damned if the sound of my name on her lips as she was coming didn't make me drop my soap in the shower.

The shower is one of the only two reasons I go into my bedroom. This past week, it's been my favorite place because Kaia has gotten herself off after my lessons with her each night. The sound of her moans has made me come harder than I've ever come in my life. Of course Charlene would ruin that after release euphoric bliss.

Over Charlene's shoulder, I see Jordan come out of the woods with her arm around Kaia's waist. Kaia is looking at the ground as she walks. I'm sure it's so people won't see the tears streaking her face, but I can. Knowing they were put there because of Charlene makes me vibrate with the anger I feel coursing through my veins.

Charlene turns. I can see her look Kaia up and down and am already making my way towards her with Dominick right next to me. I don't want her to say a fucking word to Kaia to upset her any more than she already is. That isn't who Charlene is, though. She's never been able to leave well enough alone.

Charlene shoulder checks Kaia, forcing Jordan to catch her before she falls. Kaia looks up, confusion written all over her pretty face. Charlene gasps, but not loudly enough anyone would hear if they weren't listening to her.

"You'll pay for this," Charlene hisses. Kaia's eyes widen in further confusion and a little fear as Jordan grips her waist tighter.

"Charlene!" I roar so fiercely that the kids in the pack all start whimpering. Even some of the adults cringe away in fear. Kaia lets out a small squawk and covers her mouth as she looks at me.

Charlene has the decency to at least look at me before she does something I never in a million years thought I'd ever see. Something so surprising that I, the Alpha of the most feared Shifter pack on this planet, am rendered not only speechless, but motionless as I watch.

She smirks at me, infuriating me to levels I don't know that I've ever reached. She turns her smirk onto Kaia and grins viciously. Then, she turns back to me and blows me a kiss. Her eyes turn a wicked blue, and my heart stops beating. I suck in a breath as she winks and shifts into a Wolf with tawny brown fur. She takes off running.

I nearly choke on my own saliva, but Kaia sinking to her knees snaps me out of it quickly. *Jamie, Max, Tony, Aiden, and Len! Go after her!* I wait for each of them to acknowledge me as I sink to the ground in front of Kaia. Jordan is soothingly telling Kaia to breathe.

Jamie! What the fuck! Go! Dominick yells to my eldest pack member and head of my patrol.

I look up. *Jamie! What are you doing?* I yell. *Fucking move!*

Jamie shakes his head like he's coming out of a fog. "She was there," he chokes.

I shake my head and help Jordan stand Kaia up. Without me having to ask, she helps Kaia into the house. "What are you talking about?" I growl. I don't like my orders being disobeyed, but I know Jamie. He has to have a reason.

He looks at me. The same pained expression I saw when he limped his way back to the pack house carrying his sister's body the day we were attacked is plastered all over his face. His pain takes my breath away and forces me to think of my own torment at seeing my father's body being carried back by another injured pack member.

"She's the one who killed Elsie. I'll never forget her, Kade. I'll never forget the twinkle in her eyes when she slashed her throat. Elsie died in my arms. She watched Elsie's life drain from her body before she took off, but her scent. Her eyes. I'd recognize her anywhere."

"She's... part of the same pack?" I ask in disbelief.

"How the hell did we not know that?" Dominick asks.

"She was masking her scent." I've surpassed anger and have reached fury level. I feel like I could spontaneously combust at any moment. "I fucked around with her for God only knows how long. Not once did she let on she was a Shifter. And I sure as hell didn't smell it."

"As soon as she shifted, her scent slammed into me," Jamie says. He covers his face with his hands. "I haven't smelled that scent since the day I lost Elsie and Loki." He lets out a ferocious snarl.

Loki is one of my cousins and Jamie's mate. He was adopted by Fenn and Aryan. He was a foster kid who had a lot of behavioral problems. Turns out, it was because he was a Shifter who hadn't gotten his Wolf as of then.

The Moon Goddess must have figured he wasn't in a position to get it. His parents had left him on the doorstep of the fire department when he was a newborn. No one understands why to this day. I've been helping Jamie look for Loki's parents ever since the day we lost them, but to no avail. It was just recently that Jamie decided they don't deserve to know anything about him. I think finding them in the first place was his way of holding onto his mate as hard and long as he could.

"I'm going to kill her." He lets his hands fall. "As soon as they find her and bring her back here, I'm going to tear her apart limb from limb."

I put a hand on his shoulder. Dominick does the same. "Not until after we get information, brother." I say. "Something tells me there is more to this than we know. And the look she sent Kaia's way makes me believe she knows more than we think."

"I will not stand by and allow another decimation of this pack, Kade." He glares into the woods. "I'm never going to be unprepared again. I still don't know who the hell this pack is, but I'm going to kill every single damn one of them."

I squeeze his arm. "We'll be right by your side."

She's gone. We lost her! Max tells me. *Fuck! Fuck! Fuck! We can't pick up her scent!*

I rub my head. "Fuck!" I roar.

Wait! There! Len yells.

I link with him and see they're pounding after her again. They're coming close to a creek. They all jump over it just as she shifts back to her Human form. She looks back at them and blows a kiss, like the bitch did to me, just before she jumps into a silver truck.

Get that license plate! I yell as I watch through Len's eyes.

The truck speeds off. My guards take off after it, but it's going far too fast for them to keep up with it even with their speed powers. The truck gets smaller and smaller. Len roars in frustration as they all slow.

Goddammit! Max yells as he pants to catch his breath. *Dammit!*

The license plate. Did anyone see it? I ask the question hopefully, but I know the answer. That truck took off far too quickly for anyone to have seen it.

All I saw was that it was a Tennessee plate. First letter was a D. Looked like it might be personalized, Aiden says.

I run my hands down my face. *Get back here. I want a tight perimeter set up. We're on lockdown. No one, and I mean no one, leaves the property. Everyone watch Kaia closely because Charlene threatened her specifically.*

"Hold up, Alpha. I linked with Len. That plate is custom for damn sure. It has a red mountain peak on each side of the plate," Owen says standing beside me.

Len chuckles. *That's my eagle-eyed mate. Eye for fucking details.*

Owen grins. *Just keeping up with you.*

I pat his back. "Good job. All of you. Lockdown the territory. Dom. I need you to start calling our allies. I can't be sure, but I want everyone on alert. I think this is the attack we've been preparing for."

I hear the collective gasps of everyone around me and the Wolves I've linked with who were chasing Charlene. I say nothing more, though, because my mind is completely on Kaia. I need to make sure she's okay.

Dominick jogs after me. "You think this is it?"

"Yep. Everything in me is saying whoever she's involved with is the pack we've been preparing for. She's been spying for them for a long time. Keep that in mind."

"Yeah, but this is only the second time she's been here. The first was when you took her here because her apartment was being sprayed for spiders."

"So, she said. She wasn't out of my sight, but who knows what the fuck she saw." I link with Prince and Julian, two of my Den Makers. *I want all kids and our pregnant females in the packhouse. No exceptions. Packhouse is safest.*

You got it, Alpha, Prince says.

I walk into the house and head straight for the stairs. "Make those calls, Dom."

"I'll take care of it."

We split off at the top of the stairs. He heads to his bedroom. I walk directly to Kaia's. I knock gently on the door, though I want to break it down. I need to see that she's okay. Nothing else matters to me right now.

"Kaia?"

"Go away!" she cries.

I let out a breath and reach down to the door handle. I slowly turn it, thankful it isn't locked, and gently push it open. "Kaia, I know you're pissed and -" My eyes widen. "What the fuck? What are you doing?"

She looks up at me, a mix of pain and pure anger emanating from her eyes as she throws her clothes into her duffel bag. "I'm done! I don't belong here! You've said it yourself over and over again. So, I'll leave!" She vigorously wipes at her eyes.

I close the door gently, though I want to slam it and demand answers. I make myself stay calm and turn back to her. "What you saw down there… Kaia, it wasn't what it looked like. She caught me off -"

"Off guard, Kade?" She starts zipping the bag. "I can't even stand here and be mad for it because I'm not yours, right? You haven't claimed me." She uses air quotes to drive her point home. "I have no rights to you. So, if you want to kiss another girl that you obviously have something with, that's not something I can control. But I can control this. I can leave right now and try to figure out my life without anyone else in it. I have no family. I have no friends I can turn to. I have no idea who I can trust. But

I'll do it because I have to. Because I can't figure out why I stay here. I don't understand this world. And you won't give me any answers or allow anyone else to. And the one thing I had, the library. You took that away from me, too!"

I feel like she's just kicked me in the stomach with the force of a fighter jet. "Kaia -"

"No! No, you don't get to sit there and tell me that it's not my business. That I'm not part of this pack and therefore have no rights to know anything! You don't get to say that because I've been a part of this pack for over two weeks now! I've lived and breathed this pack! I've gotten closer to Jordan than I've ever been with anyone! And for what? You don't want me here! You've said over and over that the only reason I'm here is so you can figure out who the people who were chasing me and trying to kill me are. But what about after that? Huh, Kade? What happens to me when that threat is eliminated?"

"Kaia, I get you're pissed. You have every reason -"

"You're damn right I have every reason! Not only am I supposed to be your alleged fated mate, but I don't know what the hell that entails! All I know is that whenever I look at you, I want to kiss you, punch you, and cry. I know that I have feelings for you that are intense. Feelings I can't explain that are growing at a rate that scares me so much! And I can't talk to you or anyone else about them because you won't allow it!"

"Kaia, come on. I -"

She holds up a hand. "Not done!" She's practically screaming at me now. "I cry myself to sleep every single night. Did you know that?" Her eyes meet mine. The tears fall freely now. She's not trying to stop them, and it guts me. I can't let her know that. Just like I can't let her know that I do know she cries herself to sleep every night. "Did you know that not only do I cry every night, but it feels like my heart breaks every single day. Several times. Over and over and over and over. I'm shattered every time I think of my parents. Every time I think of Leia. Every time I think of how I should have opened up to other people my age in school, but didn't. Every time I think of how alone I am and how I'm going to have to fight in this world alone and navigate it by myself."

I swallow hard as I watch her. Each one of her words feel like another dagger thrown at me. I want to sink to my knees and beg for her forgiveness. But I can't. "You won't be alone." I bite the rest of the words back. I shouldn't have even said that much, but I want to soothe her somehow. "I'll still help you, Kaia," I choke out over the lump forming in my throat.

She barks out a laugh. "So you can control my life more? No. Thank you for the offer, Kade, but I'd rather live and die alone then have you in my life in any manner. I can barely focus when I know you're gone on surveillance. I have no idea how I'll be knowing you're around, but that you're not mine. I'm fairly certain I'll be broken, but I can't research it to prepare because you locked the library and nothing on the internet helps me at all! It's all mystical rhetoric of a made up world and makes me think that this entire thing is one fucked up dream that I can't seem to wake up from! But I'm sure you don't care about that!"

"Kaia! Enough!" Before I can stop myself, I'm crossing the room to her. I grip her upper arms. "Do you think this is easy for me? Do you have any idea what it's like for a Shifter to have his mate right in front of him and not be able to claim her like he wants to? My Wolf is in my head right this very second screaming at me to kiss you! Mark you! Make you mine!"

She looks up at me in both wonder and shock before looking down at where my hands are connected to her. "You're hurting me," she whispers.

I loosen my grip but don't let go as I glower down at her. "Locking that library door was one of the hardest things I've ever done, Kaia. Because I knew how bad it would hurt you. Contrary to your belief, hurting you is the last thing I want to do! I want to protect you. I want you to be mine forever. But I can't do that because you are Human, and I can't stand the thought of losing you like I lost so many others! I can't handle the idea that the Moon Goddess could take you from me like he did my parents and brothers and sister-in-law! Do you have any idea what it's like to lose everything in the blink of an eye?"

"Yes!" She breaks free and shoves me. The force surprises me a little, and I take a step back just to keep my balance. "Yes! I do know! My parents were killed, basically, right in front of me! At least you know what happened to yours and why! I don't! I don't know why four police officers were in my house, and why they killed them! I think about everything that happened before every single hour of the day. I dream about it! I don't know how I wasn't found when I was hiding. I don't know why they left

106

me for dead! I didn't do anything! And now I've been thrust into a world I don't understand! I was trying to, though. I was really trying to. And I can't even do that anymore! So now I'm trying to figure out what my life is going to be like when this is all over, but I can't even do that because I can't see anything other than you and this pack. This life!" She hiccups as she sobs.

"Kaia, I don't have a fucking clue why my parents were killed! I have no idea why I lost nearly all of my pack! All I know is that some mystery pack came out of nowhere and killed all of them before I even got home from football practice! I didn't know what happened until Dominick and Jordan walked in the fucking house and told me! My Wolf? He blocked it all from me! And my father blocked the rest! I lost everything in a matter of seconds, just like you! So don't sit there and tell me that I don't know what it feels like!"

"I can't do this anymore!"

She shoves past me to her bag and tries to pull away from me again when I grip her arm once more. "Just stay, Kaia. You can't leave right now. There are threats all over the place against you. You won't survive out there."

"I won't survive here! I won't survive out there! Maybe you should just put me out of my misery and -"

I cut her off with a deep, all-consuming kiss. At first, she's not receptive. It doesn't surprise me in the slightest, but I can't pull away. It's getting harder and harder for me to resist her in any manner. Her pain rips me apart. Her happiness makes me feel like I'm flying. Her attraction to me makes mine grow exponentially.

Even now, her lips against mine makes my entire body buzz, like I'm standing on a live wire and being electrocuted. It's like my body is absorbing the current. I pull her closer and moan slightly into the kiss when she whimpers and starts moving her mouth against mine. She fists my shirt.

I tangle one of my hands in her hair and tug slightly. She does exactly what I want her to do, need her to do. She tilts her head, giving me easier access to take more. I swipe my tongue over her salted caramel flavored lips that I'm coming to crave more than my next breath. I know it can't happen, but I need her right now.

She wraps her arms around my waist. She's shaking, but so am I. Her tongue tangles with mine shyly. I nip hers and suck on it lightly. The motion makes her jump just a little, but she tightens her grip and moans.

Mate! Ours! Make her ours!

It takes all of my strength, but I force myself to pull away. I don't want to let go, but I push her away gently. We're both panting. Her beautiful dark caramel eyes meet mine. I can see the heat I'm feeling reflected back at me. The current I felt humming through me hasn't stopped. My eyes zero back in on her lips. I'm doing all I can not to kiss her again. I take a couple of slow steps back as she takes a deep breath and watches me cautiously.

My Wolf whimpers at the loss. It takes everything in me not to take her back in my arms. Especially when I feel her suspicion and sadness seep back into the euphoric bliss she was just feeling.

"Just… stay. Please? Charlene is a threat to you now. There are four cops out there who I believe are Shifters who are after you. I have a feeling they're connected to Charlene. I don't know why, Kaia. I wish I did. I would tell you if I knew, but I don't. What I do know is that you're safer here. I can protect you, and I will."

She watches me for a long moment before taking a shuddering breath and nodding. "Okay," she whispers. "I wish you'd talk to me… about all of this." She hugs herself and looks down.

For the millionth time since meeting her, I feel like the biggest asshole. But I shake my head. "I can't. I just can't. When this is all over, we can sit down and discuss things related to what happened. We'll discuss your future. How I can help you. But I can't discuss pack stuff, Kaia. I can't. I know you've gotten close to Jordan. I won't let her discuss pack things with you either, but that doesn't mean she can't be your friend."

She doesn't look at me. Instead, she closes her eyes and nods. Her head is still down. I know she's trying hard not to cry. I want to hold her. I want to tell her all of this will be okay. That she'll be okay and live a healthy and happy life while I'll be miserable and pining for her. Anything to make her feel better about what I'm putting her through. I want to make her understand just how necessary this is. I want to do a lot of things, but I do none of it. Instead, I turn with my own head down and slowly walk away.

She softly sniffles. "I wish you'd give me a chance. Us…," she whispers.

It's my turn to take a shuddering breath. One that forces me to put a hand against the doorframe to steady myself as I reach for the knob. I don't know how much more of her pain I can handle on top of my own before I completely collapse under the crushing weight of it.

"I'm sorry, Kaia." I say the words loud enough for her to hear before I quickly leave the room. I bypass my bedroom, the same one I haven't slept in ever since Kaia entered my life, and walk straight to my office. I close the door behind me and do the one thing I will never let her, or anyone, see me do.

Cry.

CHAPTER TWELVE

~*~ KAIA ~*~

(Two Weeks Later)

I smile over at the kids and draw soft lines in my sketchbook as I finish the drawing I've been working on for most of the day. I put finishing touches on it and admire it before I start putting my drawing pencils away.

"That's really good," Jordan says kindly. She smiles. "It really captures the emotion of the day."

I look down at the drawing again. It's of Kade and Dominick in the pool tossing a couple of the kids in the air. They all laugh and smile. Aiden and Jamie are running from a couple older kids as they play tag. Owen and his adoring mate, Len, are barbecuing. Several other pack members are around the area having a good time.

"I wanted to show the lightness of the day. It's been so dreary around here since the Crescent Moon celebration. Everyone seems happy." I smile softly when my eyes meet Kade's. I look down when he drags his eyes away. "I didn't want to forget this."

Jordan gives me a sad smile and gently pats my thigh. I look up and find Kade's eyes on mine once more. Despite the happiness surrounding us all, Kade looks upset. Sad. He's looked tense for the past couple of weeks. I've even felt some of his apprehension without even being near him. Sometimes, my heart will just start racing for no reason.

Today, though, it's sorrow. Maybe even a little regret. Every time I catch him looking at me, I see it in his eyes. They linger on me before his frown deepens, and he turns away. I know there's something weighing on him. I assume it's the threat that was made against me, and the one he feels against his pack.

"Kade! Again! Again!" one of the littlest kids says. She's in an adorable pink one piece with floaties on her arms. Her blond hair is done in cute little pigtails.

Kade smiles as she swims to him. "Again?"

"Again! Again!"

Kade swoops her up and throws her high in the air, spinning her. I smile when she squeals and throws her arms out like she's an airplane. He catches her with so much care and ease that it makes my heart squeeze. He's really good with the kids. They all have him going in different directions, but he does it without a second thought. He doesn't even look tired, even though he's been in the pool or running around it for most of the day.

Kade sets her in the water, and she jets off as she splashes around and swims towards her brothers and sister. Kade pulls himself out of the water. I can't take my eyes away from his perfectly sun-kissed body. Each and every one of his muscles are perfectly sculpted and makes me want to lick the water droplets from his body.

That thought makes me turn away, but I can feel his eyes fall on me again. Despite the sadness, he looks at me hungrily. I feel like I'm being seared under the intensity of it. Ever since he kissed me in the bedroom I've been staying in, that heated gaze is something I get more and more.

But he hasn't touched me since. He's barely even talked to me. Whenever I walk into a room, he walks out of it. Not before he gives me the sad hungry look. Which only succeeds in confusing me about everything far more. If he wants me, and I think he does, I feel he does, then why does he not give in? Why doesn't he sit and talk to me? Why won't he tell me the things I not only want to know, but need to? I just don't understand what he's waiting for. And why he's fighting it so hard.

I smile a little when Jordan giggles while she watches her mate. Dominick runs by us, barely dodging the tag of a teenager around my age running after him. He laughs and runs faster. I have to wonder if he's pacing himself to make it seem like the girl has a chance of catching him but really has no chance at all.

I feel Kade's eyes on me again. My throat tightens. I glance at him before taking a breath. "I think I'm going to head inside. It's starting to get a little chilly."

Jordan looks up at the sky. "Mmhmm... Kade will make everyone go inside soon anyway."

"Right. The sunset curfew." I can't help but smile a little more and glance at him again. He cares so much for all of these people. Shifters. His pack.

"He means the best," Jordan says softly. "He really loves all of us. He's protective."

"I know." I gather my things as I stand. "It's one of the qualities I actually really love about him."

Jordan smiles up at me as she stands herself. She giggles when Dominick runs by again, once again dodging the girl's tag. Jordan moves quickly and bumps him into the pool. I can't help the laugh that bubbles out of me. Kade cracks up. When Dominick resurfaces, he looks wounded, but I can tell it's all an act.

"Fucking shoved in the pool. By my own mate!" he bellows.

Jordan laughs harder. Kade grabs his sides. I smile because seeing him laugh makes my heart flutter. Jordan takes my arm and skips away with me, glancing over her shoulder and blowing a kiss to Dominick as he climbs out of the pool and immediately gets tagged. This causes Kade to laugh even harder and fall backwards into the grass surrounding the pool.

I giggle as we enter the house. "I'll admit. That whole thing was adorable."

Jordan laughs as we walk up the stairs arm in arm. "He's going to make an amazing father."

I smile. "I can definitely see him in that role." I turn towards my room.

Jordan keeps our arms linked and walks with me. "It won't be long now. Just under nine months."

I furrow my eyebrows as we walk into the room. "Until what?"

She giggles. "Until he becomes a father, silly!"

It takes a second for her words to reach my brain. But then I turn to her with my jaw nearly on the ground. "Oh my God, Jordan! What?" My eyes drop to her stomach. "Are you pregnant?"

She bites her lip and blushes as she nods. "It's a little different with Shifters," she says quietly, like it's a big secret she shouldn't share with me. She probably shouldn't, considering Kade's rule. I put my sketchbook down. "We don't need pregnancy tests. We feel it. I mean most mother's feel it, but we... well, we feel it almost from the moment of conception." She lowers her voice even more. "Our hearing is so sensitive that we can hear the baby's heartbeat. It's faint. Other Shifters won't be able to hear it for a little while, until it's a little stronger. But I can hear it almost the second it starts."

I can't stop myself from gently placing my hand on her stomach. I swear I feel it, but I don't want to fool myself into believing that. It's a silly thought. She's just a couple of weeks pregnant, but I feel like I can feel her baby.

I smile and look up at her. "Does Dominick know?"

She shakes her head. "I plan on telling him tonight. I have a cute little card that I made. I was going to put it on his pillow while he's in the shower. It just says goodnight, but I signed it with my name and baby. And the card itself is yellow with a bunch of baby things. Like rattles and bottles and pacifiers."

I squeal. "Oh my God. So adorable!"

She squeaks and takes my hands. We both jump up and down excitedly. "I know! I'm so excited!"

"What's got you two so excited?" Kade's deep, smooth timber makes me shiver and melt.

I jump a little when I turn to him because I didn't expect to see him standing in the doorway. He's leaning against the frame with his arms across his chest. The easy smile he has on his face as he watches makes my heart palpitate.

"Girl stuff!" Jordan says with a giggle and sly wink. I can't help but giggle along with her as she squeezes my hands.

He chuckles. "Well, can I borrow Jordan for a second? I won't be long. Then you can have her back and do more girl stuff." He gives me a smirk as he flutters his hand.

I let go of Jordan's hands as she giggles. She follows Kade out of the room. I smile after them, but I'm restless. Something about today feels off. The way Kade kept looking at me is just as confusing as he is. One second I could feel him undressing me with his eyes. The next, an overwhelming sense of grief seemed to pass over his entire chiseled face. Like he already lost me even though I'm right in front of him.

The situation with Kade, at least the physical part of it, makes me wish I had some type of experience to compare it to. But all I can think of is him. I've never wanted anyone else. I didn't know why, but as soon as I started seeing the Man in the Moon, nothing else compared. No one else interested me. Even though I never really saw his face, just brief snippets, there was something about him. I never told anyone, not even Leia, but I believed that whoever he was, I was meant to be with him.

While I felt crazy at the time, being here and around him and this pack has cemented that very belief. I believe my Spirit Guides, his parents, were leading me down a path that would bring me directly to him. What I'm still baffled about is why. It seems as though Kade is perfectly content in his world and doesn't need me in it. No matter how heated his kisses are or what he says his Wolf says to him.

I sigh and wander to the closet in the room. I don't have many things, so I've never looked in it. I assume it's probably rather small, considering the door to it is the size of any regular sized door, but when I open it, I am pleasantly surprised.

"Oh, wow." I blink a few times before stepping inside.

The closet is huge. I find the light switch and flick it on so I can fully appreciate it. It's far from a closet in my eyes. There's a giant dresser. There's a bench to sit on. There are long racks where clothes can be hung set back in a cutout within the wall. Across from it is a full length mirror. But it's not just a regular mirror. It spans the entire wall and looks so clean, I wonder if this room is somehow climate controlled so that no dust or dirt particles can settle or even be created.

At the back of the closet are several cubbies. I assume they are for shoes, but there's something in one of them that catches my eye. I tilt my head as I walk closer and reach into the cubby. My hand falls on a soft, leather-bound book. I pull it out and sit on the bench while I study it. I turn it over in my hands and notice the front cover. It's etched with the initials C.D.

"C.D.," I whisper and nibble my lip, staring at the black leather. The pages look old and are yellowing, but the leather itself seems to be completely pristine. There are no cracks or wear at all. My heart races because the only person I can think of who has those initials is someone who long ago passed. "It can't be…"

It is. I'm glad you finally found that.

My eyes snap up to meet Connor's. "But… how? How is it so new…?" I look down at the book again.

Connor crosses his arms over his chest as his ethereal self leans against the doorframe of the closet. So much like his son. *This room used to be a playroom for Jordan. Sometimes, she'd pretend she was trapped. Others, she'd pretend like this room was her own entire castle. She'd have tea parties and make Kade and Zeke join her. They were always her guards. Never anything else. Either they'd save her from whatever danger she cooked up in her head. Or they'd guard her from any outside evils. Usually fire-breathing dragons. When she got older, Dominick was always her Prince Charming.*

"That's adorable. Just like a regular kid. Not some powerful being." I smile softly and trace his initials.

That's what we are. Just normal people. Some, like Jordan, Kade, Zeke, and all the others in this pack, have been gifted with extraordinary powers. That doesn't mean they aren't still Human. They still feel like Humans feel. Think the same thoughts Humans think. Jordan still imagined her wedding day and planned it down to every single detail while she played with dolls and acted it out. They might be Shifters, but that doesn't mean they don't make the same mistakes that Humans do. They may be powerful beings, but they aren't invincible. And they are certainly not infallible. They aren't all-knowing. They walk the same path through life as Humans do. Their feelings may be more intense than a Human feels, but down to the bone, they are one and the same.

I nod and close my eyes for a moment as his words sink in. "You're saying not to give up on Kade."

I'm saying… that you're a smart girl. He smiles and looks at the journal. *I used to write in my journal in this room while Jordan was*

115

playing. I was not immune to having to share tea with her, but to her, I was the King. So, while I wrote, she would serve me tea and quietly play at my feet. When I was finished, all bets were off. I was expected to fully engage in her games. And I did. I truly cherished those moments. That's mostly what the journal talks about. Moments like that. There are a few more… some would say important things. Maybe they're important now, but not then.

"Like what?" I ask, genuinely curious.

Things that should have mattered to me a little more then. Had I paid a little more attention, maybe things would have turned out differently. Sadness and regret pass over his eyes.

I look down at the journal. "The cover is still so pristine."

This room is climate controlled. You were thinking that a little earlier. I did that so it was not only healthy for my kids, but comfortable. He looks around the room before I hear him speaking again. *You know, I've stayed relatively silent on the matter, kiddo. But I think it's time I said this. I know things are scary and new.*

"That's the understatement of the century."

He chuckles. *But you aren't the only one in this family or the world, for that matter, who has a fated mate that isn't the same species as you. My mate is a Wolf. Not a Shifter. And I'm not a Shifter. Aryan isn't a Shifter. Fenn is not a Shifter. Belle and I had a little easier time accepting it. Fenn and Aryan, while it didn't take them long, did resist it for a bit. Fenn's pack talked to him and made him realize the exact same thing I'm going to tell you. A fated mate is your soulmate, Kaia. There isn't another being in the universe that is made just for you. Well, I suppose that's not entirely true. Sometimes, lightning strikes a few times for lucky individuals, and they find love with multiple people. You will see there are a few triads in packs and even a few quads, but those are even rarer in packs. That's not how it is for most of us.*

"You're saying I need to fight for our love even if I feel like he doesn't want it."

He smiles. *I knew you'd get it. Yes. You need to fight for your love because Kade is scared. He doesn't want to lose you like he lost everyone else important to him. He thinks he's doing the right thing. I can't tell you what to do. I can't tell you how to do it. That's considered interfering. I don't want to push my luck and lose my Spirit Guide powers. The Moon*

Goddess already took us away for a couple of weeks for helping you the way we did. But it was worth it.

"Is that why I didn't see you, even when I begged?"

He nods. *Spirit Guides have rules. We can guide, but we can't interfere. We can give advice, but we can't tell you what to do or what direction to take. If we see something unexpected coming at you, we can warn you, but we can't push you out of the way. We could have led you away from your house and out of danger. But we aren't allowed to interfere in anything beyond that. What I did when I shielded you from the bullets was quite far out of the scope of what I'm allowed to do. Would I do it again? Absolutely.*

I hug the journal to my chest and smile softly. "Thank you for saving me. I haven't gotten the chance to really tell you that. But you should probably stop telling me things like this. Kade put a ban on people talking to me about pack things." A thought occurs to me, and I look back up at him with a hopeful smile. "But he never said you couldn't tell me…"

No… he didn't, did he? Connor chuckles. *But I'm not going to. Not because I don't want to or can't, but because Kade is the one who needs to have the conversation with you that you're asking me to.*

I slump slightly. "I knew you'd say that." I look at the journal. "I need to get this to Kade." I stand with a new sense of determination and straighten my shoulders. "Thank you."

He winks as he shimmers away. *Anytime.*

I smile as I hug the journal to my chest again and traipse to Kade's office feeling a little lighter at having gotten at least a little bit of information into this still very new and confusing world. It may seem strange to some, but the little tidbit has given me enough strength to go through with this. Maybe if Kade realizes that I'm not just some regular Human who is everything he seems to think… Weak and stupid or something. I don't really even know what he thinks of Humans. He's said himself that his father and sister-in-law were the strongest Humans he's ever known. Maybe if he realizes that I'm stronger and willing to fight for him and us, he'll stop fighting all of this.

"You don't have to do this," Jordan whispers. I stop in my tracks. I don't want to bother him. I want him to trust that I am following his orders about leaving me out of pack business, which is what this sounds like.

117

"You can give this a chance, Kade. She fits here. She gets along with everyone," Dominick says just as low as Jordan. It's then I know they're talking about me. I'm rooted to the ground, even though I want to go back to my room and leave them to talk.

"You think I don't want to storm into her room and claim her the way my Wolf wants me to?" Kade growls in a whisper. "The way I want to? You think I don't want to be with the woman who makes me weak in the knees just by smiling? Who brings sunshine to my own personal hell? The woman who makes me laugh when she gets all surprised when one of the kids catches her, even though she's running her fastest? Fuck. Do you honestly think I don't want to be with the woman who can calm my anger and frustration just by the cute sounds she makes when she's sleeping?"

"That's exactly what I'm saying!" Jordan, still whispering, exclaims. "You love her. You know what a perfect fit she is here!"

"Fuck that. You know what a perfect fit she is with you," Dominick growls.

My heart beats faster and faster. I take a quiet breath. Does he really think all of that? Do I really have a chance of him seeing that I feel the same way? That I want to stay here with the pack, with him, and make a life here more than anything in the world?

I jump when something seems to shatter against a wall. "I can't!" Kade's voice becomes louder than a whisper but still quiet enough that I wouldn't hear him if I weren't standing right here. "I can't let myself be with her because it puts her and the pack in danger. I have to reject her."

"Kade, you don't -" Dominick begins.

Kade cuts him off. "I don't have a choice, Dominick. The ritual is the only way to make sure she is safe. If spending the rest of my life alone means that she is safe, then I will do whatever it takes to make that happen."

Reject me? I think to myself. I don't know exactly what that means, but my heart doesn't like the sound of it. Just the word makes me tremble in a way that I only would at a devastating loss. Like I did when my parents were killed. *Ritual?*

"Kade, this is a horrible idea. If you do this, neither of you will ever be the same," Jordan says sadly.

I close my eyes and take a deep breath before I force my feet to carry me the last few steps to his office. I knock lightly just as Kade is

118

about to say something. I'm sure something else about how he doesn't have a choice. Yet another excuse. His eyes snap to mine. Jordan and Dominick both slip out the door as I slowly walk in with my head down. I blink away tears.

"How much of that did you hear?" he asks me. His voice cracks.

I choose not to answer. Instead, I look up at him with a soft smile, though my heart feels like it's breaking once more. I don't know how. I feel like it's been broken so many times, it isn't possible for it to hurt anymore. He manages to prove me wrong each time, though.

I hand him the journal I've been holding onto like it's a life raft in a very choppy and angry ocean. "I found this in the closet in my room," I say quietly.

He takes it and turns it over in his hands. "My father's journal?" He slowly opens it. His breath catches when he sees Connor's handwriting. I can't help but smile, even though it's sad, when his fingers trace the letters on the page he's opened to. "I remember him writing in this. I haven't thought much about it since I was a kid." He looks up at me. "Kaia..." He swallows hard. "This is incredible." He reverently places it down on his desk. When he looks up at me, his eyes are sparkling with unshed tears. "This means so much to me. Thank you."

I try to keep the smile on my face, but it falters. I clear my throat. "Sure." I wipe my eyes as I turn.

Kade's hand reaches for my arm. It's gentle this time. It slides down to my hand. I close my eyes as my skin feels like it's caught on fire. "How much did you hear?" he whispers as his hand finds mine. He tugs me back to him. I want to compose myself and leave the office, but my body obeys his silent command to turn back to him.

When I do, he's standing so close I can feel his warmth. "All of it," I whisper. I look down at where his hand is still holding mine. I reach up and wipe my eyes again. "At least enough to know you intend on rejecting me at some ceremony."

"Kaia, I..." His hand, usually so steady, shakes just a little. If he wasn't holding mine, I wouldn't know. With his other, he gently cups my chin and tilts my face up to his. I don't want to look at him, but he makes that impossible. "Please understand that I don't have a choice."

"There's always a choice." I try to turn away, but he doesn't let me.

"This… is the only choice. The only way I can protect you."

I shake my head as more tears fall. Hot. Angry. "If you won't fight for us, for what we could have, why should I? You've made up your mind. So, just get it over with. Please. Because I'm broken. I'm so, so broken I'm not sure I'll ever be able to put myself together again. And it's something I don't understand. I hardly know you. Yet, I feel like I've known you my whole life. Longer than that. Eternity. I don't know how anyone can feel like that when they don't know anything about the other person. Yet, I feel like I know everything about you." I pull away because his hands on me both hurt and make me want to melt.

"It's because of all of those reasons and the reasons I can't tell you that I have to do this, Kaia."

I glance up at him and can see all of that pain I saw earlier. Only it's worse. So much worse. "I guess I know why today has felt so different. Why you've seemed so different." I hug myself as I turn. This time, he doesn't try to stop me. He'll never know how grateful I am for that. When I get to the door, I turn, but don't look at him. "I think you're taking the coward's way out, Kade. You could have sat down with me and told me everything. Answered my questions. We could've worked through all of this. Together. And maybe when it was over, we would've come to the same conclusion you have. That I couldn't handle this. That it's best for me to leave. Or maybe we would've decided that it's worth a chance. Worth the fight." I finally look up at him. He hasn't moved, but he looks so hurt and conflicted. "But it would've been together. Isn't that what mates do? I don't know a lot about it. I won't pretend to, but it seems like that's what they do." I take a breath. "I won't waste my time or yours fighting for something you don't want."

I swallow hard once more and close the door behind me. I feel like he needs privacy. Maybe to work through his feelings. Maybe to yell and scream. Whatever it is, he needs to do it alone. I hurry away from the door before I turn around and beg him to not do this. To tell him I'm crazy about him and to please want me.

But I don't.

I won't. I won't beg him. I won't lose the last shred of dignity I have left. He's taken the rest.

As I walk into my room, I make the decision that I simply can't stay here anymore. Kade can reject me if he wants to. I doubt there's anything I can say to convince him otherwise, and I won't go to him sounding desperate. It makes me no better than the weak person he seems to think I am.

I won't be here for it, though. I won't be here for the hurt and humiliation this ceremony will entail. I don't know anything about it, but I know about ceremonies. Most of them take place in front of others. Which means my humiliation will be public. I can't go through that.

I quickly pack what little belongings I have. My sketchbook won't fit in my bag, so I carry it. I'd put it in my backpack, but it's ripped and tattered. My sketchbook would fall out of it. I'd rather just carry it. I've done so many new drawings of everything that's happened here. Things I never want to forget even if Kade doesn't want me here.

I quietly leave the room and walk as fast as I can past Kade's office. I glance at the door. It's silent in there. I wonder what he's thinking, but I keep walking. I hurry down the stairs towards the front door. My heart hurts. My whole body hurts. Over the chaos in my mind, though, I hear Connor.

Don't give up on him. Fight.

I shake my head and wipe my eyes because there is no point in fighting for something only one of us wants. I glance up the stairs towards his office, then shake my head again as I continue for the door.

"Kaia?" Jordan says quietly. She's walking towards me from the kitchen holding a cup with a straw. She furrows her brows. "Where are you going?" She eyes my bag before looking back up at me. Realization dawns on her. "Oh, Kaia. Don't go. Please."

"He's given up. Or rather he never tried." I look down. "Why should I?" But I want to. I want to try so badly. I don't say that. Instead, I bite my lip to stop the tears, but it's useless. They fall anyway. I turn towards the door again and turn the handle. I open it a crack and turn to her once more. "I've never felt like I belonged anywhere as much as I felt I belonged here. I still feel it. I doubt I'll feel it about anywhere else."

She puts her hand on my arm. "He's wavering. I know it. I feel it. So does Dominick. He thinks he's protecting you by pushing you away, but the other part of him, the rational side, knows that he's wrong. Kaia, just try one more time. Tell him everything. Tell him how you feel. Make him listen."

Fight for him. Fight for you.

I look up at Connor's voice and know I can't run. I have to fight. For me. For him. For us and the future we are entitled to. Jordan smiles when she sees me closing the door, but her eyes immediately widen.

I don't have any time to react or turn to see what scared her so badly because the door suddenly slams open with such force, my sketchbook and bag go flying as I fall into Jordan. Large, rough hands grip my hips and pull me back into a tall, hard body. One of those hands fly over my mouth. I scream into the hand and reach for Jordan as she runs towards me right into the arms of another tall man.

I hear Jordan scream just as I see the man push a needle into her neck. I feel a prick against my skin just as everything begins to fade. I fight the sick feeling that suddenly overcomes me. Jordan screams and fights, but it looks to be in slow-motion. I don't know if it's because of whatever she's been injected with or if things look so distorted because of what I have flowing into my system.

Everything is suddenly very cold.

Heavy.

Jordan and I are thrown against cold fabric that I slide right off of. I'm thrown into Jordan by those same large, rough hands. At least I think they are the same. I can't see anything anymore. I can only hear a roaring before I feel like I'm sinking under water and drowning. I fight and claw my way to the surface, but to no avail. Darkness overtakes me.

Kade! I scream, panicking. My lungs feel like they are being crushed. *Kade!* His face is the last thing I see before I completely lose the fight and give into the abyss.

Everything falls silent.

CHAPTER THIRTEEN

~*~ KADE ~*~

As soon as she closes my office door, I sink to my knees and fight to breathe. I've been going back and forth on this decision ever since I first laid eyes on her nearly lifeless body. Holding her close to me as she healed from her injuries, as I healed her and took care of her, was the beginning of the end for me. I felt more powerful and weak in that moment than I've ever felt. Powerful because I felt the mate bond, something I've longed for. Weak because I was terrified she'd be taken from me before I ever had the chance to claim her as my own. To explore everything she had to offer.

And then I turned around and fucked everything up with my idiotic rule that never really seemed to be all that bad to me. The pack members I have who have a human mate are still cared for. Protected. They aren't in the compound. But I'd never allow them to break from the pack completely. Even those that broke the bond aren't alone. I don't want anyone to experience that type of pain. At least this way, I feel they're relatively safe.

But Kaia has me thinking that logic may be completely irrational because sending her away and leaving her to fend for herself, even though

I'll always be there behind the scenes helping her, is something I'm beginning to think is the stupidest thought I have ever had. I always thought I understood love. I love every single one of the members of my pack. Human, Wolf, and Shifter alike.

It's obvious to me right now, though, that I don't know what the fuck that means. If I had, I'd have seen long ago that my no Human rule was and is ridiculous. How could I, the Alpha of the Deimos Pack, the most powerful Shifter pack in this entire fucking world, have been so blind?

I can't do it.

I can't go through the rejection ceremony. I can't reject her.

The realization has my Wolf cheering and me feeling a tingling sensation throughout my entire body. Like accepting her completely is somehow filling in all of the cracks and holes I've never allowed anyone to see. Some I didn't even really know I had.

I slowly get to my feet. I need to make this right. I don't care if that involves getting down on my knees and groveling at her feet. I need to fix this. She said she's broken, and I hate that I'm the one who shattered her more than she already was. She lost everything, just as I had so many years ago. At the very least, I had Dominick and Jordan. I had the members of the pack who survived. All Kaia has had this whole time has been me and a bunch of other complete strangers in a world she probably never knew existed.

"Fuck," I whisper. "I need to fix this." I stride to my door and open it just as I hear a scream followed by what sounds to be some kind of a thunk. "What the fuck?" My head snaps towards the front of the house, suddenly feeling very sick at the thought of something happening to Kaia.

Dominick meets me at the top of the stairs. "Shuffling," he whispers.

Kade!

I swear that's Kaia's voice, but it can't be. She doesn't know how to use our mind link. I haven't even told her about it.

Kade!

"Fuck," I whisper. I know that was Kaia this time.

We quickly and almost silently run down the stairs, hitting the hardwood of the ground floor at the same time. My heart is racing completely out of control. I know I need to calm it down, but I'm panicking because I know what I'm about to see before I even reach the door that's ajar.

"No!" I roar, shifting as I leap after the black SUV without plates that's speeding away from my house, kicking up rocks and dirt as it becomes smaller and smaller.

Dominick is right behind me. *They've got Jordan and Kaia!*

I hear multiple roars from my pack and skid to a stop.

They have Haley and Emma! one of my female Shifters whimpers.

I look at Dominick in horror. *Back to the compound!*

He wastes no time in hauling ass back in the direction we came from. I'm right beside him. Our paws pound against the dirt, sending up a cloud of dust behind us.

Camilla and Avery! They're gone! Prince screams. I shake my head. I need to clear it and focus because all I can hear are pained howls from many different Wolves in this pack.

Lexi! No! Julian yells.

Dominick and I reach the packhouse just as Jamie and Don are pulling two guys to their feet. They're tied up and definitely look like they lost a fight. Their eyes are swollen. One of the guys is bleeding from his nose and mouth. His cheek is cut open. His eye is coated in blood.

Dominick and I both shift to our Human forms. "What the fuck happened here?" I growl viciously, glaring at both of the captives in front of us.

"We caught these two trying to shove Cora and Millie into a van with Camilla, Avery, Lexi, Haley, and Emma," Julian snarls. "Van took off. Len was holding on, but one of them pistol whipped him and almost ran him over."

"What?" Dominick barks. "Where is he?"

"He's okay," Don says. "Leg is scraped up, but he's good. Ana is patching him up." The captive he's holding jerks away. Don digs his fingers into his upper arm and shoves him so hard, his face hits the ground when he falls. There's no way he can catch himself. His hands are bound behind him. Don pulls him back up.

"Get those two down to the basement in the pack house. Cage them," I growl far more dangerously than I just had. I've never had to use the cages below the packhouse, but I installed them during our rebuild just in case I needed them. I tried to prepare for everything.

Julian and Don say nothing more. They simply drag the captives to the cages like I told them to where they will sit and rot until I decide to talk to them. Max and Prince follow, not wanting their mates out of their sight. Jamie stays by my side. My Wolf is howling in my head, begging me to find Kaia, Jordan, and the rest of the girls taken, but I can't listen. I need to figure out what happened before I can even begin to take a guess where they are, or who has them.

I force my composure to settle over me and turn towards the two girls crouched next to each other. They are both hugging each other and crying into each other's neck. Their parents are huddled protectively around them.

I kneel down next to them. "Girls," I say, letting my voice soothe them as only their Alpha can. They both look at me. "What happened? It's after curfew. Were you all still out?"

They both tremble, but it's Cora who speaks. She's the oldest of the two sisters. "We were helping pick things up. Mom and dad were with us. Prince was near. All of the sudden, a big black van came skidding to a stop. Six guys dressed all in black ran out of it." She sniffles and looks down as Millie cuddles into her. "It was chaos, Alpha. Before any of us knew what was happening, they were shoving girls in the van. Two of them tried to grab us, but Julian got to us. Jamie and Don were right behind them. They got us and the guys trying to take us. Len leapt to the van just as they were taking off and closing the door."

"They had needles," Millie whispers. "They tried to hurt us with them."

I reach out to both of them and join in the group hug. I sigh, relieved on one hand, beyond pissed on the other. "I'm glad the two of you are okay."

"We were heading in, Alpha," Millie whispers as she looks up at me. Tears are still silently streaming from her eyes. She's only twelve and looks slightly terrified as she holds onto her sixteen year old sister. "We weren't being bad."

"I know, sweet girl," I whisper. I kiss her forehead and nuzzle her. "Go inside now. Be with your family."

"Will you find the other girls?" she asks hopefully. "Emma is gone." She cries even harder. Cora hugs her harder.

"Emma is her best friend," her mom whispers.

I nod. "I'll find them, little one. I promise." I hug them all hard but comforting before I stand. I give Dominick and Jamie a look as I storm to my house. I'm doing all I can to stay level headed, but it's far from easy.

Jamie follows Dominick and I inside. "Holy fuck," he grunts, sniffing the air.

"I know." I lean over the back of a chair and squeeze the wood so hard, I'm a little surprised it doesn't shatter.

Dominick sniffs. "That's the same scent Charlene was giving off."

I nod. "Yep."

Dominick just sits on the floor and puts his head in his hands. "They have Jordan."

"Who the hell are these guys? How did they get by us?" I growl.

Jamie shrugs. "My guess? Lots of surveillance. They used Charlene. Maybe they have other people observing us."

I throw my head back and cover my face. I scream in frustration, though it probably sounds more like a roar. "How the fuck is this all happening all at once?" I bellow. I look at both Jamie and Dominick. "We need to get everyone back. Which means we need to figure out who the fuck this pack is and where the hell they reside. What do we know?"

"We know the license plate had a red mountain, and the plate was personalized." Dominick wipes his eyes. He holds his head and stands. "I can't... I..." He looks at me. He's in obvious pain. "I can't feel her. I can't connect with her, Kade."

"Feel her heartbeat, Dom," Jamie, always the calm one, says.

While he focuses on Dominick, I pace. Rage consumes me. How dare anyone think they can come onto my territory and steal my pack members? Kids, no less. Not a single one of the girls taken are over the age of eighteen besides Jordan and Kaia. It infuriates me more, because what the fuck is the point of that? Were they targeted somehow? Was Jordan a target? I already know Kaia was.

How in the hell can anyone think they can take what's mine? My pack. My sister. My fucking mate! Do these fuckers not know who the hell I am? I'm fucking powerful in and out of the Shifter world. No one fucks with me. Just like no one fucked with my father. Hell. Even my father's brother, who was dead long before I was born. He was a damn billionaire as I am. No one dared mess with him either.

Of course, he ended up being killed by Fenn for abusing Aryan and trying to kill her, but no one knew what was going on behind closed doors. Until that moment, not even my dad knew what he was doing. I say good riddance. Aryan got all of his money and gave it to my dad to use for the pack. It was a happy ending.

Up until the point where we were attacked and slaughtered. The thought that this pack is that same pack makes me roar once more in frustration. My entire body is shaking with a stormy intensity that makes me want to explode.

"Fuck!" I scream in outrage and kick the duffel bag at my feet. It skids across the floor, sending some kind of book flying. It takes me a second to realize it's Kaia's sketchbook. Several loose sketches scatter across the floor.

"Christ, Kade," Jamie says. He squeezes my shoulder.

I take a deep breath. "This isn't going to get us anywhere. I need to think." I kneel down and start picking up drawings. There are several of me and other members of the pack, but those aren't the ones that catch my eye. "What the fuck?"

Dominick kneels next to me. "These are really good drawings." He picks one up with him and Jordan. He inhales sharply. His hand shakes a little, but he clenches his fist, crinkling the drawing a little.

"Holy shit," Jamie says, seeing what I see.

I look up at him as he picks up the drawing I was looking at. "Look familiar?"

The drawing is of a male I recognize very well. Someone who is supposed to be dead. Behind him are a group of four or five people huddled together. It looks like he is both holding and defending them. Considering who I'm looking at, it doesn't surprise me at all.

"This can't be," Jamie whispers. He looks back down at the drawing and sits down on the floor. He shakes his head. "How is this possible? Who drew this?" He looks up at me again and swallows hard. His eyes are shining with tears and swimming with emotions I'm sure he has no idea how to handle.

Fuck. I don't know how to handle them. "Kaia," I tell him.

Dominick moves to Jamie's side and looks at the drawing. "No way," he whispers. Still holding the one of him and Jordan, he starts picking up other drawings. The same man is at the forefront of so many of them.

Jamie closes his eyes and pinches the bridge of his nose. "It looks like they are trapped somewhere and Loki is protecting them." He breaks into shuddering sobs at that moment. Dominick hugs him.

I continue picking up drawings one by one. Each of them has a different, much darker depiction. One of them is someone being tortured. Another is of a few women chained together in darkness, but behind them is a mountain peak. Red.

"Well, fuck." I show Jamie and Dominick as I link with Owen. *Take a look at this.* I turn the drawing back to me so he can see what I am through me.

What the hell? What am I looking at? Is that a drawing? Where did you find that? I can feel his confusion.

Kaia. Her sketchbook is here. Look at the red mountain peak. Does that match what you saw on the plate of the vehicle Charlene got into?

Exact replica.

Thank you. That's all I needed to know.

Jamie is still looking at the drawing with Loki. He traces it with his finger as he slowly draws his eyes to mine. "Does this... mean... he's alive?" he whispers hopefully. Tears that he hasn't bothered to fight are streaking down his cheeks.

"I don't know." I pick up the rest of the drawings and put them back into Kaia's sketchbook. "I don't know where these drawings came from. I mean, I don't know why she'd draw these. Like if they're visions or something. I have no idea where these came from. All I know is that it's definitely drawn with her hand. Very detailed. Right down to the tears in the women's eyes."

"These aren't all new. This one looks a little older than the one with Loki. They had to have come to her in a vision or something. Like you did. The Man in the Moon," Dominick says.

"They get darker and darker. Look at the dates." I point to the dates at the bottom corner of the page. "The ones she did a few years ago aren't as dramatic and, I don't know, doomsday-like. These newer ones are downright scary."

"I can't believe how detailed they are," Dominick says. Jamie is still clutching the one with Loki. "Look at this one." He turns one he's picked up towards me. "These two girls look like they've been cut. She drew blood."

I reach for it. "She also drew a symbol." I tilt my head. "It's small, but it's that same mountain peak." I squint and hold it a little closer. "And there's two words underneath, but I can't make it out."

"Maybe Owen can," Jamie whispers. He hugs the drawing to his chest as he stands. The tears are still flowing. Jamie doesn't bother to wipe his eyes. I want to keep all of the drawings close to me, but I'd never dream of taking that one from him.

I also know that Owen might see something in them that I don't. I gather the rest of them and put them in the sketchbook. I stand and hand them all to him. "Take them all to Owen. Maybe he sees something none of us do."

Jamie swallows hard and nods. He takes the sketchbook. "I'll find you, Loki," he mumbles with resolution.

I nod towards the door and look at Dominick. "Go with Jamie. Question those fuckers. I'm going to look in my father's journal, and see if there's anything in there that will help us."

Jamie raises his eyebrow as he stops and turns back to me. "I didn't know Alpha Connor kept a journal."

I smile a little at the memory of him writing in it. "I'm not certain many did. Kaia found it and gave it to me just a little while ago." I know fury probably crosses my features, because I'm forced to bite my tongue to keep from roaring again. My Wolf is howling in both agony, loss, and complete fury.

Dominick, refusing to part with the drawing of him with Jordan, simply nods and follows Jamie. I don't miss the same look in his eyes that is burning in my soul, though. He may feel the same loss that I do, but he also feels the same all-consuming anger that I do as well.

I'll find you, Kaia. I'll find all of you. Whoever they are won't get away with stepping into my territory and taking what's mine.

I don't know if she can hear me or not, but I pray to the Moon Goddess she gets the message and knows I'm coming for her.

Stay strong for me, Kaia. I'm coming for you.

CHAPTER FOURTEEN

~*~ KAIA ~*~

"Mmm…," I groan. I brush at my cheek, feeling a dry gritty substance against it. The feeling doesn't go away, and my mouth feels just as gross. Like I swallowed sand.

I shiver and reach for my blanket. The movement sends wave after wave of nausea over me. I feel like my veins have glass flowing through them instead of blood. I try to open my eyes, but they seem so heavy and dry. Just like the rest of me.

"Eat that. You'll feel better," a deep male voice growls right before I feel fingers tangle in my hair and tug me up.

"Ow!" I scream. My hand automatically flies to the wrist of the man tugging me to a sitting position, but my arm feels heavy and slow. I don't reach his wrist before he's slamming my back into something hard.

"Leave her alone!" a female voice screams.

"Jordan…?" I sniffle as I try to breathe through the shock of being slammed so hard into something.

"Shut up!"

I hear something that sounds like a fist connecting with bone. The woman screams, and a body crashes into me. I scramble to stay sitting up, but I fall to my side into that same sandy substance. I hear a clang. Metal against metal.

My entire body hurts, but I force one hand to move to my face. I need to open my eyes, but they burn. Like pieces of dirt are in them and caked around them. Or maybe it's the same glass that's seemingly replaced the blood in my body.

I force myself to sit up when soft hands grip my arms and start to help me, but I can't hold back the whimper. "Ow…"

"Kaia, I'm so sorry. I saw them too late. I couldn't even scream for help or react before they were injecting me with something." The pads of her thumbs gently brush something from my eyes. "Are you okay? Please say you're okay."

I lean against whatever she probs me against. Bars? I groan again. "Everything hurts," I whisper. "I feel heavy. I don't know where I am. This doesn't feel like my bed."

She sniffles and gently hugs me. "I'm so sorry."

I slowly open my eyes and blink a few times. "Why is it so dark? Am I blind?"

She shakes her head in my neck and hugs me tighter. "We're in some kind of dungeon. Like a jail cell. I don't know where. I just woke up a few minutes before you. It took me a few minutes to get acclimated. It will take you longer since you're Human."

I swallow. "A dungeon?" I try to move to hug her, but I can't follow anything she's saying or move right now. My eyes slowly begin to adjust. I can make out bars and dirt as well as a cement wall. "My brain feels foggy."

She nods. "Just take a few minutes to adjust."

She slowly lets me go and sits on her knees in front of me. "Jordan…," I whisper when I see who she is. At least she is who I thought she was. The pounding in my head makes me want to close my eyes again, but I'm afraid if I do, I'll never open them again. So, I keep them open and make myself adjust to my surroundings.

After a few minutes, the pain in my head begins to fade into a dull ache. The glass running through my veins slowly turns back to blood. Instead of feeling like I'm being pierced from the inside, the pain turns to a tingle. The heaviness begins to subside, but moving still makes me want to throw up.

There is light, but it's faint and doesn't reach inside the entire cell. Cell.

I'm in a cell. Complete with bars, a cement wall, no windows, and several other cells. As far as I can see. The ones on either side of us look empty. The ones I can see across from us also look empty, but one of the ones a couple of cells down from us seem to have a couple of people. They look small and fragile.

Kids.

"I'm not sure what happened… Where are we…?" I ask Jordan.

"I'm not sure, but I can't feel Kade or Dominick. I'm very disoriented."

"Me too," I whisper with a sniffle. We both sit next to each other for several minutes before I hear Jordan's stomach grumble. I suddenly remember the food, but it's all over the ground now. I whimper. "The food. You need it, and it's ruined now."

Jordan shakes her head. "I don't trust it. I'm not touching it."

I lean forward, shakily and pick up a bottle of milk. I inspect it to see if it's been opened or tampered with. I don't see anything, but I'm not stupid. I tip it upside down. A tiny stream of milk leaks out of a small hole that I didn't see.

I sigh and put it down. "I was hoping at least that wasn't tainted. You need nutrition. You both do."

She leans her head on my shoulder. "We need to figure out where we are. Whatever I was injected with, though, is making me really groggy. I came out of it sort of quickly, but I can barely keep my eyes open now. I think I need to sleep it off, and clear it out of my system. Then I can focus on getting us out of here."

I nod. "I feel very wired now. Opposite of you. I think I have adrenaline coursing through me. I'll stay awake. If anything happens, I'll wake you."

She yawns and blinks sleepily. "Okay." She crawls to the small cot in the corner of the cell and curls up into herself. I know whatever she was injected with must be having a terrible effect on her because I don't believe she'd be able to sleep, or want to, if it weren't.

133

I have to wonder if we were injected with the same thing. The longer I am awake, the clearer my mind becomes. I feel more and more alert. Observant. I remember more and more of the events leading up to waking up in the dirt. I was just turning around to heed Connor's advice after acting rashly and nearly leaving after hearing about the rejection. I still don't know exactly what it entails, but I do know that I won't let Kade do that to us. I don't think he wants to any more than I do.

I planned to make him talk to me, but I smelled something awful, like a forest fire. It scared me beyond belief. My heart jumped into my throat. When I saw Jordan's eyes widen, I knew there was trouble. But I hadn't quite figured out what before I was being dragged to a vehicle and pushed into it.

Right before I was thrown in, something pricked my neck. I was immediately immobilized. Not long after, everything faded. I watched Jordan get pricked with something as well. It all happened so fast, I couldn't even scream for help.

Everything after that is not even a blur. I felt like I was being pulled into a fast current I couldn't get out of. Waves crashed over me and dragged me further and further down into the deep. When I woke up, I was so disoriented.

The more I come out of it, the more scared I become because I'm starting to recognize my surroundings. Not long after I was led to Kade, I have been having dreams. Almost every night. The dreams are vivid. Each night, they are different, but only in the events that occur. The location is always the same.

I'm in my dream. I would recognize it anywhere. It's Hell in my dreams, and now I'm here. Living in it. The dirt floors. The cells. The smells. The bone-seeping cold. The darkness. It's all exactly as it is in the vivid nightmares that haunt me.

As if all of that didn't convince me, though, the glowing red mountain drawn on the wall would. How it glows, I couldn't begin to understand. Glow in the dark paint, probably. I don't want to speculate, but cold isn't all I feel here. Fear isn't either.

It's the power.

Danger.

It's nothing like what I feel with Kade's pack or on his territory. I feel peace there. A sense of safety and protection. There's something evil here. Something sinister. I felt it when I dreamt it, but the real life feeling is indescribable.

I look up and stay still when I hear commotion. The girls in the cell down from mine jump and huddle together in the corner. They are more hidden in the dark than they were. I have the overwhelming feeling that that's a good thing.

I watch as the cells start filling up one by one and observe there are two to a cell. Never more. Never less. I don't know if that's significant, but it's a small detail I intend to put in the back of my mind for safekeeping. It might come in handy later.

Everyone is shackled together. When they reach their cell, the people controlling them unshackle them and throw them quite violently into their cell. Some stumble. Some fall. Those that fall seem just as disoriented as I felt when I woke up. Those that stumble turn back towards the guards with a vicious glare, but they don't try to attack. I have to wonder why. They seem stronger than the others. Surely the several of them could overpower the few guards.

It's one more thing to remember for later. Like when Jordan is awake. With her being pregnant, I don't know if she'll be able to fight much, but I have seen her at her best during training. She's fast and strong. With her, we might have a chance of getting out of whatever this is.

Two girls are shoved into the cell next to us. They both fall. They look dirty. The clothing they are wearing looks tattered and has holes. The shoes have holes in the toes. They both look incredibly malnourished and very weak. They crawl to the small cot in the corner and curl up together.

Moments later, one man is shoved into the cell on the other side of us. I don't look at him directly. I am too afraid to make any sudden movements, but I notice that he doesn't stumble or fall. He lets out a low rumble of a growl and slowly turns around. I don't need to see him to know he's glaring at the guard viciously because as the guard locks his cell, he smirks back at him before continuing on his way. Almost like he knows he's the one with the power.

The man stands in the middle of his cell just within my peripheral vision. His clothing is torn, but looks a little newer than the two girls. His shoes, though old and worn, aren't as beat up. His jeans look worn, at least from what I can see. His black shirt hugs all of his muscles, like it's painted on. There's a tear in the sleeve and it looks old, but still in okay shape. He's the only one I can see who is alone in his cell. It strikes me immediately as odd.

I don't know who he is, but he looks like he's in better shape than all of the others. Even those who didn't fall looked slightly weak. Whoever this man is, I feel like he's the Spartacus of this entire operation. He's the one who can get us out of here.

"If you're going to sit on the floor, move back so your back is against the wall." His voice is low and growly. He doesn't move from his position in the middle of the cell or look at me. Instead, he watches as the guards put every single person back into their cell. "Never have your back to any of these motherfuckers."

I don't say anything. I just nod and crawl on my hands and knees to the back of the cell. I sit against the wall and shiver. It's cold. I pull my knees up to my chest and watch him. From what I can see, everyone here has lost some muscle tone. Even those that didn't fall into their cell look weaker and stoop when they walk.

Not him. He stands tall. Like he refuses to be beaten down or let any weakness show. He's tall. Really tall. Like Kade. His hands clench into fists at his sides while he watches the guards turn back and leave this dungeon-like place. The same one who shoved him in his cell smirks again as he walks by him, but this man shows no reaction. At least none I think the guard can see.

When the guards are out of sight, the man takes a deep breath. His shoulders slowly rise and fall. Suddenly, though, his head snaps to me. His eyes are wide. My mouth falls open in shock and I scramble to my feet.

"Kade?" I squeak.

He's at the bars so fast, I have to take a step back. His eyes are locked onto Jordan. He grips the bars hard. "Jordan?" He rattles the bars. At least as well as he can. It's not like they would move anyway. "Jordan!" he yells louder.

"Kade…" I stare at him sadly and hug myself. "This is all my fault."

He narrows his eyes at me. "What happened?" he growls.

I look at my feet and hug myself tighter. The anger radiating off him slams into me like a truck. "I was leaving after you said you had to reject me. I understood. I'm Human. I understand you were trying to protect me, but I couldn't do it. The humiliation and shame would be enough, but the hurt I already felt was excruciating, Kade. I -"

He holds up a hand. "Stop. Just stop. Why are you calling me by my dead brother's name? Why the fuck is the sister I thought died with my parents and brother fourteen years ago unconscious in a cell with you? And who the hell are you?"

My eyes widen more and more with each of his words until I'm standing in front of him dumbfounded. I shake my head, trying to speak, but the words won't form. My head is suddenly swimming.

"Are you… saying Kade is alive?" someone across the corridor asks. I look at him but still can't talk.

"That's not possible, Loki," the man who I thought was Kade growls. "Start… talking… Now!"

His voice makes me jump. My eyes snap to his. He looks exactly like Kade. The same hair. Same strong jawline and cheekbones. The same eyes. He's the same height. The only differences I can see are that he's more muscular, though not by much. He's more intimidating than Kade. And he has a scar on his neck that looks a little like tooth marks.

"I…" I close my eyes and force myself to breathe. I have to stay strong. Kade may not have wanted me to be a part of this world, but I am now. And I have to stay strong. I open them and meet his eyes. "It's a very long story," I say quietly.

"Well, I have all fucking night," he growls even more dangerously as he grips the bars, I wonder if he could break them. He never takes his piercing glare off me.

I nod slowly and make my way back to the wall. "Okay." I sniffle. The man continues to stand. "A little while ago, I guess a month or so ago, I graduated from high school and was on my way to an all-night grad party. I had heard there was a possibility the chaperones were going to make it sort of a birthday celebration for me. I was just turning eighteen. I was getting ready when I heard commotion coming from downstairs in my house. Screaming. Shuffling." I close my eyes. "I saw some people that were wearing police uniforms attacking my parents. They were killed."

"Police killed your parents? Why?"

I shrug and sniffle. I wipe my eyes at the memory. "I wish I knew. But I don't. I hid. I don't know why or how I wasn't found. One of the men was in my room looking for me. I was under a lot of clothing and things in my closet. He kicked at the pile. His foot connected with me a couple of times, but I refused to move or say or do anything. I stayed as still as possible. He left, but I stayed under the pile for hours. Until, finally, I dared to move. I didn't know what to do. I put my sketchbook in my backpack after I decided I needed to leave in case they came back. I didn't know where to go or who could help me. When I found a Sheriff's badge on the floor in my room, I knew I couldn't go to the police. I had decided I was going to pack things and hopefully get help from another town. But that didn't work out so well. They came back while I was packing."

"What does this have to do with my brother and sister?"

I look up at him, trying to figure out how much to tell him before deciding to tell him everything. If he's Kade's and Jordan's brother, then he's probably a Shifter. Which means he'd know all about Spirit Guides and won't think I'm insane.

"Ever since I was a child, I've seen what I came to call the Moon Wolf. She was like a guardian angel. A guide. When I got a little older, I started seeing a man. I called him the Man in the Moon. He never spoke to me. I couldn't really make out most of his features. I knew his eyes. I knew the outline of him. But I never knew what he looked like. At least not fully. Just specific aspects of him. That night, the Moon Wolf came to me. It wasn't unusual. I'd spoken to her several times. She has always been around to give advice. That night, it was a warning. A warning to get out because they were coming back."

He watches me for a few moments while I wait for him to understand where I'm going with this. Finally, he sits with his back to the wall next to me with the bars between us. "Okay."

I play with my fingers and focus on my nails. "She got me out. She held the door somehow until I was able to sneak out my window. All I had was my backpack. I didn't know where I was going, but I trusted her. I ran across the roof and got down to the ground. But the man, who was in uniform, started shooting at me. She told me to run to the woods. She led me. I followed. Bullets were flying past me. Some should have hit but didn't. I turned around and saw someone I'd never seen before." I chance a glance at him. "Someone who looks like an older version of you."

He inhales sharply and looks down at his own hands. "You're talking about my mother and father."

I nod and look back at my nails. "Belle and Connor. I didn't know their names then. But they not only led me to the woods, they saved my life. Connor shielded me from the bullets. Something he got in trouble for. Both of them actually. I thought they abandoned me, but Connor told me just before I was taken that he broke the rules and the Moon Goddess punished him."

He chuckles. "My father and mother have never been ones who followed rules."

I smile softly. "They saved me, but the men caught up to me and beat the hell out of me. They left me for dead. When I came to, I was in a strange bed in a strange room surrounded by the scent of pine and something so spicy and stupidly intoxicating that it comforted me instantly. I met Kade. I found out I was his mate, and that he didn't want anything to do with me. I studied a few things about Shifters and packs. I learned a lot. But he put a stop to that. I asked over and over why I stayed, but then I realized two things. One, he said he'd help me figure out who killed my parents and protect me from them until it was dealt with. And two. I had no idea where I was. Just somewhere up Blood Mountain in what he called the Deimos territory."

"So, you're Kade's mate. I had a dream once where he found his mate. She was Human. He said immediately he needed to reject her. I told him he was an idiot." He chuckles. "Sometimes, I think I hear him and Jordan, but I shake it off. I see my father and mother, too. They give me strength to keep fighting, but I figured they wouldn't let me go on believing my brother and sister were dead if they weren't."

"I don't think they are allowed to. It would be interference. They don't want to lose the ability to see you anyway they can. And as for Kade..." I shake my head and look at Jordan. "You don't need to worry about him having a Human mate."

"I'm not worried. I don't see a problem with it."

It's my turn to chuckle as I look down at my feet. "Well, he doesn't agree. After his father and sister-in-law died, he imposed a new rule. No Humans. Including Human mates. He thinks Humans are weak and can't protect themselves or something. He feels like he needs to protect them as Alpha." I shrug again slowly. "At least that's what he told me right after I found out he planned on rejecting me as his mate. I don't know what that entails, but it was his plan."

He sighs heavily. "I guess I can see his reasoning, but it's flawed. Very flawed. Humans weren't the only ones to die that day. Wolves and Shifters died right alongside them."

"That was Jordan's argument." I let my head fall back against the wall. "It doesn't matter now. I was leaving but decided I was going to fight for whatever we had. Even if it was only a small spark. But I was injected with something. Now, I'm here. Jordan is here. And it's all my fault." The silence around me is deafening. I close my eyes. "So, who are you? You look exactly like Kade. I assume you're his twin brother. Zeke."

"Yes. I'm his twin brother. He's older by a couple of minutes, but I'm the more level-headed one. Kade has always made rash decisions based on emotion. But he was the natural born leader in every sense of the word. The protector. He was Captain of the football team and the one we all looked to for just about everything."

"I can see that," I say softly. "So, I remember reading something in the family history. I didn't think of it until now. I guess the shock of seeing you got me. It says you were killed in a big battle like your parents and brother and sister. But here you are."

"I am."

"I'm Kaia. Kade's rejected mate." I chuckle to myself at my own joke.

"You haven't been rejected yet."

I roll my head to the side and look at him. "How do you know that?"

"Because you're still standing. If he'd rejected you, you wouldn't feel like you can breathe. Your heart would feel like it's completely missing from your chest. You'd feel lost. Alone. Even in the middle of a crowded room, you'd feel broken. And that's only if he didn't mark you. If he did, you wouldn't be able to survive without him. You may think you would, but you'd be so weak, you wouldn't want to live. If the loneliness itself didn't kill you, you would kill yourself. Because anything is better than the pain you'd feel without him."

I nod and close my eyes again. "I had a feeling you'd say that."

I hug myself as I shiver. My eyes start to get heavy again. The exhaustion I feel that I was trying to fight overcomes me. I don't want to fall asleep, but I feel like I need to conserve my energy if I want to get out of this. Maybe whatever I was shot with is having a bigger effect than I thought it was.

Stay strong for me, Kaia. I'm coming for you.

A soft smile turns up the corner of my mouth. Thinking of Kade warms me from the inside. Even if it is just the thought of his voice promising me he's coming for me. I'm not sure how that's possible, but I'll allow my brain to think whatever it wants as long as it keeps me calm.

The shivering starts to subside. I slowly drift off, unable to fight it any longer.

CHAPTER FIFTEEN

~*~ KADE ~*~

There's nothing better than finding the one you belong with. The feeling is indescribable. It's almost like falling into a giant vat of your favorite treat. Only better. I can't wait until my kids feel it. I have a feeling I know who Jordan's is. She's spent a lot of time with Dominick most of her life. You'd think Dom would hate having a little girl around, but that doesn't seem to be the case with him. He invites her to go places and seems to want to spend just as much time with her.

I couldn't be happier. My kids finding their mates has been something I've wanted to see ever since they were young. I don't know who Kade's is. I'm sure he'll find him or her soon. Zeke recently found his. A kid named Maverick, who recently came to me and discussed his options. He didn't get into much detail, but he said he doesn't like the pack he's a part of. I sense there is more to the story and him. I believe he'll tell me when he joins our pack completely, which is what he wants to do. I respect him for coming to me to discuss this matter. It shows what a respectable individual he is. Zeke's mate is a good one.

"Oh dad." I turn the page of my dad's journal and wipe a stray tear from my eye.

I've been scouring his journal for any kind of hint leading me to Jordan, Kaia, and the rest of the girls taken from my pack. It freaks me out that I can't feel any of them. Just a few brief moments. It lets me know they're alive.

The Devil's Peak Pack is starting to piss me off. We eradicated them long ago. They really shouldn't have resurfaced. I've been keeping a close eye on them, though. I don't like how they're growing. They're alliance with us feels fake and forced. They came to us not long after we killed their Alpha and a few others who tried to attack us many, many years ago. Belle feels it, too. She, to this very day, hates that her brother turned into what he did, but she doesn't regret that he was killed in the name of protecting us and this pack.

He's mentioned this Devil's Peak Pack several times. Apparently, they came after him just as he was starting his pack and beginning to grow. They didn't like the challenge he presented to them. How much power they saw in him. I didn't know any of this growing up. I had no idea that my mother and her parents were kicked out of the Devil's Peak Pack because they weren't Shifters, but her brother was allowed to stay because he was.

I didn't know two Wolves could create a Shifter. I was never told otherwise, but I always thought I was smart. The process of deduction would say that's not possible. When the Moon Goddess is involved, though, anything is possible. Including two males being given the gift of a child. According to my father, that is something else that happened many years ago. It's rare, but Gunner and Lucian, who were both male Wolves, were gifted with a child.

Thinking back, though, that child was a Shifter. I was never told the child was theirs. I think I thought he belonged to someone else and just enjoyed hanging out with the two Wolves. Or that they adopted him or something. I'm not sure it was ever meant to be a secret. It was just something I never thought about. It wasn't part of my world, so I didn't give a shit.

Growing up, I'd always been kind of a dick. I didn't care about much except football and my family. I was just starting to show an interest in everything expected of me as an Alpha when the attack occurred. Gunner and Lucian were killed right along with their Shifter son, and I still didn't think about it. I was too busy wallowing in sorrow and making stupid as fuck rules out of my own guilt or something.

I don't know how many times I was told it wasn't only Humans who were killed that day. But Humans being killed were what I fixated on. It's not that I didn't know Wolves and Shifters were also killed. But Fenn and my mother, in my mind, were just as strong as Shifters. It was a flawed way of thinking, but it helped me cope. Justify my reasoning.

Reasoning that has not only taken a dramatic turn, but has also made me realize just what a terrible fucking Alpha I really am. Telling people to leave the sanctity of this territory to live relatively normal lives with their Human mates was so, so stupid. And selfish. Looking back, I think the only reason I made the decision was because seeing Human mates around Shifters and Wolves reminded me of my family. The family I am never getting back.

I growl in frustration and flip to the last page of the journal. There's a mountain peak colored red. The same as the one Kaia drew. I've stared at it so many times. It has to be a symbol that the Devil's Peak Pack uses, but I'm struggling because this is something I've never been told. My father never mentioned this pack.

Reading about it and all of the destruction they've caused us over the years pisses me off, but what makes me even more angry is that my father didn't tell me about them. He didn't warn me. Maybe if I knew, I could have found them earlier. Maybe I could have stopped them.

Kade. Stop it.

I look up when my father appears. *Dad.* I fight tears. *Why? Why didn't I know this stuff? Why did I have to learn it now? Through a fucking journal?*

I didn't tell you about them because you weren't ready. You were just starting to accept your role as the future Alpha. Everything up until that point I had tried to teach you went in one ear and out the other. That's the entire reason Alpha's don't go through the Alpha ceremony to become an Alpha until they are twenty-one, unless there are extenuating circumstances.

I run my fingers through my hair and stand. My dad sits on the edge of my desk and watches me. *Why didn't you tell me after?*

Because we have rules we have to follow, Kade. I can't tell you everything. I can guide you to finding the answers yourself, but I can't tell you. Just like I couldn't tell you who your mate was and when you'd find her all those times you asked me. And just like I nearly lost my powers as a Spirit Guide by protecting Kaia from being killed when I shielded her as I did. That would be the worst pain I could ever experience, son. Not being able to be here like this. Not being able to be your Spirit Guide.

I look at him as I soften. *Sometimes, I wish I could feel you hug me again. Or feel mom laying on me to comfort me.*

He shrugs. *You still can.* He looks up at the ceiling with a soft smile.

Moments later my mom appears next to me. *It's just a little different now, Kade. Now you have to work a little harder to feel it.* Mom sits next to me and leans into me.

I close my eyes as I kneel next to her. It takes me some time, but I do start to feel her weight. I feel her soft fur against my cheek as she nuzzles me. But it's when I feel my father's arms encircle us both that I gasp. Slowly, so very slowly, the tension vibrating through my entire body begins to uncoil. Just like when I was a kid, their love cuts through the bullshit and helps me think more clearly.

Until today, the brief touches I felt were enough. My dad patting my shoulder. Mom nudging me with her snout or head. Today, though. Today... I needed this. I needed to feel all of this to give me the strength I need to continue.

I startle when my office phone rings and open my eyes. I can still feel them both, though, and that gives me some comfort. I stand and walk towards my desk. I put the phone on speaker as I sit. Both of my parents stand in front of my desk.

"What's up, Chief?" I ask when I see the caller ID.

"I'll be honest, Kade, I don't know. What I just stumbled on is... It's above my paygrade. I'm too old for this. I'm about to call in the Feds."

I raise an eyebrow. "What happened?"

"We've had a rash of missing girls for the past few years. We obviously don't like those kinds of calls, but having one or two during the year... Well, I hate to say it, but we can deal with that. Over the past month, we've had over a hundred girls from just this area and surrounding areas go missing. Kids, Kade. Kids. Ages fourteen to eighteen. Mostly girls. A few males. There's no trace of them. It's like they just vanish into thin air. But that's not the worst thing."

I shift in my chair, suddenly very uncomfortable. "It doesn't get much worse."

"That's what I thought. But it does. How much of the news have you seen?"

I cross my arms over my chest and lean back in my chair just as Dominick comes into my office. He says nothing. Just sits down. My parents haven't moved. "You know I don't watch it all that much. I haven't had time lately with everything going on anyway."

"Well, Kaia fits the type of girl they've been going after. She's in the age group. One thing that bothers me now that didn't then is that they didn't take her. They tried to kill her after killing her parents. I've been investigating from the standpoint that her parents saw something they shouldn't have, and the deputies there that night were trying to cover it up. When you got me that badge, I identified one of them based on it. He's dead. Died in a car accident. But his daughter? She's gone missing."

I hold up a hand. "Wait, wait. You're telling me this guy was there and partook in the murder of Kaia's parents. Then he was killed and his daughter was taken. Is that what you're getting at, Jeremy?"

"Yep. This has the kind of bullshit my father constantly turned a blind eye to. The kind of shit that I always went to your father about. I don't know how the fuck he solved the mystery, but he did. Since I took over as Chief, I haven't had anything like this happen. Not until now. I've been going over the cases. I see a lot of similarities that we hadn't seen previously." I can hear papers shuffling on the other end.

"Let me guess," Dominick cuts in. He leans forward and rests his elbows on his knees. "You've noticed a pattern. This happens every four years. Except not just here. Around the entire world. And you've noticed that the parents they are taken from are either killed right away, or killed after they report their kid is missing."

Jeremy is silent for a few moments. "How did you know that?" he finally asks.

"Because last night we had several of our girls taken. One of them was Kaia. Another was Jordan," I answer for Dominick.

"Oh, shit," Jeremy says. "Kade, you need to get them back. This is a very dangerous situation. I have more information. Many of them are never seen or heard from again. But some have been killed."

I think it's time you let Jeremy in on our little secret, my father says.

I nod. Things are starting to make sense. "How long has this been happening? How far back did you track it?"

"Since just after your father died."

I can't help but chuckle. "Do you think that's a coincidence?"

"I do not. I just don't know why."

"Ever seen Twilight?"

Jeremy laughs. "The sparkling Vampire who falls for a morosely bland excuse for a human? No. Never saw it."

Dominick cracks up. I smile and shake my head. "Why don't you come to the house? We need to talk. But don't leave your office. I'm sending some people to you."

"Why?"

"Because I didn't get to where I am in this world by trusting people. I trust you. I don't trust the rest of the world. Things are dangerous. You know too much."

Jeremy is quiet for a long time before I hear him take a breath. "Why am I not surprised you'd say that?"

"Watch your back, Chief. I'll send some people for your wife and daughter, too." I don't give him a chance to argue and hang up, but I know I'm right when I say he's in danger.

Dominick leans back in his chair. "What are you thinking?"

"I learned a lot from my father's journal. Tell me what you found out first."

"The mountain peak. It signifies a pack called Devil's Peak. I think this is the ghost pack that we've been hearing about. The pack that's been growing, but that no one seems to be able to find."

I nod. "One thing mentioned in my father's journal. He was watching them. Keeping up with them." I pause a moment and lean forward. I rest my arms on my desk. "Ever since he killed Devil's Peak's Alpha. Who, coincidentally, was my mother's brother."

Dominick folds his arms over his chest and furrows his brows. "When did that happen?"

"We were too young to remember. It was just after my mother and father found each other. I don't even think Jordan was born yet. He says in his journal that they needed to keep an eye on them. And he did. Right up until the end. He knew they were growing, but didn't know they were planning an attack. It's the reason he started making everyone train so hard, though."

I quickly use the link to send a few of my guys to Jeremy and his family.

"So, what do we do, Alpha?" Dominick asks.

"Well, we see what the Chief has. Then we go from there. I don't like waiting, but I suspect he has answers to the blanks I have. What else did our captives tell you?"

"A lot of shit. They didn't give us a location, but they confirmed the name. They said Devil's Peak is coming for us. That they're almost to the point where they can take us out for good. They did say one thing that didn't make sense to me, but it does now, knowing what your father said. They kept saying they'll take care of us this time. Like they've gone against us before. But I didn't remember them. I still don't. All I remember from that day is the chaos, the blood, the fight, and getting to Jordan. Saving as many as I could."

"I was always pissed at my father for blocking me that day." I look up at him with a soft smile. "It took me years to realize why he did it."

He smiles. *To protect you as both my son and the next Alpha of this pack. I knew you could make it grow. It wasn't how I wanted it to be, but you took it in stride. Now it's time to bring them home.*

I chuckle and look back at Dominick. The soft smile on his face tells me he may not see them, but he knows they're there. "I know they're watching over us. Jordan tells me all the time, but I still miss them."

Oh, honey. We miss you, too, mom says. *We wish we were his Spirit Guides, but his parents have taken that role.*

"They miss you, too," I say softly. "And are happy your parents are your Spirit Guides."

Dominick smiles as he nods. He looks at where my parents are for a moment before taking a steadying breath. "Back to the problem at hand. He said they took the girls because one of them is supposed to be the most powerful Luna. They don't know who. They keep the girls until they are eighteen. When they are supposed to get their Wolf. If they don't get them or sooner, as some of us do, they are auctioned off in some underground slavery ring or some shit. If they do get their Wolf, they are kept there as slaves to the Devil's Peak Pack."

I shake my head. "What the fuck purpose is there to that? If they get their Wolf, they still need to find their mate. If they aren't mated to an Alpha, they'll never become a Luna."

He shrugs. "I don't know. I think they are hoping to mate the girl to the Alpha. I guess it's said that when it happens, the Luna and Alpha will be unstoppable. Like control the whole fucking world or something."

"Not if the Luna isn't mated to the right Alpha. She'll never get her full powers, whatever they are, unless she's mated to the right Alpha. Just like that Alpha will never reach his full potential until he's mated with his Luna. And that's not the full legacy anyway. I remember my mother telling me something about it. She used to make up a whole fucking story around it and tell it to us at bedtime. That was the story Jordan loved to act out."

Mom and dad both nod at me proudly and smile as they begin to fade. It means I'm on the right track. I stand and stride out of my office. I grab the key I have hanging on my wall and walk to the library.

Dominick follows. "You onto something?"

"I don't know. But something about that legend. It struck a chord with me." I unlock the door when I reach it and immediately start searching for the book I want. "What else did they say?"

"Nothing. They stopped talking after that. I think they may have been told by their Alpha to shut the fuck up or something because nothing we did got them to say another word. They are both locked in their cells awaiting your orders. Jamie wants to kill them. I'd love to let them starve to death. A nice slow and painful death."

I browse the vast array of books and nod. "I don't want them near my pack. If we can't get any more information from them, let Jamie do what he wants. We have enough to go on. I doubt we'll get a location out of them if an Alpha's order was just handed down." I pick up a book. "Here." I flip it open, looking for what I want.

Dominick stands next to me and looks at what I'm reading. "Fables and Legends."

"All fables are born from legends," I say. "Fables all hold an inkling of truth to them. It's something Aryan always said to us. They had to come from somewhere." I find the page. "Here. The fable is that a powerful Luna will rise into power after mating with someone the Moon Goddess deems the most powerful Alpha in our world."

"So, what the fuck is happening? Is the Alpha of Devil's Peak marking all these women when they get their Wolf? And if he doesn't get this huge power surge…" He shrugs. "What then?"

"First off, I think he's deemed himself some kind of fucking God or something who is in the favor of the Moon Goddess. Maybe he thinks by doing this he is gaining her favor more and more. But I don't think that's all. I think he's using them to build his pack back up. I think he thinks if he can grow bigger than us, he'll be able to defeat us. Which is what the goal is. My father took down their Alpha. So, they want the ultimate revenge. He thinks he can do what the previous Alpha couldn't. Take down our pack. Take me down."

"With our allies? Hardly." Dominick smirks.

I chuckle. "Second. I don't think he realizes what the actual legend is. I can't remember all of it. I thought it was in this book, but I can't find it. It looks like a few pages are missing. This was Jordan's favorite book, though. When we get her back, I'll ask her. Learning the full legend might help us figure out their full game."

"This is so fucked up, Kade. How did we not know what was going on before?"

I shake my head and put the book down. "I don't know. But there are a couple of things we need to do. Firstly, call in our allies. I'm sure we aren't the only pack who have had girls taken. The way the Chief was talking, this is a worldwide thing. We have allies everywhere. We need them here. That pack is somewhere in Tennessee if we can go by the plate we have seen. Then we need to talk to the Chief. Jeremy needs to tell us everything he knows. In the meantime, we need to stay alert. I assume those that were taken are probably drugged or knocked out. I feel Jordan for a couple of minutes before she's gone again. All she said when I got through to her was dungeon."

"I heard that, too, when I got to her. I'll call in our allies. I've called a few already. They were on standby, but I'll let them know the time has come. We need them."

I nod as Dominick takes out his phone and leaves the library. I let out a breath and lock my fingers behind my head as I stand in the middle of the library. I close my eyes and prepare to fix the hardest decision I ever had to make. This will be one of the easiest things I've ever done since becoming Alpha.

I focus on each of the pack members currently not in our territory. The ones with Human mates. *It's time to come home.* I say. *I made a mistake, and I'm sorry. I'll spend the rest of my life making up for it. I never should have made any of you leave our territory. I shouldn't have isolated you. I did it because I believed I was protecting you and your families, but I was wrong.* I take a deep breath and sit in a chair. I lean forward as I continue. *There is something you should be aware of before you do. There's a danger coming. Something unlike anything we've ever experienced. And I mean that in every sense of the world. Some of you may remember the Devil's Peak Pack.*

They were the pack that attacked when you were just a cub. Alpha Connor and Luna Belle dispatched of their Alpha many years ago, Devon, one of the oldest pack members says.

Yes. We have since found out they were the pack behind our pack's massacre fourteen years ago. There were grumblings, but we had no definitive proof. We knew they lost a lot of their pack just as we did ours, but we had no real idea of who it was that came after us. We do now. And we aren't the only ones they've come after. We've found out that they've been taking kids.

My granddaughter, Devon says. *She was taken three days ago.*

Then we know the kids being taken are Shifters and Humans alike. Which proves my theory. Last night, they took Jordan and several of the girls here. Right from our territory. I also have my suspicions that they were behind the car accident that killed Aisha and Evan. I now believe they may have taken Leia. I take a shaky breath. *And here comes the hard part. I made you all leave because you all have a Human mate. I never broke the bond with you and kicked you completely out because that's just not who I am. But I truly believed you not being here would be the safest option. A month ago, I met my mate. It's a long story on how. Something I will explain to you all when you're home. Until last night, I had planned to reject her because she's Human. I planned to reject her for the same reason I made you all leave. I wanted to protect her. She was taken last night, too. Right before it happened, I decided that I was wrong. I was wrong to do what I did to all of you. And I was wrong to think she or any of you would be safer out there. I was just going to tell her when she was taken.*

Shit, Kade, Jayden, another of my pack says.

151

The point is, I fucked up. It took her to make me realize just what a fucking asshole I was. It was a stupid move. I can feel the disappointment from every single member of our pack who are no longer with us. Fuck. I can feel it from everyone still with us. My job as Alpha is to make sure my pack is taken care of. I failed you all. I'll understand if you don't want to come back here. But here is where you belong. I'm sorry it took me this long to realize it. I realize how me suddenly coming to this conclusion after I, myself, end up with a Human mate makes me look, but it's time for me to make it right.

I wait a few moments before I hear a female voice. *I think I speak for us all when I say that we're coming home, Kade,* Kenzie says. A chorus of yeses follows her declaration, and a huge weight feels like it's been lifted off my shoulders. *We understood your decision when you told us. We didn't hold it against you. None of us felt like we were truly kicked out of the pack. We knew if we ever needed you or anyone, you'd be there for us. Even the ones who did truly break the bond.*

I didn't think my granddaughter's kidnapping had anything to do with another pack, but I was about to contact you. There's been a lot of kids taken from this area. The police seem overwhelmed, Devon says.

I nod. *I'm aware. I have the Chief and his family coming here now. He knows way too much. I want you all home. We need to be together. I was wrong to think you'd be safer away from us. I'll send some people for those who chose to truly break from us. I hope they'll come home, too.*

We're coming, Kade, Kenzie says. *We all are.*

I nod again, satisfied that we'll be unified once more. I link with a few other pack members to bring the others home. Those that can no longer hear me through the link. The thought brings a slight amount of peace to the chaos we find ourselves in. Now that my pack is coming home, I can focus on the other most important thing right now.

Finding my sister and family that Devil's Peak thinks they can steal from me, and righting the wrong I caused with Kaia. Hopefully, she'll forgive me after this and stay because after I finally admitted to myself that she is the other part of me, losing her is something I won't come back from.

I rub my temples and lean back in the chair I nearly collapsed into. *I don't know if you can hear me, Kaia, but I'm sorry. I'm sorry for everything I've put you through this month. When I get you back, and I mean when, not if... When I get you back, I'll make it up to you. All of it. I'll tell you everything you want to know. All of the questions you have, I'll answer them. I'm sorry I pushed you so fucking far away and made you feel unworthy. No more, baby. Stay strong. I will find you. And those that took you will regret it. I'll destroy them, Kaia. I promise.*

I hear the front door open and Dominick's voice saying to come in. I stand and head to my living room to greet Jeremy and his family. I hope he has some information that will lead me to Devil's Peak. If he doesn't, I'm liable to burn the entire fucking world to the ground in my quest to end this.

CHAPTER SIXTEEN

~*~ KAIA ~*~

I don't know if you can hear me, Kaia, but I'm sorry. I'm sorry for everything I've put you through this month. When I get you back, and I mean when, not if... When I get you back, I'll make it up to you. All of it. I'll tell you everything you want to know. All of the questions you have, I'll answer them. I'm sorry I pushed you so fucking far away and made you feel unworthy. No more, baby. Stay strong. I will find you. And those that took you will regret it. I'll destroy them, Kaia. I promise.

My body jerks awake, and I look around the cell I'm in. I pant as if I just ran a marathon. "Kade?" I whisper. I rub my throat and wipe my eyes when I feel they're wet. I try to rub out the lump forming in my throat. It's so dry. Scratchy. I shake my head. "I heard him. In my dreams, but I heard him. I know it's not real, but I heard him." My words are barely above a whisper. "I need water." I reach for the water I see on a tray near me, but a hand stops me.

"No, Kaia," Zeke says to me. "I haven't gotten the okay yet. We don't know if it's safe."

"What do you mean?" I ask. "How would you know? How can you tell?"

"I have someone on the inside who knows and tells me if it's safe to eat or drink. If it's not, he brings food or water that isn't tainted."

I think of the needle mark in the milk I had planned to give Jordan earlier. I don't know why, but my already high frustration level shoots like a missile into the stratosphere. I want to scream, so I do. Only it comes out like a scratchy whisper. It only manages to make me more angry. I throw an all-out tantrum, complete with pounding my fists into dirt beneath me and kicking my feet as I scream as loudly as I can.

When I'm done, I collapse against the wall behind me and the bars next to me and cry. "I want to go home," I choke out. "I want my parents back! I want my bed. My clothes. I hate it here! I want to wake up from this stupid nightmare!" My voice is still barely audible, just like my screams, but I don't care.

"That's good, Kaia. Let it out. Get pissed. You have every right to," Zeke says as he reaches through the bars and rubs my thigh soothingly. "Get it all out."

"It's not fair! What is going on? Why is this happening?" I croak.

He squeezes my thigh. "I'll tell you, but you need to stay strong and calm -"

"Mmm…," Jordan moans as she stretches. "Ow… Fuck…" She sits up slowly.

"Jordan?" I crawl to her side. "Are you okay?"

"I'm okay. That sedative or whatever it was is wearing off, but I feel like pins and needles are sticking all over my body."

"The serum has a worse effect on Shifters than it does Humans," Zeke says. Jordan's head snaps towards where his voice comes from. I smile softly when he smiles. "Hey, kiddo. You miss me?"

Jordan blinks. "I… want to… say Kade, but you… don't smell like him."

"That's because I'm not." Zeke stands slowly and grips the bars.

"Z-Zeke?" Jordan blinks at him several times. "It's…" She shakes her head. "It's not possible! You… you're… we thought…"

"You thought I was dead?"

She nods as she stares at him. I stand slowly. A little weakly and sit on the bed next to her. She watches him for several moments. Zeke doesn't move. He just watches her the same as she is him.

After a long while, I hear a strangled sob as Jordan launches herself at him. "I thought you were dead!"

He hugs her the best he can through the bars and kisses her head as she cries. "For a long time, I wish I had been. It would have been less cruel."

I watch quietly as Zeke and Jordan hug each other. Jordan's cries eventually subside. I can't hear the whispers Zeke speaks in her ear, but they must have a calming effect on her because, eventually, she's pulling away and wiping her eyes as she looks up at him. I move further back on the bed and pull my knees up to my chest.

I'm glad they've been reunited. I'm happy he's still alive, but it's all bittersweet. We're stuck here. I see no way of getting out. Maybe his words were on the right track. Maybe it would be better to die.

It's not like it would matter to me anyway. I have no one and nothing to go back to. Jordan has Dominick and the pack. She has the baby growing inside her. She has Zeke. Zeke has his entire family and pack who will be happy to see him. I have no one. I'm just the rejected mate of an Alpha in a world of Shifters that I know very little about. My parents are gone. My entire family is gone. I don't even have friends to turn to. I never had time for any after Leia was taken from me. I didn't want to lose them, too.

"How are you here?" Jordan asks quietly. "What is this place?"

"This is Devil's Peak territory," Zeke answers. "I've been here since they attacked us. Those they didn't kill, they took as slaves."

Jordan shakes her head. "But we couldn't feel you. No one could. Not even Kade, and he's your twin. He couldn't tell if you were alive or dead."

"Part of that is because of me," a low, deep voice rumbles. I look up at a guy just as tall as Zeke. He's not quite as muscular. His hair is lighter than Zeke's. His eyes, though. Those are a piercing green. So vivid, I can see them clearly from where I am sitting.

Jordan and I watch as he unlocks Zeke's cell. He casually steps inside, like this is something he does every day. Jordan takes a couple of steps back and looks at him warily. I just watch in confusion, already on the verge of giving up completely.

I don't know what I'm about to see happen. Maybe him beating the hell out of Zeke. Maybe him coming to our cell and doing unthinkable or unimaginable things to me and Jordan. What I'm not expecting to see is no one else reacting to him in any of the other cells. They are all looking to him for guidance or something for some reason.

The man kisses Zeke long and passionately. Zeke tangles his fingers in the man's hair and lets out a quiet moan. I blink a few times in shock. Jordan backs up a few more steps and drops to sit next to me, not taking her eyes off them.

The man pulls away slowly, but keeps an arm around Zeke's waist. He turns to us. "I don't mean to interrupt. Zeke called for me. He thought I could help explain things to his sister and his twin brother's mate."

Jordan and I look at each other, baffled. It's Jordan, though, who finds her voice. "What?"

"Jordan. Kaia. This is Maverick. My mate."

Jordan's eyes widen. "Oh, my gosh! I remember just before… it all happened, you brought him home."

Maverick nods. "I never got the chance to tell your father everything. I didn't want to risk it. I planned to leave my pack and join yours. When the official break happened, I was going to tell Connor what Devil's Peak was planning. I went home that day, and pretty much no one was there. But I heard Zeke calling for me. He was in serious trouble. I felt as much as I could hear him. I tried to help, but I couldn't get there in time. I was lucky to be able to save Zeke and those I did. I didn't know that the Alpha was intending to take him and the others as prisoners, though. He thought killing the Alpha Connor and taking his son as slaves was the perfect form of irony. Destroy the Deimos Pack and make the next in line Alpha his bitch. But Kade wasn't with the others, so he thought he'd been killed with everyone else."

"I was being drugged after we were taken. We all were. For the first few months, I don't remember anything. I didn't even remember who Mav was. Then things started to become slightly clearer. I started to remember bits and pieces of things. I remembered Mav. It was during that time that we sealed our mate bond, but just after, things got hazy again. They were upping the drugs because they were starting to have little effect on us. We were fighting it off quicker. Mav had no idea it was happening. Not for years."

"Not that I didn't try to find out, but I grew up thinking I was nothing more than the bastard son of the Alpha's mistress. It wasn't until just recently I found out the truth."

"And what's the truth?" I ask quietly, enraptured by the story they're telling us.

"The truth," Zeke chuckles. "The truth is his father was the Alpha of this pack. The one who took over after dad killed mom's brother, the previous Alpha of Devil's Peak. Not long after he took over, less than a year, he was killed. Maverick's mother was killed with him. It was very mysterious circumstances, but Maverick grew up believing he was just a bastard son of the Alpha's mistress. We found out, though, that the reason his father was killed was because he didn't like the way the pack was being run. He wanted to do it differently. He wanted to form an alliance with us."

I stand and pace. "I don't really know much, but from what I have read, I thought that the Alpha had to be blood related. So, wouldn't that make you the true Alpha? I mean if your father was killed?" I stop in front of the bars and lean tiredly against them.

Maverick smiles. "You're correct. But I'm not supposed to know I'm the true Alpha of this pack. As far as anyone here knows, I'm just the bastard son of this Alpha's mistress."

"How did you find out the truth?" Jordan asks. She rubs her head. "Ow. I still can't reach Dom. What if something happened to him?" She looks up at Zeke with tears in her eyes.

Zeke shakes his head. "Don't. Don't try using the mind link right now. The poison needs to wear off. The more you try to use your powers, any of them, the more it will make you sick." He looks at me. "You, on the other hand."

My eyes widen. "Me? I don't have any powers."

"You said Kade is alive," Zeke says. "You have a connection to him. Even if you haven't been marked with the bite of your mate."

I shake my head. "I'm not like you," I hiss. I rub my throat. "I really need water."

"Don't drink what they gave you. Or eat anything on that tray," Maverick says. "Your tray has been drugged."

I slump. "I'm about to say I don't care."

"Well, I do," Zeke says. "Mav will get you something as soon as the guard shift changes. Why do you say you're not like me?"

I just blink at him. "I'm not a Shifter," I say quietly.

"I know. You told me," Zeke says.

"We all can sense that anyway," Maverick says.

"I thought you may have forgotten because Humans do not have powers."

"Wait," Jordan says. "You never explained why we couldn't sense you. I mean, even if I couldn't, Kade should have been able to. He's not only your twin. He's the Alpha."

"Because of Maverick. Kade wouldn't have been able to sense me because of the drugs, but after we sealed our bond, I became part of his pack. Not only did I think Kade and you were dead, because that's what I was told over and over and over again, but my allegiance and Alpha became him. Even though we didn't know at the time he was the true Alpha. Not only that, the drug that is being given to us all by the Alpha of Devil's Peak is blocking us to this day. Up until you two were brought here, I didn't know Kade or you or anyone else had made it, Jordan."

"But Kade owns a huge worldwide publishing company," Jordan says. "How could you not know?"

"Jordan, I don't have any access to the outside world here," Zeke says. "And neither does Mav. Remember, he's little more than I am here. He has access to food and water, but not enough for everyone down here. He can get it for the ones who would be able to fight, but not everyone. I have to eat some of that shit in order to keep suspicions down. All of us do. And it fucks with me. The poison is stronger now than it was. Sometimes, I'm out for days. Not only that, but the Alpha here can block us all from any communication with the packs we came from."

"We don't have television up here anyway," Maverick says. "We're pretty far in the mountains. We have books for entertainment. When we have time for that."

"Most of their days are spent doing what the Alpha tells them to," an unfamiliar and very smooth, deep male voice says.

Jordan and I both jump, but we take our cue from Zeke, who doesn't move. The man steps into our view. He's as tall as Zeke is and just as toned and muscular. Other than that, he's exactly the opposite of him.

He's blonde and blue eyed. His skin is tanned. He's carrying a tray, or maybe a few stacked on top of each other.

Behind him, is a small woman, but I can't see her face. She's also carrying a tray or two. She clears her throat. "Should I give these to Loki?" she asks the man quietly. I furrow my eyebrows because I recognize her voice. But it can't be…

"Yeah, baby. The usual cells. They'll need all the strength they can get." I see her nod. Her dark brown hair just grazes her shoulder as she turns towards the cell across from the one I'm in. The man slips into Zeke's cell. "We need to move. Tonight. He's planning another sale for the morning. He said this group is ready to go."

My eyes snap to him. "Sale?"

Zeke sighs and rubs his temple. "Jace. Meet my sister, Jordan, and my twin brother's mate, Kaia."

"Kaia?" the girl says, nearly dropping her tray before the guy in the cell across from me grabs it.

Jace's eyes widen. "Shit. I thought they were dead."

"That's what I thought," Zeke says. "I couldn't feel them, but it turns out it's another of your father's tricks."

I'm about to ask what the hell is going on, but the girl is suddenly gripping the bars of my cell. "K-Kaia?" she squeaks.

I turn to her when she says my name again and my eyes nearly pop out of my head. "Oh my God! Leia!" I run to her. We hug each other the best we can through the bars. "I thought you were dead!"

"It's such a long story, Kaia. Holy shit, so much has happened." She squeezes me tighter. "What are you doing here?"

"Another very, very long story." I burrow my face in her neck. "I missed you," I whisper.

"Leia. Baby, I hate to break this up. I really do. But we need to discuss getting them the fuck out of here. Before my father can go through with his plan," Jace says.

She nods and slowly lets go. "He's right."

Jace and Leia hand out trays to people, Zeke included, but he shakes his head. "Give it to them. Kaia needs something to drink. I don't know when they ate last."

Maverick eyes him. I can see he's torn, but he allows the request. Jace unlocks our cell and hands Jordan the tray. Finally, Maverick kisses

Zeke. "I'll have Jace come back with something for you. If your brother is alive, I need to get to him. Now."

"How are you going to get out of here?" Zeke asks worriedly. "It's not like they'll just allow you to take a vehicle."

"Nope," Jace says. "But they will allow me." He reaches in his pocket and takes out keys. He takes off the hoodie he's wearing and hands it to Maverick. "You're about my size. Put the hood up and take my car."

"We aren't far from where Deimos territory used to be. If Kade is alive, I doubt he'd leave the territory. Especially if Kaia and Jordan and some of their pack were taken," Maverick says. "Besides. I have an idea." He winks and kisses Zeke again before he strolls out of the cell with a wicked grin.

"That fucker lives up to his name," Jace says as he shakes his head. He looks at Zeke. "I'll grab you food. It might be a little bit." He leaves the cell and drops a kiss to Leia's head. "Stay here. Shift. The girls need warmth. Jordan doesn't have the strength, and if Zeke does it, my father will sense it."

"Okay." Leia walks with him to our cell and unlocks the door. She shifts into a gorgeous gray and brown wolf.

My mouth drops, and my knees buckle. Before my eyes, Leia is no longer Human. I've read about Shifters, but I haven't seen it happen like that before my eyes. It's not like I fear Wolves in the slightest. But seeing her shift into one before my eyes is shocking. I sit down and just look at her.

Leia nuzzles me and looks towards the bed. Jordan sits down with the tray of food. I crawl to the bed and dust myself off as I use it to help me stand. I snuggle into Leia as Leia jumps up on the bed. She wraps herself around us, and I instantly feel warmer.

"I'm going to unlock everyone's cell doors," Jace announces to everyone. "You need to trust me and stay in the cells. Don't try to get out. Rest. Save your strength. Help is coming. Tonight. When you get the command from Zeke, everyone can storm out. Those who have the poison running through their systems are going to be weaker. Those with the strength need to help them. Those with the most strength need to fight to get everyone out of here. You'll have some defense from those on our side."

161

I hear a murmur of agreement throughout the cells, but I'm too busy enjoying the warmth and water. I've given Jordan most of the food. She needs it. I watch as Jace makes sure the cells are closed but unlocked before he makes his way out of the dungeon area.

After a few moments, I look over at Zeke. "I've tried to be quiet and just let everything happen around me, but I really don't understand what's going on. I have so, so many questions, I don't even know where to begin."

He chuckles and sits on his cot. He leans forward with his elbows on his knees and clasps his hands together. "Jordan is still fucked up from the drugs. I'm being blocked. But you... you can reach Kade. He needs a warning."

"I told you that I have no idea how to do that. I'm not a Shifter. I can't... I can't..." I shake my head.

"You can. And you will. Close your eyes, Kaia."

I look at Jordan. She smiles softly and encouragingly. I obey and close my eyes. "Okay. Closed."

"Now, focus on Kade. Bring him up in your mind's eye. Think only of him. Clear your mind of everything else and just concentrate on him."

I let out a breath and think about my dream. "He said he was coming for me in a dream I had. But I don't think that was really him. I think it was just wishful thinking."

"Shh... Focus. Think about the dream if you want to, but concentrate on him. Think of him right in front of you. Like you're talking to him instead of me."

I take a deep breath and let it out slowly. I let Kade enter my mind and focus on him. His tall and toned body. His large protective arms. The tattoo I saw on his bicep. His dark and broody looks. The sexy scruff on his face that he typically shaves off each morning. I smile when I think of his lips on mine. His rough hands on my hips.

Kade...? Can you hear me...? I set my jaw and try to push the thought to the apparition in my mind.

"You're too tense, Kaia. You need to relax," Zeke's voice filters through softly. I feel Jordan's hands on my shoulders, helping to release the tension.

I take another breath and try again with a sniffle. *Kade...?* I wait for him to answer, or to at least feel him somehow. Some way. When I don't hear or feel him, I slump. "It's no use. He wanted to reject me. Maybe he did." I open my eyes and wipe a tear away.

Jordan shakes her head. "He didn't. I believe that he wouldn't, but I also know he didn't. You'd feel the break."

"Even if he did, it sometimes fails. When the Moon Goddess gives us our mates, she doesn't like when we go against her wishes. Sometimes, she refuses to allow the rejection. But even if he rejected you and she didn't allow it, you'd feel it. Now, close your eyes, Kaia. You said you heard him in your dreams."

"Think about that. Like you're talking to him in your dreams," Jordan whispers. I close my eyes again and bring up Kade in my mind once more.

"Tell him we need his help. You need him. Tell him Maverick is coming," Zeke says quietly.

I let myself relax. I tune everything else out and think of myself in Kade's arms. I stare up into his eyes after he kisses me and see nothing but him. *God, Kade. Please hear me. We need you. I need you. Someone named Maverick is coming to lead you to us. There's so many of us. Kade... Please...*

CHAPTER SEVENTEEN

~*~ KADE ~*~

"You haven't slept. You haven't eaten. You haven't had anything to drink." Dominick shoves me onto a stool at the kitchen counter and puts a sandwich and glass of milk in front of me. "Seriously. Eat something. How the fuck do you intend to save her or any of them if you can't even see straight? Even I've eaten, and I'm going crazy without Jordan."

"I can't even argue with you," I grumble and take a bite of the sandwich. "I just can't think about anything other than what a fucking asshole I was to her this entire time. And now she's gone. Not only is she gone, but my sister is gone. Girls from my pack are gone. And they were all taken from my territory because I was too fucked up over her to pay attention to anything else."

He smacks me in the back of the head. I glare up at him with the sandwich halfway to my mouth. "As your friend, I'm going to have to tell you to shut the fuck up. As your Beta, I'm going to say this one time and one time only. Stop feeling sorry for yourself. Our allies are on their way. We need a fucking plan. We need our Alpha. Because there are pack members in danger. My girl is in danger, and so is yours. So, get it together, Alpha, and lead our pack."

I chuckle. "I needed that."

"Happy to be of service. Now, what do we know?"

"Well, we know it's the Devil's Peak Pack that's causing all of this fucking chaos. We know other packs within our circle have had kids taken. It's not just us. We know it has something to do with that fable about the most powerful Luna. We know the Devil's Peak is based in Tennessee. We do not know more than that, and that's fucking frustrating as hell." I take a large bite of the sandwich and angrily chew it as I glare at the plate.

"We need to figure out where they are. How do we do that?"

I take another bite and chew thoughtfully. I still haven't been able to contact Jordan or anyone else through the mind link I have with them. But I try again because I'm nothing if not fucking stubborn. I get that from my mama.

...de...? ...rick... coming...

I choke on the last bite of the sandwich and grab the milk. I swallow several gulps. Dominick watches me and pats my back. After downing the entire glass, I set it down and take deep breath after deep breath.

"What the fuck?" Dominick asks. "You okay? What was that?"

I shake my head. "I swear to fuck I heard…" I shake my head again. "It wasn't clear. It was broken up, but I think I…"

"You think what?"

I take a breath. "I think I heard Kaia." I look up at him. "Just broken up words, but I swear it sounded like Kaia."

Dominick stands back on his heels and crosses his arms over his chest. He furrows his brows. "How is that possible?"

"I don't know, man. I have tried telling her with our mate bond, at least what little we have, that I'm sorry, and that I'm coming for her, but I didn't think she could actually hear me. Not when I haven't claimed her. Fuck, I still don't know. I just did it to comfort myself. Keep myself from tearing down the fucking universe."

"Well, if you think that was her, try again. Tell her you hear her or something. Maybe the bond with her is stronger than you think."

I let out a breath and focus on her. Not like it's hard. She's all I've thought about since I first laid eyes on her. *Kaia? I can hear you, baby, but it's broken. You need to focus on me, honey.*

Dominick sits next to me. "I wish I could at least feel Jordan. Just to know she's okay."

I give him a pained smile and squeeze his shoulder. "I know."

A few minutes of silence go by before Dominick sighs. "I still can't feel her. Did Kaia say anything else?"

I shake my head. "I'm starting to think it was my imagin-"

Kade? Her voice is soft and unsure, but it's Kaia.

I can hear you, baby. Fuck, tell me you can hear me, and that you're okay, I say, closing my eyes.

I can hear you. I can hear the tears in her voice. *I don't know if you can hear everything I'm saying to you, but we're okay. Jordan is with me. And your brother.*

What? Wait, Kaia. My brother? He's dead! I glance at Dominick. I don't need to tell him that I've got Kaia. He can tell just by watching me.

He's not dead. Devil's Peak has him. That's the pack that attacked you all those years ago. They have a lot of prisoners here. I don't know everything or understand it all, but Zeke is helping me. Us.

Hang on, baby. Jordan. Is she okay? I can't reach her.

She's okay. The stuff we were injected with is harder on Shifters than Humans. She's still fighting the effects, but she's okay. Zeke can't contact you because if he does, the Alpha here will feel it.

I shake my head. *That doesn't make sense. He's part of my pack.*

Kade, I don't know. I don't understand it all. All I know is that Devil's Peak has us. They are the ones behind this. We're in the mountains somewhere. I don't know where.

You need to find out for me, baby. Ask Zeke. If he's been there for fourteen years, he has to know. At least has to have some kind of inclination.

Dominick and I both snap our heads to the front of the house when we hear scuffling outside. Like someone is fighting right outside my door. We both say nothing as we get up and make our way to the front of the house.

"What the hell is going on?" Dominick asks quietly.

Kade? He says -

166

Baby, hang on. There's something going on outside. I hate having to interrupt her, but the hair on the back of my neck is standing up.

Kade! It's Mav-

"You think you're so tough hiding behind daddy? Well, your daddy ain't here now to hide behind," a deep voice snarls as we hear another thud.

I look at Dominick. "The fuck?"

The door slams open. A body comes flying through it, skidding across my floor and landing near mine and Dominick's feet. A tall man with light brown hair shoots daggers at the body that's curled itself into a ball.

The man stalks into the house not taking his eyes off his prey. He picks him up by the throat and slams him against the wall. "Oh, how the tables have turned. Not only do you now have to face me. But I bet you ain't going to like going up against this fucker either, you little pissant."

I stare in pure fascination at the scene unfolding before me. So much so, that I put a hand on Dominick's shoulder when he tries to step forward to stop it. "Hang on."

The other guy, now pinned to my wall by his throat, is much smaller than the one pinning him. He's bleeding profusely from his nose and mouth, but it doesn't stop him from grinning. "As soon as my father knows what you've done, your life is going to be over. No more leeching off Devil's Peak." He croaks the words out, but I have to give him credit. Fucker has some serious attitude.

I fold my arms over my chest. "Devil's Peak, huh? Interesting. Please. Continue."

The smaller guy's eyes flick towards me. His grin starts falling slowly, though, until I can see the fear in his eyes. "W-what?"

The smirk on the bigger guy's face turns wicked as he snarls. "What's the matter? Can't reach anyone? How does it feel to be the weak one? To be at the mercy of your enemy? To face the wrath of your Alpha?"

The other guy's eyes widen in shock. "H-how…? You're not supposed to know!"

He laughs. "I've known for quite a while. I'm the true Alpha. And guess what? No way in fuck you'll be able to reach your daddy. Not tonight. Not ever." He slams his head against the wall with enough force to make me wince. The smaller guy's head lulls forward as his eyes close.

The bigger guy rolls his eyes. "He'll live." He turns to me after dropping him to the floor. "Kade. Nice to see you again. We thought you were dead." He holds out his hand for me to shake.

I look down at it and then glance at Dominick before I look back at him. I slowly reach out to shake his hand. "You have me at a disadvantage."

"I suppose you've only seen me once. You may not remember me. It wasn't long after we met that Devil's Peak attacked your pack." He shakes my hand and lets it go. "Maverick."

"Maverick." It takes me a moment, but then I remember. "You were Zeke's mate."

"Am. Am Zeke's mate. We have a lot to discuss." He glances at Dominick then back down at the guy on the floor before looking back at me. "Do you have a place to keep him? I'll keep him from contacting his father or anyone else."

I look down at the guy. He looks like a kid. "Uh… yeah." I link with Aiden. *I have a guy in my hallway who needs a room in the You're Fucked Hotel. Want to come get him?*

Aiden chuckles. *On my way. Dare I ask?*

You can ask. Don't have answers yet, though. Bring Jamie.

We'll be right there.

"Okay. Care to start talking? Because I am literally made of questions," I say.

"Good thing I have answers. Maybe not all, but a lot."

"How about we start with what the fuck is going on," Dominick says.

Kade…? Did he get there…?

Hearing her voice makes me smile. At least a little. *Maverick?*

He's Zeke's mate. I tried to tell you he was going to you for help. I'm not good at this yet. That may not have gotten through the… whatever this channel is.

Maverick chuckles. "I'm happy to answer all of the questions you have."

He's here, baby. We're talking to him. And it looks like he brought us a gift.

Good. I don't know what that means, but good.

He threw some kid through my door and said something to him about hiding behind his daddy. Any ideas? I escort Maverick to the couch in my living room after Aiden and Jamie pick up the kid.

Zeke is cackling with laughter. He says it sounds like the fake Alpha's youngest. Spoiled brat that he is. His words, not mine. I guess he follows his daddy around like he's a God or something.

Okay. Rest, my girl. Listen for me. I'm talking to Maverick now.

I have so many questions, Kade.

I know. I promise I'll answer them when I get you back. Just be strong for me. Please? Stick next to Zeke.

I will.

Good girl. I sit next to Dominick as Maverick makes himself comfortable. "So, Maverick. What the fuck is going on?"

He rumbles a low chuckle. "I should probably start from the beginning, but we don't have a lot of time."

"As much as I want my girl and my family back, I'm not going anywhere without answers. I'm not walking into a fucking ambush."

He holds his hands out. "I understand. Believe me. I know where you came from. I can't blame you for that. But I am making this quick, Kade. We don't have time to fuck around. The Alpha of Devil's Peak, fake as he may be, is planning a sale. Human trafficking. Shifters are sold as slaves to other packs or to Humans with no morals. It's been going on for years. He does one sale each year. I don't know why, but he's fast-tracked this one."

"Probably because some of the girls are from our pack," Dominick growls with an angry shake of his head.

I hold up a hand. "I have theories, but why sell them?"

"It's complicated," Maverick says. "For many, many years, the Alpha's in the pack have believed a legend that has to do with the most powerful Luna. Her powers and her love and heart, will make the Alpha she mates with the most powerful Alpha. The Alpha's of our pack have been looking for her for decades. Far longer than I've been alive. Or you. Anyone in either of our packs. They don't believe that Wolves will be the bearer of this Luna. They believe it will be birthed by a Shifter or Human who mates with a Shifter. They sell Humans to Shifters. The Shifters, they keep. The new Alpha, however, changed that. He sells Shifters to both Humans and other Shifters, but not before he mates them first."

"Why?" I shake my head. "There are so many holes and flaws in everything you said, I can't even begin to point them all out. But the biggest one is what if one of those Humans or Shifters who are sold becomes or births this Luna?"

Maverick nods. "So, you understand why there has been unrest in the pack. More so over the last few years. It was not that long ago that one of the Shifters who were around when I was born came to me and asked me if I knew the real story behind my birth. I told him what I believed to be the truth. I came from the mistress of the Alpha who leads the pack today. I am the middle son. No claim to the throne, and no real place in the pack anyway. I've been treated as little more than a slave for as long as I can remember. But he told me the real story. Then directed me to where I could find all of the documentation to back up his story.

I chuckle. "And that's when you found out the truth."

Maverick nods. "He warned me to do all of my research in secret. I did. I'm the real Alpha of Devil's Peak. My father and mother were both killed under very mysterious circumstances after my father said he wanted to change how our pack was run. He didn't like the bullshit going on with the trafficking and kidnapping from other packs and kids from all over the world. He had actually managed to rescue a lot of the kids who were sold the year he took over. The Alpha who is leading now didn't like that. Neither did a lot of others in the pack who liked the way things were. It wasn't long after that he turned up dead."

"Why not kill you, too?" Dominick asks. "He had to know he doesn't have any real control over the pack with you still alive."

"Good question. One I can't answer. I don't know. It would have been the best option. Maybe he thought raising me as his own but making me a slave to him would show everyone that he's powerful and isn't to be fucked with."

I scrub my hands down my face. "How far away is Devil's Peak's base? If what you're saying is true, we need to get there."

"It's just over the Tennessee and Georgia border. It took me about an hour to run here in Wolf form. The little pissant followed me, but I cut off his communication. No one knows where I went. He didn't have time to warn anyone."

"I'll get some of our guys together," Dominick says as he stands.

I nod. "Split them. Half stay here. Half go with us. This is a rescue mission. This time. Next time, we're going in full fucking force. And Dom? Jamie comes with us. No way is he going to be willing to stay behind. Not with the chance to get a little payback on the pack that took his mate from him."

Dominick nods. A dark expression crosses his face as he leaves the house. I recognize it well. It's the same one I'm sure is crossing my face right now. I have to allow that determination and anger to supersede everything else right now because if I don't, the loss I am feeling is going to drag me under.

Maverick watches me. "What else do you want to know? While he's gathering your people."

"I don't think we have the time for you to answer my questions, but one thing I do want to know is why didn't you come to me sooner?"

"I had no idea you were alive. We're far up that mountain. We don't have television. He keeps everyone pretty fucking secluded from the outside world. Zeke couldn't connect to you because of the drugs they were giving him. By the time we figured out what was going on and I was in a position to help with it, we were all convinced the Deimos' didn't exist anymore. It's taken me a long time to get where I am right now. Do you have any idea what it was like for me standing by and watching my mate go through the shit he went through and being able to do nothing? Or seeing all of the bullshit the man I thought was my father was doing but not being able to stop it?"

"I honestly can't, man. I didn't grow up like that. I don't know what it was like. What I do know is I want it to end. I'm only trusting you because Kaia was able to somehow figure out a way to contact me with our link and confirmed Zeke is alive. I know that makes me sound like a complete dickhead, but -"

"But you need to be cautious. I get it, Kade. You don't need to explain that to me." He gives me a half smile that for some reason goes a long way in easing some of my fears of going into this blind. "I have some men that are on my side. The guards around Zeke and the rest of the people who have been captured are on my side. You might not like this, but my Beta is the fake fucker's son. He has been on the fence for a long time, hating what his father has been doing. He has been helping me with the prisoners for years. At least as much as either of us could. He officially switched teams just a couple of months ago when he found his mate was one of the people my father kidnapped. She'd been a prisoner for two years before she turned eighteen. Well. You can imagine how he reacted to that." He nods at me.

"I can only imagine he was pissed enough to tear the bars off the cage."

"Jace pulled her out of the cell and marched right up to his father. Told him he was no longer going to be a participant in his bullshit. And then leaned down and did the mate bite right there in front of him, me, his mom, and Tristan, the little fucker I beat the hell out of. Surprisingly, Leia was well aware of Shifters and didn't react negatively to his claim."

"Wait. Leia?"

He nods as he stands with me. We walk towards my door. "The asshole killed her parents. Cut their brake line. They drove off a cliff. Well, they were forced off a cliff. He stopped them as they were leaving their house. He took her and sent them on their way. They had no idea that during the struggle, one of his guys was tampering with their vehicle."

I look at him. "I knew there was something very suspicious. They had reached out to me. They needed help. Next thing I knew, I couldn't hear or feel them anymore. I heard about the car accident. I pushed the Sheriff's Department to investigate it. They said that their car lost control. My contacts couldn't get access to the official report. Everyone was just told it was a tragic accident that claimed the lives of them all. I couldn't get any other information. Not for lack of trying."

"He owns the Sheriff and all of his deputies in this area. The Sheriff is his Beta."

I chuckle and shake my head. "That just put one giant missing piece into place in a fucked up and complicated puzzle."

Dominick meets us both in the middle of our compound. "I pulled fifty guys. Are we going to need more?" He turns his dark gaze onto Maverick.

Maverick shakes his head. "That will be enough, but we need to take vehicles. The prisoners are weak. Some are still fighting the effects of the last drugging session. Some have just more or less given up. Those are the ones he intends to sell."

"No one is getting sold. Fuck," I say.

"I have another twenty guys on my side, and we -" His head snaps up as he cuts himself off. He turns to me. "Time to go. Now."

I nod. "How many prisoners?"

"There are thirty," Maverick answers. "Not counting me, Zeke, Jace, or Leia."

"One person per vehicle," I command. "I'll take Maverick and Dominick with me. Everyone follow. We move in fast and hard. Our goal is the prisoners."

"My guys will have them ready to move. The fighting will be minimal. At least, that's the hope. Those that betray the Alpha, will be scrambling to leave with us. We need to get in and out fast, and expect retaliation."

"Everyone who is left here, I want our pack protected at all costs. Gather everyone in the pack house. There is safety in numbers. And it will keep the kids calm. The allies who haven't shown yet will be moving in tomorrow to help with a perimeter and protection."

Everyone begins moving quickly. I jog to my garage with Maverick and Dominick following. I jump in the SUV and take off. SUVs and vans move in behind me. Soon, there is a fleet of Deimos vehicles.

Kade...? Something is happening. A lot of commotion.

We're not far away. Get ready, baby. We're coming. And we're bringing you home.

CHAPTER EIGHTEEN

~*~ KAIA ~*~

I press myself as close to the corner as I can. Jordan and I both hug each other. Zeke stands, gripping the bars of his cell. He's ready to create a distraction if he has to, but the hope is that we aren't seen at all. That the Alpha will just keep walking by us.

Jace came back just a few minutes ago. He got Leia out of our cell and Zeke food, but he also said that his father has guests. Guests who arrived early and want to see the goods they are bidding on up close and personal. The statement set every one of us on edge, but no one more than me and Jordan. The look Jace gave us sent chills down our spines. Not because we fear him. We fear what he knows and isn't telling us.

They're coming! I swallow down my tears and try to stay as silent as possible. I focus on Kade because he's the only thing keeping me sane. His promise that he's coming is what is keeping Jordan from fully falling apart. She won't admit that, but I can feel it.

Who's coming, Kaia? Kade's deep voice asks in my head.

I still don't know if I'm imagining everything, but I can't allow myself to think like that. *The Alpha! Kade! Please, please hurry. Please! I think he's coming for me and Jordan!*

Not on my watch, he growls. *We're almost there, Kaia. I promise. Just a few minutes. You have to hold on for me.*

My head snaps to what sounds like a door being opened. "This is where we keep everyone," someone says. He sounds friendly but more dangerous than anything I've ever come against in my life. His friendly tone is fake. Just like he is.

Jordan turns my head back to her. "Shh…," she whispers. "Don't draw any attention to yourself."

"We just got these two a couple of days ago. I haven't had the chance to check them out myself, but they're up for purchase. I would like to get rid of them quickly," he says as he stops in front of our cell. I squeeze my eyes closed.

"Why do you want to get rid of them quickly?" someone asks. I can hear the suspicion in his voice.

"Because of where they came from. Too close for comfort. It's why I specified that these two specifically need to be taken by someone far from here. You're an excellent candidate. They both fit your specifications to a tee."

"I asked for a Shifter and a Human. They both look rather weak. I want to break them myself."

"Oh, and you will! They're just drugged right now. When you pick them up, we'll drug them again. You'll be able to do exactly as you wish once you get them home."

"Well, let me see them. I don't purchase anything without seeing it first."

"Very well. You two!" the Alpha barks. "Get up! Show yourselves!"

Oh, God. Kade! I tremble violently and grip Jordan as tightly as I can.

"Zeke has our back. He won't allow anything to happen to us," Jordan whispers as she gently pulls me up with her. I can just make out the sound of Zeke growling.

"Faster! Move!" the Alpha barks.

I jump and stumble over myself. I crash back to the ground, taking Jordan with me. "I'm so sorry," I whisper.

"Get up!" he yells.

"It's okay. Zeke won't let him hurt us," Jordan whispers as she helps me up.

"I'm supposed to be the strong one," I whisper back. "I can't even do that right."

She nuzzles me. "We'll be okay."

"Step closer!" he commands. Jordan follows his order and moves us both to the middle of the cell. "What are you two? Lovers? Move away from each other so your new owner can see you. And for Christ's sake, look up at us!"

I take a breath and look up slowly. My eyes widen. My heart stops beating. My blood freezes and quits circulating through my body. I take an involuntary step back as my eyes lock onto the man standing behind the man in charge. He grins at me and winks. I know he recognizes me.

"I'll take them both," the buyer says.

"Well, you still need to bid."

"I don't care if someone bids ten million. I'll double it. I'll see you in the morning." He nods to both of us and turns around. He leaves the way they came in.

The Alpha watches him a few moments before shaking his head and leading the rest of the group further down the corridor. "Now, these next ones are still very young. They haven't reached age yet, but they are Shifters. The deal, though, stands. I sell them, they return to me at eighteen. Because of that, they will be sold for less. If they don't suit my needs at that time, you can have them back. If they do, I'll give you your money back and a new girl. Or boy. If your tastes run in the other direction."

He stops outside the cell with young girls that I recognize from Kade's pack, but I can't focus on anything, but the man in front of me with his arms crossed over his chest and the man standing next to him. Both of their smiles turn to a grotesque smirk. The taller one, the one my focus is on, steps forward and looks me up and down. I've forgotten how to breathe.

"You recognize me, don't you?" His eyes meet mine again. They are cold. There is nothing in his eyes but hatred. I can hear low, furious snarls coming from Zeke and Loki's directions. "I made a mistake when I left you for dead. I should have taken you. Could have had some fun myself before giving you up. I thought I was doing you a favor. Being a nice guy, you know?"

"Wh-what?" I squeak out quietly. I feel dizzy.

"Oh, you know. We killed your parents because they poked their noses where they shouldn't have. Knew far too much." He grips the bars. I thank my lucky stars that he doesn't grip the part that opens. "You weren't part of the deal. At least not at first. We didn't know about you until we were at the house searching for the evidence they had against us. When we didn't see you, we figured you were at that all-night grad party being held at the high school."

I stare as the other one watches Zeke. "You know, you were promised to me long ago." He nods towards his partner in crime. "Beta there. He promised you to me years ago."

"Like fucking hell...," Zeke growls. He doesn't move away from the bars as he stares the man down. The Deputy. One of the ones who killed my parents.

"I was promised you both. You and your little fuck puppy."

Zeke smirks. "So, you know about Maverick? Good. He's going to be your downfall."

"That he's the worthless bastard of the Alpha's?" The man in front of me laughs. "You think that weak ass fucker is going to be able to do anything to us?"

Zeke glances at him and shrugs before turning his gaze back on the Deputy. "Maybe. What do I know? I'm just one of Devil's Peak's slave boys, right?"

The Deputy glares. "And don't you forget it, boy. You belong to me. Even if you don't know it yet. He may have claimed you through his bite, but I know that piece of shit hasn't claimed your ass. He isn't brave enough to go against the Alpha by doing that."

Zeke gives him a dangerous chuckle. "Little do you know."

"Enough. Both of you," the Sheriff growls. "We don't have much time. We need to wait until the Alpha leaves before we can do what we want to them."

I feel the bile rising as my knees start to buckle. *Kade. Please. Please. Hurry!*

Baby, I'm coming. We're almost there. Hang on for me.

Baby. He keeps calling me baby. It warms my heart. My entire soul. The hope of that one word and what it could mean gives me the strength to keep going. To trust that he's close. That he's ready. I have to stay strong. For him, if not for me. For Jordan, and her baby.

The Sheriff stays next to the bars, but turns his head towards the Alpha and his guests. He watches as they leave. The Alpha pats his shoulder on the way out. I can hear Zeke growling low again as he eyes the Sheriff and Deputy, but he's not the only one. There are several men in the cells near ours who are also watching them closely.

Oblivious, the Sheriff continues watching me. "But then there you were. We figured the best idea would be to kill you like we did them. I thought we did. Imagine my surprise when my mate came to me and told me that you were with Kade Deimos."

Jordan shakes her head. "Charlene is your mate? But… she has been with Kade."

The thought of that makes me sick to my stomach. I look down. "Gross," I whisper.

The Sheriff laughs. "She's my daughter. Convenient, huh? I got elected as Sheriff three years ago. Charlene was very happy to help me keep an eye on the infamous Kade Deimos."

"You make me sick," I growl as bile rises in my throat. "You whored out your own daughter."

"Oh, now, now." He chuckles and waggles his finger. "I didn't need to whore out anyone. She knows her place. She knows that she has to do whatever it takes to make sure that the Devil's remain on top. And she was more than willing to use the pack who killed the man she was betrothed to."

"We didn't kill anyone who didn't deserve it," Jordan growls.

"You don't remember much from that day, do you?" the Sheriff growls right back. He turns a vicious glare to Jordan. "You don't remember that you're the reason they tore out his throat."

I shake my head and glance at Jordan. "What?"

"I remember him. Rat-like eyes. Tawny hair. Skinny like a twig." Her eyes remain fixed on the Sheriff. "Maybe he shouldn't have trapped me and Alyss."

"Maybe you should have been a good girl and come quietly," he hisses.

"Have you forgotten that Devil's Peak slaughtered my entire pack? My family?" She goes to lunge towards him.

"Jordan," Zeke warns. "Not. The. Time."

Jordan clenches her fists at her sides and spits at the Sheriff instead. "I will kill you one day."

He laughs and ignores her as he wipes the spit from his face. He looks back at me. "My only regret is that I didn't take you the way I wanted. But, hey. There's still time." He moves towards the door to our cell.

My eyes slide to the right when I catch a flash of movement in the shadows. I take a cautious step back, instinctively pulling Jordan with me. From there, though, my feet feel like they're stuck to the ground.

"Now!" Zeke roars. He shoves the door of his cell open, banging it against the Deputy's head. The Deputy falls backwards and smashes into the bars of the cell across from Zeke. Like a flash, Zeke is launching out of his cage. "Girls! To the back of the cells!"

There's a sudden flurry of movement. Cell doors are opening. People are running in from the stairs, shifting into their Wolves in mid-air as they lunge at the Deputy and Sheriff. But they aren't the only ones being attacked. It looks like reinforcements are coming in to help the Sheriff and Deputy as some are attacking those that have fled the cells. The reinforcements are taken off guard when they are fought off with a strength they weren't aware their victims had.

The Sheriff turns towards Zeke. "How the fuck?"

He doesn't see the man behind him, who is also out of his cage faster than the blink of an eye. I hear Zeke's command for the girls to get to the back of the cells, but I can't move. Jordan, though, tugs me to the back of the cell with her. I look down the line of cells as we crouch down in the corner by the cot. I can't see all of them in the darkness, but the ones I can see, the girls are moving as quickly as they can.

The last thing I see before I burrow into Jordan is Zeke tackling the Deputy while someone else launches at the Sheriff. The cells have erupted in complete chaos. I don't know who all of the good guys are and who all of the bad guys are because it seems like everyone is fighting someone else.

The yelling and screaming and grunting and roaring make me want to make myself as small as possible, but I know I'm still too visible. I wish I could make myself disappear. I don't want to draw any attention to myself. None at all.

"Time to go," someone says.

I jump and try to scurry closer to the wall as I look at whoever just put their hand on my arm. I'm ready to fight. Scratch. Claw. Kick. Scream. Whatever I have to do to keep the person from taking me from the relative safety of this cell.

"Dominick!" Jordan screams before launching herself at him.

My racing heart takes a moment to catch up before I realize who he is. "Oh, God." I almost immediately start crying in relief.

"We need to go, baby. Now. We'll have plenty of time for catching up later." Dominick reaches out a hand for me. I take it, and he pulls me up effortlessly.

Dominick pushes us in front of him and covers us with his body as he moves us quickly through the many people fighting and clawing. Wolves and Humans are clawing and throwing kicks and punches.

I try to look behind me as Dominick propels us up the stairs, but all I see is him. "What about everyone else?"

"Don't look back. Just move, Kaia. They'll be saved. All of them."

I turn back and run when he starts to. Jordan takes my hand and leads me to an SUV. Just as we reach it, I hear a pained groan. I can't help but turn to look in the direction it came from. There's so much blood around. Bodies lying on the ground. People stumbling and holding their wounds. I'm positive one person on his knees is holding something inside himself just before he slumps to the ground.

Out of the corner of my eye, I see the bloodied form of the Deputy launching out of the building and taking off for the woods as he shifts in midair. He lets out a loud, long howl as he runs. Someone gives chase but is stopped by another and pushed in the direction of the SUVs.

But there's only one person that my eyes can really focus on. One person who is slumping to the ground holding his arm and side. One person who has blood oozing from a cut on his lip. His head. One person who, despite his injuries, is still trying to hold someone off him.

I scream and turn to run towards him. "Kade!" I rip my hand away from Jordan and sprint towards him. He doesn't take his attention away from the person attacking him, but I can see his strength is waning. He doesn't see the Wolf launching itself at him. "Kade, look out!"

Dominick grabs me around the waist and spins me around. He shoves me into the back of the SUV, but I fight him with everything I am. "Kaia! Stop!"

"You have to help him!" I shove him away, but he only steps one step back.

"Kaia! Get in the fucking vehicle!" he growls. I'm sure the dominant tone would work on me in any other moment but this one.

I try launching out of the SUV again, but he stops me. "Dominick, help him! Help him!"

"Kaia! Stop fucking fighting me! Kade will be fine! Get in the SUV! All you will do is distract him!" He pushes me with more force and closes the door behind me.

I scramble for the door handle, but in my panic and tears, I can't see or grip it when I finally find it. "Kade!" I sob uncontrollably as I claw at the door handle.

"Go!" Dominick slaps the top of the SUV. It takes off on his command.

"No! Go back! Go back!" I scream as I try to open the door.

I feel a set of arms wrap around me and pull me back when I try to scramble over the seat to the back of the SUV. "Trust them," the weak and tired male voice says. "They got us out."

I don't know who he is, but when I feel his tears against my back, I cry harder because he's right. No matter what happens, we were saved. Jordan and I aren't the only people in this SUV. There are a couple other girls huddled in the back and two young boys in the seats next to me. Jordan is in the front hugging herself and crying just as hard as me. The driver is speeding away from the complex.

While we may have been saved, I still feel lost because I don't know if my life will be worth living without Kade. He may not have accepted me as his mate or sealed whatever bond we have, but I know now that I need him. I need him whatever way I can get him. I need him to survive.

After watching him surrounded by enemies, though, I don't know if I'll ever see him again.

CHAPTER NINETEEN

~*~ KADE ~*~

I watch as Dominick struggles to get Kaia into the SUV, but I have no time to tell her to listen to him because another fist comes flying at me from out of nowhere. I'm barely able to block it before hearing her screaming at me to watch out. I duck out of the way of a Wolf with bared teeth ready to latch onto my neck with no time to spare.

I glance back at Dominick and see him yelling at her to get into the vehicle before he finally gets her to obey. He slams the door and slaps the roof. The SUV speeds away with Jordan and Kaia safely inside. I let out a breath of relief knowing they're safe, but the feeling doesn't last long.

A fist I don't block in time lands against my jaw and knocks me on my ass. The attacker is instantly on top of me with one hand around my neck. My hands automatically go to his arm to pull him off me, but he only squeezes my throat tighter and punches me in the ribs and face with the other hand.

I switch tactics and punch up, crashing my fist into his jaw as hard as I can. I hear a satisfying crunch, but it's not until Dominick kicks him in the head that his grip loosens. He flies to his side. Dominick is on before he hits the ground and snaps his neck.

"Thanks," I grumble.

"We need to go, Kade. His warriors have called for backup. If we want to get everyone to safety, we have to go. Now." Dominick pulls me up.

I hiss. "Fuck. Oh, fuck." The pain is blinding, and I nearly crash to the ground.

Dominick supports my weight and practically drags me to the last SUV. "I can't drive."

"You don't need to. I can tell your right leg is broken." He helps me into the back of the SUV. Someone in the back drags me across the seat.

"Son of a bitch!" I yell between clenched teeth when pain radiates from my shoulder, down my arm, and into my hand. "Oh, holy fuck!"

I'm a fucking Shifter. I've never been in any situation where I've come out like this. I've had broken bones before. I've had bumps and bruises. Not once have I ever experienced this kind of pain. Not even the day I lost my whole fucking family. I could manage that. This? I'm about to black out.

"Oh, shit," Dominick says after sliding in next to me. My head is on someone's lap. My leg is on Dominick's. He takes off his shirt.

"No. Not that one," a female voice says, but I can't see who. My vision is blurring.

"He's losing blood. He might be an Alpha, but he's not fucking immortal," Dominick growls.

"We might be Shifters who can heal wounds, but we're not immune to blood infections," she retorts sharply. "Here. This one. I'll use mine," the girl says. I can see the outline of her as she leans over the seat. "Hold his leg still. It's going to hurt."

I watch as she ties it around my knee. Dominick holds it still. "Ah! Fuck! What the hell!" I try to jerk away from him, but he holds my leg still. I'm starting to see black spots. My breathing quickens. She tightens it even more. "Ow, fuck!" I scream again. I try to pull away once more, but Dominick doesn't allow me to move.

"There," she says. She points to someone in the back. "Give me that jacket."

I nearly jump out of my own skin when I hear a gunshot. I look around wildly and try to get up, but Dominick pushes me down. "It's Maverick. He's shooting at someone trying to follow. Looks like he hit his target, too, because the car is careening off the road."

"Bullseye! Take that, you sadistic fucker! You ain't gonna force your fat ass on no more kids! Fucking immoral son of a bitch."

"Good. Serves those fuckers right." I groan and squeeze my eyes closed when someone moves my arm. "Fuck, stop torturing me." I try to push whoever it is away from me, but fail with epic proportions, realizing in that moment how much strength I've lost.

"I have to tie this off, Kade. You've lost so much blood, and your bone is sticking out of your elbow." She ties something above my elbow before I can even open my eyes to look.

"Ah!" I scream. "Holy fuck! Fuck!" The driver hits a bump that sends me into a different dimension of pain. I scream again. When it begins to shoot in so many different directions that I feel like I'm being stabbed with butcher knives all over my body, I beg for the Moon Goddess to take me now.

Like she's answering my prayers, the pain begins to fade. I slip into a peaceful darkness.

~ ~ ~

Coming out of the fog I've been fighting my way through is anything but pleasant. I've felt pain before, but nothing like this. Every breath I take sends me spiraling right back down into the dark abyss I've just clawed my way out of.

"Fuck me," I whisper as I open my eyes. I immediately squeeze them shut and groan.

"You're healing okay, but don't try moving around yet," a super soft and sweet voice says.

I let a smile drag at the corner of my mouth but leave my eyes closed. "My how the tables have turned." I feel the bed I'm lying on dip under her when she sits.

She presses a cold cloth to my forehead. "With one huge difference. When I woke up, I was completely healed and felt like I'd just returned from a spa."

I attempt a chuckle but cough and groan instead. "How long have I been out, Kaia?"

"Long enough to convince me you weren't pulling through," Kaia whispers. She moves the cloth lightly down my face. "It's interesting watching a Shifter heal himself. A little scary." She moves the cloth away from my face.

I slowly open my eyes and see her shoulders slumped. She's staring at the cloth in her hands as she plays with the ends. "I'm doing okay."

She nods slowly. "Much better than a few hours ago." She sniffles. "I… I didn't know what to do. Your leg was broken. Your arm was broken. You were covered in blood. Dominick wouldn't let me anywhere near you."

I look at my arm and leg. Both have been set in a makeshift splint, but they don't feel like they're broken anymore. Not that they don't hurt. The pain I am in is still intense, though maybe not anything like what it was. I don't remember them splinting me or cleaning me up. I don't even know how I got to my bed. Kaia reaches up and wipes a tear off her cheek.

I can't help but reach out and squeeze her thigh. "Kaia. Come here."

She shakes her head. "I want you to heal." She takes a deep breath before looking at me with a soft smile. "Do you need anything? Water? Something to eat?"

"You. Come here, baby. Please." I watch the shock register across her face, but she turns and sits closer to me. I gently take the cloth from her and toss it into the bowl with water she's put on my dresser. "Come lay with me." I hold out my good arm, inviting her into my side. "You look exhausted."

"I haven't exactly slept. At least not more than a couple of hours. And I was sitting up," she says quietly. When she sees I'm not moving my arm, she takes a visible breath and lays down next to me, but she is very careful not to touch me.

I can't help but chuckle a little as I drop my arm around her and pull her closer to me so she's plastered against my side. "Better."

"Kade, I don't think this is a good idea," she whispers. She stays very stiff next to me and completely motionless. I'm not certain she's even breathing.

I rub my hand up and down her arm and let myself do nothing but feel for a long while. Her warm, soft body next to mine goes a long way in easing the pain. And not just the pain from the fight. The agony I put both of our hearts through.

After a few more moments, she finally takes a deep breath, but she's still tense. I can't blame her. "What about the rejection?"

"How about we start from the beginning? You had a lot of questions I refused to answer for you. I promised I would if you held on for me."

She hugs herself, and I wish like hell she was hugging me. But I haven't earned that yet. "Why me? Why was I the one chosen for you?"

"I can't answer that fully. But not because I don't want to. Because I don't know. I don't know how the Moon Goddess works. All I really know for sure is that it's a grand design that none of us have any real say in. Sort of like your God. Or the God that Humans believe in. Not everyone believes in the same one. There are a lot of religious differences. Some don't believe in any God. But those that do, well, all of the Gods have one thing in common. They all have a plan for everyone. Fate. No one can control it. For us, the Moon Goddess is fate. She controls it all. And we celebrate her for it. We celebrate the good and the bad because it's all a grand design. Her grand design for us is each other. Our entire lives have been spent working towards each other. I never found a mate when I was supposed to because she was and is you."

"That's why I saw you all those years when I looked at the moon…"

"And why I saw you in my dreams."

She's quiet for a few moments. I keep rubbing her arm soothingly because I feel like it's all I can do right now. "Were your parents my Spirit Guides to lead me to you?"

"I think so. Maybe more to get you at least a little bit used to this world. More my mother because my father was Human. Not Shifter or Wolf. The Moon Goddess wanted to prepare you for my world in some ways."

She lowers her head. "If I am your mate, and you saw me in your dreams, why were you with others? I would have thought you would have waited for your mate. That you were faithful only to her. Even if you hadn't met yet. Maybe I'm being naive… or stupid. I'm just… trying to understand it all."

"To an extent. You have to understand that when you were born, I was fourteen. I didn't start seeing you in my dreams until a couple of years ago, but I never actually saw you. Just parts of you. I never felt the mate bond. If my mate isn't eighteen, I don't feel her. Dominick is two years older than Jordan. He didn't feel a mate bond with her until she was eighteen, but he had feelings. Like inclinations. With you, when I started seeing you, I started believing maybe there was someone out there for me. Until then, I believed I was meant to be alone."

"But you were with Charlene during the last couple of years."

"Baby, I'm about to sound like an asshole, but she was nothing more than a release for me. No girl I have ever been with has been anything other than that. I mean, you had to have been with someone else, right? Or had some kind of an attraction to someone."

She stays quiet for so long that I actually look down to see if she has fallen asleep. "I had school girl crushes, but I was never with anyone. I just…" She sighs. "This is going to sound really dumb, but I always compared the guys in school to you. They didn't measure up. When I…" She trails off and shakes her head as she blushes.

I raise an eyebrow, genuinely interested in what she was going to say. "When you…"

She shakes her head again and hugs herself tighter. "Nothing."

I bite my lip and fight a grin when it all suddenly hits me. I can't say why I want so badly for her to say it. "You don't need to be embarrassed about anything, you know."

She blushes even more furiously. I drop my arm and hug her tighter. I feel the tension slowly start to leave her body. "I felt so strangely intensely for you when I first heard your voice. You didn't even have to be near me for me to have a reaction to you. I just needed to be surrounded by your scent. It was enough for me. And I wanted to just… be with you. Take care of you. Be near you. All the time. I never truly understood that. It was more than attraction. It was, well, is, it is so much more."

"The mate bond is intense. It hits hard and fast. And it's not just attraction. For me, I want to take care of you. I don't want anyone else to touch you, or even look at you. I want you to be mine in every way. But mostly, I don't want to share my life with anyone else. I want you by my side. Always."

"Why did you hate me so much?"

"Fuck, baby. I never hated you." I let out a breath and close my eyes. "When my parents were killed, practically my entire family and pack, I wanted to figure out a way to stop that kind of pain from ever happening again. All I was focused on was my dad and Aryan as well as the other Humans killed that day. In my mind, I was protecting the few who were left in my pack from suffering the way I had. I thought making a no Human rule would somehow alleviate some of the pain I felt. And others who lost their Human mates that day. In the back of my mind, I knew that we lost Wolves and Shifters, too, but to me, they were stronger." I open my eyes and stare up at the ceiling.

"But they died, too."

"I know. I can see it doesn't make sense. I think deep down I knew it then, but I didn't care. I thought I was doing the right thing. I couldn't see that my actions hurt my pack. And when I realized that, I allowed myself to feel how much it hurt me. They should have been around their pack to heal. Splitting them only caused more pain. It's one of my biggest regrets. The other is hurting you, and making you feel like I hated you. Or that you weren't worthy of me. That you weren't good enough for me. You're so much better than me, baby. It's me who isn't worthy of you."

She falls quiet again. It takes her time, but she finally looks up at me. "What about the rejection?" she whispers. "What does that mean? Zeke… said… it doesn't always work."

I sigh. I didn't want to answer this question, but I knew I'd have to. "A rejection is when one mate tells the Moon Goddess that they don't want the mate they've been given. It can only be done on the night of the Blood Moon when it's at its highest point in the sky. Zeke is right. It doesn't always work. The rejection, while a statement from me, is a request to the Moon Goddess. She can accept my request, or she can deny it."

"Oh." She looks down again and hugs herself impossibly tighter.

I look at her. "If she'd accepted it, the pain would have been unbearable. You would have felt like you were dying. You'd have been angry. Hurt. But mostly, you would feel like I'd ripped out your heart and crushed it right in front of you. Eventually, for you, the pain would lessen. You'd be able to move on with your life. You would never feel truly at home anywhere, and you'd never be truly in love. For me, though, that pain would never go away. You'd feel like a piece of you is missing. It's a benefit to being Human. Me? I would feel like half of my soul is gone. You'd be taking my entire heart with you." I tangle my fingers in her hair. "The pain for me would worsen until I'm not only a shell of myself, but also a weak Alpha. I wouldn't be able to function."

She shakes her head. "I don't understand. Why would you want to do that?"

"To protect my pack from a fate I had dreamt in my head. A fate that doesn't make sense to me now, but it did then. To me, sacrificing myself for them is always the right path. To an Alpha, the pack is the most important thing. My father knew that. It's the entire reason he blocked the fight from me. I wasn't here when the battle started. I felt it. My Wolf felt it. But I had no idea what was actually happening. Not until Dominick carried a bruised and bloodied Jordan into the house and told me. And I knew right away why I didn't know until it was over. My father blocked it all from me so that I would survive. So that I, being the future Alpha, could be here for those that survived. So I could carry on his legacy. And I did that. At least I thought I had. But I failed them. And I didn't realize it until you."

"I think everyone here is really happy."

"They are. But there's always been a little bit missing. The rest of our pack that I sent away. I was still in contact with them, but they were basically isolated from their family. That was a truly difficult thing for me to do, even though I thought it was right at the time. I realize now that it isn't. I called them all back home. They are here now. Even those that broke the bond completely. We're all whole again."

"What about Leia? I... saw her."

I'm surprised, but I'll have to circle back to that. I told her I'd explain things to her. "Her father was Shifter. He was part of this pack. He left because his wife was Human. When they were in the car accident, they reached out to me. I couldn't answer them quickly enough. They were killed then. But I reached out to the Sheriff and asked for a full investigation. I got the runaround, but I always believed something was fucked up. It never sat well with me."

"The Sheriff." She moves closer to me, but I'm positive it's because she's scared. My heart seems to stop, both because she's closer to me, and because of whatever she's about to say. I tighten my grip. "He was there. He was at my house. He killed my parents. But he was also at the place we were taken to. He's Devil's Peak's Beta. Zeke said that's like a right-hand man?"

"More or less. Dominick is my Beta. I trust him with this pack as much as I trust myself. If something happens, Dominick would take over since I don't have any kids. Dominick would be like my right-hand man. Someone I go to for everything. A left-hand? Well, that would be like someone who doesn't have any morals. Well, they have some morals, but are willing to do whatever it takes to protect the pack. Someone who does things I can't stomach. I don't have one of those. I guess, technically, it would be Jamie, or maybe Koda, but really, they have just as many morals as me. A left-hand man would be someone who does all of the bidding for the Alpha and Beta because they don't want to get their hands dirty. From what I know of left-hands, they spend a lot of time away from the pack traveling as they take care of any threats to the Alpha or the pack in general. In other words, they do the work that the Alpha can't because they are meant to look clean and upstanding."

"I wonder who that would be for them... They didn't seem to me like there was much either of them didn't or wouldn't do." The thought causes her to move closer. I hug her tighter because I sense she needs it.

"For them, it would be someone they didn't give a shit about. Someone who didn't mind being the bad guy and didn't need to worry about his reputation."

"Maybe the Deputy. He was there, too. From what I heard, it sounds like he wants Zeke."

I glare at the thought, but choke back a growl. I don't want to scare her. Not when she's gotten this close to me and is finally starting to relax. "They all might seem like bad guys, and they are, but it wouldn't be him. He also has a reputation to uphold. At least in the public eye. And they need a good reputation when it comes to the public so what they do in the shadows is never found out." I hug her closer when she nods against my chest and shivers slightly. "Cold?"

She shrugs and shivers again. "A little. I'll get the blanket I was using." She starts to get up, but I pull her back to me.

"I'm not ready to let you up yet," I manage to choke out over the lump forming in my throat. "I don't know what happened to you there, but it's my fault it happened. I don't want you away from me."

She simply nods and moves around just enough to slide under the blanket I'm lying on top of. But she does manage to get closer and snake her arm around my waist. I'm not ecstatic about the fabric between us, but the fact that she's put her arm around me shows that she's opening up to me a little.

"How's the pain?"

I chuckle. "The closer you are to me, the more I forget about it."

She ducks her head. "Be serious."

"I am. With my mind on you, I don't think about what my body is doing to heal itself. I don't think about the pain. I focus on you and the answers you're asking for."

"What changed your mind?" she asks me after another moment of silence.

"You mean, about you and this mate thing?" I smile when I feel her nod. "You. Your words. My feelings for you. Thinking of everything you've done for me, even though I've done everything in my power to push you away. The fact that you cleaned up my office when I wasn't in it, and then moved out of my room so I could have it back. I know that was hard for you because I felt the emotional turmoil you were going through the second it happened. You felt protected in that room surrounded by my scent, even though you wished it were me."

"That's true. Something else that made me feel crazy."

My heart breaks a little. "I never meant to make you feel like that, baby. I really didn't. I thought I was doing the right thing for me, my pack, but mostly for you."

"I understand." She takes a deep breath. "This is the hardest question. Leia. She was there, too. She's here with us now. She was saved because her mate is the Alpha's son. Apparently the same day he met her, he confronted the Alpha and told him she was off-limits. That he wanted nothing to do with any of his shit, and to stay the hell away from his mate. Then he claimed her through a bite right there in front of everyone. I think he is Maverick's Beta now. He helped us get out. He's here, too, now. Is Leia part of this pack?"

"No. Well, that's complicated. She was. Her parents were from this pack. Evan's brother, Stetson, was actually my father's best friend. He was the Beta at the time and died with all the others. He actually died trying to save my mom. He killed the Shifter attacking her before succumbing to his own wounds. Evan was one of the ones who survived. Aisha was here. She hid in our house because she was closest to it when the attack started. Imagine my surprise when I opened my closet and saw her curled up underneath the shelves my shoes are on with Leia tucked underneath her. Quietest baby I've heard."

I feel her smile against my chest. "Leia has always been one to roll with the punches. She's remarkably calm in the face of literally everything. And had this really strange innate sense of danger. She actually once grabbed my hand and pulled us both out of a restaurant when we were supposed to have a double date one weekend. She took one look at my date and said no, we're leaving. She rearranged with her date, saying she was sick, but she refused to let mine near me. I never understood before, but she wrinkled her nose. I think she might have thought he was a Shifter. I found out later on that he was arrested for killing someone he crashed into going ninety miles an hour. No one knew how he survived the crash. I guess now that I know what she is, it makes sense that she had that sense. As for him, I am starting to think he probably was a Shifter. It's the only thing that makes sense. Unless he was a Demon or Vampire or something."

I laugh. "I won't even try to tell you that those don't exist. I can't vouch that Vampires don't exist. I've never encountered one. But I never believed in Demons until I came up against one. Hardest fight I've ever been in."

She looks up at me with wide eyes. "You're joking!"

I shake my head. "Nope. I swear on your life. Which I value the fuck out of, by the way." I grin as I look down at her.

"You can't possibly expect me to believe Demons exist. I didn't see any books down there on Demons!" she squeaks.

I laugh. "It's there. I'll show you. Next question." I'm waiting for her to ask the question I know she wants to but isn't sure she should. "The one asking me why I started calling you baby."

"Well, that, and why am I lying in your arms right now? Why aren't you pushing me away?"

I smile and shift slightly. I groan at the twinge of pain in my side. I'm not sure my ribs are totally healed. But they're getting there. Kaia quickly sits up and watches me. I slide up the bed as much as I can and smile.

"What can I do?" she asks worriedly.

"Put a couple pillows behind my back. Help me sit up."

"Okay." She quickly obeys and helps me sit up so I'm comfortable.

Once I'm settled, I hold my arm back out. She settles back into my side where she belongs. "I don't want to fight this anymore. I've wasted an entire month of our lives together because of my very fucked up idea that Humans have no business being with a Shifter. Not that I had any problems with any of my pack having a Human mate. I didn't and don't have an issue with that. Not at all. I just didn't want them around because I believed that it was safer that way. That's why I kept pushing you away. I had no intention of ever letting you go completely. I planned to still be there to support you. Just not as anything more than a friend. The problem with that, though, is I'd never be able to do it. Seeing you with another guy would kill me. But not after I killed him for even looking in your direction."

She blushes and looks down. She's gone back to hugging herself instead of me. I can't say that doesn't sting a little bit, but I tighten my grip on her a little because I need to feel her close. I just need to feel her.

I tangle my fingers in her hair and tug slightly so she looks up at me. Her eyes are so pretty. Pretty enough to get lost in if I let myself. Letting myself drown in her is all I want to do. I wouldn't be able to stop myself from leaning into her lips even if I wanted to.

She closes her eyes. My gaze falls to her lips. Full and perfectly pink. They part just slightly. Invitingly. Like they're begging me to claim them. It's like she's a magnet, and I'm the force drawn to her.

I close my eyes just before my lips meet hers. Soft. Velvety. They move with mine like they were made for me to devour. And they fucking were. They're mine. She's mine. Now that I've admitted just how much she means to me, there's no way I'll be able to stay away from her.

My grip on her hair tightens. I deepen the kiss, sliding my tongue between her parted lips. When I touch mine to hers, it feels like my brain explodes. It can't handle all of the sensations that one motion brings.

My entire body feels like several tiny fireworks all going off at the same time. I can feel my dick thickening and straining against the gray sweats that I have no idea when I put on. The fabric may be loose, but it has nothing on the massive wood I'm sporting.

I suck on her tongue. When she moans, it's nearly my undoing. I pull back slowly because if I don't, I'm not going to be able to. She's smiling softly. Her cheeks are beautifully flushed. Her lips have that perfect just kissed look.

She doesn't need to say or do anything. I already know when it comes to her, I'm a goner.

CHAPTER TWENTY

~*~ KAIA ~*~

Not unlike the other kisses Kade has broken down and given me, my toes curl. My body erupts in tingles. Things happen between my thighs that make me blush. But unlike the others, this one feels different. There's nothing behind it but tenderness and a sweetness I questioned several times if he possessed. I began to think it was all an act.

"Am I dreaming again?" I whisper without opening my eyes.

A deep rumble of a chuckle escapes his throat as he brushes his lips over mine. "No. At least I don't think so." His hand slides slowly down my back to my waist and then over my hip. I sigh in pleasure.

And then he pinches me.

My eyes fly open, and I squeak. "Ow!"

His beautiful eyes twinkle with the laughter he's hiding behind his cocky smirk. "Not dreaming."

"Little do you know," I poke his chest gently and give him my most serious look. Inside, though, I'm cracking up. "I dream in color and feel everything."

His eyebrows raise. "Really? Isn't that a sign of a sociopath?"

My mouth drops. "It's the sign of a creative mind, you asshole."

He laughs and gives me a soft peck on my lips as he squeezes my hip. "A beautiful sociopath."

I laugh. "Kade!"

He grins but looks up as his door opens slowly. Zeke pokes his head in and smiles. He leans against the door and crosses his arms over his chest. "Nice to see you sitting up, Shortstack. Someone's feeling like a lazy Wolf."

"I'm shorter than you by a centimeter. If that. What do you want, Trigger?"

Zeke shrugs as he smirks and walks towards the bed. "A centimeter is a centimeter."

I can't help but giggle as Zeke sits down on the bed. "Why do you call him trigger?"

"Because his temper comes on fast." He grins at Zeke. "Damn, I missed you."

Zeke smiles and reaches over to gently squeeze Kade's leg. "How do you feel?"

"Like I got hit by a truck. But I consider that improvement. When I woke up, it was a train. I think the bones are healed. My ribs hurt a little, but I can move my arm and leg pretty well. Not too much pain."

Zeke nods and starts to remove the splints. "It was pretty touch and go there. When you passed out, I thought you died in my fucking arms."

"Nah. Though, I will admit. That pain was excruciating. Never felt anything like it."

I look down and pull my hand away when I realize I'm inadvertently tracing his abs. "Seeing you in that fight was the scariest moment of my life. And that includes being shot at."

Kade kisses the top of my head as Zeke finishes removing the splints. "I know, baby. All I cared about, though, was getting you and everyone else the fuck out of there." He squeezes me close.

I feel myself melting into him. It's impossible not to. He's quite right. Fighting the attraction and bond is exhausting. I've spent a month here getting to know not just him but everyone. I don't only feel like I belong here. I feel like I belong to everyone. The entire pack. But mostly, I feel like I belong to Kade. By his side.

I don't think I have the energy to go back and forth about it. It's just something I need to accept as much as he does. The issue is I don't know if he's going to change his mind when he's feeling better and throw my entire life into a tailspin if I do allow myself to feel everything for him that is in my heart.

"I came up here to check on you, but also because I wanted to talk about everything," Zeke says. "Not just about when Kaia was around, but everything I know about what the fuck they're doing up there. I'm sure you have questions."

"Mostly, Zeke, I'm just happy you're okay. But yeah. I need to know what happened to you, and what they're doing up there. I have a few answers from Maverick. First, though, how is everyone doing?" Kade hisses as he sits up a little more. I stay quiet but help him as much as I can. Truthfully, I want the same answers. I want to know why they took me and Jordan and the others. Why they took Zeke.

"Healing. Some of the girls are scared out of their minds. A few of them have no recollection of what happened, so when they started to come to and were with their families or with people they don't recognize, they freaked out. Jamie was both surprised and relieved as fuck when he saw Loki. They're reconnecting. The shit they drugged us with fucked him up more than me. At first, when Maverick started telling me not to eat or drink and that he'd get me something later, he could only get enough for me. It took a long time for him to be able to help the others."

Kade shakes his head. "We might have to revisit that because there's a lot of questions about what happened to all of you. It might be better to wait for that explanation for when we have our pack meeting after we're done talking here. I just called everyone in. I need to know everyone is okay. Who survived? Who was taken prisoner that I didn't know about?"

"Loki was one. Me. Amelia. She was one from our pack. Phoenix, Aryan and Fenn's daughter. Kent and Rowan. They were both our age. Leia was taken a couple of years ago. I didn't know it, but Dominick told me she was from this pack. Her parents were killed. Her cousin was taken, too. He was presumed dead. He was taken a couple of years before she was. His name is Asher. From our pack, that's all."

"And they're all doing okay? Acclimating?"

"For the most part, yeah. The ones from other packs are here for now, but their packs have been contacted. Most of them come from packs

197

that are our allies. A few of them are Human. Some have been reunited with their family. Others lost their family and have no one."

"Those that have no one will have us," I say. I rub my chest and sit up a little more. I lean back against the pillows and look down at my lap. I can feel them both looking at me and realize very quickly that I blurted that out. "I'm sorry. I was just thinking that I know how that feels. It's scary. And then I blurted it out like I have some kind of authority or something."

"You do," Kade says. I look up at him, surprised. "As my mate, it makes you the Luna of this pack."

"What… does… that mean…?" I tilt my head slightly.

Kade smiles. I love his smile. I also love the way his hand is lovingly caressing my arm. There's no other word to describe it but lovingly. "A Luna isn't exactly a leader, not in the sense that the Alpha is, or even the Beta, but the pack still looks to her for guidance. And she takes care of them. The Luna makes sure they are looked after and don't need anything. A pack should never need anything. They should already have it. If they need anything, they would go to the Luna. Then if she was unable to help, she would go to the Alpha." He pauses as if searching for the right words.

I lean on his shoulder and take a chance in touching him again. I hesitantly place my hand on his stomach and revel in the way his skin feels underneath mine. I watch as tiny goosebumps pepper his skin.

"I think I understand," I say as I trace patterns on his skin.

He nods as he continues. "Some pack members may also feel more comfortable going to the Luna for advice or to inform her of things they may have noticed that they don't feel comfortable going to the Alpha for. That's not to say that they fear the Alpha or feel like they can't approach him or her. The Luna just has a more of a… comforting presence. She is able to soothe even the most standoffish member of the pack. Does that make sense?"

"She's a calming force," I say, beginning to understand more and more of what my expected role in the pack is. It explains why the pack members reacted to me the way they did. Like I am an extension of them. A person they can trust.

"She is. She's kind of like… Well, here. A good example of the different tiers in a pack. It may help to explain it more." He trails off and looks to Zeke then back to me. "I know you have done a little research in the library. Did you come across Den Makers?"

"Sort of. They look after the kids in the pack," I answer with confidence but curiosity. I want to know everything. I love that he's finally telling me. I feel more and more like I belong.

"It is a role that I was and still am very passionate about. The Luna may be the heart of the pack, but the Den Makers are the pure soul of it. It's a role I had hoped to take when I was old enough. Now, I have a different role. But you can be certain that our pack will have our own Den Makers. In fact, we have two already. I'm sure in time, we will add two more to their ranks," Zeke explains.

"That's only part of their role. Den Makers look after the whole pack overall, but have a more active role with the cubs and kids in the pack than the adults. Well, not including the parents, obviously. They have some kind of sense about them that puts everyone at ease. I've never understood it, but they are very nurturing. They are the ones who do the school runs, take the kids out to the park. They cook the main meals for the whole pack. Not just the kids. They are respected by the entire pack and held in high esteem. While they are able to help each member of the pack with what they may need, their responsibilities to the children take priority. If the pack was attacked, they would save the children first. Then think of the adults in the pack and themselves. And they are never disrespected." He pauses as if what he is explaining is difficult.

Zeke interrupts seeing his struggle. "I remember before the attack. One of the newest members tried to target Loki for being a male Den Maker. He would mock and belittle him when no one was around. He got caught trying to force himself on him. Spitting slurs about how if he wants to take on the role of a bitch then he can be taken like one. Aisha heard Loki's shout and the slurs. She didn't hesitate. She ran straight to Evan's brother, Stetson. He happened to be coming to the house from the woods with my father, Jamie, and Fenn. She didn't need to say a word. The terror on her face and the shouts they could hear were enough. Jamie took off without a second's warning, slamming so hard through the door of the pack house that it broke in half, just to get to his mate."

"Was Aisha the Beta's wife? I mean, I know they left the pack later, but was Evan Beta?" I ask.

Zeke shakes his head. "No, but she was close to the family. Evan was dad's best friend, but he wasn't Beta."

Kade looks down at my hand and takes it in his. "Dad wouldn't let me in the pack house, but I overheard later that they took him somewhere to be punished. He was there for at least a week being interrogated before dad allowed Jamie to give out the final punishment. Jamie told me later that he tortured him slowly for hours, but that was only once he was able to be more than a few minutes away from his mate. I won't go into details, but let's just say if he had lived, he wouldn't have been able to procreate or use that appendage any longer."

I just blink at him before cringing. "Gross."

Kade chuckles a little and squeezes my hand. "Back to the Den Makers. That memory just popped in my head when I was saying that Den Makers are respected by everyone in the pack. If they're attacked like that, the whole pack will defend them, no matter who they are." He chuckles again and smiles. "Even the cubs have tried to defend their honor when they feel like they have been disrespected. Even if they are being teased."

"I think in that situation, the whole pack would defend anyone, no matter their status," Zeke says. "But you get the point."

"The Luna is sort of like a Den Maker in the respect that she's nurturing," Kade continues. "Except she is more there for the entire pack. She is able to give advice and guidance to the pack. She can be a confidant for those who feel like they can't lean on their mates or families for one reason or another. Usually out of a misguided fear made up in their own minds. I saw my mother reassure many members of the pack and send them back to their mates with bright smiles. Luna even has the ability to heal minor injuries to pack members. It's very limited because the healing effect is only meant to be used in dire circumstances, and from what I have heard, usually only between mates. That's why I was able to heal you. I've never tried to use it on anyone else. I haven't needed to."

"You can't heal others? I thought I read something about that."

"I can. But like I said. It's to an extent and only in particular instances. Taking advantage of the ability could result in me losing my Alpha status and everything that goes with it."

"Well, that seems unfair," I grumble.

Kade chuckles and lets his hand drop down to my hip. He squeezes lightly. "I don't make the rules, baby. The Moon Goddess giveth. The

Moon Goddess taketh away. We may not agree, but it's not our choice." He kisses my forehead. "The Luna is also instrumental in making sure that the Alpha is keeping himself healthy while he may be more focused on the others in the pack. He may forget to eat or sleep in times of trouble or stress. She makes sure that he does. An Alpha who leans on their Luna for strength in their times of weakness is an even stronger Alpha to their pack because they know they have others to lean on. They are not pillars of strength alone. The most powerful of Alphas all have a Luna at their side who gives them the strength to be that powerful Alpha."

I blush when he smiles and look down at my hand splayed across his stomach. "You're saying that both the Alpha and Luna draw strength from each other."

"Exactly," he says. I can feel his pride in my understanding.

Zeke smiles and chuckles a little. "The Alpha has this particular tone of voice he can use to enforce his rules or commands. Our dad had one that made people stop in their tracks. The Luna has one of her own. Mom had a mom voice, but also this other voice that struck fear into anyone. She didn't use it often."

"It isn't as effective on the rest of the pack as it is on her mate, but it has its own strength to it. Mom, though. Fuck. No one messed with her."

"The Luna's order, while not being an Alpha order, is almost always followed just as respectfully, and in a timely fashion. If you want to put it in a listed order, it would go Alpha, Luna, Beta, Gamma, Den Makers, then the rest of the pack. Usually, in a Wolf Pack, there would be Omegas, who would be the lowest of the pack. But we never have and never will have Omegas. My mother hated how they were treated in her pack. She always feared her first cubs in her previous pack would end up Omegas after she was kicked from the pack. She spent year after year trying to discover what happened to them."

"She didn't find out?" I ask sadly as I look up at him.

Kade hugs me a little closer. "A few years ago, I came across a scraggly looking man. Well, he came across me. I have a restaurant I own just a couple of miles away from here. He came in looking for a job, but he could barely stand up. I recognized his scent, but I thought I was fucking crazy. Then I heard my mother's howls. She made a very sudden appearance and nuzzled him as best as a Spirit Guide can. My dad materialized next to her to wrap around them all. He practically broke down sobbing when he saw her. I had no idea what the fuck was going on."

My eyes widen. "Oh my God."

"Are you saying what I think you are?" Zeke asks. I watch Kade, hanging on every word.

He nods. "It was the cub she could never find. Fenn was her other cub. He left after his brother claimed the Wolf he thought was his mate. Just after Fenn left, his brother was ousted from the Alpha position. Instead of killing him, he just treated him like a slave. An Omega. Mom's biggest regret has always been not taking them with her. But she really didn't know what to expect when she went to dad. Obviously, she hoped for the best in that he would accept her. She hoped they'd live happily ever after. But in the back of her mind, there was that little voice that made her very hesitant. She was terrified of what would happen to them."

I furrow my brows. "I thought I read that Fenn and his brother weren't Shifters."

"That's what we thought. It's what Fenn thought. But I asked about it. Fenn's brother, Koda, said he found out he could shift after mom was kicked from the pack. Fenn was still in the pack at that time, but they already had a huge rift between them because of the Wolf that Fenn thought was his mate. Koda felt the mate bond with her, but they didn't want to hurt him."

"Sounds like a soap opera." Zeke chuckles.

"A little. Anyway, Fenn left. He didn't want the fighting. Koda let him because neither did he. But not long after, Koda was overthrown, if you will. His mate, of course, was as well and fell to the position that he did. Eventually, he just got so beaten down. He gave up. But he didn't know anything other than the pack. A few years ago, though, he just said he couldn't do it anymore. He left the pack. His mate had been killed by a hunter. He didn't have anything left. He walked into the restaurant because he was hungry and needed to figure out how to live as a Human. He didn't even remember his mom. Had no recollection of her. All he had to remember her by was a scent. No other details. Just that his father told him she was dead."

"That's so heartbreaking," I say. I cuddle closer to Kade. "I hope I never forget my parents."

He rubs my hip and sends delicious tingles throughout my entire body. "You won't, baby," he whispers in my ear. I shiver. His grip on me tightens as he looks back at Zeke. "The meeting at the pack house is in an hour. I love you. I'm happy you're home. But get the fuck out so I can finish what you interrupted." He gives him a teasing grin and a wink.

My mouth drops. "Kade!" I hiss. I can feel my cheeks turning a furious shade of red.

Zeke laughs. "I'll grab Mav and get everyone settled." He throws me a wink over his shoulder as he walks to the door.

As soon as he closes it, Kade's mouth is on mine. I squeak in surprise as he pulls me on top of his body, but I melt into him. My body molds to his. My arms wrap around him, careful of his injuries. My eyes flutter closed. I let myself be consumed by him. When his tongue swipes across my lips, I let him in.

I can't resist him.

He's all I want.

He's all I need.

CHAPTER TWENTY ONE

~*~ KADE ~*~

I tug Kaia's hair and kiss down to her neck. I lick and suck lightly as I grind into her. I groan when she arches herself into me and rubs herself against my dick. I have to fight with all of the strength I have to keep myself from tearing off mine and her clothing and plunging my cock into her.

"Fuck, Kaia," I growl against her neck. I want to seal our bond right now. My Wolf is screaming at me to do it. Some unknown force is begging me to claim her in every way.

"I feel like I've waited forever for this," she whispers against my neck. "For you." She licks my neck and kisses it, digging her fingers into my shoulders while still being careful to not hurt me. Her need to make sure I'm okay makes me want her more. I press against her center harder. "I want you so much it scares me."

I groan and give in just a little. I nip her neck but don't allow myself to bite down like I want to. "You're killing me. You taste like fucking Heaven." I let one of my hands move down her side until I reach her breast. I'm shaking with the effort not to touch it. Squeeze it. Rip her fucking shirt off and bury my face between them.

Her fingertips spear my hair and tug. She arches and turns just enough that her breast falls into my hand. "Kade…"

"Fuck," I groan and look down at my hand. It's not that I've never touched anyone's tits before, but hers feel unlike anything I've ever felt. Like they were made for my hand. My mouth. Me. I close my eyes and squeeze just a little, flicking my thumb over her nipple. It pebbles immediately.

"Mmm…" She shivers underneath me. She keeps rubbing herself against me.

I can feel myself getting closer and closer to losing complete control. "Kaia," I whisper against her lips as I squeeze her nipple. "We need to slow down, baby. I'm close."

"Me, too." She wraps her legs around me. "Please, Kade. Don't stop. I feel like we need to do this. I have no idea why I feel this so intensely, but I need you. It's like this deep, pulsing ache that is calling out for you. And only you can satisfy it. Please, Kade."

I kiss her and groan into her mouth when she jerks herself against me. I know exactly how she feels because I feel the exact same thing. My need for her is so intense that I'm vibrating with it. I guess that's okay, though, because she's trembling and practically clawing at me. I slide my hand down and grip her jean-clad ass. I pull her up into me and grind my dick harder against her.

"You have no idea what you're doing to me, do you?" I don't give her a chance to respond before my tongue is dancing with hers again. "No idea at all." I suck on her tongue and nip her lower lip lightly before diving right back into the oasis that I can't seem to stay away from.

"Oh, Kade," she whispers as she starts bucking her hips into me.

"Holy fuck." The base of my spine starts to tingle. My stomach clenches. I need to pull back before I make a mess of my sweats, but I know she's close. Her thighs are trembling. Her breathing has quickened and become nothing short of heavy pants.

"Kade!" Dominick calls as he knocks on my door. Kaia freezes. Her eyes fly open. She grips me harder as she lets out a tiny squeak.

"Go away, Dom. I'm busy," I growl.

"The pack is getting restless."

205

"They can wait." I push myself against her core. She bites my shoulder and pushes into me. Her head falls back, and she moans quietly. She bucks into me as her eyes roll back.

"You say that, but those cubs aren't going to be kept back for long. They need to see their Alpha is okay. And little Isa is close to tears. You know how Prince hates when she cries. You remember what happened the last time you inadvertently made his littlest girl cry?"

I grin as I watch her come as she bucks against my dick. "I do remember. But I'll take the lashing he'll give me. This is far more important."

"Kade! Stop getting your dick wet and get down here! You're making my littlest girl cry! I will do far worse than just chili powder in your pants this time!" I hear Prince's thunderous steps on the stairs.

Kaia puts a hand over her mouth as she whimpers through her orgasm as quietly as she can and holds back laughter. "Chili powder?"

I laugh. "Prince is kind of an asshole. No one fucks with the kids. I was playing keep away with her, and she didn't like it very much after a few minutes. She started crying. I consoled her. It was all good. Prince didn't forgive me as easily. Fucker made it so I could barely piss without it burning like a motherfucker."

"Kade!" He slams a hand against my door. Kaia jumps and her mouth drops as she stares at the door in shock. "Five minutes. I'm not fucking close to kidding!"

"Okay! Okay! Both of you get the fuck out of my house!" I wink and grin at Kaia as I get off her so she knows it's all fun and games.

"Better make it a good orgasm, Kaia! I'm warning you, Kade! Five minutes, you asshole!" Prince bellows as he storms away from my door.

She squeaks. "What did he say? He did not just say that!"

"Oh, he did. I also don't want to know what he'll do to me this time." I crawl off my bed and reach a hand out for her. "And if I know him as well as I think I do, he sees you as pack now. You won't be excluded from his retribution."

"He does? Really?" She smiles when I nod, but it falls slightly as she takes my hand hesitantly and looks up at me. "How is the pain?"

"Well, we've gone from being hit by a train to being run over by a truck. Right now..." I pull her up and cup her cheek. I lean down and kiss

206

her softly. "I'd say it was more like fell off a horse and rolled down a hill. Took a few bumps and bruises, but I'm okay."

She eyes me suspiciously but nods. "I don't know how your body works, but I will learn." She eyes my shoulder and arm. "The bruises are gone. And your arm and leg? How do they feel? The bone was protruding through your skin." She looks down at my leg and back up at me. "You're standing on it."

I smile and nod. "Baby, I'm okay. I promise. I'm healing. Right on schedule for a Shifter." I tuck her hair behind her ear. "You're already acting like a Luna. You remind me a lot of my mom."

"Speaking of…" She looks down shyly. "Will I still see her? Now that I'm here with you?"

I chuckle. "The job of a Spirit Guide is never over, baby. She'll be around to guide you throughout your entire life. So will my father."

She nods. "Good." She looks at me through her lashes. I lick my lower lip because she's so fucking beautiful it hurts. "I should get changed."

I smile. "And I need to get rid of my problem." I raise an eyebrow and glance down as I turn and stride the closet where many of my clothes still are. I didn't move everything to my office.

"Well, now I feel bad I got release when you didn't."

I laugh. "Not the first time. Won't be the last." I glance back at her before disappearing in my closet. "Get changed. And hurry. Prince is getting impatient."

She nods and hurries to the dresser as I turn and find a pair of jeans. I quickly change and tuck my very painful erection away. I pull on a t-shirt and running shoes. I glance out the door and see Kaia is changed and pulling up her long, gorgeous hair into a messy bun. I'm sure she thinks she looks plain or something, but she's fucking sexy as hell. I'd love nothing more than to tug the hair tie out of her hair and wrap it around my hand as I ravish her, but Dominick is right. I need to talk to my pack. They need to see their Alpha is alive and kicking. I need to make sure they are all safe and healing.

I stand and leave my closet. I take Kaia's hand and link my fingers with hers. I lead her out of the bedroom and down the stairs. She follows, giving my hand a squeeze that makes me smile. We make our way to the pack house.

"Why was the need to be with you like that so intense?" she asks quietly.

I smile down at her. "Because of our bond."

"It seems totally insane to be going at each other like that."

"Well, you have to remember that we've been fighting this. At least I have. I was also closed off to you. I didn't want to feel the full effect. I didn't want you to either. Now that I'm not fighting it so fucking hard, it feels different. More intense. Stronger. But I will admit, something about our connection feels different than what I've seen from others. It feels like things are meant to move quickly for some reason. Almost like we're being pushed to seal our bond."

"Is that normal?"

"Honestly?" I open the door to the pack house. "No. I mean, there's always a pull. But from everything I've learned and have been told, this is different."

Prince glares at me when I open the door. He's standing with his arms crossed over his chest. "She's crying. My littlest girl is crying. Do you know what that does to me? I feel like she's using my heart as a teething ring." He steps aside and points to the back of the house where the pool is. I smell the grill, too. "Fix her."

I smile and squeeze his shoulder on the way by. "Promise. She's just upset because, out of all the kids, she's taken quite the attachment to me. Like her father, she has the characteristics of a future Den Maker. She probably felt something was wrong."

This brings a smile to Prince's face. "Man, I hope so. I'd love for her to take after me. I can already see so much of Don in Conrad."

"The Moon Goddess did good when she gifted the two of you with kids," I say as I walk out the sliding glass door to the backyard of the pack house.

Kaia tugs my hand. "Adoption?" she whispers.

"Nope. Biological. Don carried them," Prince answers for me.

Kaia looks up at him when he stands next to her. "I have so many questions."

He grins. "Magic."

"Kaze!"

I laugh as I kneel down when Isabelle runs up to me. "Hey, Isa. How's my favorite girl?" I wrap her in my arms and stand.

She snuggles herself into me and hugs me as hard as her three-year-old body can. "Kaze kay?"

I kiss her hand when she places it on my cheek and look her straight in her pretty gray eyes. "I'm okay, Isa. I promise."

She looks at me suspiciously and purses her lips. "You tot owie." Her lip quivers.

"I did. But I'm okay now." I hold her above my head and ignore the twinge of pain I feel in my ribs and shoulders. "See?" I turn her so she can inspect my whole body. "All better."

She squints her eyes and shakes her head as I bring her back down. She puts her hand on my shoulder. "Der." She frowns and leans forward. She gently places her cheek against my shoulder and sniffles. "Owie. Sil owie."

I raise an eyebrow. "How do you do that, kid?"

"Da," she says quietly. She looks at me. Her eyes are filled to the brim with tears. She points to a chair.

"Okay, sweet girl. I'll sit. But no crying." I kiss her nose gently. "Or you'll hurt my heart."

Her eyes widen. Her hands cup both cheeks, and she shakes her head. "No!" She points to the chair again with an adorable look I'm sure she thinks is stern and demanding. All it does is make me grin. "Bown!"

I look down at Kaia and wink. "She's just like her father, I swear. She thinks she can boss around the Alpha."

"Uh…" Kaia smiles. "It looks like she's got you wrapped around her adorable finger."

I laugh. "She does." I follow her orders and take a seat. I settle her on my lap knowing full well she won't want to leave my side. I look up at Kaia as I pull a chair closer to me. She sits next to me and takes the hand I offer her shyly. I squeeze it as Zeke sits down next to me.

"Ready?" he asks.

"As I'll ever be," I say. I turn my attention to the pack as they all start settling down. "First, how are you all doing? I know several of us were injured."

"We're okay, Alpha," Jamie says. He's happily wrapped around Loki.

"Fuck. Loki. Nice to see you back." My voice is raspy as I look around at my pack. I see familiar faces that I haven't seen in a very long time. It's not just Zeke who has been returned to the pack.

"Kade," Loki says with a nod. "You've grown up. I saw Zeke every day, but I still had a vision of a kid in my mind when it came to you. How are you? You were pretty banged up."

A couple of my pack members sniffle. I smile in reassurance. "I'm good. I am. I passed out from pain, but I am healing nicely. The splints kept me still. I think Kaia had a lot to do with the speed I recuperated. I've never healed a broken bone that quickly." I look down at her and smile.

She blushes but looks at me with an adoration I didn't know I needed from her. "All I did was make sure you were still breathing."

I chuckle. "I think you did a lot more than you realize. But I'll explain that later." I look back up at my pack. "I'm sure you all see a few new faces here. I know I do." My eyes meet those of someone who seems quite bewildered at what he's seeing around him. I give him a soft smile and nod before I move on. "Make them feel welcome. Help them get reacclimated to a world where they're free to do as they please. Humans and Shifters who have no pack to go home to are welcome to stay and find a home with us." I pause as a few who catch my drift begin to smile. "You are correct in your thoughts. I'm rescinding my no Human rule. I realize now just how wrong I was. Pack is pack. I'm sorry that I made anyone feel otherwise in my misguided ideology that keeping Humans out was the best way to protect them. I did nothing more than isolate them and other pack members who had Human mates."

"It's all forgiven, Kade. We have far more important things on our plate now," Devon says. He hugs his granddaughter.

It turns out that her kidnapping had everything to do with another pack. He was wrong to think it wasn't, but I don't blame him. She's Human. He wouldn't think another pack would kidnap Human girls. Or boys, considering I am seeing a lot of kids that don't belong to our pack who are male.

"The only other thing that I have before I turn this all over to Zeke to explain what the fuck happened to everyone is about Kaia. I told you all to not give her information regarding the pack or answer her questions. I said I was rejecting her as my mate. I'm also rescinding that order. Kaia is my mate and your not-so-far-in-the-future Luna. For me to treat her as anything else was wrong. To order you all to treat her as less than what she is was me being stupid. For that, I'm sorry. Now, let me let Zeke take over. Everything he's about to say is news to me, too." I glance at my brother as he stands.

"Hey, everyone. I don't know a lot of you. Some of you, I do, and I'm happy you all survived," he begins. "I want to begin by taking us back to when all of this shit started. The day of the battle that changed this pack."

"You aren't kidding," Jamie murmurs.

Zeke smiles. "There are a lot of questions on many of your minds. I know you all know about the battle, but you don't know who was behind it. It was Devil's Peak." He waits a moment while people gasp and look at each other. "That's right. The same Devil's Peak that my father battled when Kade and I were just cubs. It wasn't much of a fight. We know the Alpha at the time barely brought any of his pack with him when he attacked. He didn't even bother to shift, even though he could have. He underestimated Connor Deimos. Even then, he easily overpowered Devil's Peak."

Maverick stands next to Zeke. "That was in fact part of the plan all along."

Zeke grins. "Everyone. This is Maverick. Maverick is my mate. I'll fill you all in on him in just a minute."

Maverick smiles back at him before addressing my pack again. "What wasn't part of the plan for Devil's Peak was for my father to be named Alpha when their at-the-time Alpha was killed. The Alpha in charge now set the entire thing up. He knew that the Alpha didn't stand a chance against Connor Deimos, but he told him that Connor was weak. He didn't have a pack. He had no protection. He was just a human who had a Wolf for a mate. The Alpha's sister, actually. The Alpha wasn't aware that his parents and sister had been booted from the pack. Not until much later, and by then, the Alpha who had adopted him had completely brainwashed him. It wasn't that difficult to convince him to take out Connor before he became a threat."

"Only our family history shows us that wasn't true," Zeke continues. "Our dad already had strong alliances with other packs. He was already using his powers to grow our pack. When he was confronted by the Alpha, he already had allies on the way. The fight was over quickly and almost before it began. Dad thought that was it. He hadn't heard anything about them after that."

"Well," I cut in. "He did, but it was just grumblings. At least, according to what he wrote in his journal. He was always prepared for threats, but he wasn't prepared for Devil's Peak. He'd only just heard that there was a chance they had resurfaced. Up until then, he'd been keeping a close eye on them and didn't see any signs that they were growing in the slightest. He knew there was a chance they'd come after us for revenge."

"We didn't hear anything about them," Loki says.

Zeke nods. "I think that was intentional. Dad never wanted to worry anyone. I think he thought he was doing the right thing by keeping up on training. He never told me or Kade either." Zeke looks down at me. I shrug my shoulders to show I didn't know either. Zeke nods. "At least until Kade read the journal."

"Which wasn't until the night Kaia, Jordan, and our girls were taken," I put in. "But it wasn't until Kaia managed to contact me through our link and bond that I knew with certainty that it was Devil's Peak who not only took our girls, but also who attacked us all of those years ago. I didn't know Zeke or anyone else had survived that day."

"And the reason for that," Zeke jumps in. "Well, it's because I was being drugged. We all were. It was a way to not only weaken us but control us. It not only blocked our connection to our Alpha and our pack, but to our Wolf, too. While we were taking the drug, we were unable to Shift."

Maverick nods. "By the time I was able to figure out what was going on, the brainwashing had already been intense and done for years. Zeke and all of the others didn't believe their Alphas were alive. And neither did I, because after my father was killed, I was taken in by the Alpha who took his place. I was too young to have any idea what was happening. I had always thought I was the bastard son of the Alpha in control now. The son who came from an affair with a woman who wasn't his mate. I was looked down on by those in the pack who didn't know the truth. As for the Alpha who claimed to be my father. He treated his two sons like princes. Me? Little more than a slave." A dark and foreboding shadow crosses Maverick's face. Kaia shivers. I put an arm around her, and she cuddles closer to me.

Zeke lays a comforting hand on Maverick's arm. "Maverick wasn't privy to a lot of the information. Everything he did find out was by accident or by eavesdropping. Information he'd given me. Much that I didn't remember because of the drugs being injected into me or fed to me in the food. A lot of shit he found out wasn't until over the past couple of years."

"And that was only because of me," a deep voice says from near the back of the crowd.

Zeke smiles, but I narrow my eyes. Isabelle climbs off my lap, seemingly satisfied that I'm okay and jumps on her dad's lap. Keeping my eyes on this new person, I suddenly have the urge to protect Kaia. I pull her into my lap. She settles into me as I eye the guy suspiciously. She, however, doesn't seem at all nervous about him. I don't know why, but her reaction to him eases me just a little.

"That's Jace. You haven't met him," she whispers. "He's Leia's mate. He's the one who's been helping Maverick."

I nod and kiss her shoulder. "That makes me feel better. Thank you, baby." I hug her tighter and watch as Jace nudges Leia off his lap and stands.

He joins Zeke and Maverick. "I'm Jace. Maverick's Beta. I'm the son of the current Alpha of Devil's Peak. I've known for a while what was going on, but I wasn't in a position to help. At least not fully. I didn't have enough of the pack on my side. That changed when I started helping Maverick, but when I discovered my mate was among those who my father kidnapped, everything stopped. I refused to be a part of his shit. I claimed Leia right in front of him just after I found out who she was, but I also started doing all I could to thwart his plans. I fell out of his good graces fairly quickly, but by that time, most of the pack had fallen to the side of right anyway."

"The pack is, by far, smaller than the Deimos Pack," Maverick says. "But he has allies all over the world. It's not going to take him long to recover his losses. Meaning those who were killed during the rescue mission and those he lost to me, who are here right now with us."

"What was the plan? Why kidnap everyone?" Prince asks.

"Good question," Zeke says. "The answer is because of a legend. Legend says that a powerful Luna is just waiting to come into power. She will make her Alpha the most powerful Alpha in the world. No one will mess with them or their pack. Her power, according to the legend, is great enough to make even the most dangerous of Humans, Wolves, and Shifters feel at peace."

Jordan tilts her head. "I get why they kidnapped me and Kaia. I understand the Human boys and girls. I even get why they took you, Zeke. And why they took Loki and the other male Shifters. Well, at least some of them. The ones they made slaves. But why the other male and female Shifters they didn't intend to make slaves?"

Zeke looks down at her. "Because of the legend. No one knows who the Luna is or who will birth him or her."

Jordan shakes her head. "That's not the legend, Zeke. The legend is that the Luna will be a Human who is given a Wolf. But before she even gets her Wolf, she will not only have proven her skills as a peacemaker, but she will also have given up everything to prove herself to her pack and Alpha. It's said the Luna will have nothing to give but herself. And she does. She gives herself fully to her pack and Alpha. The legend is that the Luna is a female. She's not a Wolf. She's not a Shifter. She doesn't come from a line of Shifters. She is pure Human. And by pure, I mean that in all aspects of the word. She's never been in trouble. She's innocent in all ways including her virginity. And she's rare… There's only one Luna given this type of power in a lifetime. And only when war and chaos threaten our world and its secret." She looks down. "I always thought for us, it was our mother. She just had this way about her. But she didn't totally fulfill the legend. In my mind, though, she did."

Everyone falls silent. I watch eyes fall onto Kaia. My heart catches in my throat. My stomach clenches. Surely, what I'm thinking can't be true. If it were, there's no way that is something that would have been kept from me by my mother and father. That's not something they would have been able to hide from me. Would it?

I know Kaia is completely oblivious to the reason everyone is suddenly focused on her, but I can feel her sudden nerves. Her body has grown tense as she slowly raises her eyes to everyone else's.

I clear my throat. "And when she seals her bond with the Alpha?" I hug Kaia a little closer.

Jordan smiles softly. "Then that Alpha becomes the one all other packs look up to. He's looked at like a God. The most powerful Alpha in the world. But it's because he's the one who helps to keep our world from tearing itself apart with war and conflict. He can't do that without his Luna. She's the one who truly helps him keep that peace because she's the one who is the embodiment of that calming force. But it's not just any Alpha. It's obvious they don't know the whole legend. Or maybe they forgot over the generations. I don't know. The Luna, though, can't just mate any Alpha and fulfill the legend. The Alpha has to be her one true mate. The Alpha can't just know the legend and start mating all of these Humans or anything like that. The Luna has to be his one true love. His one true mate."

I just nod as I nudge Kaia up. I stand behind her when she looks up at me with the most adorable bewildered expression I have ever seen. I turn towards my pack. "I know this was a lot to take in. It's time for bonding and healing right now."

Dominick glances at me. *What are you thinking?*

I kiss the top of Kaia's head and take her hand. *That everything just got real fucking complicated extremely quickly. I want you and Jordan dealing with the Humans. This is their home if they want it. If not, help them get wherever they want to go. We have unlimited resources at our disposal.*

Zeke crosses his arms over his chest. *What are you going to do?*

I take a breath. *Explain to my girl what the fuck just happened and calm her down because she's scared out of her mind.*

Good idea, Zeke says. *If what Jordan just said is true, we need to keep Devil's Peak from ever learning that information.*

Fuck. You're telling me. I lead Kaia to the house as Zeke continues telling everyone what happened when they start hurling questions at him. Questions I'll get answers to later. My only concern right now is Kaia and easing her fears.

And probably some of my own…

CHAPTER TWENTY TWO

~*~ KAIA ~*~

I slowly take Kade's silky length in my mouth again and again. He tangles his fingers in my hair and moans. He thrusts up as I take him deeper and deeper until he's touching the back of my throat. I swallow with a grin.

He jerks. "Fuck… Fuck, baby."

"Mmm…" I hum around his dick and swallow again. I've learned quickly that he really likes when I do that.

"Oh…" His head falls back on the pillow.

He begins pulling my head back and pushing it down quicker. I've learned he enjoys the control, and I don't mind giving it to him. I'm still a little unsure what I'm doing, so I like when he guides me. This is how I know what he needs me from me.

Each time his dick touches the back of my throat, I swallow and hum around him. He bobs my head up and down faster and faster while he thrusts into my mouth. I love the feel of him. He's so hard. Thick. Long. I've never seen a cock up close and personal, but I have online when I was exploring how things looked. Kade Deimos is far above average. I can't take his full length in my mouth. I'm as far as I can go and it's only halfway.

When I come back up, I scrape my teeth lightly over the vein that runs his length. I've also learned he likes that. It makes him grow impossibly harder. Before long, his dick is even thicker and slightly reddened.

"Kaia, fuck!" He pushes my head down again. I smile as he comes hard. I swallow everything he gives me as his hips jerk into me, and his dick throbs with each spurt of his hot come. Once he's finished, I lick him clean. I can't get enough of his taste.

I giggle and lick the corner of my mouth as I crawl up Kade's long and strong body. He groans and slowly opens his eyes. His arms automatically wrap around my waist, and he pulls me down on top of him. I snuggle into him and kiss the side of his neck.

"What is it with you not letting me just leave it at you being satisfied?" he teases. "Always have to make me come, too."

I close my eyes and smile. "I never thought I'd say this to anyone." I hug him tighter. "But in the past week since you quit fighting the bond, I feel this craving. Like I just need you all the time. Any way that I can have you. I read that it's normal, but I honestly thought I was insane. Or like those sex-crazed teenagers everyone talks about."

He laughs. "So, you're telling me that you've decided it's okay to want me because a book told you it is?"

I swat him. "You know what I mean."

He laughs again. "Well, I'll be honest. I've never felt the mate bond until you. I asked both Zeke and Dom what it felt like for them. They both told me that they wanted to seal their bond right away. Zeke said he pretty much did. At least as soon as he remembered who Maverick was. Dom said he made himself wait a little bit out of respect for me and the fact that Jordan is my sister, but that only lasted a couple of days because Jordan started trying to climb him like a tree. So, in comparison, you and I are doing pretty damn good at controlling the urges."

He runs his fingers through my hair. The smile falls from my lips, though, and I look up at him with a sigh. "You know, in the Human world, this would be so fast. I mean, we go from fighting the attraction to not fighting it and talking about sealing a mate bond and not keeping our hands off each other. This would be crazy."

He tugs my hair a little when he reaches the end of my strands. "You aren't in the Human world. At least not in the sense you're talking about it."

I rest my head back on his shoulder and close my eyes again. "I've started to think of it like a whole other dimension completely separate from where I came from." I start tracing the tattoo on his bicep. The bicep I've committed to memory. Just like the words written in blood red on his skin. *Once you become fearless, life becomes limitless.* Words to live by. Words Kade lives by.

"You can't do that, baby. Our worlds aren't separate. They're the same. Human's just..." He trails off as he tries to find the right words. "They just don't want to know there are other things in the world other than them. Things that go bump in the night. It means they may not be the superior beings. They would either wage war to eradicate anything different from themselves, or they'd seek to enslave us all for their own gains. But without us in the shadows silently protecting them, Humans wouldn't be the superior beings they think they are."

"Maybe that's for the best."

He chuckles and tangles my hair around his hand. "Maybe. Maybe not. There's always a flip side to the coin. There are far more dangerous things out there than Shifters."

I shiver at the thought. "You mean like Demons."

"Demons are one. Are they worse than us? Better? Depends on the Demon and the goal. Most don't have a goal of world domination. Most just want what everyone wants. To love and to exist."

I fall silent for a few moments before I look up at him. "I'm still a little afraid of my role in all of this. Do you really think I'm the one they talk about in that legend?"

"I don't know, baby. I really don't. There's no way to be sure of that. Do signs point to it? Yes. I've seen how the pack reacts to you. I know that when I feel like I'm in a turmoil, your presence relaxes me before I even realize you're near. And my father did say something about a lot of big things happening. So did Fenn. You even told me yesterday that my mother seemed strangely at peace when she visited us."

I shrug slightly. "I also said it could be because she finally has the survivors of her pack back together. Aryan and Fenn have their daughter, at least. And their adopted son. They are all safe again."

"Also very true. So, the answer to your question is, I can't be sure. Instincts say yes. But I've been proven wrong before."

"Does something big happen when we…" I trail off and bite my lip.

Kade runs his thumb across my lip and cups my cheek. "There is nothing in this world that would make me force you to seal this bond, Kaia. If you were a Shifter or a Wolf, we'd have done it already, but that's because of the animalistic instinct to do it. I don't want to sleep with you just because of some mating ritual of Shifters. It's way more than that."

I take a breath and nod as I sit up slowly, straddling him. "Maybe I'm being naive right now, but…" I look down at his abs. His hands trail up my thighs to the hem of the t-shirt I'm wearing. I don't know what he did with my panties, but the feel of his satin encased and very long shaft settled against my naked ass makes me both wish for them and hope I never see them again.

"Talk to me, Kaia. I can feel the confusion flowing through you. And that's without the connection I have to you." His thumbs rub small circles over my thighs as he looks in my eyes.

The waves of conflicted emotions I feel start to calm. "I just… feel… this overwhelming sense that we need to seal our bond." I shrug and look back down, focusing on his stomach. He's perfect. "But I'm… just… I don't think I'm ready for everything."

He sits up slowly and lets his hands travel across my butt and up to my lower back. He kisses my chin, then me. "You're not ready for anything more sexual than what we're doing."

I nod. "It's that, but I feel like this overwhelming need to do everything I need to do to seal our bond. Like I'm being pulled to do it. Like if we don't do it now, we won't be able to. I feel like something bad is coming at us, and that we need to be one unit to get through it." Something changes in his expression, and he nods. I tilt my head. "I'm right, aren't I?"

He lets out the breath I didn't know he was holding and kisses me so lovingly that I shiver and melt against him. He hugs me tighter. "I think Devil's Peak is going to attack soon. And I don't think they'll be coming at us with anything less than all they have." He buries his face in my hair. "I've always been told that an Alpha is strongest when he has his Luna by his side. His pack is the strongest when he is the strongest. Without his

Luna, he's just not." He kisses my neck softly. "I have the same feeling. The feeling that we need to seal our bond as quickly as possible."

I let out a shuddering breath because his words prove all of my feelings right. "I talked to Belle last night when I woke up and couldn't go back to sleep," I whisper. I hug him tighter.

He chuckles. "I talked to my father just after you fell asleep last night. He said that I need to trust my instincts."

I smile. "That's what Belle said."

He lets his teeth scrape lightly over the sensitive flesh just under my ear. "We can partially seal our bond. I can give you the bite. We don't have to seal the physical part of it, but it's better if we do it at the same time. If we don't…" I feel him smile against my neck. "The cravings we have right now will intensify until we have no choice but to give in. We also won't receive all of the Moon Goddesses' blessings until we have completed the full bond. I don't know what exactly we would be blessed with when we claim each other through the bite. It's different with every pair. I just know we won't have it all until we do."

I take a deep breath and snuggle closer. "Maybe that would be better for me. Like… ease me into it?"

"I understand now. You're afraid of what's going to happen to you when I bite you." He pulls back just enough to look at me. "You're apprehensive that if I bite while we're making love, and that's what it will be, making love, you're scared that all of these crazy things will happen. Like you'll turn into a Wolf or something."

I blink at him for a moment before biting the inside of my cheek. "Kind of. Yes."

He grins. "Baby." He squeezes me. "Nothing that crazy is going to happen. I'll get faster. You'll be able to feel me and sense where I am. Things I can do with you already. Sense me. Know when I'm near. Feel if something happens to me, good or bad. And my ability to do that with you will only get sharper. Better. It's not going to be like you see in the movies. When I bite you, you're not going to turn into a rabid beast. I can tell you that it will hurt, but it will quickly fade into a state of euphoria. Trust me."

I sigh a little in relief. "I do."

"How about this? We take it one step at a time. We both feel like we need to seal the bond. Let's do that first. Okay?"

I nod and take a deep breath. "Okay." I watch him carefully.

I talked to Leia and Jordan about how they felt when they were claimed through the bite of their mates, but I don't know if it would be the same for me. They are both Shifters. I'm not. I don't know how it works for me.

Kade drops his head to my throat and kisses it softly. He sucks lightly before kissing to the side of my neck. He moves one hand up my shirt and rests it on the middle of my back. The other, he moves to the back of my neck. He rubs it lightly and sucks softly on the side of my neck. He licks and kisses it, then kisses up to my jaw until he reaches my lips.

When his tongue swipes across my lips, I close my eyes and fall into him. His kiss. Kade's hands move down to my hips again, and he flips us so I'm on my back on the bed underneath him. I tremble in both excitement and a little apprehension.

Kade's lips never leave mine. His hard length against my thigh makes my entire body erupt in goosebumps. His body is so warm. I instantly regret the t-shirt I'm still wearing. I would tug it off and let my body take control, but I'm pretty sure if I did that, I'd end up doing everything I'm not certain I'm ready to experience.

One step at a time.

He kisses down the side of my jaw to the other side of my neck. "I'm going to bite." He licks my neck. "Right here. In this exact spot." He kisses it. "And you're going to do the same," he rumbles.

My eyes widen. "What?" I push his chest. "I... can't do that, Kade!"

He smiles encouragingly. "You can, baby." He points to a place on the side of his neck. "Here. Hard. You need to draw blood."

My mouth drops. My heart quickens. Tears sting my eyes at the thought of hurting him. I shake my head suddenly feeling like the world's biggest failure. "Kade... I can't... I'm not..." I blink at him in horror. I flail a little as I try to get up.

I'm dizzy.

I can't breathe.

"Kaia..." His beautiful voice cuts through the panic and somehow eases my fear. Like a giant wave of water dousing huge, out of control flames. He grips my wrists and pins my hands above my head. "Breathe, baby." His lips meet mine in a heated kiss that has me melting into him. I feel his massive length twitch against me.

I squirm underneath him. My entire body aches for him. Everything I thought I wanted changes in the blink of an eye. I can't think of anything but how good he'd feel inside me. The aches. The tingles. The shivers his tongue elicits when it swipes over my skin. The sensations are too much.

"Kade," I moan. I arch into him, trying to get closer.

Needing.

Needing to be closer.

My lips hungrily kiss his shoulder. His jaw. His neck. Anything I can reach, but it still isn't enough. I don't understand how it's always like this with him. How do I surpass just wanting him and catapult into needing him more than air in seconds?

He runs his fingers through my hair and tugs lightly. My head falls to the side, baring my neck even more. He gently scrapes his teeth along the soft flesh as he kisses. I follow each of his movements, but I'm not sure it's even a conscious effort. My mind feels like mush, and all I can think of is him.

His tongue flicks across my skin, and he nips. I jerk into him and close my eyes, relishing in the feeling of what he's doing to me. I sweep my tongue across his skin and nip. He shivers and rumbles against my neck. It feels possessive. Like with just that one sound from deep within his throat, he's telling me I belong to him.

Only him.

He sucks the sensitive flesh into his mouth. Hard. Taking my cues from him, I do the same with a soft moan I'm sure doesn't sound possessive at all. But it doesn't matter because the sound that comes from my mouth makes his body jerk against mine. I feel his teeth sink into my skin, but before I have a second to scream at the agony, it fades.

Mine, he growls, but I don't know if it's out loud or in my head. Maybe he didn't say anything at all.

I feel his teeth attached to my neck, but my body falls limp. A warm, soothing feeling rolls through me like a hot breeze on a Summer day. Euphoria. Suddenly, I feel like I'm falling through the softest clouds and landing on a bed of down feathers in the sky.

They embrace me.

Wrap around me.

Envelope me in a protective cocoon of warmth and comfort.

What feels like hours later, but still far too soon, I open my eyes. I'm breathing hard and sweating, though I'm unsure why or what happened to cause it. I'm trembling, but Kade's touch calms me. I don't know how he does it.

He hugs me close to him. Tight. "How's my girl?" he whispers against my neck.

I don't know how I got onto my side and snuggled so closely against his warm and hard body. I look up at him slowly. My body feels like it's going through aftershocks. Like I've just been struck by lightning, and the current is still jerking through me.

And then I see it.

I whimper when I touch his neck.

Blood.

"Kade," I whisper. I don't even remember biting him.

He smiles and rests his forehead against mine as he shakes his head slowly. "Don't," he whispers back. "You were following instincts." He gently presses his thumb against my lower lip and slides it gently across it. "Does your neck hurt?"

"No, but -" My eyes zero back onto the mark on his neck as he silences me.

"Shh…" He kisses me softly. "If yours doesn't hurt, is there a reason mine should?" He smiles against my lips.

I sigh quietly and meet his eyes. "I didn't hurt you?"

He rumbles a low chuckle. "The only way you could possibly hurt me, baby, is by leaving me. I wouldn't survive it."

I kiss his chest softly and snuggle as close to him as I can. "Did we do it?" I ask, suddenly feeling like I can no longer keep my eyes open. I blink several times.

"Yes," Kade mumbles. He pulls me closer.

I tuck my head under his chin. "Why do I feel so tired…?" My eyelids fall closed.

"Because as our bond and abilities strengthen, it depletes our bodies of energy," he whispers.

"Mmm…"

Kade whispers something else, but I don't hear it. The sleep world pulls me in and envelopes me. In Kade's arms, I fall into a peaceful state of bliss.

CHAPTER TWENTY THREE

~*~ KADE ~*~

"There isn't a single solitary thing in this entire universe that's going to stop me from killing you," I growl to the man trapped in the cells below the pack house. "The only thing you need to decide is if your death is going to be quick and relatively painless, or if you want me to allow Aiden and Jamie, or maybe Koda, the most sadistic fuckers I've ever met, have their fun with you." I grip the bars and lean forward, resting my head on my arm with a dangerous grin. "What's your choice?"

"Go to hell," my prisoner growls.

I chuckle. "Little Tristan. I admire your loyalty to your pack. But I'm done playing fucking games with you."

"I'm not saying a goddamn word," Tristan says. He attempts a growl, but judging from his weakness, I can't imagine it will ever sound like more than the whine that just came out of his mouth.

I can't help but laugh. "Fuck it. We'll bypass Aiden and Jamie. How about I just hand you off to Koda?" I grin. "I bet you he'd love to fuck you up. Get a little revenge for what you've done to this family." I wink and laugh more at the fear I smell wafting off him.

At the bottom of the stairs leading to my nice little dungeon of terror is a man I've watched morph right in front of my eyes. He's wearing jeans and a long-sleeve, black, Under Armor shirt that clings to the muscles he's more than earned. The brother I never thought I'd ever meet. His light-brown hair is just starting to show signs of a dark gray.

His arms are folded over his chest. One leg is propped on the wall behind him. "I can grab Aiden," he rumbles quietly. "He might enjoy the game. Get a little revenge."

"I think Aiden and Jamie have enjoyed him enough. Your turn."

"What do you want to know?"

"He knows his father's plans. Knows his next move. He knows his end goal. I have an idea. I have what Jace has told me. Maverick and Zeke have given me a lot. But there's just something that doesn't make sense. Some piece of the puzzle is missing. He's got a whole trafficking thing going on. I want to know why he doesn't just keep those he kidnaps. And I want to know why he was so adamant on selling Jordan and Kaia."

"Especially with Jordan pregnant," Koda says.

I nod. "He would have heard the heartbeat. Dominick heard it as soon as he had her back in his arms."

Koda pushes off the wall. "I'll take care of it."

"Thank you." I jog up the stairs as he casually strolls to the cell housing Tristan.

Koda might just be darker than any of the men I have ever used as an enforcer in my pack. I'm quite thankful that he found us, but even more grateful that fucker chose the right side. I'd hate coming up against him in any battle. He gives no shits, but he's protective as hell of those he cares about. Namely, the people in this pack.

On the way to my office, I glance at the training going on. After watching a few moments, I decide the inclusion of our allies with my pack's training regime is a good and very smart decision. Everyone is working together very well.

A damn good thing because I don't want to wait much longer to go after Devil's Peak. I want to end them as quickly as possible. They've been allowed to breathe the same air as the rest of the good people in this world for far too long. Now that I know who the fuck they are, their days are numbered.

I continue to my house where Dominick should have gathered all of the Alphas and Betas in the large meeting room. I'm hoping my chef prepared something incredible and large because I'm starving.

The reason why makes me smile.

Kaia.

Sealing my bond with her last night exhausted us both, but when we recovered from it, we were both starving. I'll take the hunger pains over not feeling this close to her any second of the day, though. My father was right. Feeling the mate bond is the most incredible feeling in the world. It's like a piece of me that was missing has finally been filled.

As soon as I walk in my house, I can smell delectable foods. I groan when my stomach growls. "Fuck." I detour to the kitchen on my way to the meeting room, but stop dead in my tracks.

A slow grin tugs at the corners of my mouth. I lean against the door frame and cross my arms over my chest. Kaia is wearing one of my t-shirts. She's so much smaller than me that it looks almost like a dress on her. It hits her mid-thigh.

I let my eyes wander down her very shapely legs and back up to her hips. She's dancing to music that must be in her head because there isn't any playing from the stereo in the house. I don't see headphones.

I stay quiet and watch her. She hasn't had time to learn how to use her senses. If she had, she'd know the second I opened the door. I'm secretly thankful, though, because she's shy as hell. If she knew I was standing here, she probably wouldn't be doing the seductive little dance I'm enjoying the fuck out of right now.

I raise an eyebrow when she stops mid-sway with a spoon halfway to her lips. She tilts her head and sniffs the air. I bite my lip to keep silent as I watch her. If she were a Shifter, she'd be able to not only sense me but sense my arousal, as well. Not that she won't see it as soon as she turns around, but I'm curious if her developing Luna powers will eventually give her that strong sense of smell I have.

After a few moments, she goes back to dancing. My throat goes dry, but I force myself to push off the wall and move towards her. I slip my arms around her as soon as I reach her and lean down to kiss her neck.

"You need to trust your instincts," I rumble low and deep against her neck.

"Kade!" She jumps and lets out an adorable squeak.

I smile against her neck and hug her closer. "Did you think you sensed me, then decide that's not possible?"

She melts into me with a shy nod. "I thought it was just that this is your house. I smell your scent all over it."

I chuckle and slide my hand down her hip to her thigh and across to that sexy little sweet oasis that only I'll ever get to touch. I slide her panties aside. Her head falls back against me. Her eyes close. She grabs my wrist when I push my middle finger deep into her hot, wet center.

I kiss her cheek as I thrust slowly and smile when she almost immediately clenches around me. "So needy, little girl," I tease as I slowly pull out.

She whimpers and whines. Her eyes open, and she pouts. "So not fair."

I laugh and pull her back against me. "Feel that?" I grind my hard cock against her ass. "I have a meeting right now that I should be in. I'm going to have to walk in there with a rock hard dick and face razzing from all of them. How am I supposed to be taken seriously when my cock is jutting out like this?"

She giggles and pushes back against me, making me groan. "Too bad you don't have time for me to take care of that."

I pull away before I can't anymore. "Brat." I swat her ass. She giggles. I look over my shoulder as I leave the kitchen and make a show of adjusting myself and sucking her off my finger. She blushes a furious shade of red as I walk to the meeting room.

Everyone is seated already and waiting for me. Lunch is spread across the table. A variety of meats, cheeses, fruits, vegetables, breads, crackers, and condiments. I know instantly this was all Kaia. My cook would have put out the meat and cheese with bread and let us have it. Ever since Kaia entered my world, food for all of us has become far more balanced.

I sit down after gesturing to everyone to dig in. The respect we all have for each other and who is leader on each of our territories is something I'm sure other packs don't have. It's all about power and control. With me and my allies, it has never been that. It has been and always will be about mutual respect for one another.

Before I have a chance to open my mouth, Koda walks in, wiping his hands. "Sorry to interrupt. Just wanted to pop in and let you know what I found out."

Dominick laughs and grins wickedly. "Is anything left of him?"

Koda's grin is far darker. "I thought he'd like to join his pals. I had a couple guys bring them all up to a bear's den a little way up the mountain."

"In case I haven't told you lately, I'm glad you're with us," Dominick says.

I nod and chuckle with a shake of my head. "Go for it. We're just starting."

"I'd be on the lookout for a surprise attack. It's something they've been planning for a long time. Asshole didn't hold back when I started breaking bones one by one. But I think it was when I put the glove on and started prodding him with molten silver that he really decided it wasn't in his best interest to hold out. He told me lots of fun shit."

I laugh. "You're a sick son-of-a-bitch."

He grins and shrugs. "Fucked with my mom. Or at least came from the same family."

That statement sobers me a little. "What else?"

"Well, you asked about what he wanted with Kaia and Jordan. Kaia was specifically targeted because of what her parents saw. They thought they killed her. They weren't expecting her to survive the beating she took."

I raise an eyebrow. "A nice missing piece to our fucked up puzzle. What did they see?"

Koda props a foot against the wall when he leans back. "They saw the Sheriff shift. But not just shift. The three others he was with also shifted. Remember that City Councilor that went missing?"

I nod. "Something about being involved in Human trafficking."

"Not just that. Evidence suggested he was the leader. Kaia's parents were out for a walk the night of the murder. They witnessed the entire thing."

Jace leans back in his chair and folds his arms over his chest. "I didn't think about it until just now, but the plan was to pin it all on him so my father could continue what he was doing. It just put the focus on someone else. After his last kidnapping rampage, the media covered all the missing girls, but they kept going back to the Councilor and saying that the police were investigating his contacts."

Koda nods. "They knew they had a witness that night, but didn't know who. Didn't see anyone, but they tracked the scent. He said they came up with a plan before they attacked Kaia's parents. They knew about her, but she wasn't originally a target. She didn't match the description for any of his clients in the market for a slave, Shifter or Human. It was Tristan, your little brother who made the decision to go after her. No witnesses. No one knew what she knew, if anything. Best to be safe."

"So, they came here for her and took the others just because they have a death wish?" I ask incredulously.

Koda shakes his head. "Nope. Jordan was taken because she was there. Their other target? The Police Chief's wife and kids."

This draws a few inhales from the others. "Okay. Why?" I lean forward and rest my arms on the table.

"That's a two part answer. First. the Chief knows too much about Shifters," Koda says. "Looks like you made the right decision in sending them on a nice, long vacation. Hopefully, they're enjoying the Icelandic volcanoes. I hear they're gorgeous this time of year. Second, and this turns even my stomach, it turns out that our little Tristan has a thing for younger girls. He saw her one day and went to his father demanding he have her. Apparently he loves the way they beg and scream for him." His lip curls in disgust as he tells us. "I'm sure the bears will enjoy him. If they could speak to us, they might ask why the fuck his dick was shoved down his throat."

I wince at the thought. "As painful as that sounds, I'm all for it."

"Told you he was a sick fuck," Maverick mutters. "But not even I knew that shit. I thought I'd figured most of it out."

Jace shudders with a grimace. "You're telling me. I grew up with the douche and didn't realize how depraved he really was."

Dominick shivers. "Good riddance."

Colton Pearce, Alpha of the Pearce Pack from Australia, chuckles. "I don't think even my enforcer has ripped a dick off anyone and made him eat it."

Braden Levin, Alpha of the Leviathan Pack out of London, the largest pack in the United Kingdom, laughs. "He didn't say he made him eat it, exactly." Braden is one of those other people I'm glad is on my side.

I'd never want to battle this son-of-bitch. He could probably rival Koda in just how far he'll go. Not a bad guy at all. Just not someone I'd ever want to fuck with.

Koda smiles. "True. Just choked him with it. His balls on the other hand..."

I laugh. "Anything else, Koda?"

"Nope. I got the information you wanted, but when he told me that, I lost control. He wasn't useful anymore anyway."

I nod. "I called us all in here to touch base. I was going to go over the plans for our attack on Devil's Peak, but I think we all know our roles. Instead, given that new information about Devil's Peak planning an attack, I'd say I want more guards around the territory, but I learned very well when my father did that. I don't want our forces spread out over miles. I want everyone close."

Maverick furrows his brows. "Wouldn't you want guards on the territory's perimeter to warn us he's coming?"

I shake my head. "Nope. That's what he expects. But I didn't get where I am by doing what's expected. I don't want our pack spread out. That's part of how we got in trouble before. By the time the pack guarding the outer perimeter got to us, everyone here was overwhelmed. Then, Devil's Peak ran. It spread us out more. We're not doing that this time."

Very good, son. Those are the lessons I want you to learn from my failure. Learning is what makes a good Alpha, my father says from the corner of the room he's standing in. I watch Zeke look up at him and grin before looking at me with a nod.

"I'll post my guys around the compound," Braden says as he leans forward.

"I'll send the few guys I have here with them," Maverick says.

"We have more within Devil's Peak who are still there right now," Jace says. "When my father shows up, those that are on our side will join us. It will drop his numbers by half, but he'll still have many. He has a lot of allies, too."

"Many follow me," Maverick says. "But we'll have our work cut out for us."

"I want some within the compound, as well," I say. I finally grab some of the food after seeing everyone else has had their fill.

While I eat, the other Alpha's in the room discuss where they'd like to position their warriors and guards. When it's all said and done, I feel confident that my pack will not only be protected from any kind of an unexpected attack, but that my guards and warriors will also have all the backup they need.

Even if it doesn't happen, and our plan to attack Devil's Peak in their territory comes to fruition, there will be enough of an army left here to guard everyone. It gives me a lot more confidence in leaving my pack and taking the fight to Devil's Peak. No Alpha wants a fight on his or her own territory. I certainly fucking don't.

After I excuse everyone from the meeting, I expect to be left alone, but Zeke hangs back. I look at him as the staff starts coming in to clear the food and drinks from the table. When he doesn't say anything out loud, I start to stand, figuring he wants to talk alone, but he doesn't stand. I raise an eyebrow.

Zeke crosses his arms over his chest and leans back. *I don't want to sound like an asshole, but this fight isn't going to wait.*

What are you getting at? It's a question I don't really need to ask. I already know.

We can't wait for her to be ready, Kade. I know how that sounds, but in order for our pack to be at its strongest, our Alpha needs to be. And you know you're not. Not without a complete seal of your bond with Kaia.

I sigh. *She's a virgin, Zeke. Things are... complicated. She's not ready.*

He shrugs. *Speaking as your brother, I get it. But speaking as someone who knows this fight is going to be hard, you need to be at your best.*

All fights are hard.

Zeke nods as he stands. *True. But this one... it's coming fast, Kade. And it will be the most dangerous fight of all of our lives. I've faced them when they weren't at their best. Imagine how they'll be now when they are.* Zeke says nothing more. He turns and leaves the room, allowing me to think about his words; allowing them to sink in.

The truth is, it's not something I haven't already thought about. I told her we'd take things slowly. One step at a time. I've held true to my world, though I have no idea how. I crave her. The need to claim her in all ways is so strong sometimes that I have no choice but to walk away. Or go for a drive to our Wolf Refuge. Sometimes, I think she's in the same boat as me. Then, I feel her fear as she pulls away again.

But Zeke is right. If we expect my pack to be at full strength, I need to be. Kaia needs to be. We both need to be. If we aren't, it's a weakness. We can't have weaknesses. Not at a time like this. Not when we're so close to avenging my family and those we lost so many years ago. The culmination of my entire life is this.

I stand slowly with a sigh and make my way through the house and up the stairs to our bedroom. The talk I need to have with Kaia is not one I'm looking forward to, but the girl has surprised me at every single turn. She's been open to so many different changes in her life and trusted both my pack and me to lead her through them.

Hopefully, she'll understand what needs to happen because, as seems to be the norm in our relationship, I feel like the world's biggest asshole. No man worth his salt wants to go to his girl and tell her that he needs to fuck her to complete a mate bond so the two of them and all of their pack is at full strength when they go to war.

I groan and open the door slowly. For the second time today, I stop dead in my tracks and just stare. Another norm in our relationship is that I never quite know what to expect from her. Even after blinking a few times and telling myself to wake up, I still don't quite believe what I'm seeing.

She watches me curiously and sets the books she's reading down. "Doing okay there, Alpha?" she asks quietly with a gorgeous, shy smile.

Her teasing makes me smile and gives me enough sense to at least close the door so others don't see her naked in the middle of my bed. Our bed. I take a deep breath before I turn back. I need to at least remember what I had to talk to her about. Not that easy, though. I can't even remember my own name right now.

My breath is heavy. My heart is definitely nowhere near steady. My entire body feels like it's on fire. My stomach is quivering. All of the blood in my body has rushed directly to my dick. I slowly turn back around.

The candles in the silver candelabras I have never used are lit and are the only light in the room. They flicker silently and bathe Kaia in soft light. She sits up a little more. One leg is bent just enough to give me a hint of what's between them. It's not that I haven't seen what's hidden, but something about this time feels far different.

Maybe it's because of the conversation I need to have with her. Or maybe it's because I don't think I need to have the talk with her at all. Truthfully, I don't know which of those options scares me the most, but I do know I'm terrified. A feeling I might allow myself to explore a little more if I could think of anything other than her.

She's perfect. Her eyes are sparkling. Her sun-kissed skin is glowing. Her scent is driving me crazy. That vanilla mixed with honeysuckle brings me to my knees, but when it's fused with the scent of her sweet arousal, it takes my breath away.

I swallow in an attempt to wet my dry throat, but I know there's only one thing that can quench my thirst right now.

Her.

"What are you doing?" I ask just barely above a raspy whisper.

She smiles softly. "I'm so in love with you." Her voice is so sweet, but it's taken on a little bit of an edge I can't quite place. "I've been the one fighting this…" She trails off and looks down. "This need. This… urgency." She plays with her fingers. "But not because I wasn't ready. I think I was still coming to terms with having my one true mate be someone who is part Wolf." She shakes her head. "And then I got to thinking…" She looks up at me. "I feel like I've known you my entire life. Like I just… know you. Like I've known you my whole life. Longer."

I force myself to stay still. If I don't, I'll ravish her. "And you think that makes you crazy."

She gives me that soft smile again. I don't think she realizes just how fucking sexy that look is. "I'm still pretty convinced I'm dreaming. But if I am…" She shrugs. "If I am, I don't want to wake up. Because that would mean you'd just be the Man in the Moon again. My parents would be alive, but I'd just be that girl that no one pays attention to anymore. Invisible." She bites her lip and looks down at her fingers again. "Not that I didn't play a hand in staying that way."

It's with those words that my feet carry me to her, not of my own accord. I was content basking in her beauty. Somehow, my shirt comes off on the way. By the time I get to the bed, my jeans and underwear are gone. My length is jutting straight out and at attention. Kaia hasn't looked up at me. Inwardly, I beg her to. I want to see all of her. From her adorable toes all the way up to those sexy bedroom eyes.

Mate! Mate! Mate! My wolf is leaping around in my head because he knows he's about to get what he's been pleading for ever since we caught her scent.

She looks up at me with wide eyes. She's never heard him before. When I blocked the bond, it also blocked my Wolf's access to our bond to speak with her. I've never even transformed in front of her. Though, I know she is curious about my Wolf. We're one in the same, but I'm not sure she quite understands how that works yet. I lean down and crawl slowly into the bed.

I kiss her and hold myself over her. "I came up here to talk to you about finishing our mate bond. I was going to tell you that until it's done, we're vulnerable. I was going to say how much of an asshole I feel like for pushing you into it before you were ready for it. I was berating myself the entire time."

She smiles and kisses my jaw as she cups my cheek. She shakes her head. "I understand why it needs to be done. And like I said. It wasn't that I wasn't ready. It was that I was scared. A little. I've spent the past hours since the mate bite exploring those feelings. I've even talked to Belle about it."

I groan and hide a grin in her neck. "Secretly, I'm happy as hell you have a good relationship with my mom. But talking to her about our sex life?" I nuzzle her neck and kiss it. "I need to draw the line."

She giggles when my scruff tickles her. "So, I shouldn't tell you that I also talked to Jordan and Zeke?"

"Fuck… Let me just die here of embarrassment." I smile wider and lick her neck where I kissed.

"Or that I got into details about Jordan's first time just so I'd know what to expect?"

I laugh. "If you keep talking about my sister's sex life, the hard cock against your leg is going to go down and never come back." I try to pout, but the stupid smile plastered to my face won't go away.

"Or how loudly Maverick roared when he claimed your brother?"

"Fuck. I don't know if I should be impressed with the way you're teasing me, spank you for the blatant disobedience…" I kiss across her throat and down her collarbone. "Or if I should tease you until you're a dripping mess underneath me." I lick and nip my way to her already pebbled nipples and suck each of them in turn into my mouth, lavishing them with my tongue.

She arches into me. "Oh, Kade…" She tangles her fingers in my hair. With the other hand, she lightly scrapes her nails across my shoulders.

I slide my hand underneath her hips and squeeze her ass. The animalistic instinct in me to claim my mate is trying very hard to take over, but I won't let it. I can't. I'd break her if I gave into how much I want her. Need to be inside her.

Continuing the sweet attention I'm giving her nipples, I slide two fingers into her pussy. I've only ever given her one, so when she arches into me with a quiet, shocked scream and almost immediately starts pulsing around my fingers, I keep them still.

I nip her nipple and tangle my fingers in the silky strands of her hair as I look up at her. "Ready?"

She nods shyly and blushes. I slowly start moving my fingers inside her and kiss down her stomach to the wet crux between her thighs that I'm slowly working my fingers in and out of. I lick her clit. She jerks into my tongue and fingers. She gets wetter and wetter the more I thrust and lick her. She must have been on edge, though, because she's as close to the brink as I am.

I gently pull out of her and kiss my way back up to her mouth. I give her a tender kiss and try to hide the fact that I'm trembling. My Wolf is screaming at me to take her. Make her fully mine. Claim what belongs to me. The effort to not just plunge into her is making me sweat, but I force myself to take my time. She deserves that.

I deepen the kiss and throw all of the passion I can behind it while I twine my tongue with hers. She holds me tightly against her body. I watch her get lost in a state of delirium that I only up a notch when I grab my dick and slide the tip through her wetness.

Slowly.

From her clit to her pussy and back again and again.

I position the head of my cock at her entrance when she starts trembling underneath me. I pull away from the kiss slowly and wait for her to open her eyes. When she does, I search them in an attempt to read if she is really and truly ready. She's seen my size. She knows I'm not average. I'm thick. Long. She's about to have nearly ten inches seated deep inside her. I need to know if she's prepared for that.

She doesn't break eye contact with me. Her pretty eyes look like they're on fire. Flecks of gold I'm not even sure I've ever noticed before sparkle and dance as she looks up at me with so much love and adoration that I feel like my heart might actually burst.

Feeling like I'm drowning in her and unable to stop myself, I slowly push myself into her. I feel her clench. She grips my shoulder and hisses. Her head falls back onto my arm, which I've snuggled behind her, and she squeezes her eyes shut.

I stop immediately and start to pull out but can't. She's squeezing me so fucking tightly that I couldn't move even if I tried. I drop my head to her chest and groan. "Fuck, Kaia. So tight, baby girl."

"Mmm," she whimpers. Her nails dig into my arms. She holds her breath.

I kiss her throat softly and move my hand down her body, rubbing soothingly. "Relax, baby. It's going to hurt more if you clench like that." I kiss up to her neck and keep still. My Wolf whines when he realizes she's hurting.

"Sorry," she whispers against my neck. Her grip loosens slightly.

"Don't be. You don't need to be. I promise it will feel better when you get used to my size." I continue the massage. She relaxes more and more. "Ready?" I whisper in her ear.

She nods. "I think so."

I kiss her jaw and leave a trail to her mouth. I push in a little deeper until she clenches like a vice around me again. But I don't stop the gentle massage or soft kisses. When she relaxes, I push deeper until, eventually, I'm as deep as she can take me.

I run a thumb over her lower lip before wrapping my arms around her. "Doing okay?" I lean down and lick the tear sneaking from her eye.

"Maybe just stay still?"

I chuckle. "I have a better idea. Do you trust me?"

She nods. "Always."

Staying still inside her, I shift so I'm leaning more of my weight on my arm. I keep my eyes on hers and let my hand slowly slide down her body. When I reach her clit, I lean down and kiss her neck while gently rubbing the sensitive bundle of nerves. Her breath comes out hitched as she moans.

I didn't think it was possible, but her pussy gets tighter. I'm about to come, and I haven't even moved. "Oh fuck, Kaia…," I whisper against her shoulder. Embarrassingly, I'm not going to last much longer. It might be a good thing, though, because I know she's not going to.

"Kade… Oh…" She arches into me. Her pussy gets wetter and starts pulsing.

I take a chance and start moving with slow, deep thrusts. I make sure I don't pull all the way out because I know if I do, it'll hurt her when I go back in. All I want is to give her as much pleasure as I possibly can.

Reading her and trusting my instincts to guide me, I allow her to set the pace. It doesn't take too long before she's holding me tighter and meeting my thrusts. She wraps her legs around me and pulls me into her. I fight it a little because I'm close to being sunk into her balls deep, but she doesn't allow me to hold back. Her legs tighten even more.

"Kaia, holy hell." My spine starts to tingle. My stomach tightens. My cock thickens, stretching her even more.

"Kade, yes!" Her thighs tremble. She arches into me one last time, taking my dick as far as it will go. Her pussy tightens more, squeezing my dick harder than I'd ever be able to do with my own hand.

I press down on her clit as I rub. "Come, Kaia. Come for me, baby."

"Kade! Yes!" She pulls me down, biting hard on her mate bite, and comes hard. "Mine! Mine! Mine!" She growls low into my skin. If I didn't know she was Human, I would have thought she was a Shifter with the rumbles she is releasing.

My mouth drops slightly, but fuck if those words don't make me love her more and come harder than I've ever come in my life. As our bodies jerk against each other, I hug her tighter and bite down on my own mate bite as I fill her pussy.

"Mine," I growl low and possessively. "All… fucking… mine…"

My Wolf howls. *Yes! Mine! Mate! Mine!*

Yours! Always and forever. Yours, my mate. Yours!

Stars explode in my head. Or maybe it's around us. Maybe the both of us have burst into our own light show. But her speaking to my Wolf as he claims her shoots me into a different universe. I feel numb, but in a very good way. Like I'm floating in space, and she's the only one who can bring me back to Earth.

When the aftershocks subside, I gently pull out of her and pull her as close to me as possible. Everything is as it should be. Calm. Peaceful. Our mate bond is completed. The Moon Goddess is shining her light and happiness down on us. Pride at how far we've come in a relatively short period of time. It's all as it should be.

But as Kaia falls asleep in my arms and my eyes get heavier, I can't help but feel apprehensive of what's on the horizon. It's too calm. Too peaceful. Too perfect. With Devil's Peak lurking, I know this isn't going to last.

As we both fall into a deep slumber while our powers and strengths fully come to us, I wrap tighter and more protectively around her. I know more danger than we've ever faced is right around the corner threatening everything my father and I have built.

But the fuck if I'm going to let it ruin this moment…

CHAPTER TWENTY FOUR

~*~ KAIA ~*~

I giggle and throw my head back as Kade kisses my neck and tickles me with his scruff after our shower. "Kade, what are you doing?" I wrap my arms over his shoulder.

His hands slide under the towel I have wrapped around me. I can feel his cocky smirk against my neck. "Nothing." He licks his mate bite and slides a finger deep into my pussy from behind.

I jerk into him hard and clench tight around him. My eyes roll back in my head. "Oh…" I'm almost instantly panting, and I know he can feel just how wet he makes me. I'd blush at how easily he does it, but I'm too busy dying in the ecstasy his finger brings. "Haven't you had enough?"

"Fuck no. I'll never have enough of you." He slowly pulls his finger out and grips my ass. Just as he's about to lift me onto the counter, though, I hear what I swear is a scream. Kade's head snaps towards the bathroom door. "What the hell?"

My eyes widen. "That was so faint. I thought I imagined it." I jump when I hear it again and grip his arm as I look up at him.

Something in Kade has changed. Gone is the playful man standing in front of me just moments ago. Suddenly, he's morphed into a dark version of himself. Scary. Something I'd fear if I didn't know his heart and soul.

His grip on me tightens. "Get dressed. Now. Hurry."

He lets me go so quickly, I nearly fall. I don't, though. I scramble after him because I know he knows something I don't. He tosses me clothes and quickly pulls on his own. I gasp at the immense pain I suddenly feel. Like my heart and mind are being squeezed between the hands of a giant and ripped in half. Instead of stopping in my tracks and screaming at the sharp stabs I feel, it spurs me to go faster.

Kade grabs my hand and pulls me after him as soon as I get my jeans buttoned. He leads me downstairs. Keeping up with his long stride is not the easiest of tasks, but I do it because something isn't right. The suspicions are confirmed when Dominick and Jordan appear at our sides. Dominick looks like he's going to kill someone. Jordan looks both terrified and sick.

"I didn't expect them to attack in the fucking morning," Dominick growls.

"The kids were just heading off to their first day of the new school year," Jordan whimpers.

"I know," Kade growls viciously as he opens the door. He turns to me. "We're running. I'm faster than you, so I'm carrying you. Jump on my back. Close your eyes. Don't fucking look at anything. I need my hands free while I get you to safety. Understand?"

I just nod and do what I'm told. When he kneels, I jump on his back. I wrap my legs around his waist and arms around his shoulders. I'm trembling, but I hold on tight. "Oh God," I whisper. "I hear screaming. I feel their pain." I whimper into his back and squeeze my eyes closed.

"Jordan, behind me. Dominick, behind her. We protect them at all costs," Kade says to Dominick.

"Got it, Alpha. We're ready," Dominick says.

"Move fast. Don't stop," Kade commands.

And just like that, I feel like I'm flying. The wind whips through my hair. I hold on tighter to Kade because I feel like if I don't, I'll simply fly off him. I follow his directions and bury my face in his back. I don't look at anything going on around me.

But I feel everything.

I hear it all.

When Kade punches someone, my body jerks, but that's not what's truly concerning to me.

It's the stabs to my heart. My abdomen.

It's the screams I not only hear around me, but also in my head. I'm not sure what's worse.

Kade stops. He's not even breathing heavy, and I don't know why that strikes me in this moment. Maybe because he's the only solid thing I can force my mind to grasp. He's the only thing grounding me. The only reason I'm not trying to figure out why I'm in so much pain. Why I feel like each and every single one of my new family members are being ripped away from me and slaughtered.

Kade grips my thighs and helps me down. "I need you to help me. Can you do that?"

I nod. "Anything. Just tell me what to do. I'll do it." And I will. I'll do anything for him and this pack.

"Good girl." He cups my face in his large hands. "I need you to stand right here. Usher the kids inside. Get them to the safe-room. That's the game room. Jordan will lead them."

I nod. "Okay."

"Prince will be shoving them through. He won't come in until he has the very last one, but if he commands you to do something, don't hesitate."

"Got it."

Kade kisses me long and hard. "I love you, Kaia."

My heart melts at the words, and I nearly cry. "I love you, Kade."

He gives me a strong smile, but I can see a hint of fear behind them just as they turn a piercing golden. My heart skips a beat as he turns. I slap a hand over my mouth when Dominick's turn a striking silver. Both leap into the battle raging outside, transforming before my very eyes into large, sleek, beautiful Wolves in mid hair.

Kade, the most gorgeous, large, jet-black Wolf I've ever seen, rips the throat out of someone before he even lands. Dominick, a beautiful gray Wolf with hints of black and brown, attacks someone else. He rips off his head.

I watch in both horror and fascination. Everything looks like it's going in slow motion. I don't know who is good and who is bad because everyone is fighting. Even though it seems to be going slow enough for me to see every single detail, blood splattering and heads being severed, it still seems to be moving at lightning speed.

"Kaia!" Prince's frantic voice pulls my eyes away from the fight, but I still feel every blow one of my pack members takes.

My family.

My eyes meet Prince's as I take a small, screaming child who is covered in blood from his arms. "Oh my Moon Goddess," I whisper.

"I have three more. Go. Take her to Jordan. Go, Kaia."

I nod and turn. I flee through the pack house to the game room just as Jordan is coming back out. She takes the child from my arms. I run back to the door just as Prince reaches it. He thrusts a small, whining cub at me and says nothing before turning back and running back into the chaos. I'm just turning to go back when Jace shoves Leia in the pack house.

"Go! They need you in there, baby. Help the kids. Please!" Jace pleads.

Leia looks after him. I can see she's torn. She wants to be with her mate, but she's also a Den Maker. She'll want to help the kids just as much, if not more, than standing by Jace. I suppose it makes sense. Leia has always had a way with kids. They flock to her, and she loves them all.

She turns back to me and takes the howling and terrified cub in her arms. She buries her face in his fur and hurries back to the safe-room. I turn my attention back to the fight, keeping my eyes out for Prince to come back. I close the door enough so I can still peek out, but can close it if I need to and run.

Jordan runs back out. "The kids and cubs are safe. Julian is with them. So is Leia. I need to go help. Don't go out there, Luna. I mean it." She gives me a warning look as she slips out the door.

The truth is, I don't think I would go out there anyway. I am not a Shifter. I would never be able to help them in this battle. I'd do nothing more than get in the way. Probably get someone killed. I don't want that. I already feel all of their pain and injuries like they are my own. It makes me want to curl into a ball and cry, but I refuse. I have a job to do, and I will do it.

Prince runs back carrying a woman who is bleeding and crying. I open the door enough for him to get through. He sets her on the couch and turns to me. "Stop the bleeding. It's on her leg. She's human."

My head snaps to the woman writhing in pain on the couch. I let instincts guide me as Prince runs out of the house again. I find a towel on the bar near the door and run to the woman on the couch. She's crying so hard, my heart clenches for her.

"Shh…," I whisper soothingly. "I'm here. I'm right here." I take the towel and find where her leg is pierced. It looks like a bite. Like someone tore open her flesh. Why the gushing blood doesn't make me throw up is a question I can't answer.

I think little of it as I wrap the towel around her wound and tie it to stop the blood flow. She screams. I want to scream with her, but I know that I can't. She needs me to be strong for her. "I bet your mate kicked this asshole's ass right back to the dank hole he crawled out of, huh?" I think as many warm and comforting thoughts as I can.

After a few moments, the woman stops screaming and whimpers instead. "H-he… k-killed… h-him…" Her eyes fall closed.

"Stay with me, darling." I take her hand.

She squeezes. "Your p-presence. It helps. I feel at p-peace."

I look down at her leg, fully expecting to see the towel soaked in blood. It's not. I blink when I see the bleeding has stopped completely. I look back up at the woman. She's breathing regularly and sleeping.

Prince comes in with someone else. A male. His arm is covered in blood. His shirtless chest is covered in bruises. Behind him, a wolf with bright amber colored eyes collapses near the door. Prince says nothing. He dumps the body of the man on the chair and runs back out. I rush to the Wolf.

"Oh no." I sniffle and quickly try and find something I can set the Wolf's leg with. It's definitely broken. I find two wooden spoons in the kitchen and more towels. I hurry back. "This is going to really hurt. I'm so sorry." I blink back my tears. I don't want to do this.

I close my eyes and think of an island. Peaceful. Quiet. When I open my eyes, I'm calm enough again to help the Wolf, but I still think nothing but happy things. If I think about anything else, I'll start crying. So, I keep my thoughts on that beach and set the Wolf's leg. Even when he whines and howls in pain, I keep my thoughts peaceful and calm.

Thank you, Luna.

I look down at the Wolf. "Did you just say something?"

I said thank you. I can hear his voice whispering to me in my head. *Your touch is peaceful. Healing.*

I feel his heart has slowed. He is much calmer. I'm not sure I would be after having someone snap my bone back into place. I'm sure I'd be screaming if someone tied a towel as tightly over my leg as I have his.

I'm not sure how many injured Humans, Wolves, and Shifters Prince brings in here, and how much time has passed, but I'm thankful for it because it's kept my mind clear. I'm focused on helping the pack instead of rushing out to see if Kade is okay. Everyone in here feels at peace. They are all still breathing as they heal.

Breathing.

That's all I care about. Just that they are still alive.

After patching up the last injury, with Leia's help after another Den Maker took over for her, I catch a glimpse of Belle near the door. She looks conflicted and scared. I'm sure what's happening out there is bringing up memories that she'd much rather forget for all of eternity.

Belle? I stand and walk to her. Leia continues keeping an eye on everyone.

Belle whines and paces in front of the door. It's still mostly closed, but open enough for me to look outside. *You must keep an eye out there, Kaia. It's important. You...* She looks outside. *You might be needed.*

I nod and do as she says, but I still take glances at the wounded bodies. She's right. There are still two children missing. Prince has been searching frantically for them, but he can't find them, hear them, or feel them. I can feel his frustration and fear slamming into me in waves. I can't say I'm not starting to feel nervous about their whereabouts myself, though. Thankfully, the enemy pack seems to be thinning out. Considering I don't have all that many wounded in here, I think we're winning the war.

But that thought very quickly vanishes away when I see more people coming out of the woods that surround this compound. Everything stops. Everyone's attention is suddenly on the new people entering the fight.

My heart starts hammering in my chest when I see who it is. "Oh, God," I whisper.

Out of the corner of my eye, I see Prince drop to his knees. "No!" he screams, his eyes focused entirely on the ones everyone else is looking at.

At first I think he's injured, but that's not what it is. I put a hand over my mouth to hold back the scream. "No!"

Belle is shaking near me. *He has our kids!*

The Alpha of Devil's Peak strolls slowly and cockily up to Kade. Kade shifts into his human form, as do all of the other Shifters who had been in their Wolf form. I watch in horror and disgust as the two packs seemingly split. Our pack gathers behind Kade as he stands. The Alpha and the Deputy of Devil's Peak stand side by side holding two kids who can't be any older than ten in front of them. It's a standoff. There is no other word.

"I think we've let this go on long enough, don't you, Deimos?" the Alpha says with a glare. He shifts the position of his arms on the little girl he's holding against him. His forearm goes around her neck, the other across her forehead. He turns her head slightly.

"No," I whimper as I hold my stomach when it clenches. He's going to snap her neck. I can feel it. I can feel her terror.

"You're the stupid fuck who brought this fight to us," Kade snarls. "Why don't you tell me? Have you lost enough of your pack yet? Or do we need to kill more of them?"

The Alpha howls out a laugh. His grip on the girl tightens. I can't see who it is, but I feel like it's Millie. I hear her crying. I feel her reaching out for help. The girl has been through so much in such a short period of time. She doesn't need this. None of us do, but especially not innocent children.

Stay still, little one, I say. I don't know if she can hear me, but I'll try. I'll do everything I can to keep her calm.

Luna! She's rather far away, but her pretty gray eyes meet mine. *I'm scared, Luna. I'm so scared.*

I hug myself tighter but refuse to allow her see or feel any of my fear. She needs me to be calm. *I know, sweet girl. Be strong. Stay still.*

I keep my eyes trained on her and will all of the calm, peaceful thoughts I can at her. I don't know if it helps, but it seems to work with the injured Humans, Wolves, and Shifters in here. Maybe it's one of those strengths Kade speaks of. Maybe this is my strength. My superpower.

I've never used the link to speak to any other pack members. It's possible I've had that ability all along, but I don't think so. I think it might be another strength I've gotten since my bond with Kade was sealed. I feel different today than I had even after the mate bite was completed. I feel stronger. Closer to Kade, for sure, but also closer to this pack. Bonded to them in a way I never imagined was possible. I don't feel invincible, but I feel more powerful.

The Alpha laughs. "You think for a second I feel any of them? Do you think their deaths weaken me?"

"It damn well should." Kade gives him a dangerous smile. "But that does prove the theory correct."

The Alpha's glare turns more vicious. "What theory? Does little Kade Deimos think he figured out the Big Bad Wolf's secret?"

Kade actually laughs. "I figured out a lot of shit over the years. Mostly in the past month or so." He grins, but no one should be fooled by that. It's dark. Just as vicious as the Alpha of Devil's Peak. "I know you orchestrated my father's death and the destruction of my pack. And when that shit didn't work, you laid in wait and came after us again when you thought you'd grown bigger, stronger, and larger than us."

The Alpha shrugs. "It worked, didn't it? I didn't count on you, though. That was my mistake."

"One of the many you've made over the years." Kade's hands are at his sides. If I wasn't paying so much attention to him, I never would have seen the small hand gesture he made. When Maverick comes out of the woods with Zeke, the Alpha looks a little thrown off.

He recovers quickly, though. "Funny. I was told you were dead," the Alpha growls as Maverick takes his place next to Kade. Zeke stands at his side.

"Too bad you ain't my Alpha," Maverick says with a shrug. "You would've been able to feel me even with me blocking my link with you."

The Alpha raises an eyebrow. "You think you're of any importance to me? You're nothing but an unwanted burden. We should have drowned you at birth."

His words hurt my heart, but it doesn't seem to affect Maverick in the slightest. Maverick simply stands there and stares him down. It seems the entire complex is shrouded in tense silence. No one moves.

Except one small being. The little boy the Deputy is holding tightly against him. Nathan, I think. He whimpers. I can feel his rising panic and see the reason behind it. The Deputy's grip is tightening around his neck. He moves Nathan's head so it's more to the side. I realize with horror that he's planning to snap it, as the Alpha plans to do with Millie.

No, Nathan. Don't. Don't struggle. You must be strong.

His terrified green eyes meet mine. *It hurts, Luna. He's going to break my head!*

No, Nathan. He's not. Kade won't let him. Trust your Alpha. You must be calm. Close your eyes, my little one. Close your eyes and imagine you're in your treehouse high above your house overlooking the compound.

I watch as he closes his eyes. I work hard to make sure he feels nothing but peace, but I feel my own energy starting to fade slightly. I won't allow that to bother me, though. I feel more than ever that I need to follow Belle's request and keep my eye on what's happening. I can see Connor and Fenn next to Kade. It makes me feel better knowing he has them guiding him. Protecting him.

"Is this all you have left?" the Alpha says to Kade. "It looks like your forces have dwindled. Getting my sons back won't be as hard as I thought."

Kade's chuckle is menacing. "You think the brat is still around?"

The Alpha's glare fades for only a moment before he school's his expression. "Of course he is. I'd feel if my own sons had been killed."

From behind the main house, Jace appears and walks with purpose towards Kade. "You sure about that?" he asks his father.

For the first time, the Alpha looks slightly afraid. His fear forces him to pull Millie closer to his body. "I'm done playing games, Deimos. Give me Tristan, or I will snap this girl's neck."

"Not a chance of either of those things happening," Kade growls.

"You know, it's too bad it's come to this," the Deputy snarls with a glare at Zeke. "You and I could have ruled the world right alongside the most powerful Alpha in existence."

Zeke growls. "I already have a mate."

The Deputy laughs. "I could have been your true mate. Pleasured you. Protected you. Now, you'll never know. You'll die right along with that weak piece of shit standing at your side."

247

It's Maverick's turn to growl. Only his is deeper and far more murderous. "You will never get your hands on my mate!"

"You will never get the chance to touch my brother ever again," Kade snarls. "You've shown us your forces. How strong your pack is. Let us show you how strong we truly are!" Kade's head falls back and he lets out a scream. Only it's the furthest thing from a scream I've ever heard. It's not even a howl. It's a roar. A loud roar that rattles the windows of this house.

More people I've never seen appear from all over the compound. They all stand behind Kade. Some stand to the sides. When everyone appears, the compound is filled. Those with Devil's Peak are almost surrounded. They could be, but I suspect Kade's allies expect more of Devil's Peak to be hidden.

"You have always called me weak. A waste of breath. A bastard." Maverick steps forward. "But that's not exactly true, is it?" Maverick pauses as he glares hard at the Alpha. Somehow, I see even more fear enter the Alpha's eyes. Confusion appears on more than one of the faces of the pack surrounding him. "I wonder how many know the truth about who I really am."

"What are you talking about?" the Alpha says, but it's more for his pack than a question for Maverick to answer.

Maverick lets his eyes drift over the pack before landing back on the Alpha. "My lineage is not what you think it is. I am not the bastard child of your Alpha and his mistress. In fact, my father was someone with a lot more integrity, more respect, and he was one hell of an Alpha before he was murdered." He smirks slightly.

I hear gasps and whispers come from a few of the pack as they glance between their Alpha and Maverick.

"That's right. Your so-called Alpha is not my father. My father's name was Avery Rivera. My mother's name was Carmen Rivera. For over a year, my parents brought the Devil's into peace. They were making changes. Drastic changes that would have created treaties with multiple packs. They would have started to right the wrongs of their predecessors. They tracked and found as many of the girls and boys who had been taken as they could and returned them to their families. Your Alpha didn't like that. He didn't like that when the previous Alpha died, my father was the one blessed to be chosen as Alpha. So, he bided his time... waited for the right opportunity… and murdered them both in cold blood. He made it look like a simple car accident."

"That's a damn lie!" the Deputy yells. The Alpha, however, stares at Maverick in both shock and more than a little terror.

"Truth is, you fear what I could be. The strength I have. Well, let me show you how powerful I truly am." Maverick's smirk turns into a wide grin. "My name is Maverick Rivera. And I. Am. Your. True. Alpha!" Like Kade had moments before, Maverick lets his head fall back and roars. I grip the door frame and cover my ears. I have no idea how, but it sounds even louder than Kade's and shakes the entire foundation I'm standing on.

Several more pack members come out from their hiding places and stand behind Maverick, but I don't think that's what shocks the Deputy or Devil's Peak's fake Alpha the most. It's when several of the pack members behind him walk to Maverick.

This act of disrespect seems to have momentarily stunned the fake Alpha. He watches them before fury starts to replace his shock. I can see his grip tighten on Millie. The Deputy follows his lead and does the same to Nathan. Only I can feel Nathan's pain worsen. His neck is dangerously close to being broken.

Stay calm, little ones. Calm, still, and quiet. We want them to forget you are in their grasp. Alpha has a plan. I know it. Just stay as still and quiet as you can. I tighten my grip on the frame as I feel my strength returning.

Prince is still on his knees glaring at the fake Alpha with his mate at his side. Kade is standing tall and proud. Maverick has taken his role as the true Alpha of Devil's Peak. All of our allies are a true show of force, but I know better.

History has shown over and over again that even the strongest armies fall. The mightiest of warriors are eventually defeated. While Devil's Peak may have a small number of fighters left, they should not be underestimated.

They are pure evil.

Vengeful.

And they still have our kids.

CHAPTER TWENTY FIVE

~*~ KADE ~*~

I stay ready for any attacks that may or may not come. Not that I'm all that worried. We outnumber his measly pack by a lot. I pulled every single ally I have all around the world. I know some of them have taken out several of his forces before they even got to the compound. We've been overpowering him since this battle started.

Not to say I'm underestimating him or his forces. A man cornered is a dangerous man, but a Shifter? Fuck. You don't corner a Wolf. They'll fight to the death to get out of the trap. It doesn't matter how small his pack is compared to mine.

As if to agree with me, his entire demeanor changes. The fake Alpha of Devil's Peak vibrates with anger. It slams into us all in waves, but none of us move. We only darken our expressions to match his.

"Let Millie and Nathan go," I tell him dangerously. "You have no idea what's going to happen to you if you don't, but I promise you don't want any part of it."

"Oh, so you're telling me I shouldn't snap her neck?" He smirks and twists her head more. My heart beats faster. I don't know how the two of them are being so calm, but I have a feeling it has something to do with Kaia.

Kaia.

I don't dare glance at her, but I know she's standing in the pack house with the door open slightly. My mom is sitting in front of the door watching the fight. I feel her pain. She hates seeing this. It brings up memories that she still hasn't completely shared with me. I don't blame her. I wouldn't want to talk about that day either if I were her. I still don't like talking about it, and I'm not the one who ended up a Spirit Guide.

Thinking of my parents and family losing their lives to this motherfucker pisses me off. But today, I get revenge for them. Redemption. Today, he's not getting out of this with his life. The world will be better off without him.

"Let. Them. Go," I warn through clenched teeth.

I know as soon as the words are out of my mouth that there's no chance of him letting them go. Not unless he's forced. I glance at Dominick to make sure he's on the same page as me. He nods, and we both bolt towards the fake fucker and his Deputy.

But there's no way we'll make it in time. They both have them in position to snap their necks in seconds. I don't think I can handle watching two kids killed right in front of me. It might send me over the edge. I'll lose control so fucking fast, no one here will know what happened.

Just as they're making their move to kill the kids, two black plumes of smoke appear in front of us. "*Hi, assholes...,*" dual deep, rumbling voices sing-song from somewhere within the fog. "*Bye, assholes!*"

Dominick and I slide to stop and watch in utter amazement as they vanish almost as quickly as they appeared. We aren't the only ones, though, who don't know what just happened.

I've only seen one creature who can do that shit, I say to Dominick as we both back up quickly towards our pack and allies.

Demons, Dominick answers. He looks around. *Holy shit. They brought the kids to Kaia. She's got them.*

At that moment, three black plumes of smoke appear next to me. I take a step back. My heart jumps into my throat. I've fought Demons before. Almost lost my heart. Literally. The only thing that saved my ass

251

was a truce I made with them. I pray to the Moon Goddess they aren't here to take it back. They say never trust a Demon.

"Have kids, they said. It'll be fun, they said," a deep, rumbly voice says just as he takes on his human form. He facepalms, shaking his head before lowering his hand as the other two chuckle.

"Come on, dad. You have to admit that was the perfect moment for that," one of the twins, I don't know how he tells them apart, says with a smirk as he turns his gaze on the pack in front of us. His smirk becomes a dangerous grin.

"Daemon... Kaine...," he sighs exasperated. All three are taller than me. Standing at almost six foot five. Probably more muscular. Maybe even a bit darker. All are similar in looks, but for the piercing blue eyes on the eldest. Those could probably cut through souls. For all I know, they do. He rolls his eyes with a chuckle turning his gaze to me. "One thing we don't fuck with... is kids."

"Fuck, Alaric," I whisper. "I didn't know you were going to show up."

He chuckles and pats my shoulder but doesn't take his eyes off the men in front of us who still have yet to pick their jaws up off the ground. "I sensed something was wrong. We stayed out of it for a little while, but you weren't getting to them before those kids got hurt. You know us. Kids are off limits in my realm."

"Well, I'm glad you showed up," I say genuinely. He's right. We weren't going to be able to get to them before their necks were snapped.

It only takes seconds before the fake Alpha roars. He doesn't have as many as us, but what he does have is strong. I just hope we're stronger. I hope the three Demons that just joined the fight will be our tipping point.

Because I'm getting tired.

All of us are. I feel everyone's energy is waning. The battle has already been long. Just when we think we've gotten the upper hand, more join the fight. Fake Alpha has learned well. Take out those who are tired and replace them with the ones at full strength. Though, how he's getting by with that shit considering the amount of forces I have is something I need to figure out.

Quickly.

Unfortunately, all I can think about is the multiple attacks being thrown my way. As soon as I thwart one, another comes at me. They are relentless. It's obvious I'm the target. Take out the Alpha, weaken the pack. Weaken the pack, dominate them. It's what they did with my father. As soon as the pack felt his death, they all got weaker and were overcome with an immense amount of sadness and grief. It's how Devil's Peak was able to overcome them as they did. Something I learned from Zeke since I got him back.

"Argh!" I yell as I block a punch. I grab the wrist of my newest attacker and break it as I slam him to the ground.

"Ah!" he screams. I waste no time in ripping his head off.

"Kade! Left!" Zeke yells as he punches someone.

"Fuck!" I duck out of the way of a Shifter who just shifted to his Wolf form. I shift to mine and tackle him to the ground.

He rolls me onto my back. His teeth snap at me. Way too fucking close to my neck. I push my paws against him with as much strength as I can and jump back on him when he flies off me. I bare my teeth and rip out his throat before jumping right back into the fight.

But each and every kick or punch to my abdomen, legs, neck, and head take their toll. My movements are slowing down. This fight seems to have raged on for hours. The energy of my entire pack is wearing thin. We're all struggling. Devil's Peak may not have as many forces as we do, but what they do have is relentless and won't give up.

After fighting yet another attacker off, I can't stop myself from ducking behind the pack house. I shift back into my human form and kneel. I have to catch my breath and regain some of the energy I've expended.

Kade? I don't see you. Where are you! Kaia asks me worriedly. Her fear slams into me.

Catching my breath, baby. I'm okay. I feel a warm, tingly sensation flow through me and have to smile. *I don't think you realize what you're doing, baby, but thank you. Save it, though. Save your energy for when this shit is over. You'll need it. We all will.*

I'm sending you warm, healing thoughts.

I know. And you're giving me my strength back. But you need it. Pull it back, Kaia. Trust me. I'll explain it more later, but what you're doing takes your energy and strength. Too much will weaken you. You need to be strong. Pull it back.

When I feel the peaceful sensations slowly fade, I jump back into the battle. Just in time. Dominick is being held against the body of the Deputy. He doesn't see me, though. I run as fast as I can and slam into him hard from the side. He jars enough that Dominick is able to break free.

Dominick recovers quickly and knocks the Deputy back into me. I wrap one arm around his neck and the other across his forehead. I grin evilly. "You ready to pay for all your sins?" I growl in his ear.

I watch his eyes widen. "Kade, I was under orders! You have to believe me!"

"Oh, I do. But everyone has a choice, asshole. You picked the wrong one." Before the moronic fool can say or do anything else, I snap his neck.

"One more down," Dominick growls as he launches at someone else.

From behind, someone shoves me. I hit the ground on my hands and knees. I have no time to recover before I get a swift kick to my side, sending me sprawling on my back in the dirt. I launch myself up, coming face to face with fake Alpha. I don't know his name. I don't give a fuck. It's time to end this shit once and for all.

"Finally. I'm about to kick you back to the hole you crawled out of," he growls.

It makes me laugh. "I didn't come from a hole. Some say I came straight from Hell. I'm inclined to agree."

He gives me a grin that would probably terrify a lesser man. It does nothing for me but feed my anger. "Cocky fucker, aren't you?"

I shrug, secretly thankful no one but him seems to give a shit about me. It gives me time to gain a little more much needed strength. "My last name literally means God of terror and dread. One of my best friends is a fucking Demon. I'll go with a confident fucker."

His grin turns into a vicious snarl just as he attacks.

But I'm ready.

I grab his neck just as he jumps at me and flip him over my back. I twist his neck and revel in the satisfying break of every single bone. He doesn't even twitch when he falls to the ground. I stare for a moment and shake my head.

"Way too easy," I mumble.

"Kaia, no!" Maverick howls. I turn just in time to see him running at full speed towards me.

I narrow my eyes. "The fuck?"

And then I see her. My heart skips a beat and comes to a screeching halt. Kaia is running full speed at a Wolf with bared teeth. A Wolf I would recognize anywhere. Her eyes are completely focused on me. Her claws look just as razor sharp as the points of her teeth.

If this were a movie, like my mind seems to think it is, her claws would just catch the sun. They would look like diamonds. She'd be moving in slow motion. And I'd be frozen to the ground with wide, surprised eyes unable to move even though my Wolf is screaming at me to.

Move! He screams at me.

This can't be real. It's not happening, I shake my head as she bears down on me.

"No!" Kaia screams. She launches herself past me. Charlene lets out a vicious growl and snarls just as Kaia hits her full force, sending her off course. Kaia flies through the air and hits the ground so hard, I'm positive she's dead. They both roll a few times before coming to a stop. Charlene recovers quickly, though she is stumbling slightly, and towers over Kaia with bared teeth.

"No!" I scream.

A black plume of smoke appears next to Kaia and Charlene. As one of the twins takes on his human form, he shoves Charlene off her. I run towards Kaia as the Demon slams a yelping Charlene into the ground hard enough that she sinks into the hole made with her body. He slams his fist into her chest as she howls and screeches in agony. He rips his hand out, holding her heart, as she falls silent.

Before I reach Kaia, someone slams into me head first. I turn in midair and grip the face of him. I claw at his eyes, and even though I land on my back, I have the upper hand. My fingertips dig into his eyes. He automatically grabs my wrists as he screams. I don't care about anything but getting to Kaia.

What I do not expect is this douchefuck to jab me in the throat and punch me in the chest. I let him go because I'm suddenly on the defensive. I punch him in the windpipe, but he still hits me. Every contact he makes with me hurts even worse. If I didn't know better, I'd think the son-of-a-bitch was a Demon. Nothing seems to faze him.

Or maybe it's because my strength has been completely depleted. He scratches my neck, shoulders, and chest before I roll him so he's underneath me. I see black plumes of smoke jumping in to help my pack eliminate the remaining Devil's Peak Shifters. It gives me enough strength to finish this one off.

"Argh!" I yell as I punch him over and over in the face with hard, devastating blows. I feel the life force draining from him with each hit he takes. He starts flailing more than punching. I punch him so hard in his neck that I feel his windpipe snap. Using the rest of my energy, I rip off his head. Blood splatters me as I fall backwards onto my back.

My pack is expended. I'm exhausted. I'm grateful to the Demons because they seem to have a limitless amount of energy. Alaric finishes off the last of our enemies just as I realize I'm far more hurt than I realized.

"Kade!" Kaia screams. I watch her as she shakily crawls to me. She grips my hand as she puts her other hand over my heart. I feel it shaking. "Kade, what do I do? Tell me! Tell me what to do!"

But I'm too weak and I'm holding something in my side that shouldn't be coming out. It could be my stomach. It could just be blood. Whatever it is, though, my hand is shaking and soaked in it.

I'm sorry, Kaia. I'm sorry this is ending so soon. I'm bleeding out. I can feel it. The sounds have dwindled down to silence. Judging how I suddenly feel serious sadness radiating from my pack as a whole as they start to gather around, they know I'm in trouble, too.

"No! No! This is not how our story ends, Kade Deimos! I won't allow it! We're just getting to know each other! I'm only beginning to understand this life and world. I haven't gotten the chance to love you!" Her grip tightens on my hand. She trembles as tears stream down her face. She lays her head on my chest as she sobs. "I haven't had time to love you!"

I feel myself fading more and more, but Kaia's love flows through me like a warm, gentle breeze. I let my eyes fall closed and just feel her as my heart shatters. *I shouldn't have pushed you away. I shouldn't have fought our bond. I could have at least loved you like you deserved during our short time together. I didn't know it would end like this.*

I feel her shake her head, but it's so faint I'm not sure if I imagined it or not. *Stop talking, Kade. Please. I won't lose you. I can't.*

In my mind, I'm holding her close and comforting her. I'm okay. I'm not dying. In reality, I'm watching this trainwreck from back by the trees. I'm crying so hard that it hurts my chest. I want to move, but I can't. It's not that my legs won't let me. It's that I'm tethered right where I am.

Kade. You must fight, son. This isn't supposed to be how the story ends, my father says from next to me.

I try to run to her. *I can't move. What did they do to me?*

You were clawed. You're bleeding out. But you can stop this. Fight, Kade!

I fight harder, but I'm sinking. The ground is swallowing me whole. Kaia is crying and clinging to my physical body that I no longer possess. I see her small body overtaken by sobs. My pack members are hugging each other as they watch the life slowly draining from my body. The Wolves are howling. Everyone is huddled together.

I can't die like this, I growl. *It's not time.*

Then stop whining and fight, boy! A deep, rumbling voice barks. *You have the life that I always dreamed of having. A peaceful, growing pack. A family that loves and adores you. A mate who will stand by your side through the good and the bad, and love you eternally throughout. Never wavering.*

I look up at a dark, imposing figure of a man I've never seen. *Who the fuck are you?*

I'm your mother's brother, Kade. Thanks to my father, rather, the man who pretended to be him, I was never given the chance to grow into a respectable Shifter like you. My path was laid out for me the moment I was born. I never had the courage to walk away and follow my parents and your mother after they were kicked from the pack. By then, I felt that it was too late. I never had the chance to redeem my wrongs. I knew going into that final fight that I wouldn't be walking away. If I hadn't died that day, I would have shortly after. The only good part of that day was that I got to see my sister one last time. To see her happy and settled in the life she always deserved, with a man that loves and adores her.

Why? Why did you go after my father? I furrow my brows when my father places his hand on his shoulder.

Because I was weak. Because dying that day was a better option than the one I faced if I went back. I would have been overthrown and killed. I had given up. There was nothing left for me. That's why I put up as little of a fight as possible and made sure I took the strongest of my pack. *The ones who wanted me dead. Without them, I hoped Devil's Peak would end with me. I was wrong. I didn't realize how deeply the deceit had gone. The only good thing that came from that is I was able to make it right with my sister when I came back as her Spirit Guide.*

I slip further down. *Fuck. I feel so weak.*

Fight, Kade! Fight! Be the Alpha this pack deserves! my father commands. *Be the mate Kaia deserves! Focus! Fight!*

I look back at Kaia. While we have been talking, she has shifted position. She's kneeling over my body with her hands pressed over my stomach. Like she's trying to stop the blood flow. I can see from here that her shoulders are shaking with sobs as she begs me to stay with her. Somehow, I am starting to feel stronger. If I didn't know any better, I would say her hands were glowing slightly.

What the...? I blink, looking down at myself.

The entire world seems to fall silent. All I hear are whimpers, cries, and howls that seem to echo just before I'm violently pulled from my purgatory and slammed back into my body. My eyes snap open as I inhale sharply and cough, like I need air that I've been deprived of for far too long.

"Kade?" Kaia's hands slide from my stomach as she looks down at me. She is swaying slightly.

"Kaia..." I sense her weakening by the second. All at once, I realize, with growing alarm, what she just did. "Kaia!"

"Kade...," she whispers. She sways again as her eyelids flutter closed. I'm still weak and not quite fast enough to catch her when her head rolls backwards. She sinks to the ground.

"Kaia!" I scramble up as quickly as I can and pull her against me. "Kaia!" I shake her slightly to try and wake her. "No! No! No!" I hold her close and rock back and forth with her. I immediately set to trying to heal her, but there's no way that's happening. I'm still not strong enough. She brought me back from the brink of death. It's going to take time for me to gain any of my strength, let alone powers.

I look up when Zeke drops to his knees next to me. He tries to pull my arms from around Kaia as Maverick comes rushing over. He tries pulling her from my arms with urgency, but I hold her tighter against me. I'm not letting her go.

"There's something I can do, but we're running out of time! Let her go, Kade!" Maverick drops to his knees. I hold her closer shaking my head. I'm unwilling to let her go. I can't.

"Let her go, Kade," Zeke says, pressing down on my clavicle.

"Ah! Fuck!" I let go of her when the pressure point he hits weakens my grip. Zeke drags me backwards and away from Kaia. If I wasn't still recovering, I'd be able to fight him off. "Let go, Zeke!" I struggle against him, but he easily overpowers me.

Maverick gathers Kaia in his arms, laying her gently down on a blanket that Jordan brings out to us. He places her hands comfortably on her stomach as he settles more on his knees. He places one of his hands on her forehead and the other on her chest over her heart. I watch confused as he closes his eyes and takes a deep breath.

Snapping myself out of my initial confusion, I try launching at Maverick to get to Kaia again. "What the fuck!" But Zeke easily hangs onto me. "Zeke! Let me go!"

Maverick snaps his eyes open as he concentrates. His head falls forward slightly as black lines slowly travel through his veins. He grits his teeth. I watch in fascination, horror, and complete bewilderment, but I stop fighting. Not because I want to, but because watching Kaia die right in front of me is the worst punishment the Moon Goddess could rain down on me to make me atone for all of my sins and mistakes.

I can't do it. I can't lose her. I already feel her pulling my heart with her the further she drifts away.

I'm begging you, Kaia. I'm begging you. Don't leave me. Not like this. Don't make me face this world without you. I'm so fucking sorry. I'm so sorry for treating you the way I did. Let me love you, Kaia. Please don't fucking leave me. Hold on, baby. Let my love be your strength as yours is for me.

I collapse against Zeke and close my eyes. With everything in me, I hold onto her. My soul cradles hers. I won't let her go. I can't.

CHAPTER TWENTY SIX

~*~ KAIA ~*~

As if I'm flying, I look down from above my body and watch as Maverick pulls me away from Kade. He lays me on the ground. I tilt my head in confusion when he places his hands on my forehead and over my heart.

Belle appears beside me. *You are lucky to be witnessing this, sweet one. It is extremely rare. So rare that I don't believe even Kade knows of it.*

What's happening, Belle? What is he doing?

She shakes her head, and I know she's not going to tell me. *This is not the place for you. You have to go back. It is time for you to be who you were destined to be.*

I look down at her before looking back to the scene before us. I notice that Prince and Jordan have joined everyone. The children are being held by their parents. The clearing is completely still. Silent. But who knew how loud silence could be?

It's not your time, Kaia.

My attention snaps to the kind, male voice I never thought I'd hear again. *Dad?*

Oh, my girl. You've grown so much in the past few weeks. He looks just as he did the day he died. Tall. Strong. A few wrinkles near his eyes. He reaches out and cups my cheek. I close my eyes and lean into his hand. It's warm. Just like he always was. *You must be strong. This is only one challenge in a long line of many you've had since your life changed.*

I wish we had told you sooner, my mom says as she appears next to my father just as I open my eyes to her voice.

Tears sting my eyes. *What do you mean?*

Mom smiles. *We knew that Leia's parents weren't like us, but we were told to keep that quiet until they found out if Leia was a Shifter or not. There were signs that she was, but girl Shifters are different from boys. They get their Wolf later. We weren't sure, and she hadn't tried to shift. Though she was a very restless girl and had some unique abilities that seemed different.*

I don't know if I'll be able to feel it, but I turn and hug them both. I sink into them when I do feel them. *I know she's a Shifter.*

Their grips tighten. My dad breathes deeply. *Yes. But we deliberately kept it from you. Even after we saw... Well, we saw a couple of Shifters murdering someone.*

I know that, too... The Sheriff who killed you told me.

They let go slowly. My mom smiles softly. *But that wasn't all. We always knew you were special, Kaia. We didn't just move to where we did so you could have plenty of room to run.*

I tilt my head curiously. *But that's what you've always told me.*

My dad smiles softly. *When you were born, we had a visitor. Someone who told us that you were destined for greatness. Of course, your mother and I thought we dreamt the entire thing. But then you started showing us the signs that she warned us about. Things like talking to yourself. We chalked it up to an imaginary friend, but she didn't go away. You kept talking about her pretty fur.*

I blush. *Belle.*

My mother nods. *The Moon Wolf.*

But it wasn't just her, my father continues. *It was how you spoke to the moon. We thought you were praying at first. We'd watch you. When you got older, you should have been interested in boys, but you weren't. You were fascinated with the moon. Specifically -"*

The Man in the Moon, I whisper. *Kade.* I look down at Kade. He's struggling with Zeke, but I know it's only because he wants to be closer to me. He's not full strength yet, so he isn't able to break free. I look at my parents. *I don't understand. You knew I was supposed to be with Kade?*

Dad shakes his head. *We didn't know that. But we did know that you were destined for greatness. There was a legend. A legend that only comes true once every hundred or so years. Sometimes, longer. It says there is a Human girl who is so full of life and love that she has a unique power to make everyone feel calm and peaceful when she is near. She is beautiful. Smart. Her life, however, is cut short. She dies trying to keep peace. But the Moon Goddess sees her potential and gives her a second chance. She gifts her not only life, but also her Wolf. That girl goes on to become the most powerful Luna of that generation.*

Nothing like a witch or sorceress, my mom continues. *She's powerful because she's respected among not only her kind, but the world. She's not able to solve the world's war and famine problems, but she does keep the world, Shifters, Humans, Demons, Wolves… everyone… from erupting into chaos.*

She's the most powerful Luna in the world. And with her Alpha at her side, the two of them go on to become respected and looked up to. The two of them keep the world relatively peaceful. My dad smiles. I feel him tug on a strand of his hair.

My heart feels heavy as I begin to understand his words. I look down at Belle. *That's me. And my Alpha is Kade. What he theorized about me and the legend is true.*

Belle nods and nuzzles my stomach. *That's why Connor and I both went above and beyond to save you. You would have died that night. It wasn't how it was supposed to happen.* She looks down below us and leans her body against my thigh. *This. This is how it was supposed to happen.*

So… I'm dead?

Yes and no. My mother frowns. *You are. But this is not your ending. You're to go on and do great things. With Kade and this pack. Things that your father and I will be so proud to watch as we watch over you. You're between worlds.*

You have a choice to make, sweet child, Belle says. *You can either accept the gift the Moon Goddess would bestow on you and return to Kade to live out the rest of your new life, or you can choose to come with us. But this decision must be your own. Not what you think we, or Kade, would want you to do. What you, and only you want to do.*

I take a deep breath and hug myself. *If I come with you, I would be dead.*

My father crosses his arms over his chest and nods slowly. *You would be. You would return as a Spirit Guide as we have. But you would be relegated to the Spirit World. Your physical body would no longer exist. Just your soul.*

I shake my head. *I can't do that. I'm not ready for that. I feel like I have so much more to do. So much more love to give. I haven't even started my life yet. Not really. There is so much I still want to experience. I haven't begun to show Kade how much I love him. I don't want to leave this world. Not yet. I'm not done with it yet.*

One of the Demons, the older one, kneels next to Maverick. "I can help."

"Don't! Don't touch him!" Zeke yells as he holds a now trembling Kade in his arms. "If you touch him, you'll break it! We must not break it! We could lose them both!"

The Demon looks at him and backs away with a nod. Sweat pools on Maverick's brow as he grimaces in pain. There is black-like tar that is traveling through his veins. It becomes more and more prominent the harder he concentrates. It lasts for a few more moments before he suddenly moves. His back straightens. His muscles stiffen as he sets his shoulders back.

I stare, transfixed, as Maverick's eyes snap open, glowing a shining gold that I have come to learn represents his Alpha status. At that same moment, he throws his head back with a mighty, deep roar that echoes throughout the clearing. A roar that is filled with pain, fear, sadness, love, and hope.

I want to fulfill my destiny. I want to go back, I say with resolution. *The world may be done with me, but I am certainly not done with it.*

Maverick's roar seems to go on forever. It feels as if it's pulling directly at my soul. His hands glow a blissful silver. I barely have time to register the roar fading out or the gold in his eyes slowly draining away before I am forcefully thrown into a dark abyss...

Go and be the best Luna you can be, my sweet girl, Belle says as I fade into the darkness. *Make sure you keep my boys on their toes and their pranks in check. Goddess knows they could get into trouble just standing still.*

Come back to me, Kaia. I came back for you. Don't leave me, baby. I'll make up for everything I've done if you'll just fight and come back to me, Kade's tearful voice says. But it's distorted. As if it's coming through a tunnel.

I feel like I'm violently slammed back into my body so hard that it makes me jerk. I grasp whatever is nearest to me as my eyes fly open, but it's very short-lived. I feel like I'm being lifted off the ground. Suddenly, I'm once again looking over the entire scene with Belle at my side.

I look at my surroundings confused. Everything seems to be getting darker but when I look down at the group below, I can see it is still daylight. My already weak body suddenly feels like it is being drained of any remaining energy I had. I stumble at the drastic change. I feel like I'm falling, but I'm not.

What's happening? I ask, terrified. *I said I wanted to go back! I can't leave them! I can't leave Kade!*

I - Belle cuts herself off. I realize she's just as confused as me.

I hear a low, pained groan. I look towards where it came from and see Zeke and Maverick. My eyes widen when they land on Maverick because he is partially shifted. Something I haven't witnessed in my time here. I trail my gaze over him taking in what differences I can see. His hair is shaggier, and a little thicker.

I let out a gasp when I see his eyes because while they no longer shine the beautiful gold I have come to love in Kade's, they are now the shining beautiful, piercing silver of a Beta. He has fangs that are still prevalent.

Gasps echo around the clearing. I initially think they are gasping because of Maverick, but I quickly realize how wrong I am when my eyes fall onto my body. Every eye is on it. Though, whether they stare in shock or fear, I'm not sure. If it were me, the fact that there's a body in front of me that is lifting into the air would send me running for the hills.

Are the Demons doing something to me? Stop them! I yell to Belle. But she's just staring as the scene unfolds. I look at the Demons, but they are all standing off to the side near Kade looking just as shocked and confused as everyone else.

All but one.

"She's… I don't believe it…" The eldest Demon murmurs shocked.

All but one head snaps in his direction. Kade shifts onto his knees, gripping Zeke like a lifeline. He doesn't take his eyes off my body. "Alaric…? Explain. What is happening to my mate?" His voice is gritty. Like he is holding back tears.

"She's… being given a Wolf…" Alaric, the eldest Demon, says. His eyes never leave my body. "But the legend… This isn't the year it's supposed to happen. It happens every one hundred years. We're on year one-hundred and two. We didn't think this would happen again. The others… they were all right on time. Right on the one hundred years."

"You know about the legend?" Kade asks.

"Just bits and pieces."

Everyone falls silent once more as beams of light seemingly shoot from all areas of my body until I'm a ball of bright, glittering light. My arms fall limp. My head falls back. My body looks like it's arching like a rainbow. I gasp right along with everyone else. Some cover their eyes at the radiance of the glow.

Oh, sweet one, Belle says with a sniffle. *The legend is being fulfilled. I've never seen it before. It's beautiful.*

I just watch, mesmerized. The sparkling luminance dims only slightly before I seem to be completely engulfed in a cloud of glitter. Everyone backs away a step as they stare. Once again, I'm pulled violently back into a dark abyss, but this time, I feel the ground underneath me. And I don't feel like the body I'm in is really mine. At least not my human one.

I slowly open my eyes and blink a few times. There's nothing around me but a bright white light and something shimmery falling around me, but it never touches the ground. Like the light, it fades slowly.

I'm curled into a tight ball in the dirt. The entire pack is surrounding me, but they've given me a lot of space. Even Kade isn't near me. Maverick is watching. His eyes have dulled from that beautiful silver I saw to an almost dull gray.

Maverick, I whisper. I try to get up, but I'm weak. It's then I see that I have paws instead of feet and hands. I have snow white fur in place of my skin. It takes me a few moments to realize that I'm not Human anymore. I'm a Wolf. A beautiful, purely white Wolf.

A small Wolf cub sits in front of me and nuzzles my nose. Well, snout. *Luna?* He tilts his head curiously at me. *Is you oteay?*

I... I don't know how to answer him. I don't even know what happened.

Kaia? Kade kneels above me. *Please talk to me, baby. Tell me you're okay.*

I look up at him. *I don't know what happened.* I tentatively lift a paw.

The Moon Goddess. She gifted you a Wolf. I've never seen anything like it. He gently cups my cheek and kisses me softly right on the mouth.

The young cub snuggles into me. Kade runs his fingers gently through my fur. I don't attempt to move, but more of the Wolf cubs and kids slowly make their way to me. I watch them just as curiously as they watch me. A few of the cubs nudge me with their snouts. The kids kneel next to me and follow Kade's lead. They run my fingers through my fur. The adults get a little closer as they look at me. Even the Demons inch towards me.

With each second that passes, my strength seems to return. It's almost like a low hum coursing through my blood. I still don't dare move because I know I need the energy. I feel it coming from those surrounding me.

I find my eyes drifting to Maverick, though. Something about what happened to him seems strange. The fact that he's between shifts both frightens and intrigues me. His eyes are on me, but they seem to become more and more lifeless. Even his skin seems ashen. His claws don't look as sharp. His fangs, while definitely visible, seem to be shrinking.

But it's not any of the partial shift that worries me. It's not even the fact that his eyes are ever so slowly falling closed. It's that he hasn't gotten up off his knees. When I last saw him, just before I was pulled back to my body, Maverick was still sitting tall.

Now, his body is drooping. He seems like he's hunching over. His arms appear to have lost all strength. The tips of his claws touch the ground. His chest barely seems to be rising and falling. I want to believe it's because he used so much energy in the fight and then whatever he did with me, but I feel with all of my heart that it's more than that.

I don't know how no one else hasn't seen what I see. It's not like the change in his posture isn't drastically different than it was before. Even Zeke hasn't picked up on it, but I think that's because he hasn't left Kade's side. He might not be able to see Maverick from where he is.

If Maverick is anything like Kade, he will be actively keeping the bond between him and Zeke closed to the best of his ability so whatever is going on doesn't flow over to his mate. Maverick is sitting outside of the circle surrounding me. Zeke is behind me next to Kade. Zeke looks peaceful. Not at all worried. I'm sure that's what Maverick wants.

The corners of Maverick's mouth try to turn up but don't quite make it. *Thank fuck it worked... It worked,* he whispers. *Thank the Goddess for blessing you with such a precious gift.*

I battle with myself because I think Zeke needs to know what's happening to Maverick, but it's not until he sways to his side slightly that I make my decision.

Zeke! I scream.

But then I realize I'm a wolf. I'm not screaming at all.

I'm howling. A piercing sound that cuts the quiet din. I don't know if anyone other than Kade can hear what I just spoke.

Everyone around me jumps back, but only slightly and not at all out of fear. They are completely concerned and bewildered. I can feel them. I'm still not strong enough to really move, so I hope that my howl alerts someone, anyone, to Maverick.

"Mav?" Zeke asks.

Several heads turn towards him. I breathe a sigh of relief and let my eyes fall closed. I'm too weak to keep them open, but I'm glad someone can keep an eye on Maverick. I know that I'm not going to last much longer. I need to rest my eyes.

As the kids and cubs begin petting and nuzzling me again, I let myself relax and soak up the waves of energy flowing at me from all different directions. I know I'll need it because I don't feel like this is totally over yet...

CHAPTER TWENTY SEVEN

~*~ KADE ~*~

I glance up and see immediately why Kaia was so concerned about Maverick. I still don't understand what he just did, but whatever it was affected him badly. He looks weaker and weaker by the second. Zeke stands and walks to him. He kneels next to him. I look down at Kaia. I can feel she's getting her strength back.

My dad kneels next to me. *There were rumors that she was the one.*

The one to fulfill the legend that I still don't know everything about, I say.

He nods. *It mostly talks about her keeping peace and risking her life for it. But it says that she will give the ultimate sacrifice saving the one her heart desires. It's a forgotten part of the legend. Something a lot of people leave out. That sacrifice is when she gets her Wolf.*

Does she stay a Wolf? I ask. I'll love her either way, but I'll miss the Human part of her. I fell in love with her as a Human. Not as a Wolf. But I don't care. As long as she's alive, I'll take her in whatever form the Moon Goddess gives me.

I don't know the answer to that, son.

She seems to be sleeping peacefully. Considering what she's been through, I doubt she'll wake up for many hours. As if to answer my question, though, Kaia's Wolf body looks as if it's shimmering once again. Everyone backs away, but I refuse. My father stays right next to me. He'll never know just how grateful I am that he's been with me through all of this.

Kaia's Wolf body seems to start glowing a brilliant white. The silver shimmer I'd seen before rain down over her as the light fades. When I see Kaia again, she's sitting with her legs tucked under her and her back to me. She's got one hand against her forehead. The other is propping her body up.

She runs her fingers through her hair and looks back at me slowly. "Kade?"

"Fuck… Kaia…" I pull her into my lap and wrap around her. I hug her hard and bury my face in her hair, inhaling her scent.

She shakily grips the waistband of my jeans. "Mav…," she whispers.

I look up. Maverick is smiling softly, but he's still in a half-shifted state. The light in his now silver eyes has faded almost completely, but he's standing. Zeke is hugging him and looking at him with both concern and love.

My eyes widen when Maverick's eyes close. His knees seemingly buckle. He slowly drops to his knees. Zeke furrows his eyebrows as he sinks with him. He runs his fingers through Maverick's hair and hugs him close.

"Maverick?" I rumble as I hug Kaia tightly. I meet Zeke's eyes and see nothing but fear. Not worry. Not sadness. Not confusion. Fear. Pure unadulterated terror.

Maverick's body deflates. He begins falling forward like all of the strings that had been holding up moments ago have been cut. Zeke pulls him into him and takes his weight. He pulls him into his lap and hugs him shakily.

"Mav!" Zeke screams. He trembles as he kisses Maverick's face. He holds him tightly to him and rocks back and forth. "Mav!" He grips Maverick's hair and pulls his large body impossibly closer until Maverick

269

looks like nothing more than a child being engulfed by a loved one in the most protective of hugs. "I got you. I got you, baby."

"He's okay," Kaia whispers.

"How do you know?" I keep an eye on Zeke and Maverick.

"Because I can feel him."

I look down at her. "You can feel him?"

She nods slowly. "I don't know how to explain it, but I feel him. I think whatever he did left a kind of echo of a connection between us. He's exhausted. He needs recovery. He needs Zeke."

I don't question her and look up at Alaric. "Get them inside the house."

He nods. With his sons, Alaric helps Zeke and Maverick up. Zeke lifts Maverick in his arms, but stumbles. He's weakened, we all are, but I know he'll never allow anyone else to touch Maverick while Maverick is so vulnerable. Alaric steadies him when he stumbles. I watch them until they disappear inside the house.

"What do you need, Kade?" Dominick asks me quietly. He's hugging Jordan close and swaying gently with her.

I look around the complex. Parents are hugging their children. Mates are hugging each other, much as Dominick and Jordan are. Some faces are missing, but I know they haven't been taken from us because I can feel them. Everyone looks a little beat up, but not a single soul in this pack was killed.

I can't say the same for Devil's Peak. No one survived. At least not of the ones who attacked us. Those who joined the side of right are all still standing tall, though they are all concerned about Maverick, the true Alpha of their pack. Even Jace, who would have become an Alpha if he hadn't chosen to become Maverick's Beta, looks distressed. Leia, though safely tucked into the arms of her mate, looks just as worried as him.

"Call the Refuge. Get our pack doctor. Bring all of our injured there. He has the equipment he needs there to help everyone." I tell Dominick. "There are a lot of injured and wounded. I don't have the strength to heal them all. Neither does Kaia. I don't think any of the mates have the strength either. Everyone is exhausted and beat up. Some are too hurt to heal quickly."

Dominick nods. "I'll take care of it."

I hug Kaia tighter. "Think you have enough of your strength back to move?"

Kaia nods. "I still don't understand what happened." She stands slowly. I follow her. We're both still shaky, but at least we're alive. "One second I'm looking over everything. Like I'm between worlds or something. The next second I'm a Wolf. I'm not a Shifter. How is that possible?"

I can't help but chuckle a little as I lean down. I kiss her softly and let my eyes close just long enough to feel her and nothing more before opening them again. I take her hand. "I think you're a Shifter now." I turn and lead her slowly to the pack house.

She looks up at me and squeezes my hand. "I still don't really understand."

"Truthfully, baby, I'm not entirely sure that I completely understand. Part of me thinks that we never will. That it is supposed to remain a mystery. That's what legends are after all. There seems to be different versions. Some are absolute fable. Others are close to what the legend says, but there are differences. What I don't totally understand is what happened with you and Maverick. I've never seen that before. It was almost like some type of Demon shit."

She giggles. The sound is melodic and warms my soul. It's something that, just a little while ago, I never thought I'd hear again. "I don't think Mav is a Demon."

I smile. "I just hope he can tell me what the fuck he did." I walk into the pack house and see a lot of bodies, Wolves, Humans, and Shifters, laying all over the room. I wince because I hate seeing anyone in my pack hurt, but I'm thankful they are all okay.

Alive.

Refusing to let Kaia go, I lead her through the house as I speak to each injured member of my pack. I know that we need to sleep to replenish our energy and heal completely, but the Alpha in me needs to be sure they are all still with us.

With me.

~ ~ ~

271

It's taken almost a week for my pack to fully recover. Kaia and I have both checked on each of them every single day. Some of the Wolves were kept at the Refuge so our doctor could make sure they were okay. They all just came home today. Maverick is still recovering. Slower than Zeke would like, but he is.

Things feel a little different. More… peaceful. Not just here in my territory, but throughout the world. There doesn't seem to be as much conflict on the news. Not to say there is none, I'm sure there will always be some. But it's noticeably less. So much so, that even Chief Jeremy Alexander said there's not a lot of shit going down to keep him busy. Things feel calm. That's okay for him, though. He's retiring next month and plans to teach new recruits at the local Community College.

We've learned Kaia has been granted the gift of being a Shifter, as we thought. Not only is she hearing her Wolf speak to her and guide her, as we all do with our Wolves, she's also slowly learning the process of shifting. We've gone on walks in our Wolf forms just so she can get used to the feel and movement of her own Wolf.

It's a little like training a newly born Shifter. Only we start from a very young age with them. All Shifters, even though they don't get their Wolves until different times in their life, show signs of being a Shifter. Some are slightly more aggressive because they have that animalistic instinct. Others are overly protective of things like toys. Things that are important to them.

Kaia hasn't done any of that. It's something I'm completely amazed by. I've always wondered how Kaia remains so calm. Even when I was rejecting our bond and being a complete asshole, she was relatively calm. She consistently set me at ease just by being near. I had noticed many times how the pack reacted to her. Some of my most difficult pack members were different around her. They are different when she's near.

The explanation becomes more clear every single day. It's who she is. Who she's destined to be. She's the living, breathing version of the legend Jordan constantly acted out with me, Zeke, and Dominick. At least when she wasn't pretending to be the kidnapped princess locked in a tower.

Kaia fulfills not only the legend, but all of my dreams. Fuck. She is my dream. She's all of them rolled into one. She's my life. My entire heart and soul. She makes me who I am. She is my other half. Funny how it took me so long to really allow myself to not only see it but feel it, too. I kick myself every single day for wasting time.

"Kade?" Kaia asks hesitantly from my office door.

I smile. She's still not comfortable coming in here. She views it as my place of solitary. I've told her a thousand times over the past couple of weeks that it's just as much hers as mine, but she still hesitates when it comes to coming into my office.

"Kaia," I say teasingly with a grin as I watch her.

She blushes and ducks her head. "Are you busy?"

"Nope. I just approved a budget for Deimos Publishing. I'm all yours."

She leans against the doorframe. "Zeke said Maverick is ready to talk. He's getting lunch but wanted to know if you were ready."

"I'm ready whenever he is, baby." I stand and cross the room to her. Unable to resist kissing her, because I always want her, I wrap her in my arms and kiss her deeply. I tangle my tongue with hers and suck on it lightly as I pull away slowly.

Kaia puts a hand against my chest to steady herself as she takes a deep breath. "Wow. You always make my head spin when you kiss me like that."

"I'll kiss you like that for the rest of our eternity." I take her hand and lead her downstairs where Zeke is settling Maverick in our living room.

"Baby, I know you're trying to help, but you're driving me insane," Maverick says with a half-smile as Zeke props his feet up on a pillow he's placed on the coffee table.

Zeke chuckles then narrows his eyes at his mate. "I almost lost you. It took two days before you could pull your partial shift back. You have only just gained enough strength to start walking around unassisted. Forgive me for being a little overprotective." He places Maverick's plate on his lap and drink on the end table next to him.

"I did not." Maverick takes a bite of his sandwich.

"The entire Deimos Pack and all of its allies beg to differ. Now be a good boy and eat." Zeke shakes his head when he catches mine and Kaia's amused smiles. "Alphas." He grins as he settles next to Maverick with his own lunch.

I can't help but laugh. "I'm an Alpha."

"Yep. And you're just as insufferable," Dominick says, appearing behind us. He sits in a chair and pulls Jordan into his lap.

Jace lets out a low rumble from the chair he and Leia are settled in next to where Kaia and I are standing. "I think it's a trait all Alphas have. I don't know how many times Leia has called him an asshole this week. I may or may not have agreed a few times," he teases with a wink to Maverick. Maverick shakes his head with a smile.

Kaia giggles and tugs me to the couch. I sit next to Zeke and pull her in my lap. "It's an Alpha thing." She smiles and kisses my jaw. "You all are stubborn."

I grin. "Yet all of our mates love the hell out of us." I kiss her nose. She wiggles it. I smile wider. "Bunny."

"Wolf," she counters. "I'm a Wolf."

"Maybe physically," I tease. "But even in Wolf form, your nose twitches as adorably as a bunny." I kiss her nose again. She wiggles it again and giggles as she settles. "Alright, Mav. Lay it on us. We're all anxiously awaiting the explanation. Now that you're feeling better, that is."

Maverick chuckles. "You all act like I was on death's door. I was just a little tired and weak, that's all."

"Ha!" I say before Zeke can start his lecture. "You were on death's door. And I should know. I was right there with you."

"Well, I ain't anymore. I'm fine. So, ya'll can stop worrying," Maverick barks. He smiles a little, though. We all know he's just as happy as we are that he's alive. "Alright. I guess you've waited long enough." He drops an arm over the back of the couch and around Zeke as he finishes his lunch. "When I was young, I found a really old, hand-written book in the library. I didn't know it then, but it was my grandfather's journal. My real one. He wasn't the Alpha of Devil's Peak. He was Alpha of another pack that eventually merged with Devil's Peak because they felt that was the only way to grow." He chuckles. "If only he knew."

"I've always thought how great it would be to know things that are going to happen," I say with a soft smile. "But if we did, we might miss the dance that leads up to it. Most of the time it's the dance that's the most fun." I kiss Kaia's shoulder.

"Maybe in most situations," Maverick says. "In some, I think if my grandfather knew what was going to happen, he wouldn't have made the decision he did. Devil's Peak had two goals. One was to have a pack of only Shifters. Keep some of the others as slaves. Extricate the others. Sell the rest. In the end, it was all about power and fulfilling the legend of the most powerful Luna and Alpha duo."

"They fucked that up," Jace grumbles.

"Anyway," Maverick continues. "In the journal he talked about his life as an Alpha, the merge, his kids. There was an assassination attempt on his kids. It was what made him decide to merge with Devil's Peak." He takes a deep breath. "One of his kids, my father, was near death. He didn't hesitate to do all he could to save his son." He lets out a long breath. "There's a gift all Alpha's have. It's called Pain Absorption." He looks down at his lap.

I furrow my brows. "Not just Alphas. We all have that ability. All Shifters."

Maverick swallows and nods. "True, but not everyone knows exactly how it works and how far it can go." He looks up at me. "Kaia, as an example. As soon as you both sealed your bond fully, she got powers she wasn't sure of. She didn't know how to use them, exactly, but we know that she sent calm and healing, peaceful thoughts to those that were injured during the attack. We know those thoughts helped the others to heal faster. We know that her love for you brought you back, but she used too much of her energy. She collapsed. To an extent, that's what pain absorption is. But there's more. It's why in the very beginning, they kept it as a secret that it wasn't only Alphas that could do it. They thought it was the right thing to do."

I'm suddenly a little uncomfortable about what he's about to tell me. "You did something different, though. I've never seen veins in both people being healed turn black like that. It's like it was being pulled."

He nods and bites his lip. "Because I was pulling it. When you and everyone else do it, it's not that you're pulling the pain. You kind of are. But you're also sending healing thoughts. Healing strength. It expends energy and doesn't work on someone who is…" He trails off. "Well, someone who is on death's door, as you and Zeke so kindly put it. The healing that you're doing sort of cancels out the pain absorbing part of it. You wouldn't see the black veins that you saw with me. And you can't do that when someone is as close to death as Kaia was. You were close, but not where she was."

His words cause me to inadvertently hug Kaia tighter. "Fuck," I whisper as I bury my face in her hair.

Jace shifts a little and raises an eyebrow. "Are you telling us you pulled her pain? Like, brought her back to life by removing what got her there? That doesn't seem possible."

"That's the point. At first, it was kept a secret that anyone other than Alphas could do it. Then, according to the journal, it was decided that the consequences of using that gift were too great." He glances at Zeke, who is watching him closely. He looks back at the rest of us. "Bringing someone truly on the brink of death back takes a lot of strength and energy. Alphas would lose their Alpha powers because the gift, while given to us by the Moon Goddess, was never used for the greater good. If it's someone's time, the Moon Goddess takes that very seriously. Messing with her grand plan is not something she takes lightly. Sometimes, however, even the strongest of Alphas didn't survive."

"Wait," Leia begins. "You're saying you could have died."

Kaia whimpers and turns to bury her face in my neck. "I... didn't... know how close I was... to dying." She sniffles. I feel her tears dampen my neck. I shift her so I'm cradling her and hug her tighter.

Zeke turns and wraps his arms around Maverick. "You told me through our bond that you could help. You said you could lose your Alpha powers, but you didn't care because we could stay here with the Deimos Pack and be just as happy and content as long as we're together." He looks up at him. "Why the hell didn't you say you could have died?" His voice cracks.

Kaia lets out a strangled sob. "I didn't know," she whispers.

"Shh...," I whisper back against her neck.

Maverick turns and hugs Zeke even tighter. "Because I trusted the Moon Goddess, my love." He lovingly kisses Zeke's shoulder. "I knew Kaia was special. We all did. We all saw how she handled the wounded that day. To me, it sealed it. I knew in my heart of heart's that she is the one. She's the legend. And I was right. I didn't care if I lost my Alpha powers. I knew they were nothing compared to what she and Kade will bring to this world."

Zeke shakes his head. "You should have told me, Maverick. I deserve to know what could have happened. Especially after all we've been through together."

"Kade is family, Zeke," Maverick says softly. "So is Kaia. Even if she had nothing to do with the legend, I would have done the same thing. Kaia took a hell of a hit when she collided with Charlene. That hit should have killed her on the spot. I don't know how it didn't. What I do know is that I was the only one there who could do what I did. If I hadn't, Kade would have been broken. Fuck, we all would have."

"The Demons. Couldn't they have done it?" Leia asks.

"They have a few abilities that are similar to ours. But you have to remember that there is always a cost, Leia," Maverick says. "They could have saved her, but they also have rules to follow."

"Save one, take another," I say. "Though, I have a feeling Alaric would have broken that rule in a heartbeat. And not because of the legend. He hates a lot of their rules. He's broken many. Including forming an alliance with Shifters. That's something that his kind has never done."

"I still can't believe we're friends with Demons," Kaia mumbles as she untangles herself from my embrace. She walks to Maverick and leans down, carefully hugging him. "Thank you. For saving me."

"I would do it all over again and again, Kaia." He hugs her tightly.

I smile when she melts into him. "So, the black veins. You were pulling her pain. I'm guessing since you're still here, you lost your Alpha powers. You're welcome here."

"I could always use a couple other Betas," Dominick says with a grin.

"Kade is a lot to handle," Jordan teases.

"Well," Maverick lets go of Kaia.

Kaia returns to my lap. "Your eyes. I saw them fade from gold to silver. I know from my reading that silver is of a Beta."

Maverick smiles as his eyes glow an even brighter gold than they were before. "I got my Alpha powers back. I think the Moon Goddess was grateful that I did what I did because after having time to heal, I am no longer a Beta. Jace is still my Beta, if he'll have me. And Koda said he'd be honored to join my pack. Only because I need someone like him. He said you have a few." He meets my eyes.

I grin. "He'd love to help you grow your pack. He's been trying to find his place in the world. Not that he's not comfortable here, but he's been a little restless."

Jordan chuckles and smiles brightly. "Who would have thought that the family, split by the idiocy of past Alphas, would be a family reunited as two of the strongest packs in the world?"

I smile. "Certainly not me." I kiss Kaia's cheek just as the front door opens.

"Kaze!" a little girl screams as she darts to me.

I grin when I turn to see Isabelle darting towards me. "Isa!" I say with just as much enthusiasm.

She giggles. "Mooooiiiiiiieeeee!" She takes my hand and tugs as hard as she can.

I laugh but don't budge. "What movie, gorgeous?"

"Pincess!"

I raise an eyebrow and look at Prince for help on that one. "Okay, I give. Usually, I know what she means, but there are hundreds of princess movies."

Prince chuckles. "Her favorite."

"Since when is Little Red Riding Hood a princess?" I ask.

"Since Isabelle decided she was," Prince says with a grin. "Your presence has been requested, Your Majesty." He bows teasingly.

Zeke cracks up. "He's no King."

Prince only raises an eyebrow. "To her he is."

Isabelle turns towards Zeke then back to me. She tilts her head and makes her way to Zeke after dropping my hand. She crawls into his lap and takes his face in her little hands. Zeke watches her with interest. Maverick grins. She tilts his head side to side as she squeezes his cheeks together so his lips look like that of a largemouth bass.

Keeping his face in her hands she turns to me with wide eyes. "Kaze! Cone!"

I laugh when I realize that while he's been around, she hasn't actually seen him up close. At least not in a situation she'd be paying much, if any, attention to him in. "That's Zeke. He's my twin brother."

Her eyes widen impossibly more as she turns back to him. "Zee! You come moie, tay?"

Zeke grins. "Absolutely. Want to help me get Maverick to the pack house? He might need you to hold his hand."

Mavericks snorts a laugh. "I won't get lost."

278

Isabelle giggles and climbs off Zeke's lap. She holds her hand out to Maverick. "I hep you no los."

"Now, how can I resist a request like that?" Maverick grins and boops her on the nose as he makes a show of letting her help him up.

Zeke laughs as he follows. Jace and Leia follow behind him. I nudge Kaia up so we can join them and smile when she quickly takes Leia's hand. The two have rekindled their friendship, but I am pretty sure it's probably far stronger. The bond between Shifters, Wolves, and their mates is something stronger than that of a conventional relationship. I'll always believe that. It's something my father taught us from a very young age. I think of anyone, he'd know the most about it. He's seen both sides of the coin.

Dominick and I follow our mates to the pack house and watch with huge smiles as Isabelle does all she can to help Maverick. He keeps leaning down on her like he's falling and making her squeak. She pushes him back up, then runs to his other side when he makes a show of falling to that side.

Dominick laughs. "Tell me mine and Jordan's kid will be just as adorable."

"As that?" I point to Isabelle. "You have a lot of competition."

"I can't wait."

I slap his back and put an arm over his shoulders as we walk into the pack house. Everyone is gathered in the family room. Isabelle settles Maverick on the couch after she shoos someone off it. After the rest of us are situated, Prince puts the movie in. Isabelle, having taken an instant attachment to Maverick, crawls into his lap instead of mine like she usually does. I'd be jealous, but the way she's trying to take care of him is far too adorable.

With my pack happy, healthy, and almost completely healed, I allow myself to relax with Kaia and watch the movie. I feel at peace. Something I haven't felt in a very long time. We have come out of this whole thing stronger than we were before.

For the first time in fourteen years, I feel whole.

Happy.

EPILOGUE

~*~ KAIA ~*~

Spending three years of my life as a Shifter and as a very powerful Alpha's Luna, I've learned a few things. One. The love of a pack is endless. Unconditional. Powerful. Stronger than anything I've ever experienced. Two. An Alpha's love for his Luna is limitless. There's no beginning. There is no end. It grows each day by measures that have yet to be discovered. Three. A Luna's love for her Alpha and her pack is exactly the same as theirs. It's deep. Fathomless.

And four. A Luna must be prepared to not only have unexplainable urges for her Alpha, but she must also be prepared for her Alpha to want to ravish her at all times. It doesn't matter if it's in a coat closet, a nursery, an office, the kitchen, the car, an airplane, or an elevator of one of the many buildings he owns. It could even be out in the middle of the large, majestic expanse of the woods that create a border for his territory.

Like right now.

"Oh, Kade," I moan as my head falls back against the large, Red Cedar tree Kade is holding me against.

His big hands grip my bare ass. His lips find each and every sensitive place along my neck. When he groans or moans, vibrations are sent throughout my entire body and makes my need for him rise higher and higher.

I wrap my arms around his shoulders tighter and pull him closer with my legs as he thrusts into me. He's so big. Thick. Each and every time we're together, I wonder how he doesn't tear me apart. I'm amazed at how I stretch around him. Like I was meant for him and he for me. Like we were made for only each other.

"Christ, Kaia," he rumbles. He nips my neck where he's made his mark and sucks.

I jerk into him when the sensation rips through me like electricity. I gasp and clench tightly around him, making him feel bigger. Harder. "Kade!"

He licks his bite mark with a low, possessive growl. "Mine, Kaia. Say it. Say you're mine."

I pant against his shoulder as I meet his thrusts. "Yours... Yours, Kade!"

"Good girl."

He pounds his dick into me harder and slams my back against the tree again and again. I feel his dick start to thicken, filling me even more. I tighten around him like a vice, clenching his dick with a possessive growl of my own.

Our moans and groans echo in the silence around us, but neither of us care. All that matters is us. Our connection. How good he feels with me wrapped around him. How incredible he feels inside me.

When I can't hold on anymore, I take his face gently in my hands, but kiss him hard. Unwilling to relinquish his need for control, Kade plunges his tongue into my mouth at the pace of his punishing thrusts, driving us both to insane heights.

"Yes, Kade... Kade!"

He slams himself into me a final time. His dick jerks. "Come for me," he whispers against my lips. "Now..." His eyes gleam with a challenge to disobey.

As much as I want to, just because I love the game, I can't. I come so hard, my back slams against the tree. It takes my breath away, but I scream for him anyway. "Kade!" I wrap my arms around his shoulders once more and dig my nails into them as my entire body jerks into him. My pussy pulses erratically as I give into my release. "Oh, yes... Yes!"

"Fuck, Kaia!" Kade's cock twitches inside me just before he groans. He closes his eyes and starts filling my pussy with stream after stream of come.

After several moments of heavy breathing, Kade finally lets me down as he pulls out. When my feet hit the ground, I feel both his come and mine dripping down my thighs. Kade smirks as he looks down at my thighs while he packs himself away.

I giggle and playfully shove him. "How am I supposed to walk back into the compound like this?"

"No one will question who you belong to when they smell and see me all over you."

I laugh as I pull my jeans up after I brush the dirt and tree off them. "So, that's the real reason you fuck me as much as you do."

He winks before laughing. "Well, partially. Mostly because I love you and can't resist you."

I take his hand when he offers it and lean into him as we start walking. "Good thing I feel the same way about you."

"Lucky me."

We've come a long way in the three years we've been together. I feel like I'm growing into my role nicely. I have Belle and Aryan to guide me. I even get to see my parents sometimes. I've always believed in Spirit Guides because of Belle, but I never thought I'd be lucky enough to have so many. Especially some of them being my parents.

It turns out after my parents saw the Sheriff and Deputy killing the Councilor, they knew they had to find Kade Deimos. They'd tried to find him at his publishing headquarters but were told that he doesn't work out of that office. They said they'd get him a message, but they never gave it to Kade. If they had, things would have turned out a lot differently than they had. I didn't know at the time, but when Kade found out that someone deliberately didn't pass on my parents' message, he ordered an internal investigation. It ended with Kade promptly firing half of his staff who were involved and hiring new staff.

I can't stop myself from wondering why the Moon Goddess felt the need to take my parents from me. If they'd only given Kade the message, my parents would still be alive. It's a frustration I struggle daily with, but I always end up telling myself that I am here where I belong fulfilling a legend I knew nothing about. I'm happy. I'm at peace.

But mostly, I'm surrounded daily by everyone that I love. The pack has become family. I have become close to Jordan. I have Leia back. Maverick and Zeke are so happy leading their pack with Jace at their side. Devil's Peak may be dead and gone, but the Aethelwulf Pack is strong and thriving under Maverick's leadership. In honor of Connor Deimos, they have even opened up their own Refuge for Wolves, continuing the work our father started and was so proud of.

Kade is truly the other half of my soul. Three years ago, I didn't think this would be my life. I didn't really know all of this existed. At least not to this extent. I think the reason I was so accepting of it is because of Belle. She's been by my side almost my whole life. I believe now that her job was to not only guide me, but also to prepare me; ease me into this.

She's done an incredible job. I feel I am who I was always meant to be. Like I'm where I've always belonged. I can't imagine my life turning out any other way. I get to travel the world with the love of my life and come home to an amazing family. No one can ask for more than that.

Kade leads me into the clearing where our compound begins, and I smile. I can tell some of the pack members are feeling a little restless. The kids are trying to climb Jamie like a tree. Loki is laughing, but I sense both of them want to run.

I look up at Kade. "What do you say to a pack run? The sun is just about to set. It's the perfect time and would settle the restless energy I feel all around us."

Kade grins. "You've come up with a lot of good ideas, but I think these pack runs are, by far, your best. We've always been close, but..." He trails off and looks over our pack. "I think we're closer because of the bonding we've been able to do lately. It's nice to not have to think of the next battle all the time while still being prepared for it."

I smile. I feel it, too. And if I'm being honest, I love it. It gives me a chance to become closer to my Wolf. We may be the same, but she has a mind of her own sometimes. Apparently, it's totally normal, and I'm doing very well for someone who is a new Shifter.

As Kade calls everyone for the pack run, we both shift into our Wolves. We're a stark contrast to each other. He's as black as midnight.

I'm as white as freshly fallen snow. Really, though, it's perfect. I'm the light to his dark. The ray of sunshine to his gloom.

I nuzzle him as everyone gathers. We've grown over the years. We've added Shifters, Wolves, and even Humans who felt like they didn't belong anywhere. We're both proud to say they belong here. Even if they don't have a mate here, we love them just the same. All of them.

I smile up at one of our new Humans when she brings us our young daughter and son. They are twins. Two-year-old holy terrors, but we love them so much. Too young to go on our pack runs, something the pack needs desperately right now.

I think they missed you, Jen says.

I nuzzle them both. *They both love being around Missy. She doesn't like going on runs that much.* I look up at Jen. *Take her to them and come join us. I feel like you need it, too. Besides...* I nod my head towards the man I know she has a huge crush on. *Dean is coming. And he's looking over here at you.*

Her eyes widen and she blushes a deep red as she scurries away. I watch her as she gives the twins to Missy, who is holding Evan's hand. Evan is Loki and Jamie's son. They named him after their best friend. Missy smiles at me as she brings the kids to the pack house. Jen shyly joins Dean when he eagerly calls her over.

You have a serious matchmaking addiction. Kade chuckles and licks my nose.

I wiggle it. *I just want everyone to have what we do.*

I don't think that's possible. What we have is what legends are made of. He grins.

I laugh because it's something Kade loves joking about every chance he gets. The legend, and how we're part of it. Jordan is constantly teasing us about being the real life version of the legend she grew up loving so much.

When everyone is ready, we take off. Our older members are up front with the kids, cubs, and a lot of the humans. They are setting a pace they can handle and are comfortable with. Behind them are our protectors. The stronger of the pack. Behind them is the strongest of the pack. Those that watch out for all of the others. Jamie and Loki are among them. Behind them are me, Jordan, and Dominick.

And following just behind us is Kade. Our Alpha. He watches over the entire pack as we run. If someone seems to fall behind, Kade is right there to help get them back on track. He makes us all slow our pace to the one who has fallen behind because he refuses to allow anyone to feel left out or alone.

After a little while, I hear a deep howl of greeting. Several of the Wolves in our pack return the howl just as Maverick and Zeke's pack, full of Humans, Wolves, and Shifters just like ours, join us as we leisurely run.

Zeke nuzzles me as he reaches my side. I nuzzle him back just as lovingly. Maverick takes his place at Kade's side. The rest of the pack blend seamlessly with ours. My heart feels like it's going to overflow and burst with the adoration I have for everyone in front of me, next to me, and behind me.

Maverick settled the Aethelwulf Pack next to ours so we're close. He took over all of the Devil's Peak territory and has expanded his territory even further as more have joined his pack. Like us, he's accepted everyone who doesn't feel like they belong anywhere and have found themselves on his doorstep.

After a little while longer, we reach the cliff our packs enjoy meeting at. There are a few cars lined up off to the side as we all run into the clearing. The cubs are playing with the kids who were too young to come on the pack run. Our Den Makers and a few others are all protectively sitting along the edge of the cliff so the kids don't get too close.

The Shifters transform to their Human selves as we reach our destination. As soon as Tyson and Aimee, our beautiful twins, spot us, they make a beeline for us with their arms outstretched. Aimee has definitely become daddy's girl. Tyson, however. He's all mine. We both lift our kids in our arms as they squeal. We hug them close.

As the sun sets, we all settle to watch it, allowing the peacefulness to wash over us. Zeke sits between Maverick's legs with a small swell to his stomach indicating the future of the Aethelwulf Pack. Kade and I snuggle our kids and look over our pack.

I lean my head on Kade's shoulder and close my eyes. Everything about this moment is perfect. My entire life leading up to this moment may have been chaotic, but if I had the chance to go back and change things, I wouldn't change a thing. This, right here, is what I have always wanted.

A place where I can be myself.
Friends.
Family.
I found my love.
My home.

THE END

THE DEIMOS TRILOGY

Available Now

Connor's Legacy
Aryan's Alpha
Kade's Redemption

Box Sets Available

The Deimos Trilogy

OTHER BOOKS BY MELONY ANN
THE BEAUTIFUL DREAM SERIES

Available Now

Loving You
My Love, My Heart
Softening Lyric
Undercover Temptations
Captain Charming
Breaking Boundaries
Crashing Into You
Tactical Inferno
Ravishing Our Queen
Cherished By The Texan
Unveiling Our Passions

Box Sets Available

The Beautiful Dream Series: Box Set: Part 1
The Beautiful Dream Series: Box Set: Part 2

THE CRANE FAMILY SERIES

Available Now

The Reluctant Mafia King
Sweet Lies
Billion Dollar Love Story
Be Mine
Protecting Her
Dangerously Forbidden Love
His Heart
Love In The Dark

Box Sets Available

The Crane Family Series

THE FORBIDDEN TEMPTATION
SERIES

Available Now

The Detective's Forbidden Temptation
The Running Back's Forbidden Temptation

THE LUCINIO FAMILY SERIES

Available Now

Rising From The Ashes
The Player's Rebel
Encrypting My Heart

MULTI AUTHOR SERIES
PIPER FALLS: FIREHOUSE 49

Available Now

Ignite My Fire by Melony Ann
Regain My Fire by Kindra White
Playing With My Fire by D.L. Howe
Fight My Fire by Darley Collins
Against My Fire by Anneke Boshoff
Relight My Fire by Louise Murchie
Harness My Fire by Ayana Lisbet
Quench My Fire by Havana Wilder

LET'S BE FRIENDS

Follow me on

Bookbub

Facebook

Goodreads

Instagram

Tik Tok

Visit my website
www.melonyannauthor.com

Subscribe to my newsletter and get a FREE never-seen-before NOVELLA
just for subscribers!
https://www.melonyannauthor.com/exclusive-content

Join my Facebook Reader Group!
Jason's and Melony's Sizzling Book Nook

The official Deimos Trilogy Playlist on YouTube
https://youtube.com/playlist?list=PLGEiD5wbQmDdILeGUdsWxGhWBh
obSXhTI

DEDICATION

To our forever. Our pack. Our family. Our home.

ACKNOWLEDGEMENTS

Brad - You're always my place to rest when the real world is chaotic.

Laura - The love of my life. You keep me on track. You keep everything on track. You're so beautiful and smart. I'm so lucky to have you in my life, and even more lucky that you love me as much as I do you.

Jay - You're the end of my movie that I never want to end.

Ayana - I've said it before, but you are honestly such an amazing soul. Thank you for being my chosen family. And thank you so much for running my social media. You don't have any idea how much you and your work means to me.

Anneke - It has not been a very pleasant couple of months, but we aren't giving up. You'll be home soon and reunited with your husband. And we can hug for real instead of virtually!

Jason - I never seem to be able to find the words when it comes to you. I stumble and fall over them all the time. You always seem to catch me before I hit the ground, though.

To the Bookstagram Community.

To my family.

To all of those who believe in me and support me.

To all of those who don't.

Cover by: Carter Cover Designs

ABOUT MELONY ANN

Melony Ann began writing short stories and poetry as a child. She continued honing her craft over the years until she took the plunge and began publishing her work, despite having severe anxiety.

Melony writes contemporary romance stories that are full of suspense and a lot of steam.

When she isn't writing, she is loving her family and working to make her life something she deserves.

Melony believes that if her writing can inspire just one person, then all of her hard work is worth it.

Her hope is that her writing allows each and every one of her readers to escape for a little while. To dive into a different world one book at a time.

www.ingramcontent.com/pod-product-compliance
Lightning Source LLC
Chambersburg PA
CBHW051526260626
47170CB00003B/807

* 9 7 8 1 9 6 1 9 6 6 4 2 0 *